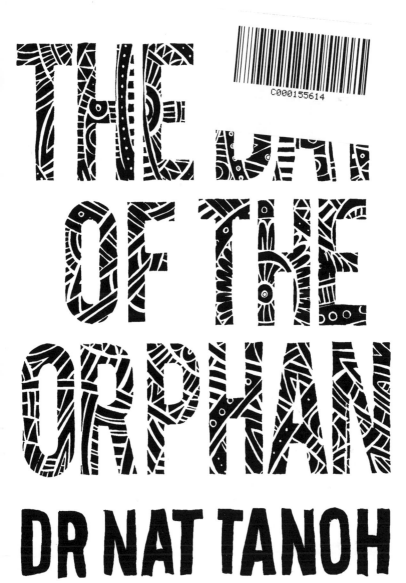

THE DAY OF THE ORPHAN

DR NAT TANOH

Acorn Independent Press

CONTENTS

PROLOGUE

Though she had abstractly anticipated the possibility of what was happening at that moment, Aba had always harboured a baseless optimism that such a day would never come. But when her husband ushered her and their oldest son, Obo, into their room, she knew the news would be bad.

'Did you have to do it now? I thought we more or less agreed that you'd wait a little longer to see if things would change a bit. Now you have gone and drawn unnecessary attention to yourself and the family, and you know very well that this foolish government is bound to find trouble with us for this. Why Nana? Why resign from the Ministry of Justice now?'

'I'm sorry, Aba. I know I should have spoken to you first but things just came to a head today. I had no choice. They came and arrested our friend, Mr Gab, for simply refusing to fire two very bright Northern Muslim chaps who work for him as junior prosecutors. A memo came from the Minister that the lads should be dismissed for absolutely no sensible reason whatsoever, though of course, we all know why. Gab refused to fire them as a matter of principle and sent a note back saying the Minister should dismiss them himself if he wanted it done so badly.'

At this, his wife gave an involuntary gasp and braced herself for what was coming next.

'Within a few hours, Zombie troops came in, handcuffed him, slapped him around in front of his staff, and dragged him away in one of those Pinzguar military trucks. You should have seen all the blood on his face and shirt and his swollen face. What had he done wrong? That was the last straw. I'm sorry, Aba, but I just couldn't remain in that office for another day. I simply wrote my resignation and handed it over to the Minister and asked him to inform the Presidency on my behalf.'

'Nana, don't apologise. It's okay and I'm also sorry. How could they do that to such an innocent, mild-mannered man with a

wife and five young children? And so brazenly as well, in front of everyone? These government people have some nerve. This is serious. Will they drive Muslims out of all jobs? Then what? No Nana – you did what you had to do. What is done is done. You had no choice.' She abruptly switched to the pragmatic without warning. 'Obo, sit with your father and make sure Saga and Emma do their homework. I'll get some bread and provisions from the shop and take it down to Mrs Gab and the kids. I'll sit with them for a while. They will need comforting, as their friends will be afraid to go and visit them for fear of getting into trouble. What nonsense is this? Call me at their house if you need me. Our lives, as we knew them, are over. We'll continue this discussion when I get back.'

Aba barely slept that night. She knew that their relatively comfortable existence would unravel before her very eyes and she was powerless to stop it. Already, her son was a marked man for his role in the university opposition against the Regime. She already knew what it was like to have a loved one taken God knows where by the police. At least he was back with them now. Her family was being hurtled along a particular path by forces way beyond her, and she knew deep down that it boded no good.

CHAPTER ONE

Unbeautiful Nature

Everyone called him Saga, though that was not what his parents had named him. He was fidgeting at his wooden government-issue desk in his very-good-for-Africa sized classroom of only 30 students. His teachers were lucky; many other teachers had to cope with as many as a 100 students or more in each class.

Unlike most of the other struggling and quasi-dilapidated secondary schools in the country, Brewman Boys High School was a modern, purpose-built affair that boasted of plush, green acreages and pristine, red-brick classroom blocks and administrative offices. It was a school named after the immensely powerful, pre-eminent President-For-Life-Until-Further-Notice. Though relatively new, it was simply 'poshest', most privileged and nicest school within the entire country.

Saga, however, was not feeling privileged to be stuck in a boring maths lesson. He was attempting unsuccessfully to absorb what his lanky, bushy-haired, crumpled-looking maths teacher was imparting to the upper sixth-form class. The word 'tedium' popped into Saga's mind and he abstractly considered it, wondering whether it accurately reflected how he felt. He quickly concluded that it didn't. Tedium could somewhat describe his tiredness and the drab dreariness of his teacher, but failed to make provision for annoyance, which for now was his number one feeling.

He was hungry too. Without warning, his stomach growled cantankerously in protest against its unnatural state of emptiness, which did not in any way help improve Saga's mood. Saga was in truth a tall, bulky young man who, among other things, seriously disapproved of hunger, especially his own. He furtively cast his eyes around the room to see if any of his form-mates had heard his potentially embarrassing stomach protestations. To his relief, no one gave any indication of having noticed.

His maths teacher, now affecting a lofty air of one who lived and breathed nothing but equations, was pontificating on how mathematics was as divinely beautiful as nature itself. This vexed Saga even further. Unconsciously, he began forming counter-arguments in his mind against this so-called beauty of nature, instead of paying attention to the lesson.

Why do people always talk about the beauty of nature in a manner that makes it look like it doesn't have an unbeautiful side? Are earthquakes, hurricanes, landslides and tsunamis with the destruction and horrors they leave in their wake beautiful? What of the rather fierce leopards, cheetahs and lions who despite looking absolutely majestic, savagely prey on wildebeest and allied beast in the Serengeti and elsewhere, according to the very laws of this beautiful nature?

In his heightened state of vexation, he averted his eyes from the teacher's face and shut his ears to his droning. He shifted his gaze to the wide, louvered windows that were open in an attempt to lure in some breeze, which was essential in combating the ever-present heat. Looking outside, he espied a gang of white-collared crows, prancing and strutting about the place. They had congregated under the vast canopies of the numerous Neem and Flame of the Forest trees that provided the school grounds with much-needed shade from the glare and blistering afternoon heat of the remorseless African sun. During the school's construction, these fully-grown trees were brazenly uprooted, at huge expense, from the protected National Botanical Gardens and replanted on the school campus to supply necessary shade for the school's elitist pupils.

Saga could distinctly hear the crows cawing and this, he thought, they did with considerable passion, with their agape beaks pointing skyward. He absent-mindedly wondered why they were not foraging for worms or bugs or whatever it was that crows found appetising. They were probably giving a crow version of praise to Providence for the shade that gave them refuge from the pitiless sun. He wished he could be out there with the crows and not in some boring math class with a dreary, pretentious, Einstein-emulating maths teacher!

It was not that school was not his thing. Saga generally liked school. Nonetheless, he liked it less and less these days since the teachers had recently become rather intense and insufferable with their incessant pressures, to the point where he was now quite fed up with them. Nowadays, all upper sixth-form students were needlessly hounded and harassed with endless assignments and constant after school study lessons.

Saga considered this grossly unfair, since it was not as though they did not understand that passing your A-levels was the surest way of gaining admission into one of the very few universities in the country. Of course, all the students further understood quite clearly that in their so-called Third World Developing Country, Less Developed Country, Underdeveloped Country or Emerging Economy – or whatever it was called according to the dictates of whatever current development *lobby-speak* held sway – having a university education was a big deal indeed. In many parts of Africa, being university-educated usually guaranteed good career prospects and a comfortable place among society's relatively small, affluent upper middle-class educated elite. Or at least that was how it was supposed to be, in theory.

Saga's unrelenting, overbearing teachers were constantly lecturing him and his mates about their future prospects. He couldn't understand how these educated folks couldn't see that applying too much pressure would not get their desired result. Those teachers should just let them be. Saga refused to get worked up about any A-levels or whatever level they wanted to bring on! Somehow, he would pass, just as he had passed all other exams. With these thoughts, Saga left the class that was now thankfully over, quickening his pace towards home and some much-needed hot food. He stopped at the school gates to meet his best friend, Ibrahim Koto, so they could walk back home together, as they always did.

Their school was not far from where they lived, quite near the centre of Cape Cove, their capital city. The route they always took home was a beautifully shaded path that bordered the Ridge Heights Children's Park and was lined with regal-looking royal palm trees and neatly-trimmed milk-bush hedges. They also enjoyed passing the well-kept expanse of lush, green grass that covered the entire park and was dotted with evergreen, bright, red-flowered Flame of the Forest trees.

The long, fairly broad, tree-lined pathway afforded them a temporary escape from the remorseless sun that blazed down all day, lending the tarred roads a hazy, shimmering look, as if they were getting ready to produce mirages that never actually materialised. This was probably just as well since the images the seemingly inefficient mirages would have most likely reflected would have been from larger, less affluent parts of the city, which were in stark contrast to such pleasantness.

For Saga, in particular, the route – with its pleasing honey-like fragrance from the red and purple bougainvillea flowers that crept up the trees and were in full bloom everywhere – always made him feel rejuvenated. This was especially welcome after such a drab maths lesson.

Ibrahim and Saga were bosom buddies who curiously could almost always agree on nothing. It was as though they had an unspoken agreement to disagree, but they enjoyed the debating. Saga hoped it would help distract his mind from his still distressed stomach. Today, Ibrahim wanted to revisit an earlier topic of debate.

'I, Ibrahim Koto, do solemnly declare that 50 Cent is a much better rapper than Eminem, and from this verdict, do not even attempt an appeal!' exclaimed Ibrahim, harking back to an earlier argument they had started during their noon break with some of their other classmates.

'Better in what sense, Ibrahim? You couldn't answer me then and I bet you still have no answers now, so pause here and permit me to school you. 50 Cent, together with all your other Rappers – the P. Diddys and the Snoop Doggy Dogs – only talk about bling jewellery, posh cars and sexy women or dissing somebody. It's always about the bling or some other pointless ostentation they can show off. Eminem talks about some social issues. You're blinded by the bling – and that's all it is.'

'What social issues, Saga? And why the big words? Ostentation, my foot! You think bling is not a social issue? You get me some serious bling and I'll show you how seriously social I can get and see the number of ladies I will blind with my bling! And I still say – 50 Cent is hotter!'

'He can be colder for all I care. I'm not saying he's bad, but it's almost like saying P. Diddy is better than Tupac. You think the only thing in this world that matters is bling? There's more to life than bling.'

'Like what, Saga? Sometimes, you sound too much like your daddy and your big brother, Obo. Those guys can get far too serious with all that heavy-duty stuff they mess with. They should have been preachers or philosophers. I thought you were different, yet every now and then, you start parroting them. And mind you, bling is money too. Have you not heard the Chinese Cantonese saying – *'Moh ching, moh meng'* – meaning – *'no money, no life'* – so there.' Ibrahim was clearly enjoying this.

'I don't parrot anybody – so kindly shut your face! I don't even know why I bother having these arguments with you. Can you, for example, say that Mike Tyson is better than Muhammad Ali? Tyson, all told, was just a brute of a boxer with passable talent. Ali, on the other hand, was a boxing genius, an effective social commentator, and a Civil Rights activist who even went toe to toe with the entire American government over Vietnam! No comparison here, not by any stretch of any imagination! Absolutely no contest! The problem with you, Ibrahim Koto, is that you are inflexible,' Saga retorted quite heatedly. He didn't exactly like being told he was a parrot or that he had parrot-like tendencies.

Ibrahim sensed his friend's mood change and sought to make him smile again. He grinned at him and said, 'Relax Saga. I'm only joking. And mind you, Muhammad Ali is my boy too and was certainly the greatest! But man, you have to admit that some of those rap-cum-R & B chicks are seriously hot and definitely all that! Check out Beyoncé and Jennifer Lopez – are they hot or what?'

It worked. Saga was now smiling mischievously, as talk of beautiful women was always a most welcome topic, and Ibrahim's assertions were something he certainly had to agree with.

'As for that – I'll say you are definitely in the right. Those ladies are seriously fine! But don't let my mom or sis hear you use that word "chicks" – or you'll get a fierce blasting. Objectification of women and all that – whatever the hell that means. But guess what, I heard that because of those fine ladies, nowadays, many flat-bottomed Western women want to have bums that poke out a little. You know the cute type that hoist up skirts like J. Lo's? So, get this – they've been injecting this thing called Botox into their bottoms to get bums. It's like having bum-lifts as opposed to face-lifts. Those women are crazy. A bottom is a bottom, for heaven's sake!'

Ibrahim was astonished. 'Botox into their bottoms for curvy behinds? Wow! Botox for bums? Why, what does this Botox do anyway? Just gives cute, curvy bums? Is there some of that Botox stuff in this country for the girls here too?'

'Are you that blind? Look around you and tell me whether the ladies here need any Botox for bottom lifts! Everything they wear is plenty hoisted already! TIA – This Is Africa, man! Or you forget? Can you imagine the havoc it will cause if these, our African women here, were to add that Botox stuff to what they've already got in such serious natural abundance?'

Ibrahim paused for a second, looked at Saga suspiciously, and asked, 'But how do you know all this stuff, Saga, when even we, the specialists on women, don't? Are you pulling my leg or what? Since when did you become a bottom inspector? And what's this hoisting business?'

They were approaching the intersection where they would have to part, and Saga sought to have the last word. 'Anyway, back to the original issue. My verdict is that 50 Cent can't compare to Eminem and, to crown it all, 50 is Eminem's creation with the help of Dr Dre, so let's leave it at that.'

But Ibrahim, however, did not care to go back to the original topic. He was really in need of more information on this astonishing Botox revelation. 'Whatever! Just forget

50 Cent, Snoop, Eminem and all those elements for now. Saga, why do you think those Americans call bums booty? Is it because it houses serious treasure or because it tails behind like a car boot? Me – I'll go for the treasure. What about you, Inspector Buttocks?'

'I'm no inspector of anything. Some things you can't help but notice, especially if you are surrounded by it. Hey Ibrahim, will you come with me this afternoon to the market to get a pair of trainers? Say around 4p.m.? The ones I've got have started to give me cheesy feet and they're not even that old! Why do trainers do that, eh?'

'Do what, Saga? It's got nothing to do with the trainers. Why blame them? It's just your feet that are smelly. But never mind, I'll come with you in sympathy for those who have to live with the pong from your dubious feet.'

Saga tried to playfully swipe the back of his friend's head in response but Ibrahim managed to dodge and trotted off home shouting, 'See you 4p.m.–ish!'

The close friends differed considerably in appearance.

Saga was tall and had a tendency towards bulkiness. He had discovered the delights to be derived from food quite early in life and consequently, had always been a couple of years ahead of his classmates size-wise. At 10, for example, he wore clothes for age 12. At 12, he wore age 14 clothes, and at 18, stood just over six feet and was developing a small potbelly, which he jokingly referred to as his budding 'designer paunch'. He carried his extra weight well as he was energetic and reasonably strong.

Taken separately, the features that made up his face could not be individually tagged as remarkable or chiselled or outstanding. But put together, most people tended to do a pleasant double-take of his appearance. It was as though, united, his individual facial objects blended quite well, but divided, they seemed to pose quite another matter.

When he could be bothered to consider his features at all, he tended to view every object quite separately, and was thus far from being impressed. He thought his nose insufficiently prominent for an African man and his lips also not full enough. But who really cared? He was just not vain. He was a warm-hearted young man with an ever-ready smile for everyone. However, he was also known to occasionally take off in deep reflective thought, becoming quite unaware of his surroundings during such moments.

Though a good two and a half inches shorter than Saga, Ibrahim was definitely designed and destined to be a ladies' man, as well as a man's man. He was also 18, and handsome in an immediately endearing way, with well-carved individual facial features that collectively produced pleasing results as well. His lean though muscular build gave the impression of reasonable height to the extent that he had already been approached by some local agencies on the prowl for talent to take up some modelling.

Though he maintained modelling was for sissies, Ibrahim knew he was good looking, even if not big headed about it. He also knew how to use it to his benefit whenever the need arose, which happened to be quite often. He was very outgoing and could be found in the middle of any argument. He was also the chief originator of almost all the outrageous pranks that came out of their classrooms over the years. He had a more thoughtful side to him that he rarely showed. Saga had been his friend forever and he loved him dearly.

What made their friendship all the rarer was religion. Too many of Saga's friends, who were mainly Christians, tended to look down on their Muslim schoolmates. Since the relatively recent 9/11, which had occurred barely three years ago, their Christian president had also begun demonising the Muslims in the North of the country, thus making matters even worse. This, Saga found ridiculous, as he had been brought up quite differently in a very liberal and tolerant environment.

CHAPTER TWO

Hop-Hip

Saga was glad to get home. He was essentially a home person. Home was where he felt most secure. For him, it was like a sanctuary away from school and the growing turbulence that seemed to be engulfing their society. He preferred his friends to visit him at home rather than having to go to their houses. His parents also generally allowed him his own space, which was conducive when his visitors came. Simply put, his home was his main comfort zone.

Saga was the second of three children. Along with his brother and sister, he lived with their parents in Ridge Heights residential Area, also near the heart of Cape Cove. Saga had often wondered why their area was referred to as 'heights', since there was not a single hill or hillock or any elevation of any sort remotely resembling such in the entire area. Curiously, there was also a similar absence of authentic 'ridges' to boot. It was specifically termed as a 'residential area', built during the colonial era to give decent accommodation and shelter to white colonial civil servants and other highly-placed officials of the mighty British Raj.

The neighbourhood boasted very spacious, double-storey 'bungalows', which had very large compounds of at least an acre each. These also had the obligatory 'boys' quarters' building, where the house-help, such maid-servants and steward boys, would sleep some distance away from the main house, maintaining the unspoken but prevalent and pervasive protocol of domestic class segregation at night.

Every bungalow was either walled or had a sturdy barbed-wire fence hidden within prickly but well-groomed hedges. Most importantly, there were trees everywhere – both within the compounds as well as lining and adorning the streets. They were mostly Neem trees. Shade had obviously been of paramount importance to the colonial masters, whose delicate, fair skins did not always take too kindly to the relentless heat from the sun.

With the coming of Political Independence from the British Colonisers, the area had for a while now housed senior government officials and Ministers of State, and others, like Saga's father, who had been afforded the opportunity to buy their homes during their tenure in Government. There were also quite a number of expatriates working for local branches of foreign, multinational conglomerates and some international agencies still residing within their locale.

Saga's mother was a senior television producer for the State-owned Zimgania Broadcasting Corporation. In recent times, it seemed to Saga that she spent quite a bit of her time at work in unending battle with the head of her production department, whom she called a 'male chauvinist excuse for a boss'. At least that was the impression Saga got from her daily answers to her husband's polite inquiries about her day.

Saga's father had been a prominent barrister in lucrative private practice before taking on a government job as Deputy Minister of State at the Ministry of Justice. He was now 60 years old, prematurely retired, and presently worked for himself as a legal consultant. He was also the landlord as well as a minority silent partner in a small family shop enterprise that catered to the daily basic (soap, tea, coffee, toilet roll, and bread and butter) needs of their local community.

Saga had no idea what he wanted to do as a profession, but for an occasional token hourly wage, he liked working in the shop on the days he did not have to go to school, or sometimes even after school. Most times, he simply worked there voluntarily. Retired Army Major Kata, the principal owner of the shop, was very fond of Saga. He enjoyed his company and diligent efforts when assisting in the shop. A mini café was attached to the shop, which also catered to the tobacco, wine and beer needs of the community, and faired very well under a cluster of trees that gave perennially welcome shade.

This café was central to comings and goings of the male component of the locality. The female component, however, said they had much better things to do than simply idling at cafés such as their 'ne'er-do-well' men-folk. This was, in fact, their roundabout way of registering some annoyance at a society that unfairly frowned upon women spending as much time as men in cafés.

Some of Saga's developing knowledge of his country and also of the larger world had been learnt in the café. Sometimes, he sat for hours, listening to the worldly wisdom of those who could afford to ramble on as a result of having too much time on their hands, as well as having imbibed sufficient levels of alcohol to guarantee verbosity. He had also learnt a lot about modern African history from his elderly friend, Major Kata.

On reaching home, Saga walked through the entrance of his large compound, passed the partially fenced-off portion his dad had set up for Major Kata's shop-cum-café, and entered through the front door.

Saga's family were waiting for him in the living room before they sat down to lunch. Because of their various work and school schedules, lunch was almost always a mid to late afternoon event in their household during weekdays. Saga often missed the family lunch as a result of those silly teachers keeping his class behind after school hours. Today's fare was traditional: pure white rice balls and peanut butter soup with chunky pieces of lamb and charcoal smoked tuna fish; one of his favourites. He could barely wait to tuck into it. The aroma had enveloped him with full force and got him salivating from the moment he entered the welcome coolness of their air-conditioned living-cum-dining room.

'Look who's here,' exclaimed Nana, his father, as Saga hurried in. 'We'd better get started as this young man looks like he'll give up the ghost any minute now if he's denied his food much longer.' They all knew Saga as one not to play around when it came to food matters.

'Good afternoon Mama, Dada and siblings all – and Dada is right, no food, no life and I'm starved.'

'Saga, don't forget to wash your hands and face first – that's Mama's law,' chimed in his bossy little sister, Emma, who was rewarded with a rude, upwardly pointing middle finger from Saga once he was sure his parents weren't looking.

'Ma, Da, did you see what Saga just did?' she exclaimed in mock disgust, to which her eldest brother, Obo, frowned.

'Stop tattling like a baby,' Obo admonished, as Saga rushed off to perform his obligatory minor ablutions.

Walking back towards the table, the food had already been laid out in large Pyrex bowls, resting on those little yet sturdy food warmers, which always reminded Saga of mini metal scaffolding with their miniature candles aglow beneath. Their rectangular dining table was covered with a white tablecloth. Saga wondered why most people preferred white tablecloths, given that they stained so easily. A black tablecloth came to mind, and he shuddered involuntarily at the grim images it evoked. They were surely better off with the white.

The sight of the caramel-coloured, thick peanut butter soup glistening quickly banished those grim images and made Saga literally weak with desire as he sat down.

He was just about to have a taste of his food from his amply heaped bowl when his sister halted his spoon in mid-air with an accusatory shriek of, 'Mama, Saga and Obo didn't say their prayers before eating.'

But Saga just stuck his tongue out at her as his spoon finally completed its maiden trip into his salivating mouth. It was, however, their father, Nana, who replied, 'Emma, why are you harassing your brothers this afternoon? You know very well that prayer is not compulsory at the table. Like I've said many times, it must be left to the individual and his or her God.'

'But Dada, you should make it compulsory.'

'I've told you before, I let every man pray – or not – how he likes. What I do believe in is peace between neighbours, and that includes those sitting next to each other around this table now.'

'But Daddy, they should be grateful and truly thankful for the food on their plates. We saw pictures in class today of many children starving in the Sudan and some of them looked very sad and had grown very thin and had many flies bothering them. It was horrible and our teacher said most of us are lucky not to be in that situation and should be thankful, and so should Obo and Saga for what they are about to receive,' she said, sneaking in a small part of her own standard thankful prayer into her reply, which did not go unnoticed by her mother, who smiled approvingly.

Emma, the last of the litter, was adored by all in her family. However, her brothers often thought that she had imbibed their mother's women lib practices rather early in life, and was often berating them in a fashion after their mother for their sloppiness. She had established herself as the deputy mother figure in their scheme of domestic arrangements.

'When are you going to stop your tattling, Emma?' Obo laughed.

'I don't tattle. I only state facts – so there!' Emma said in a sulk.

'Come now, let's eat. Laughter makes us humans one with the heavens. Providence disapproves of long, sulky faces, you know that,' her father said with a wink.

But Obo had not quite finished. 'So, tell me, Emma, how can you be sure that Saga and I haven't said our prayers silently in our minds? Do you see you could be wrong?'

'Well, I hope I am because then it is all the better for you guys with salvation now in sight.' At this, the whole family laughed. They truly adored her young quick wit.

'Enough of your salvation talk now, Emma,' Ma chided. 'Concentrate on your food before you choke from talking too much.'

But Obo had still not finished. 'And Emma, don't for a second think that we are not grateful for the privileged lives we've got. I agree that things are terrible in places like Sudan but things are equally bad in our own country as well. Do you know that 70 per cent of the people live below the poverty line right here in Zimgania? They don't have enough to eat and many people cannot afford to send their children to school or even buy them medicine when they become sick. Have you not seen the mud houses many of our people live in when you go on your school excursions outside the capital city? Or even those who live in the thousands of tiny tin hovels in the Zongo slums of this very city? It's not like our lovely private estate here! Yes, believe me, Emma, when I say our family is very, very privileged and we are truly grateful for that!'

Saga was thankful the rest of the main meal was untroubled by his sibling's politics. But it wasn't long before the topic went back to serious matters. Before they had finished their small bowls of fruit salad, his Da, looking at his eldest son, asked with obvious concern, 'Is it true your university students are planning yet another demonstration against the Government? Isn't it getting too dangerous with all the beatings and arrests that took place the last time? I heard it today at one of my meetings. What is this all about?'

But before Obo could reply Aba, their mother, intervened. She looked even more worried than her husband. She glared at her son and asked hotly, 'Obo, what is this protesting, rioting, nonsense business again? Don't you students ever learn anything? Look at what happened to you the last time with your arrest? Have you people not had enough? I want a word with your friend, Kobby. This nonsense has to stop! It must be all that hop-hip you people have been listening to, which is driving you all insane.'

Emma suddenly burst out laughing, practically choking. 'Mama, it is hip-hop, not hop-hip,' she squealed with delight. Even Saga, who was abstractly using his spoon to shove the little pieces of fruit around in his dessert bowl, could not help but also burst out laughing, and this somewhat helped to diffuse the tension that was rapidly building up at the dining table.

The Kobby their mother had referred to was the National President of the University Students' Union and Obo's best friend. Obo decided to take advantage of the lessened tension to unruffle his mother's fast fluttering feathers. She had now transferred her glare to Emma, who was still in stitches over the 'hop-hip' mispronunciation.

'Take it easy, Mama. Nothing has been decided. It's just an idea that's being kicked about. Nothing is definite. You can ask Kobby when he stops by to pick me up. You think I enjoy spending time in those filthy police jails? Don't worry, okay? Now let's stop all of this before Emma starts with her "*politics is not good for digestion*" theory,' he said, mimicking his younger sister's high-pitched voice.

'I don't talk like that, do I, Mama? And politics *is* bad for digestion – so there!' Emma responded, still giggling while looking at her mother for confirmation.

'No, you don't, darling, and you're right, so we'll stop talking politics now and it's time you also stopped laughing at me too. Hop-hip, hip-hop, hippity-hop – what's the difference? At least you all understood me – so there – to you as well,' she laughed.

Saga truly cherished these moments when all the family were together and generally at peace with each other. He loved the easy banter and the way his parents always shared in the jokes and discussions. He loved his parents for being quite open and modern-minded in an environment where personal enlightenment was generally not encouraged. The Government indeed found it convenient to keep the general population as ignorant, as uninformed and as conservative as possible. But it would only be a matter of time before the crisis within the larger society would burst forth into their warm home, sweeping all before it and leaving nothing in its wake but ruination and emotional debris.

CHAPTER THREE

Jaw, Jaw and Not War, War

The family were still gathered at the dining table after lunch without Emma, who had hurtled up the stairs to her room to do her homework, when Aba, their mother, spoke sternly to her son.

'Obo, I know you shrugged me off about the riots because Emma was here. So now, tell me the truth – what is going on? What is the matter with you people? Don't you get tired of all the beatings and suffering at the hands of these policemen and soldiers? You should stop and think before you act. You act like people who have never been to school and know no better!'

It was Obo's turn to get serious. 'Why are you doing this, Mama? You know we have no choice in this. We still don't know what has happened to some of our mates who were arrested the last time. We just don't know where they've been sent. Their parents are frantic with worry. The Government must be forced to release them. They just can't keep detaining people without trial and continue to keep their whereabouts secret. What if they're being tortured? What if they're dead? Put yourself in the position of those parents and then tell me if we are doing the wrong thing!' Obo had not minced his words but realised he had probably been too candid, as his mother was now visibly shaken.

But it was his father who intervened to soften the impact. 'The boy is right, Aba. He did not mean to sound so harsh but he's right that they've no choice. Remember how frantic we were when he himself got locked up and we could not find which police detention centre he'd been taken to? Our ordeal was for just a couple of weeks and look how we almost fell apart. It's been months now and those boys and girls must be released and all of them accounted for, and it will probably take another student confrontation with the Government to achieve this.'

In his youth, Nana himself had been steeped in the anti-colonial struggles of their country. Consequently, with his background of political activism and his overall antipathy towards illiberal government, he tended to be a touch more sympathetic towards the activism of his son.

A very unsettled Aba addressed them gently. 'Are you and Obo saying that the only way out of this mess is for the students to riot in the streets again? Obo, didn't you tell us a while back that you and Kobby with some of your other colleagues were thrashing out matters with the Minister of Internal Affairs as well as the Public Education Minister? Is dialogue not better than this rioting? Is "jaw, jaw" not better than "war, war", as Winston Churchill said, or you have forgotten your history?'

'Ma, it's not like we haven't been trying. The Interior Minister has been stalling us. These days, he sends word to Kobby and others on our negotiating team that he's too busy with "matters of national importance" to meet with us, and that we should have thought about the consequences before demonstrating in the streets. As for the Public Education Minister, he's always off on foreign trips and is hardly ever around. But we've heard from a good source that it is the President himself who has vowed to teach us a lesson. What choice do we then have?

'And by the way, we've also decided to step up our agitation for a return to constitutional rule, multi-party democratic elections, and an end to this useless border war that for us, can only be classified as a war of blame. All of this is in the planning stages but I'll keep you all posted,' Obo replied, with a very determined look on his face.

'So, is this vicious cycle never going to end?' asked Aba, feeling quite defeated.

'Not till our guys are released and we have some firm answers about the transition to democracy, plus a timetable for a phased de-escalation of the border war in the shortest possible time. Kids are dying in that war, Mama. So, I imagine it will continue for a while since those brutes at the top won't relinquish power any day soon. But we'll eventually make them. Sorry folks, but I've got to get ready now. Kobby will be here soon. Ma, you still want to interrogate the poor man when he gets here?'

'No – it's okay. You boys should take care of yourself. There's some rice and spinach and goat stew and some provisions for you to take back to campus in the kitchen. It's in a basket on the table,' replied Aba, who was further unsettled by the steely determination in her son's voice.

'Thanks Ma. Saga, I remember you saying something about going to get trainers at the market. Want a lift with us?' Obo asked his brother.

Saga thanked him for the offer but explained that Ibrahim was stopping by soon and they'd walk since it wasn't really that far.

Indeed, Saga had not uttered a word during the entire discussion. He simply noted all that was said and filed it away. He would think about it later. For now, he silently wished his brother well and hoped that he would not get arrested again. He told them it was also time for him to get ready for Ibrahim, which prompted his father to point at the centre table in the living room, saying that the envelope on it had the money for his trainers. Saga said a grateful thank you and also made to leave, watching his mother staring vacantly into space as he climbed the stairs to his bedroom.

To the extent that it was humanly possible, Aba loved her children equally. Of course, some were harder to manage, caused more trouble, and showed more affection during the various stages of their growth, which she simply saw as the normal course of things. Neither her husband nor the children themselves could say with any truthfulness which child she loved the most. She loved her children dearly and was proud of them. She showered them with all the affection she had, but not to the point of doting. She appreciated their differences, similarities, and where they complemented each other, and believed that she and Nana had done a fine job of bringing them up. She could, nonetheless, be quite clinical when it came to analysing them.

Her eldest son, Obo, for example, took after his father in more ways than one, with the only exception being his rather fair complexion, which he had inherited from her. He was now 24 years old, and would have been admitted to the bar by now as a barrister, following in his father's legal footsteps, but for the student riots at the universities, which had disrupted normal academic schedules. He was tall – standing just under six-feet – handsome with full features and very impressive to behold. He had an air of distracted seriousness about him, though not averse to joking and laughing from time to time.

Of all the children, it appeared as though he was the one who had imbibed their father's teachings the most, and was literally on a quest to save the world. He had hardly been in any serious trouble in school as an adolescent, apart from being suspended once for leading a minor rebellion against some teacher who did not wish to spare the rod. Obo was also a straight-A student. He was also the vice-president of the National Students' Union. He had a considerable following as he inspired confidence, but it was as though he was someone who people were comfortable being in awe of from a distance. It was not that he disdained intimacy. It was just that he appeared not to eagerly encourage it.

Saga, on the other hand, exuded genuine warmth wherever he went, and drew people towards him with his ever-ready smile and his unconscious air of elegant nonchalance. He did not shy away from friendships. He had always been an optimist and attributed this to his bulk. A large person like himself, he claimed, always lived in hope of being slim.

Saga was not a seriously unserious person. It was just that he had a tendency to see the lighter side of things. Yet, as and when he chose to exert himself, he was capable of producing a few A grades in class. As a rule, however, he was usually content with not working too hard, preferring to do just enough to remain within his usual top third of his class. He showed an aptitude for maths, but was more interested in discovering and using big and clever words. Even as a child of five, he had stumbled upon the word 'sagacity' and virtually adopted it as if it were his own baby. Of course, at the time, he phonetically pronounced it 'Sagakity'. He would strut around a room, asking those present, 'Am I Sagakity?' And for some time, his parents were at a complete loss as to what or who a Sagakity was. He used the word so often that after a while, he was jokingly called Sagakity by all, and soon, the shortened version of Saga became his pet name by which he became known to everyone including his parents. On filling his admission forms for secondary school, he had insisted that Saga be added as his middle name to make it semi-official. Later, in his teens, he would often joke that he knew even as a child that he would grow up to be 'sagacious' and thus full of wisdom.

Saga did not have his brother's light skin and liked to jokingly describe himself as being 'desirably chocolaty'. He had been in trouble at school a few times, mainly for covering for his friend, Ibrahim, whose pranks were often not appreciated by the teaching staff. But that was not to say he had always been entirely blameless. He had also been suspended once for smoking cigarettes in the school toilet – that had gone down very badly at home. Saga had equally imbibed his daddy's progressive thinking but was loathe to be drawn into arguments about what he truly believed in. Unconsciously, he tended to act out his beliefs rather than talk about them. Despite his overall light-heartedness, his parents sensed that Saga realised and understood a lot more than he let on, and harboured some deeply buried restlessness within him. They were quite baffled by this but were not quite sure how to broach the matter with him.

Emma had also inherited her mother's lightness of skin and was certainly very much in the front row when good looks were being handed out, with beautiful, curly hair to boot. Though lean and quite lanky, she was nonetheless starting to sprout what could be called budding breasts, and thus announcing her forward march towards puberty. She was of course too young to understand a lot of her family's liberal-minded views, but the seeds had been sown, and it could be said of her to be headed in that general direction. To date, she had at the very least firmly grasped the belief that men and women were certainly most equal *at all times.*

Nana's constant teachings, together with the force of his own example, had sunk into the collective consciousness of his children in a manner that made him also very proud of them. In recent times, however, he had nonetheless been forced to caution them not to share these sentiments too openly and indiscriminately, since they generally lived in a society where such liberal views were now viewed as harmful by the Government.

Indeed, not known to his family, his very liberal views, which he had at times unguardedly espoused in public and during conversations with his neighbours at the café over beer, had already been tagged as dangerously subversive in certain official quarters. And this, among other things, was what was ultimately to bring his family into conflict with the authorities, with harrowing and far-reaching repercussions for them all.

CHAPTER FOUR

Rude Awakening

'I checked online when I got home, Saga, and I found out that your Botox thing is used to get thick African lips like Angelina Jolie rather than for big behinds,' Ibrahim boasted, as they walked on the narrow, beaten earth pathway alongside the busy Independence Road, which led straight into the city centre. Concrete pavements were not a regular feature alongside most African roads. Indeed, a great number of the roads in many parts of their city and country were simply not tarred.

The beaten earth pathway they walked on was very close to the road, such that they could constantly feel the hurried, whooshing air of cars that passed them by. Indeed, a motley collection of every imaginable variety of vehicular modes of transportation streamed past them in an unyielding array. These ranged from high end, latest versions of very expensive cars such as Mercedes Benz, Lexus, Audi, VW, Toyota, and their counterpart SUV models to cars that were battered and at least three to four decades old – veritable metal carcasses on squeaky, rickety wheels, which simply would not quit, just like Ibrahim.

'I know you're into chicks as well, but please be aware that you are way behind those of us who are living authorities on women and womanhood! You should stick to what you know, like big words and food, and let me handle the rest.'

'Talking of food, look at that advert. The restaurant is called "Don't Mind Your Wife Chop Bar". I don't think my mama would like that at all!

The boys laughed.

'As for the Botox thing, I remember reading it somewhere. I'll find that article for you, and I keep telling you that you should be careful about this "chicks" business in front of women. Some girl is going to smack you and give you what for one of these days for it.'

'Don't worry, man – you think I'm stupid enough to say "chicks" or "babes" in front of the likes of your mom or any of those other fierce women-lib characters? Not even in front of your bossy sister, Emma! Tell me, who needs that kind of hassle?' said an exasperated Ibrahim, who was not quite at home with being deprived of what he saw as his harmless 'chicks' and 'babes' lingo.

'Hey, Ibrahim, you think it's going to rain? Look out there,' exclaimed Saga, pointing seaward at some dark clouds that for now appeared to be lingering some distance away. Though they could not see the sea from where they were, the coast was only a few miles away from their neighbourhood, and less than a mile from the market as well, albeit from a slightly different geographical angle.

'Wow – those are definitely clouds that can't wait to unleash their rain on us all. Anyway, let's hurry, as I've also promised my mom I'll do some stuff for her before it gets dark, and you'd better find that article so I can do my own investigations into this Botox business.'

They soon got to the central market, which was a vast, sprawling, open beehive of human activity, covering an area of about two square miles and dotted with mini stalls made mainly from plywood and cardboard with corrugated aluminium sheets serving as roofs. There were of course some concrete buildings that were gaily painted with advertisements and partitioned into shops.

Though Saga generally had little affection for shopping, he didn't mind the hustle and bustle of the marketplace if taken in small and irregular doses. It was a colourful sight indeed. Almost every imaginable produce and product was on display, ranging from food items such as nicely stacked fresh fruit of assorted hues, vegetables, canned fish, canned meat such as corned beef and luncheon meat, to the latest designer shoes and perfumes, cosmetics, DVDs, CDs, music equipment – you name it.

He found the incessant noise of traders loudly advertising the extraordinary and oftentimes imaginary qualities of their wares quite pleasing. He also enjoyed the ceaseless bargaining that went on at almost every stall, as buyers and sellers squabbled heatedly to get the better of each other.

The market was dominated by women who wore an assortment of brightly-patterned Western clothes, and 'traditional', multi-patterned Dutch Dumas cloth outfits and headgear. The vibrant panorama of colour made Saga feel very much alive. He sometimes wondered what it would be like to view all this interactive drama from on high, in something like a hovering helicopter. The picturesque image that came to mind from on high would be a vast sea of colourful ants, foraging vigorously in all directions from sunup until sundown.

But what pleased him most of all were the assorted aromas coming from innumerable open-air food stalls. Traditional foods such as fried plantain with beans and salt beef stew; plain rice with goat meat stew; spicy spinach stew with smoked tuna fish and boiled yams; exceedingly delicious brown rice with beans and hot pepper sauce, and 'cow-foot' stew; soft, pounded cassava balls called fufu with hot mutton pepper soup – to mention but a few of his favourites – were invitingly on display in huge, steaming, iron cauldrons perched on equally huge, fiery coal pots. The food was dished straight onto plastic or metal plates or into traditional earthenware bowls and handed over to queues of salivating customers, who hurriedly paid and sat down to eat there and then on long, wooden benches and tables, using rather suspicious-looking spoons or just their fingers. For some reason, forks and knives never came into play here. Those who wanted to take their food away had it expertly packaged for them in cocoyam leaves or cellophane bags, and finally wrapped in old edition newspapers.

Saga loved street food and enjoyed eating out in the open, though he knew his parents disapproved of it for hygienic reasons. Due to insufficient hygienic conditions, patrons of open-air cooked foods had on occasion been known to suffer from a variety of ailments. Typhoid was a major culprit in this regard. This, however, did not deter Saga, who apart from not being one to joke with his food, was oftentimes caught up in the 'forbidden fruit' syndrome whenever he came to the market.

Today, however, they'd had lunch not so long ago, and with Ibrahim in a hurry, they only bought a double portion each of *kele* – which was deliciously salt, ginger and chilli-spiced fried plantain and banana, diced into small pieces and served in aromatic banana leaves. This they munched with golden-shelled groundnuts on their way to the footwear stalls, whose proprietors had colonised a section of the market to the exclusion of other wares.

'Hey Saga, this *kele* is extra hot today. Let's stop at a drinks kiosk for some seriously iced coke or Fanta, or even some Sprite. My mouth is burning like crazy,' managed a distressed-looking Ibrahim, who was obviously suffering from the extra-hot ground chilli pepper he had requested on his portion.

'No problem – there's one at the corner of Egom Street just up the road behind those stalls. The girl who serves there is out of this world. You should see her. She's a local version of Halle Berry with extra attributes. Anyway, I warned you about the extra chilli pepper, but as usual, you have to be macho in all things. Just continue to suffer a bit more, we'll be there soon,' replied an eager Saga, who was glad for the opportunity to set his sights on the local Halle Berry.

'When are you going to stop using these big words of yours?' Ibrahim asked in mock exasperation, then asked quite excitedly, momentarily forgetting about his chilli pepper induced discomfort, 'But what extra attributes are we talking about here, Saga?'

'But you just used the word you say is big – so what's your point? What's so big about "attributes" anyhow? As for the girl – just wait and see because seeing is believing,' replied Saga, but feeling the urge to taunt his friend a little more, added, 'Ibrahim, tell me, but why do you insist on pulling your jeans down to the middle of your bum? You think you are in some "hood" somewhere in some projects in downtown Los Angeles or Brooklyn or what?'

'My boy, 50 Cent, and all my favourite rappers wear their pants that way. It's the trend, Saga. As for you, you belong to colonial times with your non-trendy retro dressing, so there!' retorted Ibrahim in an attempt to imitate Saga's sister, Emma.

'Can't you try being original for a change? And you glorify these rap stars too much like they're some tin gods. They're great and all but you forget they're also human. I can bet you my last cent that some superstar somewhere is sitting on his loo doing number two as we speak. And trust me, when he's done, the product he leaves behind won't be frozen and preserved just like it goes for all of us – *so there* to you as well!' replied Saga, hurling back the same words and causing his friend to stop and double over in laughter.

'You are crazy – you know that? And I'm just going to ignore you before I get bombarded with yet another lecture about copying only the useless aspects of an otherwise edifying culture,' said a still laughing Ibrahim.

'Good for you, and you also used a big word. You're getting there, Ibrahim, and I think there's still the possibility of redemption for you,' replied Saga, who was also now laughing at his own silly sallies.

But their happiness suddenly evaporated. A couple of policemen had descended upon a family of miserable-looking beggars who were squatting with their begging bowls at an intersection just a few paces from the drinks stall. It appeared the policemen were roughly attempting to drive the beggars away from their chosen spot. The adult beggars, along with their two filthy-looking children, who looked no older than 10, were all clad in a tattered assortment of clothes. The grime on the children made it practically impossible for Saga and Ibrahim to tell whether they were male or female.

One of the policemen was shouting quite rudely in Pidgin English – a widely-used lingua franca made up of proper English language and words from literally translated local vernacular dialects.

'Make you get out from here, you useless refugee peoples. Make you go back for your country and make you go find job before I go arrest you, plus your dirty, small childrens as well.

You de make we our country smell with your dirty ways!' And with that, the policeman gave the beggar man a vicious kick to his side, causing him to stumble and shriek in pain.

This pointless act of brutality caused many passers-by to stop and gawk. The beggar man, in his anger and humiliation at being assaulted for no apparent reason, shouted back quite unwisely, also in pidgin English, 'What be da meaning of dis nonsense? Why you kick me wen I not do nothin'? Why you be harassing me plus my family? We not worry anybody and we not hurt anybody! Like not your President that him do war for my country, you tink that I go be sitting here beg and beg for your street plus my wife and little childrenses? You tink say we like to make refugees or wat? Which fool for dis world want to make refugee, I ask you? You policemen no can find any proper thing to do wid your time wid all dem plenty crime for dis city instead of make you harass we innocent beggars that no do notin?'

Many in the gathering crowd gasped at the man's foolish daring. Being a foreigner probably meant that he had no idea that one did not exchange words with members of the security forces in a police state – be they soldiers or policemen – where they were literally a law unto themselves. And indeed, this was certainly more than enough to trigger off the policemen, who suddenly yanked out their heavy leather belts from their waists, and as if on cue, started thrashing the beggar man with all the strength they could muster. Many in the crowd were appalled by this and started appealing loudly in pidgin English, 'STOP… PLEASE MAKE YOU STOP! WHAT YOU ARE DOING? WHY YOU FOR BEAT DEM? DEM NO COMMIT ANY CRIME SO MAKE YOU STOP DIS BEATING,' repeatedly to the policemen, who paid no heed to them. Caught up as they were in the frenzy of their mindless brutality, one of the policemen started thrashing the beggar woman as well, equally oblivious to her cries of pain and terror. The crowd however did not dare physically intervene.

Saga was shocked at what he was witnessing. It was the first time he was coming face to face with the wanton police brutality he had heard so much about. As if in a trance, he started moving towards the harrowing scene, but was quickly pulled back by Ibrahim, yanking him by his shirt, 'Let's get out of here, Saga. This is bad stuff,' he whispered urgently to his friend, who appeared to be in a daze.

But before Ibrahim could hustle him away, an amazing thing occurred right before them. A tall, well-dressed, very light-skinned, young lady, who looked somewhat their age, appeared from nowhere and rushed into the fray, bravely pushing one of the policemen away from their victims, and turned to face the other, while yelling at the top of her voice, 'STOP THIS MINUTE! I SAID STOP!' There was no doubting the authority with which she spoke. It silenced the protesting onlookers.

Though her face was suffused with anger, it was plain for all to see that she was very good looking indeed. The policemen stopped, looking quite puzzled. One of the policemen who had managed to stop wheezing from his exertions, started to advance towards her and asked menacingly in regular English, 'Who the hell are you? And how dare you interfere with our work?'

The girl was unafraid and did not back off. Rather, she motioned to the beggars with sweeping backward movements of her arms that they should stand behind her, which they did. She then looked at the policeman squarely in the face, replying gently but still with undisguised authority, 'I'm Zara Yalley. My father is General Yalley, and this is what you call doing your work? Beating up people who have nothing and nowhere to go? Have they broken any laws? Answer me! Now!'

The policeman stopped dead in his tracks. The name had registered. He spluttered, 'You… you mean Minister General Yalley?'

'Yes, the Minister for Presidential Affairs. You want to see my ID?'

The policemen were aghast. After all, who didn't know the dreaded General Yalley – the chief right-hand man to the President himself, and practically in charge of all security in the land? Holy Mother of God, what were they to do? They stood there dumbfounded and very much afraid. They did not even dare offer an explanation. They knew that to risk saying the wrong thing to the daughter of the likes of General Yalley could mean very serious trouble for them. Their best bet was to just shut up and look down repentantly, which they did while studying their police-issue jack boots in abject contrition.

But the young Zara lady had no time for them. She turned and started talking to the beggars, while examining the ghastly, discoloured bruises that were fast emerging on the arms of the Tuareg-looking lady beggar. Just then, a new shiny black Mercedes Benz SUV with recognisable government licence plates pulled up, and before it could park properly, a hefty looking, very dark-skinned, bald soldier with a side arm and Staff Sergeant stripes and epaulettes rushed out and went straight to the young lady who called herself Zara.

'We were looking all over for you, young madam Zara, near the shop you went into. You just disappeared. It is only when we noticed this crowd that we came over. Is everything okay, ma'am?' he asked solicitously, while casting a baleful glare at the policemen who patently appeared to be the obvious offenders. The driver of the Mercedes Benz SUV, who was also in olive-green military attire and sported the stripes of a corporal, soon joined them. He carried a side arm in a black leather holster.

Zara explained what had happened to them.

Whether her military companions agreed with her or not could not immediately be discerned on their faces. Brutalising innocents was a favourite pastime for most security personnel. Nonetheless, both the driver and bodyguard were quick to openly side with their young charge and immediately took issue with the policemen. The military carried a lot more weight and authority than the police and were thus overall superior.

'What de wrong you police people! You make crazy or wat?' the driver yelled at the cops, and turned to address Zara, 'Madam, do you wish me to report them to your father or to their commanding officer? I can take down their names and service numbers. I can also ask them to report at the office to save time. We will arrest them if they fail to turn up. Which do you prefer, madam?'

Those in the crowd who had heard this exchange started shouting, 'MAKE YOU REPORT DEM, MAKE YOU ARREST DEM TOO! DEM NO BE GOOD PEOPLE!'

Zara then turned and gave the vengeful crowd a slightly deprecatory smile before focusing her attention on the offenders. She had half a mind to side with the crowd and get the policemen punished for their unwarranted brutality. She however did not have the heart to do so. Also, she generally didn't like using her father's position for anything. She knew very well that they would be in for some serious beatings as well as the sack. She reasoned that they probably had wives and children to feed. She couldn't be responsible for that.

The policemen had, by this time, been thoroughly cut down to size and were shifting their gaze to nervously peer at her and back at their shoes, in undisguised fear for their careers, not to mention their safety. She suddenly pitied them and told them they could go. They thanked her repeatedly and profusely, and scurried off to the sound of loud boos from the spectators. Just then, a very old woman emerged from the crowd and hobbled up to the Zara lady, placing a shrivelled, bony hand on her cheek, and said, 'Heaven bless you my daughter for your good heart. I will always remember you in my prayers. You are one of God's chosen.' And with that, she turned around and hobbled off. That was when a very amazed Saga and Ibrahim decided to also leave. They had long forgotten about their drinks and the delightful localised Halle Berry.

A very disturbed Saga followed an equally disturbed and unusually non-smiling Ibrahim Koto to the shoe stalls, where they picked a pair of trainers and paid without even bothering to bargain. They did not even care about whatever they might have gained by way of savings through bargaining to buy some other delicacy on their way back home, as had been their original plan. They were that troubled.

They were barely halfway home when the skies, as if sensing their despondent mood, abruptly turned even bleaker, as the darkening clouds emerged directly overhead. Sudden, strong gusts of wind were whipping up litter, dust and sand in a flurried frenzy, as if to announce the imminent rain in no uncertain terms. The heaviness of the initial drizzle that followed suggested the actual downpour was barely seconds away. Thus, Ibrahim wisely shouted 'time to run' and with that, tore down the street with Saga at his heels, amidst people running pell-mell in all directions, seeking temporary shelter from the oncoming tropical deluge that had the annoying habit of not giving sufficient notice of its arrival beyond taunting them with grey clouds.

'Children's Park Pavilion,' yelled a now struggling Ibrahim, who was having some difficulty pulling up his trendily-positioned jeans, which were impeding his running. He finally got the better of his pants and pointed to the approaching park as they turned and zigzagged between the mildly flowing traffic in a bid to reach their sanctuary before getting soaked. But that proved to be wishful thinking, as the heavens opened to release heavy sheets of unyielding, torrential, tropical rain.

Saga and Ibrahim soon made their way across the now thoroughly soggy grass to the shelter of the large pavilion that stood at the centre of the park, drenched and shivering slightly. They sat down on one of the wooden benches that cluttered the deserted pavilion, instinctively using their hands and forearms to swipe the water from their faces and out of their eyes as puddles began to form around their feet.

They sat in silence for a while, catching their breath and watching the heavy downpour, until a still distracted Saga asked gently through slightly chattering teeth, 'Ibrahim, why do these security people do that? Why do they pick on innocent people and beat them up for no reason? Have they no feelings? Are they not human? Don't they have families like everybody else? How would they like it if people went around beating their wives and children or their sisters and mothers? It's getting too much. Way too much.' Saga got worked up as he spoke.

'I don't know, man. It just gets crazier and crazier every day and everybody is getting more and more fed up with all this violence. But I don't think it's going to stop anytime now because…' Ibrahim stopped abruptly in mid-sentence, looked at his friend quizzically and asked, 'Saga why were you moving towards the policemen and the beggars? You know we should always move away from trouble, not towards it!'

'I don't know. I wasn't a hundred per cent aware that I was actually moving towards the action. All I know is that I couldn't stand there and just watch such a horrible display. I only realised it when you pulled me back.'

'You should be careful. You just can't mess around with those police and soldier brutes. Don't even think about getting involved. Please never again,' admonished his very worried friend.

But it was as though Saga did not hear him. He simply looked at Ibrahim and said, 'I've seen that girl before but I didn't realise till later that she's our mate Junior Yalley's sister. She looks just like him. She must be his twin. Wow – she's so bloody brave. But why did she stop them? Don't all those security thugs ultimately work for her father? I know her brother wouldn't have stopped them. He'd have probably joined in bashing those poor refugee beggars.'

'You should know her. That's silly Yalley's twin all right, and she's at Brewman Girls High. I thought I pointed her out to you a while back. But boy, that girl is pretty, and there's certainly no need for your Botox stuff there. But for her dangerous family, she would definitely be one to chase. Don't ask me why she did what she did, but I've heard she's nothing like her brother. Ask your kid sister what she's like. She is her senior in school so she must know something about her.'

The rain abated after a while, allowing them to leave amidst a gentler drizzle. The rest of their walk was, however, done in damp silence, which was rare for them indeed. Each appeared to be caught up in their own morose thoughts. The unpleasant incident with the beggars had affected them more deeply than they realised, and being belted by the downpour had done little to shift their dour mood. It was getting dark now, and they soon parted company but without their usual bonhomie.

Later that same night, Saga lay in bed, reliving the market scene over and over again, and wondered about what was happening in his country. He also thought about the tense discussion between his mother and Obo that afternoon, and knew that all was far from well, and that presently, there was no denying that they lived in what could only be described as a fear-ridden police state. Not so long ago, he had foolishly thought that much of what was going on was quite removed from him, his family and friends. That had ceased to be the case ever since his brother was arrested and detained some months ago.

And today, the market scene had rudely awoken him to the realisation that his ostrich-like approach of literally burying one's head in the sand was fast becoming untenable. Whether he liked it or not, the crisis had found its way to their doorstep and was seeking to penetrate right into the heart of the cocoon he thought they were safely ensconced in. There was also the issue of his father having felt compelled to resign a while back from his government ministerial job because of his serious displeasure at the worsening conditions in the country. Saga knew that like most genuine patriots, his father was truly heartbroken with all the troubles that were now daily unfolding in their society. These were issues he was determined to discuss with his father very soon.

CHAPTER FIVE

A Rock and a Hard Place

Saga was sitting with his father at the dining table. They had just had a delicious lunch of pounded yam fufu and his favourite peanut butter soup, but this time, with the excellent addition of chicken. It was just the two of them. Everyone else was out and Saga decided that now was a good time as any to seek some answers from his father about the appalling situation in their country.

'Dada, what do you really think about this government? In school, the teachers tell us that all is well, but that does not seem to be the case. They teach us that this is the best government ever! And yet I saw government men just beating up innocent people in the market! I know you once supported them. Is that not true? But you would not support anyone aggressive. You don't believe in that.'

'Yes Saga, in truth, I was initially a supporter of the Regime when it first came to power. President Brewman was then just a captain with ideals. Now, he has become a field marshal and President for life.'

'But Dad, what made you support such a guy? Look at the misery he has brought to our country.'

'It was not always like that, Saga. At the time, they appeared to be progressive and had grassroots backing. They were a new military government, and I actually believed they intended to create a true welfare state in which everyone would benefit from the oil deposits that had just been discovered. I believed they were just going to do a short period of political house-cleaning and then hand over power to a democratic and constitutionally elected government. They sounded so sincere and made their promises with such ardent fervour that I was completely taken in.'

'But Daddy, what changed? When did you stop supporting them?'

'When the Regime did a U-turn in the face of popular demands for the long overdue return to multi-party elections and constitutional rule. President Brewman and his government had tasted unlimited power with no one and no constitution to keep them in check. They had also made huge amounts of money from dubious lucrative oil deals. Making so much money through corruption had become so easy for them. Eventually, they decided against handing over power to any elected body or party through democracy. They had a new mission, which was to cling on to their unrestricted power and their absolute control of the country's rich natural resources.'

'Wow! So, they broke all their promises and started stealing money?'

Nana nodded, wishing the truth were more palatable.

'But Dad, that does not explain all the brutality that is going on, like what I saw in the market – even at school sometimes, between Muslims and Christians. Major Kata told me that this hostility between the various religions is a recent thing and that it was never like that before. I really need to understand this.'

Nana then proceeded to give Saga a brief history of how the current dictatorship they lived in was nurtured and consolidated by President Brewman.

Nana explained that in order to discourage increasing demands for the military to hand over power to a democratically elected civilian government, the Regime soon started arresting and punishing all those who dared to oppose its rule. It also moved to brutally clamp down on those bold enough ask about what had happened to all the promises of increased social wealth, social justice and political party elections. They then went on the offensive to constantly seek, hunt down and savagely prey on real and imagined enemies with a destructiveness that could never have been anticipated by trusting people such as Nana.

Far from its original liberal attitudes, the Regime, in a fashion after the long-expelled colonists, decided to embrace the tactics of divide and rule to maintain itself in power. It saw the use of sectarianism as a powerful tool in not only dividing the population, but also as an instrument of generating widespread fear and insecurity, which would, in turn, justify the need for strong government.

Consequently, the two principal ethnic groupings within the country – the Northerners and Southerners – were pitted against each other through the Regime's devious machinations. This polarisation was even more pernicious since the country was demographically structured in such a way that most of the nation's minority Muslims lived mainly in the North, with the majority of Christians in the Southern areas. Since the President was himself a Christian Southerner, official propaganda soon branded the Muslim Northerners as the dreaded internal enemy, who sought not only to bring the regime down and enslave Southern Christians in the process, but who, in a most unpatriotic move, also wanted to invite a neighbouring Islamic country to enter the struggle on their behalf through military invasion. They were also said to be supporters of International Islamic terrorist movements that sought to render the country wholly Islamic and introduce the much-feared Sharia Law.

Thus, in order to guarantee the internal and external security of the country, the Brewman Regime moved to declare an internal war on the Northerners through strong-arm repression, including the physical elimination or jailing of many Northern Muslim luminaries, especially their more outspoken leaders. Human rights and the rule of law were suspended as the country was placed under Martial Law. Western aid was cynically sought and readily given to combat those Northern supporters of international terror. This was soon followed by military skirmishes with the neighbouring country, said to be sympathetic to the Northern Islamic cause, citing some trumped-up charges of border violations and the creation of terror training camps within the border regions.

With the country at war and within the context of a consciously orchestrated fear-ridden society, the stage was thus set for the Regime to assume all power, and rule without reference or regard to anyone. The Regime further consolidated itself by donning Mufti, in which the President now wore Savile Row and Armani suits, as opposed to military fatigues, appointed a smattering of civilian ministers to disguise the core military nature of his government, and declared himself President-For-Life-Until-Further-Notice. He also declared himself as lifelong leader of a newly-formed political party for only Southerners, and organised farcical elections with himself as the only Presidential Candidate, winning 99.97% of the vote. No opposition to this was tolerated in any form and society indeed became very unsafe for all those who disapproved of the way in which the Regime was ruling the country.

Thus, the Regime revealed its dehumanising face by betraying the nation's trust, and transforming the country into a fear-ridden, brutal, totalitarian police state with a despotic President-For-Life-Until-Further-Notice thrown into the mix.

Saga sat silently, listening to all his father told him about their recent history as a nation. It was certainly not the best of historical narratives, though it explained quite a great deal.

His father had paused and was thoughtfully sipping a glass of water. Saga could tell his questions were wearing him out. He decided to ask just a couple more questions before leaving the man in peace. 'So Dad – all this didn't happen overnight. It took quite some time. So what finally compelled you to resign from the Ministry of Justice?'

'I am a lawyer, Saga. I believe in the rule of law and all that it represents in regulating any civilised society. As I mentioned, it came to a point when the Regime suspended the rule of law and other fundamental legal practices such as habeas corpus. This meant that the Regime could now arrest and detain anyone indefinitely and without trial. I could not justify working under circumstances where the most fundamental human rights were being denied. The oppression, divisiveness and brutality had simply become too much for me to be associated with them any longer. I thought some of us could work from the inside and make things better, but I was sorely mistaken. My friend, Mr Gab's arrest and public beating was the final straw.'

'But Dad, ever since you resigned, those Brewman snoops and spies have been hanging around us like we were troublemakers!'

'It is because they now see me as a potential dissident, and this Regime cannot abide dissidents, which is why those who oppose them are often arrested and detained. Saga, you know what a dissident is, don't you?'

'Of course I know what a dissident is, Dada. It means they see you as one of those subversive troublemakers. So Dad, are you a dissident?' Saga expectantly asked.

'Hmm Saga – yes, I am, but not in a bad way, as the Regime would have you believe. Like all genuine patriots, I want what is best for this country, and another thing I want is for us to continue this conversation another time as I am late for a meeting and you, no doubt, have some studying to do'

Indeed Nana's resignation placed him on the Government's list of potentially dangerous troublemakers who would have to be carefully watched by the teeming spies that had been pressed into the Government's service out of fear, sheer greed, malice or plain destructive ignorance.

He had initially reasoned that deciding to do something about the situation was a sole personal decision he had to make for himself. But that line of thinking proved resoundingly inaccurate as he eventually came to the grim conclusion that the Government would have absolutely no qualms about severely punishing his entire family if ever he was caught working against them. This was certainly a matter of life and death, and though all his instincts and impulses propelled him to join in a struggle against a bunch of criminally-minded people who were tearing his country apart and destroying all that he held sacred, he was nonetheless terrified of putting his entire family in mortal danger. He knew he had to be very careful.

Nana was conflicted. His family's safety was imperative. Yet, if he remained a passive bystander while his country was ruined, his children and future generations would pay the price. Morals were very expensive at this time. There was also the critical matter of self-preservation.

Nana was confident he was no coward and that if necessary, he would risk life and limb for what he believed in. But of what use would he be to himself, his family and his beliefs if he quickly became dead? People had already 'disappeared' for challenging the Government, and whether they were still alive or rotting in some lonely, loathsome jail was not known.

Nana was caught between the proverbial rock and hard place.

What he needed was a delicate balance. A delicate balance between having as much of an impact in the struggle to set things right as his abilities permitted, while preserving the lives of himself and his family. But it would be a difficult balance to find and maintain, as the Government had eyes and ears everywhere.

Brewman, the President-For-Life-Until-Further-Notice, had become 'Big Brother' and was watching everyone!

CHAPTER SIX

No Rwanda

It wasn't that Saga was an insensitive young man, impervious to his troubled surroundings. He was actually very sensitive towards other people and their problems, though he did not always show the true extent of his feelings. Not so long ago, however, he had simply felt somewhat detached from it all and it was as though he was watching some drama close to him, but one that did not touch him directly. But all that was now changing and ironically, it was not his father's or brother's activities that were soon to graduate his family prominently onto the Regime's critical list of dangerous troublemakers – but rather his own.

The official persecution of the Northerners had found its way into the schools.

Saga was initially dismayed when some of his favourite teachers were hounded out of the school on the charge that they were not teaching the students the basics of the Brewman Regime's new definition of patriotism. This new patriotism, broken down to its bare essentials, simply meant hating and hounding the internal Northern 'enemy', despite the fact that no evidence whatsoever had, as of yet, been given as conclusive proof of Northern perfidy or treason. It also meant blindly supporting everything the Government did, adulating every law they decreed into existence, praising the President like he was some non-erring demigod, and spying and reporting to the authorities those who dared to question his methods of ruling.

The thinly-disguised charge levelled against these teachers was absurd to the likes of Saga, since all of those dismissed were Northern Muslims in the first place. How could the authorities expect teachers from the North to preach destruction against their own persons and families?

Recently, a gang of Christian students attacked and beat up a number of their Muslim schoolmates. These acts of brutality created an inhospitable siege mentality within the school, and made the likes of Saga very unhappy. After all, his best friend was a Muslim.

Saga just could not understand why people who had been friends all their young lives and had shared much together as they were growing up could suddenly turn on each other with such ferocity and for no apparent good reason. Here were people who knew each other's parents, lived in the same communities, participated in many social events together such as going to each other's parties, confirmations, family weddings and even funerals of relatives, and yet were suddenly at each other's throats like a pack of wild animals, and all at the behest of a brutal dictator.

At home, Saga protested vehemently against his teachers and the government.

His father tried to explain to Saga that though he was absolutely correct to dislike the evils occurring in his school and wider society, it was nonetheless very important that he kept such thoughts to himself for now.

'Saga, I know how you're feeling and we fully sympathise with you. You know many of my friends have also been arrested and badly beaten up by these soldiers for no reason at all. Look at what happened to Mr Gab, for example, who is not even a Northerner or a Muslim. But Saga, you have to be careful about what you say and do. You have to let your head rule your heart at the moment. No one is in a position to fight the Regime head on at this stage and I don't want you to get into trouble, so you must not say bad things about the Government or the President in school or in public. Not even in the café here.

'And I am not saying that you shouldn't be disgusted or upset with what is going on in your school and all around us. And yes, your mother and I have taught you to abhor such injustices. However, all I'm saying is that there is a time and place for everything and that sometimes, discretion is the better part of valour, as you have learnt in your Shakespeare studies. Please be careful, my son,' he tried to reason with Saga.

'I understand, Dada, but something has to be done about it. For some days now, many of my friends who are Muslims haven't come to school because they're afraid. Ibrahim, of course, fears nothing, so he has been coming. But how are the others going to pass their exams if this continues? And can you believe that those responsible for the beatings are not going to be punished? And do you know the headmaster hasn't even seen it fit to announce what happened or to warn those stupid boys who conducted the beatings not to do so again? Something has to be done, Dada,' Saga replied, shaking his head all the time he was speaking.

His mother had stepped in at this stage. She had been sitting at the dining table, drawing up her weekly shopping list while listening to Saga and his father, who were seated in the part that formed the living room. She stopped to observe her son and was bothered about his intensity and the anger that was obviously burning in him. The boy was telling his father that he understood when it was obvious he was clearly refusing to understand anything, and this was not good at all! She got up, dragged a dining chair along through the archway that served as a divider between the dining and living areas, and placed it directly in front of Saga. She sat down facing him and used both her hands to raise his head to her eye level.

'Saga, listen to your father, okay? What is happening is bad but there isn't much we can do about it at the moment. It won't be forever and something will eventually be done, but right now, you must promise us that you will not go out there and do anything rash or stupid. And you will also not go about saying the things you've said here today. For now, you will simply concentrate on your exams and nothing else. Are we clear? Do we have your promise?'

The 'yes' that came from him in reply was very reluctantly given. Indeed, though Saga could understand what his parents were trying to explain, he nevertheless knew deep within that he could not take much more of what was happening to his school and friends. He was also becoming quite agitated over all the horrific stories he had been hearing lately of all manner of people being brutalised and arrested by the Government on the slightest pretext. He remembered as well the incident with the beggars at the market. The only problem was that he had no idea as to what he would do, or not do, should he be confronted again with a hideous situation such as what he had witnessed in the market. He simply could not predict how he would react, and that scared even him a little.

Watching him closely, his mother was far from convinced that the boy had truly acquiesced regarding the practical wisdom they were trying to impart to him. Consequently, she kept on at him, for the boy had to be made to understand:

'What is this feeble "yes" you are giving us? What do you think you can do about the situation, Saga? I am begging you to be wise. There is only so much we can say but please, for the sake of your family, if not for yourself, please listen to your father, okay?' And with this, she picked up the chair, dragged it back noisily to the dining table and left for the kitchen. The boy's recalcitrance was upsetting her but this was not the time to get angry. 'Temper, temper,' she kept repeating to herself in an effort to remain calm as she walked away.

Her husband watched her go in empathy and brusquely told Saga he could also leave, feeling equally exasperated with their son's attitude.

Unbeknown to them, Saga's baptism of fire was to happen shortly afterwards.

Even though Saga generally understood what his parents were saying about the need to restrain himself concerning the New Patriotism issue and how it was causing havoc in his school, he was nonetheless unsure whether he fully agreed with them in his heart.

'There must be something that can be done,' he kept repeating to himself. He had left the main house and was now sitting on a flat stone behind the café, with his repetitive thoughts as his only companion. He had gathered some pebbles in his hands and was aimlessly flinging them at the white bamboo fence that demarcated the boundaries of the café within their compound.

'Saga, has my fence offended you in some way I am not aware of? What's the matter, my boy? Why the long face?'

Saga was startled but happy to see his elderly friend, Major Kata, limp towards him. The retired Major then grabbed a folding metal chair that was resting against the wall, unfolded it and sat down facing Saga.

Major Kata was tall and had a full head of grey hair, which was in the process of actually turning lily-white. His neatly-trimmed beard was already resplendently white. He was a very quiet man and was rumoured to have an intriguing past. Not a bad past, but a mysterious one. He was said to have been once very wealthy, but had used almost all of his fortune for charitable works and now lived very modestly in a little bungalow he owned in Uso Town. Indeed, it was the only thing he owned, apart from his café-cum-shop he had set up on Saga's father's property.

His speech usually consisted of polite, monosyllabic responses when spoken to. Otherwise, he kept decidedly mute, and communicated only through smiles and allied facial expressions. It seemed the only person in the world whom the mysterious Major would actually converse with was Saga, and this baffled quite a number of the patrons, as with Saga's own parents. In fact, though the major was in his 60s, Saga was simply his best friend.

'So, tell me, my young friend, why are you looking so unhappy and flinging pebbles at my innocent fence?'

Saga told him all about the troubles and violence unfolding in his school. He explained about the unsettling atmosphere being generated as a result of some students trying to put the New Patriotism doctrine into practice. He further narrated what his parents had told him when he complained to them about these unsavoury developments.

'Ah, I see, Saga. I see,' replied Major Kata in his low, sonorous voice he barely used. 'I see,' he repeated yet again, and stared for a while at Saga, who was now getting a touch uncomfortable from the glare of his friend's relentless eyes.

'Major, is something wrong? Why are you staring at me like that?'

'Oh, I am sorry,' said the Major, as if coming out of a reverie. 'Forgive me, Saga. I was just thinking about what you said. And no – you have said nothing wrong. Rather your sentiments are spot on. You have a good heart. A pure one. And I like that about you. Yes, this Regime has to be stopped. This New Patriotism is nothing but hate-mongering. It must be stopped. That is how it all starts...' said the Major, his voice trailing off.

'That is how what starts?' asked Saga, sensing he was about to hear one of the rare stories the Major told none other than his young friend. Saga, for example, was one of the few people who knew that after resigning his commission in the Armed Forces, Major Kata, in his more youthful days, had played pivotal roles in the armed struggles of a number of African countries that actually had to engage in war with their colonial masters to attain independence. Major Kata was a veritable African Che Guevara indeed, but without the fame. So Saga knew this was going to be good.

'I was in Rwanda in the 90s during the butchery and the genocide. I went to visit an army friend of mine who was there with the UN troops that were supposed to be keeping the peace. He was a French man. A very good man.'

'You actually saw the killings in Rwanda? You really saw it?' asked Saga, who had learned about the Rwandan Genocide in school.

'Yes Saga, I saw some of it and, up until today, I wish I had never seen it. In fact, the reason why I have been limping for the past few years is because of an injury I sustained in Rwanda, trying to protect a group of minority Tutsis from being butchered. Someone slashed my leg with a very sharp machete, and I am even lucky to be alive, since it sliced the tendons at the back of my thigh and even nicked an artery. A lot of people think it's a bullet wound or shrapnel wound but it's not. You know what shrapnel is, don't you, Saga?'

'Come on, Major – who doesn't know what shrapnel is? Who doesn't know what bomb or grenade fragments are? I read, you know,' replied Saga with slight exasperation, as he was eager to hear the rest of the story. 'But Major, please tell me how come someone slashed you?'

'As I said, I was visiting my French friend, then serving with the UN mission in Rwanda. He was on a college campus in Kigali, guarding defenceless Tutsis who had sought refuge in the school. A message came from the UN High Command that all UN troops should "cease and desist" from involving themselves in any aspect of the genocide that was rapidly unfolding. They were to lay down their arms and confront no one, including the Hutus chasing after the Tutsis to slaughter them.'

'So, they had no choice but to obey and abandon their protection duties?' asked Saga, who was wondering who was then going to protect the defenceless Tutsis.

'Not exactly. My friend removed his UN army jacket and insignias in disgust, openly declaring his refusal to stand by and condone inaction that would lead to the slaughter of innocents.'

'What a brave man!'

'He refused to abandon his protection duty at the school and did not leave with the other UN troops when they were ordered away.'

'And you?'

'Of course, I was not going to run and abandon the principles I fought for most of my life, including the right of everyone to peacefully co-exist on this continent!'

'So, what happened next?' asked an excited Saga, who could barely breathe, listening to a real-life account of what transpired back then.

'Hmm Saga, it was not easy. Two other soldiers, also from France, refused to leave the college and stayed to help us protect the helpless Tutsis, who were mainly women and children. Soon, we heard from lookouts that the area on the campus where we were hiding the Tutsis was gradually being surrounded by Hutus, wielding machetes and baying like wild animals for

Tutsi blood. "Kill the Tutsi cockroaches", we could hear them chanting, so we led the women and children through a back route out of the college that led into some nearby wooded hills and safety. This we managed to do, although we had to engage with a seven-man team of frenzied, machete-wielding Hutu thugs who had anticipated our plan.'

'Wow Major. This was serious. How did you escape from the Hutus with the machetes?'

'Guess what, Saga? We had practically nothing to fight them off with. The UN soldiers had taken their weapons from my friend and his other two colleagues when they left. All they had between them were two jack knives, and I was, of course, unarmed. And this was what the four of us were supposed to use against seven rabid men wielding very sharp machetes. Can you imagine how difficult that was, Saga? We had to rely on a couple of sticks we were luckily able to pick off the ground, and our bare hands.'

'You had no arms at all? Not even a pistol? Major, you guys were very brave.'

'Well the battle between us was nevertheless short and decisive. We were able to subdue, disarm, wound some, and chase away all the Hutu assailants. But both my friend and I sustained life-threatening injuries. The other two French chaps were fine. I managed to tie tourniquets around our wounds. I'm not sure what happened next because the next thing I remember was waking up in a UN medical base to the good news that the women and children we had saved had all been moved to various safer locations.'

'Wow Major. You did so well. Wow. What an experience! You saved lives. So, tell me what eventually happened to your friend and the two other UN soldiers who stayed to help?' asked a quick-thinking and still very excited Saga.

'Hmm Saga. It was not easy for them as well. Though they were privately praised for saving so many, they were all officially dismissed from their positions and relieved of their army commissions as officers. They were lucky they did not have to face a court martial in France. But Saga, what happened there in Rwanda cannot be allowed to repeat itself anywhere else. It was humanity at its worst. It was a nightmare that shook us to our very foundations. It's all about hate, and that is what President Brewman is poisoning us with. Somehow, each in his own way, we must find a way to stop him. We must stop him, Saga. Some of us are now disabled and old, but that does mean we cannot find ways to contribute. Hate is the one thing that must never be permitted to take root in this country. The dehumanising effects are too lasting and difficult to recover from.'

'I fully agree with you, Major,' replied an admiring Saga, who wished he could hear more of such heroic stories.

'I admire your brother, Obo, so much for the stance he and the student leadership have taken in fighting this New Patriotism. Maybe when it's your turn one day, you'll also help?'

'Of course I'll help, Major. Of course I will. I even wish I could help now and not wait until I get to the university first. I hate what the New Patriotism is doing to my school and my friends. I hate what it is doing to our country, but my parents keep telling me there is nothing I can do now and that discretion is the better part of valour.'

'Don't use the word "hate", Saga. There's too much negative energy involved in hating. So, let's just say you can't abide it. And your parents are right, Saga. With all things being equal, there is a time and a place for everything. But all things are not always equal, in a manner of speaking. Life is always full of surprises and it may be your turn to act sooner than you think. But always remember to have a cool head, a warm heart and steady hands. And stop with the hating. Never forget that hate corrodes and infects the container in which it is carried. So never be a container of hate, my young friend. Now off you go, Saga, and listen to your parents. I have spoken more than enough for an entire week!'

* * *

Saga had malaria and had been out of school for a few days. In the African tropics, everyone, at various unpalatable points of their existence, was bound to have some unsavoury dealings with the dreaded malaria fever. It was yet again his turn.

Malaria was a nasty business indeed. The puny, barely visible Anopheles mosquito was the main cause of depositing malarial parasites in the bloodstream of innocents, causing insalubrious and often times, life-threatening fevers in their wake.

It was late afternoon and Saga was lying in his bed, thinking about mosquitoes and wondering why they had to exist at all. He had suffered a particularly bad night of shivering as though he had icicles in his veins, and had also vomited any and everything he tried to eat.

He was completely exhausted and could do nothing but wish pure perdition on all mosquitoes! The generally accepted view that HIV/Aids was the single highest cause of death in Africa was pure fabrication, he mused. Those so-called experts ought to check their facts because it was actually malaria that was the chief cause of mortality in Africa, especially among infants! Experts indeed! He scoffed weakly and mentally added on more perdition for all mosquitoes everywhere!

He was now feeling very hot and bothered, and had cast aside all his bed cover sheets that had failed to do their job of keeping him warm the previous night. He was starving too, as he had managed to hold down just a single bottle of 7 Up all day long. Everything else he had attempted to eat had been unpleasantly and painfully regurgitated. His voice had consequently become very hoarse from the frequent vomiting, and he had shed a couple of pounds in a stressful manner.

Saga heard the house telephone ring downstairs. After a few moments, he heard his mother's muffled scream. He was too weak to muster the necessary vocal power to shout out any enquiries to his mother downstairs.

He soon heard his mother's tread coming up the stairs. She came into his room and he noticed her face was tear-stained, rendering the make-up around her eyes askew and rather unsightly.

'Saga, Ibrahim has been hurt. He and some other Northern boys were beaten up badly at your school. They are all at

Ridge Heights Hospital. It's the anti-Muslim thing, that New Patriotism thing. I am so sorry, Saga. I am very sorry.'

Saga was shocked, upset and agitated. Ibrahim was his dearest friend. He did practically nothing without Ibrahim and he knew exactly what must have happened. He tried getting up off the bed but his mother stopped him.

'I must go and see him, Mama. You know I must do that. How many times has he been to see me already since I got this stupid malaria? I must go, Mama!' he said weakly, but with growing determination.

But his mother was firm. 'You're too weak to go anywhere, Saga. You can't even walk. I know he is your best friend, and almost like a part of our family. But you are still not well enough. You just had a relapse and you have barely eaten anything for three days straight!' She gently pushed him back onto the bed and pulled his abandoned cover sheets back over him. It was obvious he was even exhausted from his slight efforts to get up. Extreme bodily weakness and malaria were bedfellows indeed.

'Don't worry, Saga. I know this is bad but you must wait till you're stronger before you go to the hospital to see him. You're lucky you're not on admission yourself in your present state. I will go and see Ibrahim at the hospital with your father when he gets home, so don't worry, okay?

That night, Saga wept. He wept for his friend, Ibrahim. He wept for his other Muslim friends who had suffered a similar fate. He wept for his school, his family and his country. Finally, he wept for his own frustration at being unable to do anything about the terrible maladies that were engulfing his world.

CHAPTER SEVEN

Baptism of Fire

It was during half-term and Saga and Ibrahim were walking home from school mid-afternoon. They had been to school just to use the library, which was still open in the holidays. For a change, their after-school discussion was of a serious nature. Rappers and bling and Botox had to be put aside, and the nicely-scented, tree-lined path held no joy or sense of revitalisation for Saga that day. He neither heard nor saw the children gleefully playing in the park either. He was still unsettled about the outbreak of violence in their school and the seemingly sudden escalation of tensions all around them.

'Ibrahim, when do you think all this chaos at school will end? I am still ashamed I wasn't around the day you were attacked. Bloody malaria! I am surprised your parents made you come back. You're a tough guy, you know!'

'Yeah, I have to be. But it was not easy. As for my parents, what could they do since I insisted? I still refuse to be afraid, Saga. My parents say we should just stay out of trouble and focus on our studies. Saga, I know you feel we should do something about all this rubbish but what can we really do now? It'll be different when we get to the university where your brother's people are always rioting and getting beaten up or arrested for it. We can join them and kick some Zombie soldier butts once we get in.

'But right now, we're helpless, and the sooner you get that into your thick skull, the safer and better it'll be for all of us. You think you're the only one who is mad at what is happening? No. You're not. Look at what happened to me! I've still got bruises. But we must listen to what our parents are saying. Right now, we just have to play it cool. Rome was not built in a day, as you know, and no one will also change this bloody system overnight. You should relax, Saga. All this nonsense in the school will blow over very soon. Just chill, man. You have to just chill. Period!'

'So, I should just *chill* and allow my Muslim friends like you to be beaten up in school? Look at what happened to Khalil, Mohammed and Ahmed as well! And what if it doesn't blow over? Have you noticed how many of them had still not shown up for classes by mid-term? They're not all as brave as you. Surely there's something we can do at least in school. Why are you sounding like some wimp anyway?' a frustrated Saga retorted quite unfairly.

'Do something like what, Saga? And you bloody well know I'm nobody's wimp. You very well know I fought back hard that day, alone, against four guys, until they overpowered me. It was tough. But they've got their bruises too. I'm simply smarter and more sensible than some I know. Have I ever wimped out on you? You're out of your mind,' replied an unusually irritated Ibrahim.

Saga was now even more ashamed for his foolish retort. 'I'm just joking, Ibrahim. I'm sorry. I know you're nobody's wimp and I hear you belted a few of those lads quite well. Nice one. They certainly won't dare again. Anyway, please forgive me. The thing just bugs me. Sorry.'

Ibrahim smiled and patted his friend on the back and said, 'No worries, Saga. We're good. I know you're just messing around because you're frustrated...'

Noticing something unusual ahead, Ibrahim stopped mid-sentence and nudged Saga, who had his head down, dejectedly kicking at some pebbles on the ground, still quite ashamed of himself.

'Hey, what's all that commotion about? Is that not Sablon's house?'

'Yeah, it is,' replied Saga, looking up. What the hell's all that about with military cars and the crowd? This doesn't look good, Ibrahim. Come on – let's go see.'

As they ran towards the house, they noticed a din that was alien to the usually quiet residential neighbourhood. They ran up to the house, pushed past the gathering crowd, and were able to enter the compound, only to be confronted with an extremely distressing sight.

Their friend Sablon's father was being beaten with batons and gun butts, and dragged on the ground towards the gate by some soldiers, right in front of his family. It was also obvious that their neighbours, having caught on that something was amiss, had rushed to investigate, only to be held at bay by menacing soldiers in their traditional olive-green uniforms, wielding truncheons and AK-47 Kalashnikov assault rifles. The victim's face was bloated and bloody. His white shirt was shredded and dirtied from being dragged on the gravelled driveway, and stained bright crimson with his blood. His wife was screaming and pleading while being held back by concerned neighbours and her son, Sablon.

'WHAT HAS HE DONE? WHAT HAS HE DONE? PLEASE LEAVE HIM ALONE. HE HAS DONE ABSOLUTELY NOTHING. PLEASE LEAVE MY HUSBAND ALONE... HE'S INNOCENT! PLEASE... PLEASE!'

She wailed over and over again, but to no avail.

Other neighbours were in the process of carrying off her two younger children, away from the premises. They knew that this was definitely not a sight for children to behold, but they had unfortunately seen too much already. The children had been reduced to a state of whimpering terror and were shaking all over.

Upon seeing what was happening, and also seeing the children who were trembling so pathetically, something in Saga's mind snapped, compelling him to lose all reasoning there and then. He threw his school bag onto the ground and in a flash, rushed at one of the soldiers who, reminiscent of the policemen at the market, was now using a thick leather belt to whip Sablon's dad. Saga hurled himself with such speed and force that the soldier was knocked right off his feet, crashing heavily into the gravelled dust with Saga on top of him before anyone could figure out what was going on. Saga's massive fist smashed into the now prostrate soldier's jaw, rendering him insensible for a while to come.

There was a sudden shocked silence. The onlookers could just not make head or tail of what was going on. No civilian dared attack any of the Regime's soldiers. Even the soldiers themselves were quite paralysed by their sheer disbelief. Saga, however, experienced no such paralysis. He was already on his feet and drove a beefy fist solidly into the abdomen of another of the stunned soldiers who had been dragging Sablon's dad up until the moment he saw his colleague crash to the ground. The soldier screamed in pain as another fist crashed into his private parts, and it was probably his agonised scream that brought his colleagues out of their momentary paralysis. They all rushed at Saga, who again managed to bring down yet another soldier with a resounding, sure-footed kick to his groin before being beaten to the ground by the overwhelming number of soldiers – six in all, as three were now out of commission due to Saga's very effective blows and kicks. They were now all over him and quickly pounded him with the gun butts and truncheons.

Everything had happened so fast that most of the onlookers were initially immobilised with shock. They soon, however, came to their senses when they saw the soldiers on Saga. Instinctively, they knew as a group that they had to act or the boy would be beaten to death in a matter of minutes. Spurred on by the boy's astonishing bravery and confidence in their increasing numbers, many of them surged forward and yanked the boy away from the clutches of the soldiers.

Already, Saga was bleeding profusely from a crack on his skull and other indeterminate cuts and gashes all over his face and body. His face was swelling up very quickly and he could barely stand. Heedless of their own safety, and ignoring the snarling threats from the soldiers to bring the boy back, almost half the crowd simply formed a protective shield around him and led him away through the gate into a waiting car. It appeared some Good Samaritan had the presence of mind to start-up his late model VW Passat car and keep the engine running. Other members of the crowd used their numerical superiority to deliberately block the path of the soldiers who were still desperate to get to Saga.

To prevent later identification, Ibrahim, who was quite perplexed as to the inexplicable suddenness of what had just happened, quickly sprang into action and grabbed Saga's school bag from the ground, which contained books that had his name on them. He then forced his way through the crowd into the car to join his badly-beaten friend just as it was speeding off.

At Ibrahim's insistence, and over the Good Samaritan's protestations, Saga and Ibrahim were driven to Saga's house instead of a hospital, as the Samaritan had suggested with some persistence. Home was probably safest now, Ibrahim reckoned, since they couldn't risk anyone seeing Saga in his current bloodied and semi-conscious state. That would generate questions that were best left alone for now. Ibrahim also instinctively knew they could not use the front entrance as it was in full view of the café, where patrons would no doubt be enjoying their drinks. Again, at his insistence, they parked in an alley that led to a side gate in a wall. The Samaritan and Ibrahim half carried and half dragged Saga into the house. They entered through the back door into the kitchen.

Emma, still in her school uniform, was alone in the kitchen, standing in front of an open fridge that was just about her height. She had just finished fixing herself a tuna and egg sandwich on a plate and was grabbing a drink from the fridge when Ibrahim and the Samaritan entered with a badly-bruised, bloodied and almost unrecognisable Saga. She took one look her brother and started to scream, dropping her sandwich in the process with a loud crash, shattering the plate on the tiled floor and scattering bits of ceramic, tuna, egg and bread everywhere. Her drink followed suit, as her bottle of Sprite crashed to the ground, scattering bits of green glass in all directions.

'What happened? What happened to him? What happened, Ibrahim? Why is he bleeding? Has there been a car accident? 'She was yelling at the top of her voice through tears that had suddenly appeared and were streaking down her horrified, contorted face.

'Shush… Be quiet, please. Be very quiet. Shush… Okay? Are your Mom and Dad in? Listen – we can't carry him upstairs to his room, so open the downstairs guest bedroom for us, okay? Hurry!' Ibrahim said with a no-nonsense authority, borne of anxiety.

'No, they're not in. Only me and the maid,' Emma managed to choke out in reply and rushed to obey, moving quickly ahead of them while sobbing uncontrollably.

Saga, who could barely talk from the sheer pain he was experiencing, was soon laid out on the bed in the guest room. Emma, who was already recovering, shouted for the maid, Massa, as she helped Ibrahim and the Good Samaritan take off Saga's torn and bloodied shirt. The maid, already on her way downstairs to investigate the commotion and Emma's wailing, entered the bedroom, saw the state of Saga on the bed, and started screaming as well. Ibrahim quickly wheeled on her.

'Don't scream. Shush! Just don't! And don't worry. Everything will be fine. Just go to the front door. Someone at the café may have heard all the screaming. If anybody comes to the door to ask, just say you were playing with Emma or you people saw a mouse or something, okay? Better still, no mouse – just you were playing. And make sure nobody comes into the house, okay?'

With tears streaming down her face, the thoroughly frightened maid stumbled off, sniffling, to intercept any well-meaning yet nosy patron from the café who might want to investigate the screams emanating from the house.

Seeing that he had done all he could do to help for now, the Good Samaritan said he had to go. He left them his name and number, explaining that he needed to get back to find out if any of the soldiers or some gutless informer got his car number plate. He was praying they didn't, since they knew what could happen to him. Saga was able to force out a heartfelt yet muffled thank you from his swollen lips, as the gentleman was leaving.

With the Good Samaritan gone, Emma suddenly took charge with a sense of purpose that was surprising for her age. 'Ibrahim, I'm going to phone Mama to come. Look in the main upstairs bathroom cabinet, you'll find a first aid kit. Bring it to me. I'll get some towels and hot water. Ma has taught me some first aid things. We also learnt some at Girl Guides. Saga – I'll look after you till Mama gets here, okay? Don't worry. I'll be back in a minute.'

She was using her bossy deputy mistress-of-the house tone, though this time, it was not with the mock gravity she usually affected when harassing her brothers to clean up after themselves. This time, her youthful voice was laced with a determined seriousness. A fairly amazed Ibrahim was off like a shot to do her bidding.

She was gently sponging Saga down when her mother arrived.

Aba took one look at Saga and at the bucket of water beside Emma, which had turned dark red with her son's blood, and her face fell, her knees almost buckling under her. She quickly put her fist in her mouth to stop herself from screaming out. What Emma had told her on the phone had not prepared her for the bloody sight she beheld, and it took all her strength not to wail at the sight of her badly-wounded son. But she too recovered quickly and took charge. Her son was in danger and she could not afford the luxury of losing her nerve at this moment. Get a grip, she told herself, and knelt by her daughter.

'Well done, Emma. Let me do that now. Saga, I am so sorry you're hurt. Ibrahim, you had better tell me what happened once I'm done here. Emma, call your father on his mobile phone and tell him to come quickly with Dr Ramsey. He should stop whatever he is doing and get the doctor here now. Tell him it's an emergency and they should come in through the back. Ibrahim, go and change this water for me. It's okay, Saga, I'm here now. I don't think it's as bad as it looks, but the doctor will be here soon anyway. You don't have to say anything. Just lie there and keep your head up a bit so your nose can stop bleeding.'

Aba of course had already surmised that there must be a very good reason why her badly-beaten son was at home and not in some hospital where he could be easily tracked down. She silently blessed Ibrahim, whom she suspected had the presence of mind during a difficult situation to get her son home where he would be at least safe for a while.

Saga tried to sit up to talk to his mother. He whispered hoarsely with his now hideously swollen face contorting in pain, 'I'm sorry. I could not help it. I didn't plan to cause any trouble. I'm so sorry about all this.'

'Hush, Saga. Never mind and don't try to get up. Whatever it is, we'll talk about it later. Right now, what is important is that we get you well. Just rest and try not to talk. I know it hurts but your father will be here with the doctor soon. Everything will be fine, okay?'

Saga nodded his head gently and gave up the excruciatingly painful mission of trying to sit up. Tears rolled down from the corners of his very swollen eyes and his mother felt hugely sorry for him. At that moment, his pain was her pain.

After what seemed to Aba to be an eternity, though only a little over an hour had passed since she got back, her husband arrived with the doctor, who immediately went to attend Saga. The doctor quickly ushered everyone out of the room apart from Emma, whom he curiously allowed to stay as his stand-in nurse.

Waiting anxiously in the corridor outside the room, Ibrahim haltingly attempted to brief Saga's parents as to what happened. It was obvious from his narration of events that he still could not understand why Saga had snapped the way he did. He had to repeat parts of his story a few times, as Nana and Aba had most of their attention focused on the door where their son's muffled screams came through as the doctor did his necessary prodding and probing. Their son was in terrible pain, which was very hard for them to bear. Ibrahim himself was wincing with every scream they heard and kept on breaking off his story. Eventually, the screams stopped and Ibrahim was able to finish.

Saga's parents were equally baffled and troubled as to why their usually unaggressive son had gone down this uncharacteristically violent route.

'Is he crazy?' Nana asked no one in particular, bowing and shaking his head in wonder. He lifted his head to address both his wife and Ibrahim. 'Anyway, you did well, Ibrahim. Whatever it was, you're not to blame, and it was good you got his bag and forced your way into the car. You were also wise to bring him home and to come through the back. We are very grateful to you. Aba, I'm going to go back to the scene with Ibrahim now to see if the soldiers got Saga's name or whether they got our Samaritan's car number. You know how vengeful these soldiers are. I'm praying that none of their spies were at the scene. It's important that they can't pinpoint Saga. It could have been anybody. Sablon and his mother of course won't say anything. It's also good that you boys were not in your school uniforms.'

'Aba, Dr Ramsey brought his own car so he'll be fine getting back. Please sort the bill out with him but I must go now. You can just write him a cheque if you're short. Ibrahim, go to Saga's room and change your shirt. Wash your face and hands as well. You've blood everywhere. Hurry and let's go.'

Ibrahim and Nana left shortly after.

Dr Ramsey patched Saga up and gave him a shot of morphine to ease the pain. He explained to Aba that despite having bled quite a lot, the boy's cuts and bruises were mainly flesh wounds, which would heal quickly, though there would initially be a lot more pain and swelling. He left some very strong painkillers for when the morphine wore off, ordered total bed rest for the patient for the next few days, and suggested that someone stay with Saga all night. Of course, Aba had certainly no intention of letting her son out of her sight for a while to come. He also refused payment on the grounds that though his actions had been rash, the boy ought to be seen as a hero. He finally praised young Emma for her bravery and asked her to consider being a nurse in future. He left with the promise of coming by the next day to check on the patient. Emma stared after him as he was leaving, wondering why he had not suggested she become a doctor instead of a nurse.

Nana was home by 9p.m. and went straight into the guest room where his battered son lay, still sleeping off the effects of the morphine. His mother sat on a low stool by the bed, staring at her son's face, deep in thought, with her own face tear-stained. She came out of her sad reverie as Nana quietly entered and quickly wiped her eyes with the back of her hands.

'How is he?' he asked anxiously, though in very low tones so as not to disturb the patient.

She replied in equally hushed tones, 'He seems a bit better. He was tossing and turning and moaning before but he's stopped now. He hasn't woken up since the doctor left. It's a good thing they're on half-term. At least he'll have some time to heal before school reopens. So, tell me – how did it go? Do they know it's him? How bad is it? I'm afraid, Nana. I'm terribly afraid.'

'Don't be. It's not that bad. They don't know it's him. If anyone recognised him, they didn't give him up. They also didn't get the name or licence plate number of our Good Samaritan, whom I've already called to thank. He wanted to know how Saga was doing and thought our son very brave. I also heard they eventually took Sablon's dad away. There was no one at their house when I got there. The night watchman said some relatives had come for the rest of the family. Aba, come here,' he beckoned to her.

She was slowly getting up unsteadily when he leaned over and gently pulled her towards him. He wrapped his arms around her and whispered into her ear, 'I know it's not easy to look at him lying there like that, all bloody and bruised. But he will be fine, okay? And we will find a way out of this mess, somehow. Listen, why don't you go and tidy yourself up and also see to Emma? She must be pretty confused by all this, though she's been wonderfully brave. Go and talk to her and grab a shower or something to get rid of the blood. I'll watch over him, okay? No need to cry anymore. It'll all be all right, and Emma will be even more troubled if she sees you've been crying. You can come back later. Don't worry for now, please.'

Aba kept nodding her head, gave him a tight squeeze, and left him to stand watch. She had heard him all right, but knew there was actually much to worry about.

* * *

Six days after Saga's skirmishes with the soldiers, Nana was sitting under the shade of the sole mango tree that adorned their back garden. There were other trees, but only one mango tree, which was his favourite species. The tree gave off the sweet, tangy smell of its growing yet unripe fruit, which he normally found pleasing. But today, he could neither smell nor savour it, for he was deeply troubled. He had been this way for several days. Saga was better now and ready to talk to them, but he was still at a loss as to why his son had suddenly turned violent without warning, and in circumstances that could have proved fatal for him.

Nana called himself a pacifist, which meant he did not believe in violence, although he did not think there was any such thing as anyone being an absolute pacifist. There were practical limits to being totally non-violent. People sometimes had little choice but to react in a world where there were, unfortunately, some senseless, soulless maniacs who were quite willing to harm their fellow men and women for no apparent reason.

Nonetheless, he did not like violence of any kind, and held that violence generally caused more violence. This was what he had taught his children and which, up until now, he thought they had understood. Maybe it was a one-off occurrence. It had to be a one-off, since Saga had generally never shown any aggressive tendencies, apart from the few scuffles that all boys got into as part of the growing-up process. The last incident had been years ago, and while growing up, the boy had not demonstrated any above average liking for aggression, as compared with his fellow mates. Rather, he had always been calm and sweet with his ready smile, and was generally known in school to be the one always breaking up fights. This was very uncharacteristic of him indeed, but for now, they simply had to hear him out in order to get to the bottom of it. It was time to ask those difficult questions. Emma had gone over to a friend's for a party and eventual sleepover, and Obo was home from the university, so now was as good a time as ever. He sighed and went inside.

Everyone was in the main living room, which was spacious and airy. The air conditioning had been turned off, the white lace curtains parted all the way to the respective corners of their wooden rails, and all the louvered windows opened. The ceiling fan was on, since Obo was smoking. He had already been home to see Saga a few times over the past week while he was healing.

Nana spoke first. 'Saga, we are all at a loss to understand why you attacked those soldiers at your friend Sablon's that day. We need to know if you understand the potentially fatal consequences of what you did. You are not a child anymore, Saga, and you owe this family some answers. We are listening. You can speak now.'

Saga was ready to talk. He still had bruises on his face, arms and torso. Stiff with pain and also sporting a bandage on his head, he sought to both apologise and reassure them.

'Ma, Da, Obo – again, I'm sorry for what I did. I've thought about it a lot, lying in bed, and I'm still not sure as to the exact reason why I did it. You all know I don't fight, so I really don't know why. All I know is that the sight of Sablon's dad being beaten and bleeding so badly in front of everybody was just too much for me to take. It was way too unfair with so many of those soldiers attacking one person and everyone just standing there and doing nothing. I was not just angry. I was more than angry and, before I knew it, I was in there, trying to fight the soldiers off.'

Obo was the first one to respond. He was in no joking mood and clearly impatient to start. He sat up on the sofa he'd been reclining on, staring at the ceiling fan. His voice was stern.

'What you did was crazy. Way too crazy and stupid as well. What the hell were you thinking? It's good to want to help people, but not at the cost of getting yourself killed and your family arrested in the process. Look here, Saga, you know I'm not afraid of those soldiers and you know we've been fighting them for a few years now on campus. But this is not the way. No one can do it alone. Even when we are in large groups having our demonstrations on campus or on the streets, we always try to avoid direct physical fights. You can't fight guns with your bare hands. Every fool knows that. Dumb is what it is! What if one of the soldiers had lost control and shot you? Where would you be now? And where would Ma and Da be? And what would happen to Emma? I'm sorry you got hurt but this should be a serious lesson to you. Focus on your A-levels. You can join the struggle when you pass and join us on the university campus, and you had better consider yourself lucky to be alive!'

'Enough, Obo!' His father stopped Obo's angry tirade. Nana knew Obo had not meant to be rough, but was worried for his brother's safety and for that of the rest of the family as well.

Nana was looking at Saga, who had bowed his head, with his face buried in his palms, and he knew the mental agony the boy was undergoing. He felt sorry for him, but what had to be said had to be said, and Obo had said it for them, albeit a touch harshly.

Aba, who had just been nodding her head to all Obo had said, now had a few words to say. 'Saga, one thing you said has made me very worried and that's the bit about anger. What have your father and I always told you children about doing things in anger? Don't you children, especially Obo, always tell me to mind my temper? Listen again, Saga – doing things in a rage is one of the most stupid things a person can do, and do you know why? A person who is angry to the point of rage is a person who is not thinking, and is therefore very exposed, as he or she is not in control. It's as though they've crossed that thin line between sanity and insanity and become mad. And you were truly a madman on that day! That must never happen again. Listen to your brother, Obo. He is right in all he's said!'

Saga was crestfallen and felt thoroughly ashamed of himself. He knew all they were saying was true and that he'd placed them all in grave danger. He knew all of this without them having to spell it out (come on – he wasn't that stupid). He also knew he had been selfish and unthinking in his actions, but that was not the most important source of what was truly bothering him.

His worst fear, which he could of course not tell anyone, was whether he could truly control himself if he ever met with such a situation again. Deep down, he wasn't so sure. Could it just be that seeing Zara Yalley in action at the market against the brutal policemen was what had probably spurred him on? He turned to look at his father, very unsure of what to say next.

'I'm sorry. It won't happen again. I promise you all. Let's also say I've learnt my lesson and I'd like you all to forgive me.'

'Okay, enough said. I guess that's it. I think he understands perfectly. Saga, what your mother is saying about doing things in anger is something you already know. Listen to your brother as well. Those soldiers out there are Zombies who are drunk on power and high on marijuana, cocaine, booze and goodness knows what else. They could have shot you for no good reason. The bottom line is to always use your head. What's done is done. We all got off lightly. We've all been very lucky. And don't waste time feeling sorry for yourself. That solves nothing. And there's no need for you to say anything more. I think we're finished here.' Nana turned his attention to Obo and in one breath, asked, 'Obo, are you staying or leaving, and please don't raid our kitchen to take food back with you. The last time, we had hardly anything left to eat in the house,' he added playfully to ease the tension.

Obo had softened up by now. 'No Dad. Can't stay. Scared of our Mike Tyson wannabe here. And everything I take or borrow is with Mama's approval. Not so, Ma?'

Obo then walked over to his brother, playfully ruffled the unbandaged part of his hair, and said, 'You're crazy, you know. Totally mad, but guess what? When I told Kobby on the quiet about what happened, do you know what that other madman said? He thinks you should be given a medal. What an ass. Anyway, take it easy, okay? This was your baptism of fire, but no more Hercules or Samson stuff, okay? Come and help me raid the kitchen. On campus, everyone is always hungry. You guys at home are lucky. Let's go.'

The parents watched the brothers leave together for the kitchen through the dining room, glad the session was over. It had been too tense and full of too many bad images. Even now, they could not be sure as to whether Saga or they themselves were in the clear. All they could do now was keep a close eye on the boy and hope for the best.

Unfortunately, for Nana and Aba, hoping for the best was not sufficient to keep their son out of trouble. Saga was proving to be one of those people who though generally slow to act on issues, could not be stopped once they had the bit in between their teeth. It was as though while he had initially appeared not too concerned with the general issues around him prior to the incident at the market with the refugee beggars, he had actually been gradually soaking up the surrounding societal tensions to the point where he had unconsciously decided that he had had enough.

Violence he knew was out of the question. He himself did not like violence, despite what happened at Sablon's. Yet, he somehow knew that he had reached that stage where turning the other cheek was out of the question. He had been fervently hoping that he did not find himself in any such situation again where he would feel compelled to resort to pugilistic means. He just wanted to get along with his life, pass his A-levels and get into the university where he could join his brother and his group to hopefully change things for the better in their country.

CHAPTER EIGHT

Orphanhood

The prestigious Brewman Boys High School sported both indoor and outdoor basketball courts, indoor and outdoor heated swimming pools, and two large football fields with athletic racing tracks to boot. There were also tennis courts, basketball courts, handball courts, two science labs, three computer labs, two large churches that could each house six-hundred or more worshippers, a vast woodwork shed, as well as over forty-five modernist bungalows for the teaching staff. To add to this was the vast administrative block, which resembled a sprawling government ministry, and a huge assembly hall, which could have passed for an international conference centre to the untrained eye.

Brewman High was indeed the envy of all schools, and it was within the confines of one of its pristine classrooms that Saga's act of public defiance in school occurred. This was an occurrence that was to quickly and significantly change things for himself, his family, his school, and the overall opposition struggle to the Regime as well. This occurrence was something Saga did not plan; it just happened.

Several weeks after his fight, a fully-recovered Saga was sitting by Ibrahim in class, chatting with some of their form mates while waiting for their general paper teacher to make his appearance. General paper was the only mandatory subject all A-level students had to take. Just as the boys were discussing whether Jack Bauer, star of the popular TV programme *24* was a more effective operative than the suave and better-known James Bond, the head prefect then came in to announce that they were going to have a public education class instead of general paper that day. A loud groan greeted this announcement.

For them, it was a fake 'subject' that the Ministry of Public Education had recently introduced to ensure that what the Regime wanted taught as part of the syllabus was *actually* being taught in the schools.

'What does public education have to do with our forthcoming A-levels?' Sablon asked his mates.

'It's just the Regime trying to indoctrinate us and get us to memorise their damned slogans,' Saga grumbled.

The announcement added to Saga's renewed vexation with most of the teachers for tacitly condoning the violence in school against Muslims by refusing to punish the culprits. It was this very New Patriotism rubbish that they taught in public education that had fuelled the troubles in the first place, and he would be damned if made to sit through any such class. Thus, he stood up and rallied the class.

'Listen you guys – this is not part of our A-level curriculum, which is why we are here. We didn't come to study any public education rubbish and I suggest we all boycott the class. Let them take their nonsense to the lower forms. We are almost out of the school and they should just leave us alone. Are you guys with me or not?'

Ibrahim, Sablon and a few others shouted in unison, 'We concur!' While others yelled and manifested their agreement by drumming on their wooden desks with their fists, rulers, pens or anything that could serve as drumsticks.

But the head prefect had to do his job. 'We can't boycott the class, Saga. We'll all get into trouble. What's more, the headmaster mentioned that a special visitor is coming in today to take the class, so please calm down, okay? You guys, let's all sit down and wait. After all, the lesson is only 40 minutes.'

Only a couple of the students murmured weak assents to what the prefect had said.

'Who says we can't boycott the class and why should we get into trouble for following the very advice that they have been giving us to focus on nothing but our curriculum? What can they do to us? Suspend us? Since when did public education become compulsory for upper sixth-formers?' Saga retorted, with an authority that surprised even himself.

And Ibrahim, who simply loved any form of trouble in class, jumped up by Saga and yelled, 'All who agree to a boycott, raise your hands!'

But before anybody could raise their hand, the headmaster walked in with their form master, together with a very well-dressed, light-skinned, obviously mixed-race, middle-aged man in an expensive-looking suit, who swaggered in with complete assurance. He had an entourage with him who halted near the door, with the exception of two burly, black-suited men with white earpieces, like the ones in the movies, which instantly gave them away as bodyguards. Ibrahim quickly sat down as a hush descended on the class. *Too late for a boycott now.*

The headmaster, Mr Money, greeted the class and immediately introduced the well-dressed gentleman as the Deputy Minister for Public Education in charge of secondary schools – Mr Com. Many of the students had of course seen him on TV before and knew exactly who he was. Mr Money explained that Mr Com was making a random inspection of schools to find out whether students were being taught properly about certain key aspects of the Government's New Patriotism. He said that since Mr Com had many schools to inspect that afternoon, he would only ask some of them a few questions and be on his way. He asked the class to stand up and welcome the Deputy Minister formally, and to make the school proud by answering all questions correctly.

After the quasi-formal welcome, the headmaster and form master hastily stood aside, moving backwards towards the blackboard so the Deputy Minister could take over by posing his questions directly to the students as part of his verification process. The bodyguards also placed themselves at the two front corners of the classroom behind the Minister, and commenced an inexplicable process of touching their earpieces with equally inexplicable regularity.

Mr Com, who now had the floor, asked if anyone would volunteer to go first, and a still very annoyed Saga impulsively raised his hand before any of the others could. The New Patriotism issue was indeed a very sore point with Saga. He was still plagued with guilt that he had not been present to defend his bosom friend, Ibrahim, when he was beaten up badly by New Patriotism fanatics who happened to be students in their own school. Subconsciously, it was as though he thus felt the urge to be the one to face any New Patriotism 'onslaught' from officialdom within their school. As to how he would deflect such an onslaught, he had absolutely no idea. It was a subconsciously inspired impulsiveness so he simply had to wing it.

'Well, well – I see we have an eager beaver in our midst,' he smiled at Saga, who did not return the smile. The headmaster, and the form master, and all the five men and one woman who made up the Minister's entourage, however, giggled rather obsequiously at this sally. They truly understood the meaning of grovelling to those on high. The Deputy Minister turned and rewarded them all with an openly condescending smile.

'Okay mister serious young man, let's start. So, tell me, who is your mother under our New Patriotism?' Mr Com boomed out his question.

Saga knew the answer he was to give and did so correctly. 'My mother is the Great South Party of President Brewman!'

Mr Com was pleased. 'Not bad, not bad,' he said, and nodded happily towards the headmaster, who gave an equally satisfied beam in response.

'And who is your father?' Mr Com boomed yet again.

Saga again answered correctly. 'My father is the Great Leader of our nation, His Supreme Excellency and President-For-Life-Until-Further-Notice Field Marshal Brewman.'

Both Messrs Com and Money now beamed in unison. The entourage and form master were not far behind in this beaming effort.

'Well done my boy, well done.' Mr Com smiled a vastly complacent smile at Saga.

'Tell me, my bright, young friend – so what would you like to be when you grow up?'

This was far from being a question about future careers such as wanting to be a doctor or lawyer or pilot. Saga knew he should answer something along the lines of wanting to grow up to be a dedicated follower of the President or the Party.

However, Saga inhaled and dropped his bombshell. 'I would like to be an ORPHAN when I grow up,' he said with utmost seriousness.

'A WHAT?' Mr Com bellowed, his face suddenly mottling with anger and disbelief. He could not believe he had actually heard what he thought the boy was saying.

'An ORPHAN of this MOTHER and FATHER!' Saga repeated loudly with assurance, his face set in stubborn determination.

The room went deathly silent for a second and then the students burst out laughing. They suddenly saw the humorous side, once the initial shock of Saga's subversive answer had subsided. What Saga was actually saying was that he wanted both his political mother and father of the New Patriotism dead so he could be orphaned and free of them!

The headmaster was aghast! He looked around him in confusion. He immediately understood the implications. He could also not believe what he had heard. This could go very badly for him. And to worsen his rapidly rising dread, the foolish students were not helping the situation with their wild laughter. They were now whistling and cat-calling as well. It was fast becoming a very noisy affair. This was indeed a much bigger and thus much noisier class than usual, since all the upper sixth-form streams were always brought together for their general paper lectures. He knew he had to do something quickly. He needed to find a plausible explanation to give to the Deputy Minister, who was shaking his head in complete amazement and annoyance. He was a truly vexed man.

'The utter cheek of this boy – the sheer impudence and impertinence! This is subversion!' shouted Mr Com. Since secondary schools were under his jurisdiction at the education sector level, he could also get into trouble with the Presidency if word got out through the wrong channels. And these bloody students thought this was funny! How dare they laugh at him – a whole Deputy Minister with an entire entourage and security detail to boot?

The headmaster saw Mr Com's face change colour in a most alarming fashion. At some point, it was dark scarlet, and it was now moving towards some hue of purple he had not quite seen before.

'He was... was... err... err... only joking... err... Sir,' he stammered. 'The... the... boy was only joking, p-please,' he croaked again.

Mr Com overrode him furiously. 'Who is this boy? Who is his father? Money – what is the meaning of this nonsense? Is this the sort of rubbish you have been teaching them here? This is almost tantamount to treason – or you don't have the sense to see?'

The headmaster was alarmed at the viciousness in Mr Com's voice. And the boys would not stop laughing, jeering and cat-calling, while Saga gamely stood his ground. He had not sat down all this while.

Mr Money knew it was time to act. He urgently signalled to the form master, who had himself been watching the unfolding drama with growing apprehension, and together, they grabbed Mr Com – each taking an arm – and speedily bundled him out of the classroom like a shot into the corridor, and as far away as possible from those subversive and renegade students, who were still laughing and now drumming on their tables! The bodyguards and entourage rushed out as well in tow, all of them quite baffled as to what had just transpired. Unlike their boss, they were yet to grasp the subversive significance of Saga's declaration.

This particular saga of Saga's was yet to play itself out.

Saga's public stance against the hated New Patriotism won him a great number of admirers within the school, as news of the incident spread wildly like a bush fire in the dry Savannah plains. The unthinkable, that which could not be said, had now been openly, publicly avowed, and Saga was a hero.

Many of the students who had long been confused and uneasy over trying to understand and imbibe the New Patriotism could now take a sturdy, principled 'Orphan' position.

The reasons for their confusion and gnawing unease was not hard to fathom. Firstly, before the Regime's switch to terrorising its own people, the President had been somewhat of a national hero, and most of these youngsters had grown up on the legend of his early days in office, when he was seen to represent progressive national development and social justice. He was then the saviour of the nation from the evils of the undemocratic one-party state and dictatorship the country had endured for so long. In fact, most of these youngsters knew of no other national leader than the existing President. He was the leader they had come of age with.

Secondly, theirs was a conservative society in which obedience to authority – be it parental or official – was deeply ingrained. It was as though parents and leaders could not be seen to do wrong in the eyes of children. That was how the conservative adult population wanted it, and that was how it was. Yet suddenly, for these youngsters, life was no longer that simple. The sheer evidence of the suffering and chaos that was occurring with the introduction of the New Patriotism under the President's dictatorial rule could not simply be ignored by them, just as the propensity of youth to seek truth could also not be expected to remain forever dormant. The evidence, which was there for all to see, starkly contradicted the official line that all was well under the President's rule. Consequently, this glaring contradiction needed resolution in the minds of many of the country's youth. In Saga's school, he had somehow just supplied the resolution of this contradiction for some of them with his public declaration in favour of orphanhood from the unholy and patently destructive parentage of the President and his all-powerful South Party.

Youth indeed sought truth as a club was born that very day in the school called the Orphan Society (Orphans for short) – whose aim was to oppose the New Patriotism within their school. But youth was also truly foolish, as this was a path that could readily lead to despair for many of them and their families. Youth, however, by its very essence, was not generally prone towards prudence. Discretion for them could not quite be understood as the better part of valour.

Saga was approached by some members of the newly-formed Orphans later that day and was asked to be the leader of the club. He was very excited about this. Not only could he now strike back at all the bad things that were causing him so much anger and distress, but he would actually get to lead the charge in his own school as well! Soon, all the painstaking reasoning his father, mother and brother had put him through, all the promises of patience and prudence simply flew out of the window with his immediate acceptance of the leadership of the Orphans.

Saga left school that day in very high spirits. He would deal later with whatever punishment the school authorities would mete out to him. This time, it was not just he and Ibrahim alone, but 10 more of their mates had joined them – all jostling to be abreast with Saga on the pathway they normally used. Ibrahim was overjoyed. This was the kind of stuff that made him tick. Their other mates were also in a state of anticipatory excitement. They knew that things were not going to be the same again at school for a while to come.

These newly-charged students, who had formed a cordon around Saga, soon reached the busy roundabout at the top of the path when Ibrahim broke out into a song, which they all took up, apart from Saga, since the song was for him: *'For he's a jolly good fellow, for he's a jolly good fellow... and he'll kick Brewman's ass!'* They were yelling so much that almost everyone around the roundabout – drivers in their vehicles negotiating the roundabout, hawkers and pedestrians – simply gawked at them in wonder. They looked like a bunch of unruly football fans whose team had just won a major victory!

CHAPTER NINE

No Pimple-Faced Youth, Please

Though Saga was late in getting home that day, he was still very much on a high. He entered his home through the side gate, via the kitchen back door, and into the living room where his parents were. He was not too troubled by the worried looks they greeted him with. It was obvious that his exploits had preceded him. What was a worried look or two from his parents compared to being a hero in the eyes of his peers? Was he not the original Orphan? Was he not 'The One' – à la Keanu Reeves turned Neo in *The Matrix*?

Saga was nonetheless surprised that both his father and mother barely said anything to him about the matter that day. His father simply told him that they would have a word with him later about what happened in his school that day.

Though quite heady, he still felt a little strange when all the patrons from the café peered at him over their drinks when he later went to look for his friend, Major Kata. Many of them had also heard of his heroics, as some had children in Brewman High. He tried to read into the looks on their faces, which were mainly admiration from the younger generation and sad and knowing looks of the more warily sympathetic adults, who understood that nothing but trouble could come out of the boy's bravery. He left quickly as Major Kata was nowhere to be found in and around the café.

Saga's father, Nana, was pensive that evening. He was back in the rear garden under his usual mango tree. He absent-mindedly did battle with a swarm of mosquitoes that were anxious to get at his exposed arms, while thinking about Saga's showdown in school. He was no fool though, and knew that one thing was certain – his entire family was marked from now on and not just him and his eldest son.

Indeed, what Saga had done placed them all in clear and present danger, since there was no possible way the matter could be hushed up in the school. However, how could he berate his boy for doing something so honourable, even if a tad rash? How could he tell him off for following the very teachings that he, Nana, had imparted? Probably things would not be so bad for them and the future would not look so bleak if more people had had Saga's courage a while back to demonstrate to the Regime that enough was enough and that they would take no more.

Right now, the President was much too powerful. Consequently, any overt opposition towards him and his malignant Regime was fraught with grave danger and involved a monumental risking of life and limb. The general populace, Nana reasoned, had been cowed by government and their ruthless employment of brutal state terror tactics. Fear was very widespread in their society, and many were resigned to the fact that the Regime was a curse that would simply not go away.

In fact, other more superstitious-minded people saw the Regime as a malignant disease, sent by Providence to probably punish them for some collective misdeeds of the past. How else could they explain this pestilential plague in the persons of the President and his brutal, zombie-like shock troops of terror and destruction? On another level, Nana could not truly blame many for being sufficiently fond of life and limb to risk them in a futile battle against a mighty Regime they saw as being there to stay – like it or not!

At this juncture, he knew he needed to call an urgent meeting of the underground resistance group he was now a part of, without any delay whatsoever. The underground resistance comprised of a dedicated group of patriots who had come together with the ultimate aim of ridding Zimgania of dictatorship and ushering in an age of democracy. The group would need to anticipate how the Regime was going to react to what had happened and, among other things, see what could be done to lessen whatever harm was irreversibly hurtling towards them as a consequence of his son's heroic intervention at his school.

His thoughts were soon disrupted by his wife, Aba. He watched her walking towards him from the kitchen. She was reasonably tall for a woman and generally self-assured. She had a pretty but subtly ageing face. Her chest had a natural forward thrust that appeared challenging, with her not insignificant breasts firm and upstanding for her 50-year sojourn on Earth. She was 10 years younger than her husband and stood a head shorter than him. The lighting outside was good and so he could see her distressed face from some distance.

'I can see you're worried.'

'Aren't you?' she asked him.

'Of course I am. Why do you think I'm sitting here? It's just that I'm not quite sure how to handle it. I'm not sure what to tell the boy.'

'It's too much! First, Obo gets arrested, then you resigning, and now even our little Saga is caught up in this? Obo has always been the one to get involved in such matters. But Saga is still too young for this. What has come over our son? He was never like that before. He is changing right before our very eyes. Maybe someone is influencing him and we just don't know about it. Or is it that rap music he's been listening to? Or is it because he doesn't have a girlfriend? Is it his hormones or what?'

Nana's heart went out to his frantic wife. She was now on a permanent roller coaster ride of worry.

'Calm down, my dear. Yes – I know it's tricky. It's not like what he did before but it's still a very bad situation. This "Orphan" business at school is bound to get out, and the authorities are going to start watching our every move, waiting for us to fall into whatever trap they will try and lay. They're going to say that either we put him up to it or what he said reflects our thinking at home.'

Aba looked desperately at her husband. 'What are we going to do, Nana?'

She was obviously plagued by innumerable questions. She covered her face with her hands and raised her voice. 'Oh God, what is all this, eh? When is it all going to end?' she lamented and stifled a sob, not feeling so self-assured now.

Her husband moved closer and placed an arm around her shoulder. 'It's okay, honey. Please be calm. We have to be strong. Please.' He held her as closely as he could manage for a few moments, before leaning back to continue. 'I've been thinking, Aba, and I believe part of the problem is that we still think of Saga as a child. He's young but he's not a child anymore and he is finding that out on his own. This matter is bigger than us. It's bigger than the family so this is what I've decided – I'm going to take him to one of our underground opposition meetings. I think it's about time. The boy needs the guidance and discipline of the wider group. We can't just deal with it here at home. He has to get a better picture of what is at stake. I'm sorry but I think it's the only way.'

Aba was looking at him as though he had lost his senses, and replied sharply, 'What on earth are you talking about? Have you lost your mind as well? The boy is only 18 and has his A-levels ahead of him. You want an 18-year-old boy to join the underground opposition? Do you want him to get killed? It's bad enough with you and Obo being in it, and now you want the poor boy to join as well? What is the matter with you?' she shouted.

'Enough, Aba! Stop raising your voice!' Nana said sharply. 'We are all understandably emotional about it all but we need to think a bit more clearly here. What do you want us to do – lock the stable doors after the horses have bolted? Listen to me, we can't stop the boy. Just wait and see. It's better if he has proper guidance so we can reason with him properly. Wasn't I part of the anti-colonial struggles at his age or even younger? And don't these kids know a lot more now than we did at their age? Look, let's leave this for now, okay? Just think about it. He'll be safe – I promise you that.'

'Seriously? Nana, are you crazy? Are you losing the plot? Christ Almighty!'

'Let's go back inside, okay? Where is Saga now?' Nana could see she was immovable.

'He's in his room with Ibrahim. They claim to be studying, but all I can hear is that hip-rap music. Okay – let's continue tonight. But in my opinion, it's even more dangerous now than when we were young. At least those we struggled against were forced to play by certain rules. But not these people in power now. They have no rules, no conscience, and therefore are exceedingly dangerous, so you think about that too! Anyway, I have to go and drop off Emma and her friend now.'

She got up, still very peeved, and left him under his tree. Nana blankly watched his wife's curvy behind as she left, without admiring her superb physique as he usually did. Rather, he was wondering about whether Saga had a girlfriend or not, while resuming his battles with the mosquitoes by absently waving them away with his arms.

Up in Saga's bedroom, he and Ibrahim had their own pressing concerns. They had exciting things to do and to work out. How were they to run the new club of Orphans at school? How were they going to recruit lots of members? Where would they get sound advice to embark on a venture they saw as holding the promise of great adventure? How were they to prevent the school authorities from finding out who the members of the Orphans were? Was that even necessary? Should they have lots of members or just a few secret ones to direct things? At this moment, studying was the furthest thing on their minds.

'Obo will know, man; he's the expert in all this. Make sure you speak to him tonight.'

'I'm not sure how on-board he'll be,' said Saga, remembering his brother's words about staying out of trouble.

'I want a full report in the morning,' Ibrahim joked as he got up to leave.

'Hey, wait, I'll walk with you to the end of the road.'

It was hot and humid and both had their shirts open down to their belly buttons – something that Saga's mother disliked intensely and was always complaining about, but she was not around to give them what-for for baring their chests and bellies in public.

The air outside the house was filled with the aroma of spicy mutton kebabs being grilled on skewers on an open charcoal brazier for the café patrons. Mutton or goat kebab on a skewer was a constantly required delicacy that went very nicely with beer and allied alcoholic beverages in their part of the world. Thus, the café owner, Major Kata, had accordingly contracted a 'kebab expert' to come in six days a week to prepare some for eager customers. On his way out to see Ibrahim off, Saga picked up two sizzling kebabs each straight off the brazier for himself and Ibrahim, with a promise to the now-frowning expert that he would pay for them the next day. The expert it seemed was not generally amenable to handing over kebabs on credit, but knew his boss was fond of Saga and so had no choice but to agree.

The boys walked along the poorly-lit street, gingerly picking at the meat with their front teeth, as it was very hot temperature-wise. They listened, as they walked, to the familiar cacophony of trilling night insects making their usual nocturnal racket, as they busied themselves with their delicacy.

Just before they got to where Saga would turn back, Ibrahim asked, 'What will be the aim and objective of this Orphan club, Saga? After all, every club or society in school must have aims and objectives. What will ours be?'

Saga had to think for a bit before replying, 'I'm not so sure ours is going to be like a regular club or society like the Scripture Union or Chess Club. This is serious business. But I still agree with you that we have to be able to tell our members something. From the top of my head, all I can think of at the moment is getting them to boycott this New Patriotism rubbish they're teaching in public education. That's supposed to be the original purpose of the club. But don't worry. I'll discuss all of this with Obo, cool?'

'Cool. Good idea. That serious brother of yours can surely show us the way forward. Okay, my man, peace out. You did great today. Catch you tomorrow. Same place, same time!' And he was off.

Back in his room, Saga thought of his father and brother. Actually, he had suspected a while back that his father was an active member of the fabled underground resistance movement and that Obo sometimes went with him in the middle of the night to their secret meetings. His adventurous nature had demanded confirmation of this suspicion. Consequently, he had one day waited until his sister and mother were asleep and had secretly followed his father and brother, who were on foot, to one such meeting at his Uncle Tiger's house.

The night watchman at the gate who knew Saga and suspected nothing untoward had allowed him through the main gate, and told him that his dad was all the way at the rear end of the very large property in some church-like structure on the compound with his uncle and some friends. Saga had cautiously made his way there and, peering through one of the windows, was able to confirm his suspicions.

He saw many people, including his father, his brother, Obo, and his Uncle Tiger in a huge, cigarette-smoke-filled hall, talking amongst themselves. Maybe quiet, soft-spoken and outwardly timid Uncle Tiger was not so timid after all. Maybe there was a reason why everyone called him Tiger. Appearances could truly be deceptive.

Saga had recognised a good many faces in the room that day – people whom he had known all his life as family friends or neighbours. There were a couple of others he had seen before in the newspapers, branded as subversive opposition leaders on the run, but he could not for the life of him remember their names. It was as though his excitement at his discovery had compromised his memory at the time.

There were about 20 of them in all, huddled conspiratorially in a circle and talking urgently amongst themselves. There was grimness, a grim seriousness about them he had never seen before, which made him apprehensive at the time. He had left quickly, telling the watchman that he did not wish to disturb them, and also that there was no need for him to mention that he had been around. A 100 Zimgania dollar note offered by Saga and accepted with alacrity and much gratitude by the watchman would undoubtedly ensure the sealing of his lips. Luckily, Saga had received some money that very day from Major Kata for helping out at the café. A 100 Zim dollar windfall – as the currency was called in short – was the equivalent of five days of the watchman's paltry salary, and could buy four small loaves of bread for him to happily surprise his usually bread-deprived children. Bread was not something that was usually affordable on the watchman's salary. Consequently, he was truly grateful to Saga indeed.

Saga remembered that day quite well and had resolved to someday follow in the steps of those quiet heroes who had made it their business to help set things right in their country. Now, he would certainly make them proud of him at his own level. Everyone would hear of the Orphans and their heroic deeds. Yes, Obo would show him the way.

That night, however, Obo did not come home. Never mind, Saga thought. I'll talk to him tomorrow. Today is Monday – there's time enough. But that was not to be, as his father told him the next morning that Obo was going to be away for a few more days. Apparently, the Students' Union had dispatched him post-haste to the Northern Territories of the country on urgent business.

'Time' unfortunately demonstrated its old habit of not standing still for anyone, including newly-created heroes, as Saga and his Orphans were to find out at school before Obo got back.

* * *

That very next morning, Saga woke up to the familiar clinking and clanging of crockery and pans coming from the kitchen, signalling that his mother and Massa the maid were busy preparing breakfast. He pulled his light Dumas cotton cover sheet off him but did not immediately get out of bed. He was quite certain that the little minx, Emma, was as usual hogging the bathroom for no particularly sane reason.

He could smell that pleasing, fresh, earthy fragrance that usually came with the rain. Only raindrops that were not thwarted by concrete slabs or asphalt and were able to make direct contact with the red earth could give off such a refreshing scent, he mused to himself.

He stretched lazily and, putting his hands behind his head, proceeded to stare at the ceiling, thinking nice thoughts about his Orphan club. Suddenly, school no longer appeared as such a drag. His mother's shouting soon disturbed all the wonderful castles of Orphan achievements and popularity he was absent-mindedly building in the air.

'Hey Saga – don't tell me you're still asleep. Have you looked at your watch? I don't think you're going to have time for any breakfast or you'll be too late. Your sister's been out of the bathroom for ages now so don't use that old, tired excuse. Up, up, up, now!'

He looked at his watch and groaned. He was now late and didn't relish getting what-for from Ibrahim if he kept him waiting too long at their morning meeting place. And blast the fact that he had to skip breakfast too when already, his tummy was growling in response to the lovely aromas of cornmeal porridge and freshly-baked bread wafting through from the kitchen. What a life! He complained to himself and shot off into the shower.

Saga walked into school that Tuesday morning with Ibrahim to the loud cheers of many of his schoolmates. Many of the students had gathered just beyond the gate within the school compound, waiting for him to appear, and the cheering started the moment he was spotted.

'ORPHAN! ORPHAN!' they chanted.

It did not look as though much would get done in the school that day unless the teachers took some very firm measures. The headmaster, Mr Money, dispatched the form masters to hustle the students back into their classrooms. The teachers, however, were unsuccessful, as many of the students were too busy cheering the Chief Orphan, and creating noise and bedlam in their excitement. They knew that everything had changed, and accordingly booed and sassed the form masters away. The original Orphan had shattered the school status quo.

Mr Money, already in a fright over what the Orphan event could do to his career, was propelled into action by his fear. To appear to have lost control of the school would no doubt seal his already shaky fate. He grabbed a bullhorn off the wall in his office and rushed to settle the nonsense being perpetrated by those renegade, unruly students once and for all.

The shock of his loud, hysterical admonitions over the bullhorn served to silence the students. He threatened serious punishment for any student who did not head to their classroom immediately. To his dismay, the students did not budge. They merely stared at him. In his panic, the headmaster went a step further by threatening to call in the much-feared riot police to report student unrest in the school. The students however remained unimpressed, and studiously continued to ignore his ranting. Instead, many of them looked towards Saga to see what he would do.

Saga became startled when he realised what was going on. What was he expected to do? The Orphans had not yet met properly to decide anything of consequence, and he still hadn't had the benefit of any guidance from his brother, Obo. Them looking to him to decide the fate of the school that morning was way too sudden and too onerous a responsibility. Yet, he knew he had to do something, since he could not just stand there and lose face forever.

His instincts, however, told him that this was not the right time and place for a showdown with the school authorities. He also knew that their spineless headmaster would not hesitate to call in the police to save his own neck, which could mean the likely indiscriminate beating of the students with truncheons, rifle butts, leather belts, etc., and Saga could not stomach the thought of his fellow students being brutalised. Yet, would walking away from this confrontation mean loss of his new-found popularity?

He finally went with his natural impulses, which would not permit him to place his own narrow concerns such as his continued popularity over the welfare of his schoolmates. He thus turned and faced his rebellious mates, raised his right arm as high as he could in a V for a victory sign salute, which immediately broke the tension and drew massive cheering from the students. He then signalled, pointing towards the classrooms that everyone should head inside. Astonishingly, they all trooped off as directed by Saga, talking loudly, jeering at the teachers, and cat-calling all the way into class.

The headmaster, in particular, felt himself rapidly progressing towards a nervous breakdown as a result of the unyielding dilemmas that continued to confront him. While seething at his own impotence and further loss of face, he could not help but grudgingly feel a little grateful in his heart to Saga for defusing a potentially dangerous situation that would have no doubt compounded his mounting problems.

He was losing control of his school and would ultimately be held responsible for what happened earlier on with Saga and the Deputy Minister, Mr Com, thus placing him in serious trouble if his luck did not dramatically change very quickly. Also, for any one single student to hold that kind of sway over his fellow schoolmates, as Saga had just demonstrated, was a certain recipe for disaster in these turbulent times, and could not be tolerated in any possible form by the school authorities. And such a disturbing influence obviously needed to be neutralised very quickly!

He was gravely disturbed by the real possibility of some strident form of student unrest within the school. It had, for example, come to his notice from one of the many spies he had planted within the student body, that some students were thinking of taking matters into their own hands in a bid to counter and combat Saga's overnight popularity and the subversive nature of what his 'Orphan' stance represented.

The core of this group comprised of a reckless band of ultra-elitist Southern students whose fathers held important positions within the Regime. These were very privileged students who wielded considerable influence within the school by virtue of their daddies' jobs. This group instinctively knew that Saga's sudden influence automatically created a new centre of power within the school, which directly threatened their special position.

This special position of theirs was not a laughable matter. It was serious business indeed. For example, they could literally do as they pleased without fear of censure from the school authorities, who dared not incur the wrath of their powerful parents. Even more importantly, no teacher would dare fail them in their internal school exams for very much the same reasons. They were the Princes of a new aristocracy and were to be treated as such by lesser mortals such as schoolteachers, on pain of consequences possibly much too alarming to even contemplate.

The presence of these Princes in the school, which was generally thought of as a special gift from Providence, could now prove to be the very cause of their undoing. Up until now, their presence meant, for example, the availability of extra funding from the State coffers, privileged access regarding admissions to the country's few universities, and much higher salaries for the teachers than generally prevailed.

In addition, teachers of the school that bore the privilege of the President's own exulted name – Brewman Boys High School – also enjoyed a host of unmerited bonuses and perks for acting as the sycophantic guardians of the Regime's possible future dynastic rulers. And such privileges could surely not be given up lightly.

The absurd logic of the times was that such extra funding and privileges had even resulted in the school becoming the finest and most elitist secondary institution in the country, regardless of purely academic considerations. To add to this, the teachers there were now also viewed as a corresponding teaching aristocracy that had the ear of the 'powers-that-be'. Mr Money and many of his staff had delightfully basked at the apex of this new hierarchy, and were daily milking it for what it was worth!

Thus, Brewman Boys High was inundated with a mile-long waiting list of eager, young students trying to gain admission, not to mention the countless applications of teachers seeking to transfer into this new teaching stratosphere that guaranteed almost instant social elevation and relative prosperity. Unfortunately, however, a negative correlation of this, which the teachers were now realising, was simply that by the same virtue of the presence of these Princes, serious attention would definitely be focused on the school as a result of the Saga-inspired drama. And this could very well prove problematic for its nouveau aristocratic teachers.

The headmaster wondered as to how this privileged cocoon they had so painstakingly built for themselves through the most humiliating forms of grovelling, obsequiousness, sycophancy and plain, old-fashioned boot-licking could be so ominously and suddenly threatened by an insignificant, pimpled-faced youth such as Saga. Had they been too complacent to realise how this privileged lifestyle teetered on such a tenuous and fragile existence by virtue of being dependent on the whims and caprices of bigoted rulers who were obsessed with nothing beyond their own vainglory and brutality to perpetuate their power within society?

Well, never mind what the facts spoke – they, the teachers, would not just stand by and let renegade youth such as Saga bring down the petty empire they had so painstakingly created for themselves. Life was too short as things stood in the country today.

CHAPTER TEN

'My Daddy Will Get You'

The Princes themselves were even more furious! How dare a non-entity, an upstart, and a certified nobody such as Saga attempt to upset the order of things as they stood? Though certainly privileged and pampered, not all of the Princes were entirely stupid. Many of them had quickly grasped the significance of what Saga had done and what could happen if such public defiance from so youthful a quarter should spread and gain currency in the other secondary schools. They realised that it was imperative that they formed a counter-movement in the school to challenge the rapidly growing influence of this hateful Orphan.

However, theirs was not as united a group as one might have imagined. The reason for the potential divisiveness among this princely group was that, for some of them, it had been difficult to simply accept the kind of injustices that prevailed both within their school and the wider community, despite their own exulted positions. Was it a fact of life that youth generally had a greater propensity, a more genuine inclination towards seeking what was true, or was it simply that some of these Princes were more fair-minded than others? Whatever it was, the more narrow-minded and aggressive of their lot won the day.

A handful of belligerent boys that imagined themselves as the natural leaders of the Princes had met and resolved to form a rival group to thwart these foolish Orphan upstarts who dared threaten the status quo. But as was to be expected, this was far more easily wished for than done. To start with, here were a bunch of spoilt, privileged teenagers who could not agree on anything. Each was much too pampered and much too self-centred to listen to any views other than their own, and each was too used to having his own way.

Their initial plenary meeting, which was held to decide the fundamentals, such as the name of their movement, aims and membership, started rather chaotically, as the Princes were much too eager to hear their own voices than to submit to any orderly process that would regulate the meeting.

Yalley Junior – one of the more notorious of these Princes – fancied himself as having the gift of the gab. He had consequently muscled his way into becoming president of the school's debating society, and as such, thought himself familiar with the protocols of managing debates and curbing unruliness at such gatherings.

Thus, he stepped up and sought to bring some order into the chaotic proceedings. He reasoned that whoever could achieve some semblance of order in what was quickly becoming a senseless, riotous fest, would undoubtedly assume the mantle of leadership, which he very much coveted. There was no telling what additional privileges could be earned from leading the group that sought to restore the status quo within the school while besting these awful Orphans as the main sport to achieve this aim.

Yalley Junior thus moved into action. 'This meeting is called to order,' he bellowed. 'Order… order,' he continued to yell above the din.

There was a stunned silence and Yalley felt an initial thrill of pleasure. I'm doing great, maybe I'm a natural born leader, he thought to himself. But he had, however, misunderstood the reason for the silence that occurred, as he was soon to find out.

What Yalley had not realised was that these Princes – being as pampered as he was – were not in the business of having themselves yelled or bellowed at. Thus, their responsive silence was due more to the shock and indignation of being yelled at, rather than recognising any particular merit in Yalley's attempt to achieve some order.

'The meeting is called to what?' one of them cheekily yelled back when the initial shock had subsided.

Everyone started talking and yelling at the same time yet again.

'Hey Yalley, are you crazy?' one of them shouted.

'How dare you scream at us?' chimed in another.

Now, it was coming from everywhere.

'Who do you think you can "order" around here?'

'Have you lost your mind?'

'Who do you think you are, anyway?'

'Foolish boy! Go home and order your sister!'

'Who made you lord and master and leader?'

'Order? What order? My foot order is what!'

It was not going to be easy, but Yalley knew what had to be done, and recovered accordingly. How were they to achieve anything if they could not even talk to each other to start with? Being one of them, he knew that only more shouting and bullying would get these lads into some order. After all, was that not the common language they spoke without realising it? Were they not always being bossy and bullying people all over the place? Yalley knew he was on to something here. He was determined to grab the leadership for himself at all costs, and give the Sagas of his world a run for their money, which would also assure his own glory within the school, with greater privileges to boot! These foolish boys needed a leader and he would give them one, whether they liked it or not.

This time, Yalley mounted a chair. 'YOU ARE ALL STUPID!' he roared again above the din. 'TOO STUPID FOR WORDS!'

Again, the shocked silence.

But Yalley had learned his lesson. He was not about to give them the time to recover and hit back at him. He slammed them again without hesitation.

'All of you should go back to your classrooms, where you have obviously left your senses! How can we achieve anything here if we can't order a simple meeting? You want Saga and his awful Orphans to call the shots from now on? You want us humiliated before the whole country, when you're aware that all eyes are on us? Are you men or sheep?'

He had them now. He had their attention. They were riveted – part from residual shock, part from Yalley's sheer audacity. Yes, he had them. Yes!

'So get out of here and be back at noon tomorrow! And don't you dare leave your senses behind again! Out you go. Shoo!'

The sullen and cowed Princes trooped out.

In his mind, the Legend of Yalley was born! Who's the man, he asked himself with barely concealed glee! Yalley's the man, he answered himself with considerable conceit. I'll ask them that tomorrow, he promised himself. He needed the assurance of his peers that he was truly the man! Leadership was certainly not for the faint-hearted, and he had coined a mother of all phrases to boot: 'Awful Orphans.' *Saga, my boy – here I come! Beware and aware!*

Yalley knew that they had to move very quickly to show them who this school truly belonged to.

Back in his classroom, Saga was flushed with elation. A different sort of confusion reigned here, as he was still being mobbed by many of his form mates, while the form master looked on with growing fury, worsened by his own obvious inability to control his class. He dared not attempt to bring the students to order.

Saga, however, was sensible enough to know that any form of prolonged disorder at this moment would not serve the Orphans well. They needed time to grow, to organise, to strategise and to assign tasks, and all this would be impossible if chaos reigned. He also knew the events unfolding in his school were already attracting the attention of the wider society. Consequently, whatever the Orphans were going to do had to be done very well, and in style. It all had to be well-thought-out and planned.

Saga had also heard that the Princes were organising themselves against the Orphans. He had no illusions about what such spoilt brats were capable of, since they cared for no one but themselves. He also knew that they had very powerful and ruthless fathers, who would not hesitate to commandeer state security resources to back their obnoxious offspring. That was a thorny problem indeed. But he would deal with that later. For now, he needed calm to prevail.

Saga stood on his chair. The teacher gave a start.

'Quiet, please,' Saga said firmly to the class.

Instant silence! Even the scowling, grumbling Princes in his class held their peace.

'Let us settle down to our books and have our discussions during break-time,' he reasoned with them. That was enough. Peace now prevailed, much to the form master's grudging admiration.

Break-time went horribly wrong for Saga. He emerged from his classroom during the noon break into the welcome sunshine and adoring looks of many of his student compatriots. Much to his pleasure, many of his own friends, as well as a mini-mob of newly-acquired followers who also saw themselves as would-be Orphans, flanked him. Though he had eaten no breakfast that morning, the sheer excitement of events had so far vanquished his earlier hunger pangs. He had even forgotten to bring with him from the classroom his mother's daily packed snack of sandwiches and fruit juice. This realisation dawned when many a sandwich was thrust in his direction from those eagerly wishing to share their repast with their new-found hero. He politely refused them all. For now, hunger had to give way to adrenaline!

There was tangible tension everywhere within the school compound. It was as though the student body had unconsciously split itself into two opposing, hostile camps. Saga and his followers had grouped themselves on the larger football field, chatting and laughing, while the Princes and their frowning followers were massed on the opposite side of the field on the paved basketball court, looking askance at those silly 'Orphan' upstarts.

The leaders of the two groups gave the nonchalant appearance of ignoring one another. This was until a group of first-year youngsters, playfully kicking a ball around in Saga's side of the compound, shot their ball onto the basketball court, where it hit the back of a Prince's head, and sent him sprawling onto the ground. The Prince in question was Yalley Junior – the very aggressive son of the Regime's All-Powerful Minister for Presidential Affairs.

This was sacrilege! How many shocks were the Princes to endure in a just a few days? Yalley was certainly not having it. In a blind rage, he charged off to teach the disrespectful Saga-lovers some sense. Others in his set, equally outraged by such shocking impertinence, dashed after him in support. Some recalcitrant ears of these insolent offenders were in dire need of a princely boxing.

Saga and his group only became aware of the impending altercation when Yalley bellowed in his charge and others in his own group had enthusiastically started the chant of 'Fight... fight... fight!' He was initially taken aback by the abrupt shattering of the prevailing tension. There was, however, no time to even consider finding out the facts. Some of his younger supporters were in immediate danger of receiving a vigorous thrashing, and that could not be permitted. The Orphans were their brother's keepers!

Thus, Saga could not again simply stand back. He rallied his supporters and they also charged in defence of the offenders. They arrived at the pending altercation site in the nick of time to form a protective cordon around the ball-booting youngsters, just as Yalley and the other Princes arrived on the scene.

'Get out of my way,' Yalley yelled at Saga. 'This is not your concern, even though you started it all! This is between me and those young fools who need to be taught some manners! How dare they hit me with their ball? I'm warning you, Saga, just get out of my way! And who the hell do you think you are anyway, getting in my face like that?'

'Calm down, Yalley. Just calm down! It was probably an accident – just calm down, okay?' Saga replied. But Yalley was neither to be deterred nor denied. He was unused to such.

'Get out of my sight, Saga, or you'll also get what's coming to you. Move, I say. Now!'

But Saga did not budge. He was unafraid and there was simply too much at stake. He was nonetheless doing some rapid thinking. He was in a dilemma.

Firstly, he could neither encourage nor ignore any open fights that would prematurely draw too much negative attention from the authorities on all of them. However, to abandon his first-year supporters to their fate at the hands of Yalley and his thuggish student followers was unthinkable. In reality, he had only one option.

'Sorry Yalley, but I'm not moving. You'll have to go through me to get to them. Why don't you go and pick on someone your own size?'

This was just too much for Yalley to bear. He lunged at Saga, and the fight was on. Following their lead, Yalley and Saga supporters threw themselves at each other.

Though caught in a grim wrestling lock with Yalley, Saga knew he still had to do something to end the fighting immediately. It was just this kind of misdemeanour the headmaster needed as a pretext to call in the police. This thought gave him extra strength. So far, members of staff were most likely unaware of the fight that had broken out, and it had to stay that way.

Mustering his renewed strength, Saga managed to throw Yalley onto the ground, sat on his chest and pinned his arms to the ground with his knees. Yalley struggled in vain. Saga was much too strong and much too heavy for his thin opponent. Yalley was fast appearing to be no match. Years of lugging boxes of provisions and crates of beer and Coca-Cola for Major Kata's store-cum-café had given Saga muscles he was not even aware he possessed, not to mention his general bulk.

Once he was certain Yalley posed no further threat and was securely pinned down, he yelled at the top of his voice, 'STOP! ALL OF YOU – STOP THIS MINUTE!'

His voice carried and everyone stopped.

'This is no good! No more fighting, please! Disperse to your classrooms now!'

Amazingly, he was yet again obeyed. He knew he had to disperse them before the teachers caught on.

'PLEASE GO NOW!' he yelled some more.

He turned his attention to Yalley beneath him. 'I'm going to release you now. If you know what's good for you, you'll help me stop this nonsense and get back to the classroom with your people now. And just leave those kids alone!' he said, panting from his exertions.

But Yalley needed to show some resistance, as there were still some students watching and listening.

'And what if I don't?' he retorted, panting just as much as Saga.

'Then you are going to get a bashing that will make your own mother incapable of recognising you!'

Yalley quickly weighed this new threat. He considered his present state of helplessness, coupled with the Princes not being sufficiently strong enough to deal with Saga and his followers at present, and relented.

'Okay – but I'm going to get you for this, Saga. It's looking like you won because I slipped, so don't flatter yourself thinking you are stronger than me! I'll get you, Saga. You are finished in this school. My daddy will get you! Now let me go!'

And Saga let him go, but he was bothered.

Such unplanned eruptions so early in the game were not a good thing. He very much needed to consult with Obo to seek advice on how to run his new movement and manage the crisis that was fast brewing in the school. For now, some further damage prevention was necessary. He had to caution his followers not to provoke the Princes at this stage. There was time enough for that. There was time enough for a lot of things.

* * *

A few days later, when Saga got home, he was pleasantly surprised to find Obo back. He was sitting on the outside porch with their father, smoking a cigarette. As soon as he could, Saga whispered to his brother that he wanted to have a private word after supper.

'No problem, and I won't be going back to campus so we've got all night,' answered Obo, who was himself quite anxious to have his own private briefing on what was happening in Saga's school. The news was fast becoming the talk of the Cape Cove University campus.

Later, with parents and sister in bed, Saga tiptoed downstairs to Obo's room to have his overdue yet much-anticipated session.

After briefing Obo as to what happened in school with Mr Com, the Deputy Minister, and also with Yalley Junior and his Princes, and the general mood that prevailed, Obo said he'd soon explain some of the possible ways in which they could organise the Orphans and other things they could generally do to help the wider effort of thwarting the Regime's detested New Patriotism.

Obo, reclining back on his king-sized bed with Saga at the edge near his feet, was glad to lecture his now-famous younger brother, drawing on his own experiences as a student leader, who had been involved in many open and clandestine struggles against the Regime and its goons. But first, he needed to ascertain what the situation was on the home front.

'Before we continue, tell me, Saga, how are Mom and Dad taking it? This can't be easy for them, especially Mom.'

'The thing is, they really haven't said much, which is bothering me a bit. I've been waiting for one of their long lectures, but nada so far, zilch, nothing!' replied a rather perplexed Saga.

'As for the lecture, it will come – never fear. This time, it's quite different from your previous Mike Tyson approach, but you can bet they've discussed it over and over again. Don't put them through too much.' Obo gave his little brother a serious look before lightening the mood with, 'So, Chief Orphan, tell me what you're up to. Word has even reached our university campus, but perhaps the story got embellished along the way?'

Saga looked bashful; he didn't really know how to cope with his new-found fame.

'In all this, there's one fundamental thing you should understand, Saga, and it's like this – this thing you have started is not child's play. This is serious business, so listen very carefully. What you did wasn't wrong. Actually, you did well – but from now on, your life is going to get very complicated and much more difficult. You're no longer a kid, and many bad things can happen. If you know you don't have the stomach for it, now is the time to quit. I'm serious, Saga. Don't waste anybody's time if you're not up to handling the can of worms you've just opened. So what's it going to be?' Obo asked quite seriously now, with his eyes fixed firmly on Saga's face. He needed to be sure.

Saga thought for a minute, then raised his eyes and met his brother's squarely. 'I can do this, Obo. I'm not afraid. It's taken a while for me to get here, but I'm ready now. Ibrahim and many others are firmly behind me, and of course, we know the dangers. And you're right – we're not kids anymore. All we know now is that we've started something that can help rid the secondary schools of this New Patriotism rubbish, but you need to show us the way forward. Please believe that I'm willing and able, and you have my word that there'll be no more fights. I will do my best to avoid fighting. I promised you and the old folks that what happened at Sablon's won't happen again and I mean it,' Saga replied with conviction.

'You're sure your friends are aware of the dangers? Do they know their parents can get into trouble as well? First-year chaps at the university not much older than you have been arrested and beaten many times by the Zombies. You think you guys can handle that kind of heat and pain? You remember the surgery I had to undergo halfway around the world in London, when the soldiers slapped me around till I couldn't hear in my left ear? That's what I'm talking about when I say it's no joke. And don't forget the students who have also gone missing.'

Saga assured Obo that he understood all that he was saying and that the Orphans were fully aware of the implications of what they were going to attempt.

Obo then pointed out to Saga the importance of what he had inadvertently started within his school, and how, if well-organised, it could positively gain currency in many secondary schools. He even let Saga into a secret that a section of the leadership of the student body in his university had approached him when he got back from the North about forming a chapter of the Orphans on their campus. That was how big this could all become. He cautioned Saga about being big-headed, pig-headed and complacent. He emphasised loyalty, the need to be each other's keeper, as their father had taught them, and the ever real and present danger of spies.

Obo emphasised yet again that though only 18, Saga and his mates could no longer see themselves as children, given what they had started in the school and the circumstances prevailing in their country at the time. The Regime, he said, was daily robbing them of their youth.

Throughout this session, Saga marvelled at Obo's breadth of knowledge and good sense for one who was only in his early 20s. There was much to think about, digest and brief his fellow Orphans, he thought quite excitedly. Life had changed indeed. A final lesson Saga learned from Obo that day, which was to prove invaluable, was simply that no one person could always fully control any situation. Life had many surprises for everyone and human beings were not always predictable, no matter what anyone said.

'Always make room for the unforeseen,' Obo had warned, 'but even then, you can never be fully prepared, so just prepare to the best of your abilities always and that way, you're better positioned to handle any surprises! Never forget that, Saga. And finally, you're my brother, so know that I always have your back. Always come to me if you need anything or are unsure about something. What are brothers for, eh?' And with that, Obo leaned forward and patted his younger brother affectionately on the back.

Encouraged by his brother's warmth and guidance, Saga confidently felt he could now set the stage for the Orphans to move into action. He knew what to do. He would call a meeting of the Orphans soon to impart his newly-acquired wisdom and tactics gained from his impressive big brother. He knew that there was a 'learn as you go' process also involved. His father's constant refrain that life was a learning curve came back to him with renewed meaning.

Yes – he was willing and able to learn! And he would!

CHAPTER ELEVEN

TIA – This Is Africa

Yalley Junior's humiliation that afternoon was killing him.

He was sitting in the plush living area of his suite of rooms, designated as 'Junior's Wing', within his father's sprawling mansion. He literally sat in an unashamed and unambiguous island of sheer opulence, in what could only be described as a general societal sea of poverty. His father's mansion was situated in the seriously affluent part of Ridge Heights, not very far from where his rival, Saga, lived.

Yalley Junior's rooms were modelled on the Premier Suite of The Four Seasons Hotel at 2880 Pennsylvania Avenue in Washington DC, one of the not so many 'Five Diamond' hotels in the world. At the invitation of one of the American defence contractors that supplied the Government with sophisticated weaponry for Brewman's elite Presidential Guard, Yalley Junior had spent a week in wondrous splendour at the enormously expensive Four Seasons in Washington DC with his father a couple of years back. The young man had come away so impressed that he had vowed to live in similar unadulterated elegance back at home in Zimgania.

Consequently, under intense pressure from his son, General Yalley had reached across the Atlantic and hired a well-known and hugely expensive firm of architects and interior designers also based in Washington DC to come out to Africa to re-design his son's rooms. He had managed to lure the initially reluctant designers across the ocean by hurling a boat-load of dollars at them, which they had of course found impossible to resist.

To his twin sister Zara's mind, Yalley Junior's quest to cause their father to spend hundreds of thousands of dollars just to convert his living quarters on a whim symbolised everything that was wrong in their society. In fact, for her, it brought into sharp focus a virulent malaise that was partly responsible for the abject poverty, human degradation and stagnation that afflicted most of the inhabitants of the wider African continent. The malaise in question was the unbridled addiction to corruption at the highest levels of government; a condition which she could only describe as 'Kleptocracy' – the rule of nation states by a bunch of thieving political kleptomaniacs.

To her, such unapologetic opulence in the face of widespread poverty and human squalor was macabre! Aghast, she had surmised at the time that the cost of Junior's rooms could have very well fed, clothed and probably housed scores of poverty-stricken families for a whole year in their country. And she was not far from the truth, given the fact the average per capita annual income of the people of Zimgania was just over a paltry $900 a year! Zara also knew that such terribly low levels of income were pitifully insufficient in the sustaining of human lives to any appreciable level, which meant that most were forced to live in dire poverty. This hideous situation was not much different in most countries in Africa.

Zara knew from her copious reading that in many African countries, a not insignificant part of the revenue from the sale and export of primary products such as oil, gold, copper, zinc, bauxite, cobalt and allied strategic minerals, as well as cash crops such as cocoa, coffee and cotton, flowed directly into the pockets of the ruling elites via the coffers of the state. Vast amounts of these revenues were also spent on pampering and equipping national armies that were either already in power through military coups, or were poised as a constant threat and menace to fledgling democratic processes on the continent.

If so much money was literally stolen from state coffers by leaders and corrupt state officials, as well as senselessly pampering elitist armies with vast sums in an attempt to lure them away from their habitual coup-staging propensities, then what miserly sums could possibly be available for human development? For public education, public health delivery, public transportation, cleaner water supplies, affordable energy, failing agriculture and overall socio-economic development? Was it thus any wonder that Africa boasted of the highest mortality rates in the whole world, with not infrequent crises of famine and starvation in which hundreds of thousands were left to die?

With acute feelings of guilt by association and disgust, Zara had protested vehemently but in vain to her father. She asked him to desist from such criminal opulence in the face of the desperate economic and social crisis that was destroying the lives of millions in their country. She had pleaded with him to give the money instead to the many charities and NGOs operating in their country, such as Oxfam, the Red Cross, the Green Crescent, the Catholic Relief Agency – to mention but a few – that were trying very hard to bring some relief into the lives of those who were even too poor to feed themselves.

Her father had summarily dismissed her protestations. He simply contented himself by telling her that the Regime's economic policies would soon generate a 'trickle-down effect' that would improve the lives of the poor. Why such policies, which had been in existence for aeons, had never done so before was a matter he chose not to address. Nonetheless, he sternly cautioned her to refrain from wasting her thoughts on issues that were of no concern of hers and to rather focus on her studies.

In a lighter tone, he even offered to also designate a set of rooms in their mansion for her exclusive use and have them renovated like her brother's so she could entertain her friends in the style becoming of her status in life. If she did not wish to go for a 'Five Diamond' option, she could opt for a lesser 'Five Star' option to assuage her misplaced feelings of guilt, her father reasoned. The 'Five Star' option was however much too pedestrian for her very elitist brother, Junior.

Zara had been horror-struck by her father's suggestion that she become a part of such criminal indulgence. And despite his warning that she desist, Zara had nonetheless persisted in her protestations to him, but to no avail. Instead, her father soon developed the twin habits of pointedly ignoring her or studiously avoiding her.

As for her brother, Yalley Junior, he had simply scoffed and made fun of her 'stupid bleeding heart sentiments and soppy, goody ways'. He had then proceeded to enlighten her on his world-view on such matters. 'Look here, Zara,' he had said, raising his right hand to eye level. 'Look at the fingers on my hand. Are they the same? Are they all the same length? Well the answer is no, they are not, and that is how God made the world. We are all not equal. Read your bible, read your history, and you'll see that in reality, some must be rich and some must be poor. So how dare you try and upset the natural order of things with your stupid arguments?

'You say I should not have my rooms done according to my exquisite tastes because some people decided to be born poor or are cursed to be poor by a higher power. Is that what rich folk do in England or America or Europe? Have you not seen their country estates and manor houses? Please don't waste my time with such nonsensical arguments. Read your *Animal Farm* again. Some people are more equal than others, so shut your face before I decide never to invite you to my Four Seasons' rooms. And finally, never forget that TIA – This Is Africa – and we who rule do as we please!'

Zara had just stared at her brother utterly dumbfounded. She knew that there was absolutely no point in arguing with him. His beliefs were too ingrained and would possibly remain so forever. Yes, she had been right. The Four Seasons' drama in her own household effectively mirrored the deep-seated horrors of the social and political actualities of her beloved country and wider continent.

Sitting in his Four Seasons-inspired suite, Yalley Junior was feverishly fuming at Saga. How could Saga possibly treat him in that manner? Was he not Yalley Junior, whom even the teachers were very careful in dealing with? His newly-acquired dislike for Saga, who by birth and social position *ought* to be in the camp of the Princes, was growing in leaps and bounds and rapidly turning into hatred. Yes, he hated Saga, and it was getting worse by the minute. Right now, becoming the leader of the Princes was more critical than ever before. One on one, he knew he was no match for Saga, but leading a bunch of privileged students in some kind of student organisation made all the difference. It had now become very personal to him, and he had to find a way to make Saga suffer seriously for causing him to lose face so badly.

He was a little nervous about running to his father to do 'something' about the situation. If word got out, he would be branded a sissy, which under the circumstances, would not augur well at all after losing that fight with his new-found arch-rival, Saga. No, appealing to his father would be his trump card, his last resort. Instead, he would make his daddy proud of him by taking matters into his own hands at school. He would restore the New Patriotism rightfully to its pre-eminent position in their school.

Yalley also had another vital card up his sleeve. He knew he could coerce many of the teachers in school, especially the headmaster, to side with him and the Princes. This he knew could prove to be a crucial tactical advantage for his group. After all, had not the headmaster and his lackeys actively condoned the elevation of him and his set to the level of Princes? Was the headmaster not in mortal dread of the Prince's fathers, who held such powerful positions in the Government? Was he also not in the pockets of these powerful men? Yes, co-opting the support of the school authorities could prove to be a decisive factor in besting Saga and his awful gang!

Yalley also reckoned that it was very important that the example of Saga's heroics did not catch on in other schools. That would do untold harm to his daddy's government. Already, the Government was facing stiff opposition from university students over their fierce antipathy towards the New Patriotism, which they foolishly deemed as hateful. The same could not happen in the secondary schools.

In truth, the Regime's heavy-handedness had so far not achieved the anticipated results. The university students were proving rather too fearless and had refused to bow to the pressure unleashed on them by the Regime. Student demonstrations calling for an abandonment of the New

Patriotism and a cessation of war hostilities had been met with stark brutality from the troops sent to unleash terror on them. The universities had also been shut down several times over the past few years due to such unrest, which was now equally focused on the release of the students being held without trial. Academic courses had, as a result, been seriously disrupted, creating a backlog of students waiting to be admitted after they had passed their A-levels. Thus, many students were simply marking time at home, not quite sure as to what the future held for them.

The Regime's handling of the university crisis had attracted some criticism from a few foreign countries. Some human rights activists were up in arms against the President, who simply ignored them all. Instead, he gave fresh orders to his security chiefs to use his troops to break the back of the student resistance by employing overwhelming force if needs must.

Yalley hated those university students with a passion. He saw them as troublemakers who were disrupting the smooth running of the country. He hated all those people who were opposed to his daddy's government, including those stupid foreigners who were always criticising the President. What did they know anyway? How dare they interfere so brazenly in the internal affairs of a sovereign country? He had heard his father say this many times. What could possibly be wrong with bashing and detaining a few unruly students who were hell-bent on causing chaos in the country by resisting the wisdom and vision of its leader? How dare they refer to the President as 'Brewman the Brute'?

Yalley approved of the Regime's brutal methods. He had absolutely not a shred of sympathy for all those who threatened his privileged existence – period! He was a product of the New Patriotism – pure and simple. As such, Yalley vowed to do all in his power to prevent Saga's example from gaining currency in the secondary schools. He had once read about some African countries where widespread student unrest in second-cycle institutions had helped bring about the downfall of governments, and that could not be allowed to happen here. If the problem was contained within his school and examples made of the Orphans, then Yalley would have done his duty to his daddy and his government.

He thus had a mission. He now had serious focus in his life – the destruction of Saga and his Orphans.

CHAPTER TWELVE

No Xbox, No Nintendo

Saga's father, Nana, was having sleepless nights. Though no coward, he was nonetheless virtually walking around with a hollow ache in his belly at all times. He was very worried for Saga and for the safety of the rest of his family. He had no fears for himself beyond the hope that he would be around long enough to continue looking after his family. But should anything happen to him, should he be killed or maimed in the struggle against the Regime, he knew that he had provided well for them. If his family remained prudent, they would not want for much for a while to come.

His anxiety was based on the painful awareness that he had taught his children too well, to the extent that he knew there was no stopping Saga from now on. He was shrewd enough to realise that a fire had been lit in his younger son, which could not be extinguished any time soon. His children were much too steeped in the sense of fairness and social justice he had implanted in them from infancy. Saga was certainly not about to stop, just when his intervention in school had woken him up to the fact that he could help change things at that level at the very least.

Saga's was truly a dangerous quest, which Nana felt powerless to halt. In fact, how could he stop the boy when Saga was simply acting out what he had been brought up to believe? How could he ask the boy to be a hypocrite or coward when it was obvious that he wished to do only what was right? How could he also ask the boy to place himself and his family above all else and abandon his fellow schoolmates, who were equally risking so much to support the stand Saga had taken?

Nana knew his children were also not cowards. He had painstakingly brought them up to understand the hopelessness and futility of irrational fear. Fear got you nowhere – he had taught them. Fear in general prevented one from leading a full life, and irrational fear was the worst of the lot. He had nonetheless been careful to point out the distinction between fear and the sensible recognition of danger. For instance, one did not go prancing about in a field full of starving lions because one was fearless! That was stark stupidity at its best.

Kindliness, patience, understanding and tolerance were not qualities that were in conflict with the general absence of fear. Bravery was not simply a question of not being afraid of physical danger. Actually, it also took a lot of courage to show the softer qualities, such as demonstrating tender sensibilities toward your fellow man or woman as and when the occasion called for such.

He also taught them not to be afraid of showing their emotions and that it was all right for a man to cry when it was necessary to do so. Crying was not the preserve of women, as was falsely believed in their 'macho', male-dominated society. Nana argued that after all, it was only a brave man who not being afraid of what others thought or said of him, and could cry when the urge arose.

And it was this absence of fear that was going to compel Saga to attempt to deepen and spread his recent heroic standoff. Nana was no fool. He knew that the first person Saga would rush to for support and guidance on how to wage an anti-New Patriotism struggle at secondary school level was his brother, Obo.

Nana knew that his sons were already in consultation about the tactics to employ in the secondary schools. He was not worried that Obo would give Saga dubious advice in this respect. Obo was level-headed for his age, and was very much aware of the nature of the society they presently lived in, as well as the dangers involved in any form of resistance against the Regime, no matter how minor.

How Nana wished his sons could be spared all of this! This was no rite of passage – he lamented. Why could they not enjoy the normal rites of passage that other children enjoyed in less turbulent parts of the world? Why could they not be playing Nintendo, Xbox and the host of modern-day computer games that were the order of the day for youngsters in the Western world, where all of such were now practically taken for granted? Why could they not spend time on the internet, gaining useful knowledge on Wikipedia or some such search engine, or having MSN, Myspace and allied cyber chats with their friends, or simply continue to listen to that loud rap music of theirs? Why was the world so unfair?

Nana hoped as never before that his children would not resort to violent methods, though he knew many students were now talking about 'fighting fire with fire' in their struggles against the Regime. He hoped his teachings against violence had taken sufficient root in their hearts and minds to prevent them from being swayed by their more aggressively-minded student compatriots.

Since he knew he could not stop his children from fulfilling what now appeared to be both their legacy and destiny of struggle, it was about time he intervened to guide and assist them in placing things in their proper perspectives. He knew that if word ever got out that he had not stopped his children but had rather egged them on with advice as to the best means to wage the struggle, he was a dead man. But there was no choice for him in the matter, as the circumstances and recent developments had irredeemably proved.

* * *

The next day, Nana was sitting under his usual mango tree in the back garden when he heard Saga come in from school. He called for him to come out back and curtly told him he was taking him to the underground resistance meeting that night.

Saga almost fell over. 'But Dada…' was all he could manage.

'But what, Saga? You have something you want to ask? Or you don't know there's an underground movement?' Nana asked tersely.

'Of course I know, Dad – it's just that I didn't know you were a part of it.'

'Since when did you start telling little lies, Saga? You think I'm an idiot? You think I don't know you're aware your brother and I are involved and that you followed us that night to Tiger's place? I just didn't say anything then in the hope that you would come and ask me directly. But you never did. Anyway, your brother will also be joining us tonight.'

'I'm sorry, Dada. Please see it as a white lie. But thank you. Thank you so very much.'

Nana then instructed him as what route to use to get to the meeting, as they would be leaving separately. The meetings now took place in the basement of Tiger's church-like structure on his compound, and no longer in the main hall where Saga spied on them previously. Saga was to go via the back wall of their home and leave through the nursery school they shared a wall with. Obo would make his way there from the university campus. He advised Saga not to run and to be wary of anyone he met on the way. He was to return home the moment he felt he was being followed. Caution was everything.

By this stage, Saga was speechless. What an honour to be invited to a meeting of the famed resistance group when he was only just a teenager. Saga did not know whether to laugh, scream, sit or somersault! He was over the moon, under the stars – he was everywhere at the same time and beside himself with joy. He just stared at his father, barely comprehending what he was saying about the need for caution, back walls – whatever! It was all meaningless to him, given the immensity of his joy. He still could not believe it! Was his father pulling leg? Did he misunderstand what his dad said?

'Dada, did you just say I am to come to your resistance meeting?'

Nana realised Saga had ceased being compos mentis at that point. He realised his invitation had left the boy in a state of bewilderment. He decided to be gentle and told Saga yet again that he was invited to tonight's resistance meeting and that he would explain the reason for it when they got there. He also repeated the precautions he was to take against prying eyes and would-be informants. They certainly lived in very unsafe times.

Nana then became stern again. 'Saga, I need not tell you that you cannot, and I repeat, CANNOT mention this to anyone at all – not even Ibrahim. Do you understand? No one outside the people you meet today should ever know of your involvement, and you must *never* reveal to anyone those you see there and what is said there. It is absolutely top secret! Do you get what I am saying?'

Nana's sudden harshness had brought Saga back to his senses. This was no dream. This was real.

'Of course I won't mention it, Da! You have my absolute word. You know I will never betray you or anyone for that matter, and I also know that this is a very big matter.'

Of course, he realised the immensity of the trust being placed in him and his obligation to remain absolutely mute about it all. This was not some personal triumph to be shared with one's friends. This was literally a matter of life and death for many people and their families. Yes, total discretion and secrecy was everything in this business!

Nana was reassured. He did not doubt his son, but he had needed to be sure.

Saga did not know how to contain himself up until the appointed time for them to leave separately that night. What was he to do until then, given the sheer excitement that was coursing through his body? Studying was totally out of the question. Where would he find the concentration needed for that? He had already developed a spring in his step as he was going about some domestic chores he had uncharacteristically assigned himself in the absence of anything to do but wait. He understood for the first time the true meaning of being on tenterhooks! Chores complete, he decided to go and help out in the café.

Tales of his heroic exploits in school had of course reached his neighbourhood, and many of the customers at their café whispered quiet praises to him, though none of them failed to mention that he ought to be very careful. He nodded politely to each of them but said nothing. Praise of that nature was not meant to be voiced aloud in public. It was much too dangerous and foolhardy. Despite the fact that most of the people in his neighbourhood were generally opposed to the Government, Saga knew well enough that one could never be sure. Some people were not averse to currying favour with the Regime by informing on neighbours.

That night, Saga dressed carefully for the meeting. He wore very dark clothes. That way, he knew it would be more difficult for anyone to follow him. The streets of his neighbourhood, like in most of the city, were poorly lit or had no street lighting at all. The Regime – far too busy with oppressing the people, indulging its 'kleptocratic' propensities, and waging unnecessary war – had lost its sense of maintenance culture. It was as though those corrupt officials had forgotten that light bulbs ought to be replaced when they expired. Such a culture was a thing of the distant past and properly functioning street lamps a relic of bygone days. For what it was worth, this state of general malaise, *vis-a-vis* the street lighting situation, suited Saga and all would-be skulkers very well that night.

Saga knew why his father had asked him to leave via the nursery school they shared a back wall with. It was common knowledge in the neighbourhood that the enfeebled watchman in charge of that compound at night was not one who toyed with his sleep. Saga knew you could literally set your clock to the commencement of his snoring every evening, which could be heard in their home and several others. Actually guarding the premises appeared to be quite an alien concept for the watchman, who seemed to think the most effective way of doing his job was to scare would-be prowlers away with fierce bursts of his cacophonous snoring.

Saga made his way carefully over the back wall. He walked across the small compound and exited through the front gate to the tune of the night watchman's unmelodious snoring onto the street that was parallel to his. It was deserted at that time of the night. Or so he thought. The street was tree-lined as well, which would make it easier to duck and dive behind them if the need arose. And the need did arise much sooner than he thought.

CHAPTER THIRTEEN

'The Mystery Wheezer?'

Bayou was an embittered middle-level official in the State Planning Ministry. Bayou was having a cigarette on his porch because his nagging wife had recently decreed that his smoking in the house was getting on her nerves. Being shoved out of the house the moment he lit his cigarette had done nothing to improve his already foul humour. Why should he be manhandled out of his own home without ceremony like a common felon whenever he wanted to have a cigarette? What was the world coming to when a man could not have a decent smoke in the comfort of his own home after a hard day's work?

Bayou had become embittered because for a long time, he felt he had been passed over for promotion at the Ministry in favour of those whom he believed were lesser men than he was. Surely, he was much better than those stupid young men who, because of their university degrees, had rapidly received undeserved promotions and thought that the world owed them a living. All they did was sit there all day and stare and tap at their computer screens while people like him did the real work in the field for the Ministry. Did these people think that having a university degree automatically gave you wisdom and made you better at your job? Did society no longer value experience? All his years of hard work had been in vain! All the years in the field, sweating under the fierce sun while collecting valuable data for the Ministry, had all been for nothing!

Bayou was a frustrated man who simply could not come to terms with the fact that he lived in a changing world, which required the use of new techniques and methods to stay abreast. He did not appreciate that he now lived in a cyber age where information technology ruled. In truth, middle management bureaucratic types like Bayou who were at the heart and soul of policy implementation before the advent of the cyber revolution had, in all reality, been failed by the Government. For such people to be able to maintain their step-by-step rise within the bureaucracy would have simply required Government to re-train them to embrace the rapid technological changes taking place worldwide. But the Government simply left them to their fate while promoting younger graduates with cyber skills to become their bosses.

But Bayou was not a wise man. He was a small-minded man. Thus, after very little hesitation, Bayou decided to channel his bitterness and frustrations into embracing the Regime's New Patriotism when it was first introduced. The divisiveness that was a necessary tool of the New Patriotism and the havoc it was wreaking suited his embittered and twisted mind very well. This way, he would be able to get back at those who had hindered his advancement at work. It also afforded him an unprecedented opportunity to strike back at those snotty-nosed, young graduate punks who had 'lorded' it over him when they received their undeserved promotions. All he needed was to find some real or imagined reason to inform on them as potential enemies of the state. Consequently, with all the fervour of the newly-converted and spurred on by his own insecurities and blind hatreds, Bayou embraced the New Patriotism with mindless ferocity.

He became a Northern/Muslim-baiter at the Ministry and informed on anyone who so much as gave a worried look whenever the New Patriotism was mentioned. Many had been sacked, demoted and arrested due to his deplorable activities. And he had become quite wealthy overnight from taking bribes from those who now saw him as a source of influence within their Ministry (due to his new-found connections with the Regime's ruthless henchmen). He had also secured what he saw as having been his long overdue promotion, as several of his bosses now lived in mortal fear of him. He had become the very personification of the bigoted citizen that the Regime wished to create.

Standing on his porch that evening, Bayou was livid that an up and coming powerful man such as himself should be made to endure the indecency of not being able to have his smoke in the comfort of his living room. He was grimly relishing all kinds of mean mental fantasies about informing on his wife to the authorities and having her rightfully tortured by his thuggish pals within the security apparatus, when he noticed someone creeping out of the gates of the nursery school, which was practically opposite his house.

Being a thoroughly suspicious fellow, Bayou was immediately on guard and knew instinctively that this was not quite what he would consider a usual development. Why should anyone be sneaking out of a day nursery at this ungodly hour? A thief? Certainly not, and also, the figure appeared not to be holding anything! What was there to steal at that place anyway? Tattered books on nursery rhymes? Dilapidated mini-chairs and tables? No, that couldn't be it! Something was amiss!

Wait; was that not the troublesome young lad from the next street? The one who had recently caused all that commotion down at the prestigious Brewman High School in their neighbourhood? Was it not one of the not-to-be-trusted, looks-like-a-subversive liberal and not-long-for-this-earth Nana's son? What was he doing creeping around at this time of night and clearly looking suspiciously around to see if he was being observed or not?

Bayou quickly extinguished his cigarette to prevent just that. It would do no good to be observed just yet. He suppressed the urge to yell at the lad to find out what he was up to at this ungodly hour. Bayou felt his excitement rising. He quietly moved to a darkened part of his porch where he could not be seen, to observe the boy. The foolish boy was obviously up to no good. To be able to pin anything serious on this boy or any other in his family would bring much praise and rewards from his persecuting peers.

Already, he had heard whiffs of disgruntled noises from high places, complaining about the untold damage that the boy's actions could cause the Regime if not dealt with. Also, he knew that Nana was on the list of potentially dangerous troublemakers and that it was simply a matter of time before the authorities got to him and brought him down several pegs before giving him his just deserts.

That uppity Nana with his liberal views deserves every bit of what is coming to him, Bayou convinced himself. If only I could speed up the process of that man's fall! Maybe this trouble-causer of a brat would provide the key. Better follow him to see what he's up to. Maybe his foolish father has put him up to something. That would be even better.

Actually, Bayou had heard persistent rumours that there was a very prominent underground resistance cell or group or whatever it was called operating within his neighbourhood, though no one had been able to provide any sensible proof or evidence of its activities up until then. What secretly frightened him was that if the existence of this underground cell in his neighbourhood was found to be true, it would reflect very badly on him.

He was an informer.

He would be seen as not having been vigilant enough.

He would be seen as having under-informed.

He would be seen to have failed.

He would be seen as not having done his job well enough.

That would be a disaster beyond belief.

Though a staunch follower of the Regime, he had absolutely no illusions about their lack of loyalty to their own supporters and the ferocity with which they could abruptly turn against their own kind if it so suited them. The brutal purges within the core of Brewman's South Party were legendary, and he was only a recent and fringe member.

All his newly-acquired friends on the fringes of power would desert him. All his new-found petty power would evaporate within a day, not to mention being dragged to the dreaded Traitors' Jail, where dreadful things would be done to him, as had been done to those he had sent there with his evil tattling. What would the inmates he had betrayed do to him? He wilted in terror at the mere thought!

He almost always vomited whenever these thoughts popped into his head, which was growing alarmingly frequent.

Consequently, Bayou was nowadays in a near permanent state of fear-induced nausea!

Bayou came back to the present.

Was it likely that this brat was part of this horrid group of malcontents who would see him in Traitors' Jail? Was he not too young? Or was he on an errand for them? In fact, was it truly the Saga boy or some other youngster?

He needed to be sure.

Though he could not quite work it out exactly, Bayou's instincts made him feel he was onto something big here and was not about to let it go. The boy was walking briskly towards the intersection that formed at the end of the road. He had a good 400 metres to go. Bayou noticed that the boy stopped frequently to look around and behind him.

He quickly moved to tail him. He ducked behind the tree in front of his house and quickly moved from tree to tree in pursuit. Bayou was not exactly fit for his age, and soon began panting after walking and ducking behind four consecutive trees that were interspaced about six metres apart by the colonial city planners of years before. For a fraction of a second, he thought of abandoning what could very well prove to be a wild goose chase, when an acute surge of his fear-induced nausea that accompanied this thought quickly brought him back to his senses and propelled him after the boy.

Saga, on the other hand, was initially confident that he was very much alone on the street, apart from a couple of cars that had driven by. So far so good. No nosy neighbours had peered out of their curtained windows as yet. He could smell the aroma of people cooking their evening meal on coal pots in their backyards, and remembered that he'd again forgotten to eat in his excitement. Maybe this entire business would yield an added bonus of making him lose weight, he thought hopefully.

He suddenly became uneasy. The rustle of the leaves beneath his own feet as he walked did not make him hear Bayou's footsteps behind him. Rather it was Bayou's laboured wheezing, totally out of tune with the rustling leaves and other night sounds that made him aware that danger lurked and he was not alone. Bayou was only two trees and thus, twelve metres away.

A clear, undisguised, strangled wheeze from Bayou made Saga halt suddenly, immobilised with shock, not fear. Just a rational acknowledgement of danger, as his father was wont to put it. Yet his anxiety soared and his heart was pounding so wildly, he could hear it in his ears.

The thought of unwittingly leading some informer to their meeting and thus endangering those who were about to honour him with so much trust sent his mind reeling. His over-active imagination produced a wild thought that it was possibly a wild animal on the loose. The thought left just as quickly as it came. There were no wild animals in the part of the country, and there was certainly no zoo around his neighbourhood for one to break out of. The National Zoo had long ago gone out of commission, with the animals probably starving to death or being butchered for kebabs and meat soups by irate, underpaid zookeepers. Also, he was yet to come across a wild animal that made distinctly wheezing human sounds. And it certainly wasn't some stray cat or dog.

Saga concluded someone was dogging his steps. Though he didn't know who or why. He quickly and quietly tiptoed to the next tree, crouched and waited to see what would happen. Lo and behold, was that not the dreadful and wholly detested Mr Bayou, their local chief informer for the Regime, who was sneaking up from one tree to another with a handkerchief clamped on his mouth?

So that was the wheezer!

Why did it have to be him, of all people? The one person in the neighbourhood who would not hesitate to bring destruction upon them all on the slightest suspicion. And why did he have a handkerchief on his mouth? Oh, to muffle the wheezing, of course.

What was he to do? He needed all his wits about him. He had to think very fast. What were his options? Had hateful Bayou recognised him?

Saga knew the notorious and sinister Bayou quite well. He knew Bayou was in no state to catch him if he decided to dash off in a sprint, despite Saga's chubby frame. Not in a hundred years could that happen if Bayou was already having a wheeze-fit after traversing the distance of only a few trees. But that was not the crux of the problem. Indeed, Saga knew of a fanatically pro-Brewman para-military neighbourhood Mobile Watch Team that patrolled their area at night, and could be summoned by the likes of Bayou on special-issue walkie-talkies, which were given to some of the more productive informers and other Government officials. They were a Rapid Response Unit and as such, could be there in no time if summoned.

His father had time and again cautioned him about these barbaric thugs who made no distinction between adults and youngsters when doling out their harsh punishments to those who broke the numerous curfews that were imposed wantonly by the authorities whenever it caught their fancy. Today was not a curfew night, however. But that did not mean they were not doing their usual neighbourhood patrols.

Saga had also heard rumours that the Bayou-types carried their walkie-talkies on them at all times. Now, since he did not know the location of the night patrol at this precise moment, Saga knew he certainly could not risk having them summoned by suddenly dashing off. He was even surprised that they had not been called at the first instance he was spotted by the odious Bayou. He suspected that Bayou probably wanted to make sure of who it was and what he was up to before summoning the patrol. Maybe the patrol chaps were quite averse to being made to rush over false alarms. He was hoping that was the case, as it would give him a bit more time to extricate himself from this truly unpleasant situation.

Saga knew that his only option was to vanish. Yes – he needed to disappear. He needed Bayou to believe he had seen a ghost of sorts, an apparition created by night-time shadows, or whatever he chose to believe along such lines. Saga's logic was that Bayou could hardly summon the patrol to chase after something that was simply not there. If he were foolish enough to summon them, where would they begin to look for this non-existent being? Surely, Bayou would not risk the wrath of these Paras that were literally a law unto their thuggish selves.

Like many things in life, some were much easier said or imagined than actually done. After all, Saga knew he was no magician. He briefly wished he had the abilities of Harry Houdini, whom he had seen in movies doing some spectacular vanishing acts.

Saga pondered his options.

The prospect of shinning and disappearing up a tree posed intractable difficulties. What if Bayou spotted him in the process? There would certainly be no escape then. Furthermore, the branches could creak and squeak noisily or possibly even break under his not inconsiderable weight.

Saga desperately contemplated shinning up a wall and jumping into of any of the residences closest to the tree he was hiding behind. But this option was equally fraught with too many difficulties. For instance, what if he landed in a yard that had a night watchman, who would promptly raise the alarm and probably shoot an arrow into his buttocks after mistaking him for a thief? Saga knew that many night watchmen in the country tended to favour bows and arrows as their guard weapons, which, though archaic and anachronistic, could still prove quite deadly. The possibility of having his bottom painfully pierced with a tetanus-laden rusty arrow while scrambling up or down a wall filled him with dismay!

Again, even if he met a watchman with pacifist tendencies, what was the guarantee that the watchman in question would have a work ethic similar to their own sleepy nursery watchman? None whatsoever!

Furthermore, what if there were dogs in the yard, which were bound to raise a racket and eagerly sink their teeth into the parts of his anatomy that were accessible to them? The wall-climbing option was fast proving no better than the tree-climbing option.

By this time, Saga's nerve was almost failing. He simply could not think of any convenient way to disappear. He was literally preparing to make a dash for it – damning the consequences in the process – when a loud, authoritative voice bellowed truculently in the dark, 'Hey, Bayou, where do you think you are going to at this time of the night?'

Both Bayou and Saga were stunned to immobility as the shrill, piercing voice shattered the night-time quiet. But they froze for different reasons.

Saga was again in a state of shock for the second time that night. For a moment, he thought the night patrol thugs had miraculously appeared from nowhere and were using their roof-mounted loudspeakers to order him to halt. He quickly recovered from that perilous thought and focused properly on the shocking development.

Then it dawned. It was a female voice. He fervently prayed it was Bayou's formidable wife and that she would save him from his current predicament.

Bayou was as startled as anyone could possibly be. His nausea came back with a vengeance and he retched. Bayou cursed silently as he struggled not to give his position up.

'Hey Bayou – are you ignoring me, or what? I asked where you think you are going at this time of the night? Answer me now, now I say!'

'Hush,' was Bayou's instinctive reply. 'I said SHUSH! Be quiet!' he added louder than he had intended in his state of frustration.

The voice hit back even more aggressively. 'Who are you SHUSHING and HUSHING? Who should be quiet? How dare you SHUSH me, Bayou? You think I am one of those people you have been picking on in a cowardly manner? A good-for-nothing like you coming to HUSH and SHUSH me? The cheek of it! You have the impudence of a dead cockroach to SHUSH and HUSH me! I said – where do you think you are going? Why are you now dumb or have you become a Zombie like your foolish soldier friends who pick on innocent people? Answer my question – I say!' Bayou's wife added even more cantankerously!

Bayou knew he was a defeated man. Though it was not public knowledge, Bayou lived in mortal terror of his wife. She was known to always stand legs akimbo, with her beefy arms folded on her vast chest, when addressing Bayou. On the surface of things, Bayou was certainly no match for this sizeable woman, who reminded him of a fortress. But it was not just her forbidding physical attributes. She was the only one in his small world who could tell him off to his face. She had no respect for the way he made a living out of informing on people, though she would never acknowledge it to outsiders. Had it not been for her children and her conservative upbringing, she would have left him long ago. And she greatly resented him for her inability to leave, and unconsciously sought to make his life at home a living hell.

Thus, she was bitter for her own reasons. And although she had never let on directly, Bayou knew his wife was very much aware of many a shady deal he had concluded, purely for cash considerations, which needed to be kept hush at all costs. He knew for sure that he was a doomed man if any of it got out, since he had hidden the proceeds accruing from his brutal benefactors within the Regime with whom he was supposed to share all illicit profits. Thus Bayou did not wish to tempt fate by seriously annoying his wife. There was no telling what the old hag would do when one of her towering rages descended on her.

Her voice boomed out again, confusing him even further. 'You still won't answer – you abominable man? Okay – let me answer for you – nowhere is where you are going! Did you hear me? I said NOWHERE, so you had better stop hiding behind those trees and get yourself back in the house! What are you doing behind those trees anyway? Spying on our innocent neighbours? Have you no shame, Bayou? Get into the house right now before I lock you out – you good-for-nothing spying and informing excuse for a husband! Husband indeed! You alone are reason enough for them to re-define the word "husband"!'

'Okay, okay – I'm coming!'

There was no way he could tell his wife what he was truly up to in the shadows of the trees. He would never hear the end of it. There was no stopping this woman when she got going. She was truly a hurricane! Better to let that Nana's brat off for now. He was not worth the grief he could catch from his wife. He meekly made his way back onto his veranda to resume his smoking, while wildly hallucinating about reporting his wife to the authorities and to have her tortured till she begged for mercy! But he knew he dared not. What if she sang his secrets while in their custody? He certainly could not risk that. He would simply have to bow to fate and take his frustrations out on the people he informed on.

Saga was free! He could hardly believe it! Relief flooded through his entire body. This was truly an 'in the nick of time' situation. Saga secretly blessed Bayou's wife. He had heard the entire exchange and was quite delighted that Bayou was getting what-for from his no-nonsense wife. He certainly deserved a drubbing for having caused Saga such grief! What a narrow escape!

In his euphoric state, Saga completely ignored his father's warning and dashed off as fast as his legs could manage towards the meeting venue. It was only when he was almost there that he remembered and slowed down a little – but fortune was now on his side, and he managed to arrive without further incident.

CHAPTER FOURTEEN

'Goliath of a Regime'

Saga's Uncle Bazo, whom everyone called Uncle Tiger, was a very calm and quiet man. Nobody had ever seen him angry before, and he was viewed by many to be a rather timid person. Consequently, for many of his acquaintances, the fierce nomenclature of Tiger that had been bestowed upon him did not make much sense. Unless, of course, it was a name they simply called him in jest.

Beneath the exterior of calm timidity he displayed to all was a layer of very tough steel.

Uncle Tiger – as only those very close to him knew – was a very brave person who neither feared man nor beast. He was nonetheless very spiritual and was almost always in constant personal meditation, which gave off the appearance of an exceedingly calm, distracted timidity.

Uncle Tiger was a true Freemason who did not belong to any Masonic Lodge. He was at odds with Masonic Lodges in Zimgania. He felt that most Masonic orders had lost touch with the true and ultimate purpose of Freemasonry. In their country, for example, Masonic meetings, beyond observing a few tired rituals, mainly consisted of unbridled banqueting in which copious amounts of the richest of foods and the most expensive alcoholic beverages were consumed with frequent regularity. In the days when Uncle Tiger belonged to these epicurean Masonic orders, it normally took him two to three days to recover from each such bout of fearsome wining and dining.

For Uncle Tiger, the core principles of Masonry were: the spreading of enlightenment; the constant, conscious effort to better oneself spiritually; and to seek '*ordo ab chao*', which meant 'Order out of chaos', which was a very key tenet of Freemasonry.

Consequently, as a true Mason, he had come to the unambiguous conclusion that since the current regime of President Brewman was so diametrically opposed to any notion of enlightenment, and rather sought to create and perpetuate chaos, it had become the absolute and sacred duty of every true Freemason in their country to vigorously combat his Regime and end it! And this, he believed, each Mason must do with all the resources at his or her disposal.

Indeed, the fact that almost all Masonic Lodges in their country had decided to remain conveniently 'apolitical' did not deter Uncle Tiger from his chosen path of dedicated resistance, which, in turn, had catapulted him into the top hierarchy of the underground resistance movement aimed at toppling the Brewman regime and restoring 'enlightened' democracy.

Uncle Tiger lived in Uso Town, which was the next residential neighbourhood south of Ridge Heights towards the coastline of Cape Cove. Though he lived alone, aside from his all-in-one trusted-houseboy-cum-factotum-cum-driver-cum-assistant in a modest three-bedroom, single-storey bungalow, the sheer size of his compound was, however, very far from modest. It was a sprawling, wooded, four-acre compound, which was a rare find in the increasingly land-scarce capital city. Nobody knew how he had managed to acquire this mini ranch in the heart of the city.

At the back of this wooded property stood a splendidly designed Masonic Temple that he had had constructed a few years back from his own resources. He had intended it to be a centre of Masonic worship in their city. That was before he had fallen out with his Masonic brothers. In recent times, with it having ceased to be a centre for all Masons due to the falling out, Uncle Tiger worshipped and meditated alone in his handsome temple.

Under the temple was a vast and concealed basement that Uncle Tiger had specially commissioned to store the innumerable Masonic artefacts, statuary and relics he had acquired over the years from various countries around the world and at considerable expense. And it was to this basement that Saga was headed for his initial meeting with the key figures of the underground resistance movement.

Uncle Tiger had offered his temple as both a sanctuary for those on the run and in need of hiding from the Regime's security forces, and also as a well-concealed meeting place for the movement, away from prying eyes. Like his elder brother, Nana, Uncle Tiger, the renegade Freemason, was a staunch pillar of the 'resistance', as the Zimgania Resistance Movement was called for short.

Many of the resistance members assembled already knew Saga and were generally pleased to see him, as they were also privy to his recent heroics. Some were nonetheless more than a little perplexed as to his presence there. This was a serious meeting for adults and not adolescents.

'Saga – what are you doing here?' asked his soft-spoken Uncle Tiger, who was equally baffled at his nephew's sudden appearance in their midst. What alarmed him most was Saga's knowledge of the recently adopted password, which had allowed him entry at the main gate. That was certainly a breach of security. Uncle Tiger sought a proper explanation.

'My father asked me to come and wait for him here. He said to tell all of you that he would explain why I'm here when he comes.'

A few heads nodded assent, while others wondered what had possessed Nana to send his son here! What they were involved in was dangerous and nobody's idea of child's play. Was Nana losing it with all the pressures being heaped on him on a daily basis, Tiger wondered. But then again, Nana was not known to deal in foolishness, so it might probably be best to wait for his explanation, he wisely reasoned.

They did not have long to wait, as Nana soon entered after observing the necessary security precautions. Obo had arrived a few minutes before his father but had been unable to shed any light on Saga's presence when questioned. Obo came with another youngster named Kobby, who was the President of the National Students' Union, also at the heart of the struggle against the Regime. Kobby and Obo's maturity, bravery and good sense in leading the university struggles had earned them places on this council of resistance. It was a privilege indeed.

Saga himself had started to feel quite uncomfortable, but ultimately had faith in his father's judgment. Consequently, his excitement was not dimmed in any way. He simply found a place in the corner of the basement to sit and made himself as unobtrusive as possible for the time being.

The group consisted of mainly men and a few women from all social classes and walks of life. Age-wise, the gathering was made up of youngsters in their early 20s to veterans in their 60s. This expanded Steering Committee of the resistance comprised of twenty-four men and seven women. These patriots ranged from intellectuals-cum-professionals, such as Nana, to woman activists, student leaders and workers representatives. There was also a smattering of a few eminent resistance legends, who had been publicly branded as wanted dissidents and 'enemies of the state', and were thus on the run and in hiding. They all had one thing in common and that was to work and fight tirelessly to end the oppressive dictatorship of President Brewman and his excessively corrupt government. Their collective aim was to usher in constitutional democracy for their beloved country.

'I called you all here for this emergency meeting as a result of some recent developments that require our immediate attention,' Nana started quite formally, once the usual protocols had been observed and the co-chairman, his brother, Tiger, had given him the floor. He continued, 'I know many of you will be wondering about Saga's presence. I asked him to come for the simple reason that he is central to these developments I speak of, and which I'll soon address. My not telling you of his attendance beforehand is not intended as a sign of disrespect to this body. You all know me. I would never do that to any of you. There was simply no time to do so, and I thought the matter at hand sufficiently pressing for me to make that judgment call. As to the security concerns that his presence raises, I want to assure you that Saga is my son and I have taught him well. Neither of my sons will ever betray us, either consciously or unconsciously. They would rather die than do something so unholy. You have my absolute word on this. Kindly rest assured.' Nana paused to let his words sink in.

There were murmurs of assent and acknowledgement of his reasonable explanation so far, stated with such clarity. They knew that Nana was not one to make snap judgment calls. That is why they had elected him as one of the leaders of their movement.

He continued, 'You've all no doubt heard of what Saga did in his school the other day. Though what he did may appear impulsive and rash on the surface of it, he was nonetheless brave enough to accurately express single-handedly the sentiments of most of us in this country, both young and old. Also, though this happened barely a week ago, news of the incident appears to have spread far and wide. We've even heard from reliable sources that chapters or groups calling themselves Orphans are being formed with rapidity within many secondary schools. The question that immediately arises is whether this development is good or bad for our cause, both in the short and long term.

'Before attempting to answer this question and seek your views on the matter, I want us to first understand one unalterable fact: that whether good or bad, this development is the reality, whether we like it or not! It is a reality that has been sprung on us and must be dealt with. The next question that confronts us is how best we can harness and channel this to aid our cause, which is to liberate our beloved country from this inhuman government and help introduce long-lasting democracy as well as the social and economic development we so desperately need. Before I sit down for our debate to begin, let me also point out that the Regime will be quick to realise the dangers that these Orphans pose and will be considering methods to neutralise them. Finally, and most importantly, we need to answer the question we have so carefully avoided because of our love for our children and our wish to keep them out of harm's way. This question, which can no longer be ignored, is: is it time for us to include the secondary schools in our struggle? Ladies and gentlemen, my own view is that the new reality precipitated by my son over there has effectively answered the question for us. Thank you for listening. Mr Chairman, the floor is yours once more.'

The debate began in earnest. Pappy, a seasoned, grey-haired veteran of the anti-Brewman struggles, who was also co-chairing the meeting with Tiger, decided to order the debate by clarifying what he thought to be the most pertinent issues. Pappy had grandchildren in Saga's school and was gravely concerned.

'Nana was right to send his son, Saga, here today. He is also right in saying that Saga has drawn the secondary schools into the struggle, whether we like it or not. So to endlessly debate the question as to whether it is good or bad for us is what I call a bootless venture. For me, it is both good and bad. Good, because it broadens the base of our struggles. It gives us the promise of further support from those adults on the fence who now cannot just sit back and watch their children enter the struggle while they do nothing at all. And bad, because it places our children in unprecedented danger. There is also the added danger that, if not properly monitored and guided, these very children could bring us grief in the long term with their propensity for random acts of aggression. We can't have these children running around, stoning security personnel all over the place, or going around with slings and catapults, imagining themselves to be reincarnated versions of David against this vicious Goliath of a Regime. The real question for me then is how do we guide them to wage the struggle at their level, while keeping them relatively safe from open acts of brutality by these Zombie policemen and soldiers?'

They all agreed with Pappy. The children should be prevented at all costs from adopting a confrontational posture against the Government's security personnel. They had to be made to understand that aggression was not a solution, but would rather lead to more violence from those only too eager to employ brutal methods. It was thought that, as and when appropriate, the students could further the resistance cause by organising sit-ins at their schools and by boycotting classes in support of a future general strike or something along such lines.

Obo raised some important questions. 'How are these Orphan groups to be formed? Should it just be any student who wishes to join or should it be a group of core members whose mission is to guide the rest of the students in their respective schools?'

This was a thorny matter indeed. To allow every Tom, Dick and Harry to join could prove very tricky, as it would probably result in large, unmanageable groups of students who could easily resort to problematic, unruly and unsanctioned wildcat actions. Students on their own without being provoked could already be quite the nuisance. To thus create the conditions for unruly group action in a context of peer pressure and turbulent times was a certain recipe for disaster.

On the other hand, to turn students away was equally problematic and could cause the Orphans to lose support. Furthermore, it could generate the impression of elitism, which was one of the very things they sought to combat and reverse in the country. They needed to find a middle ground to resolve this dilemma.

After debating the matter for a while, Raba, a striking, middle-aged female rights activist and university lecturer, who had recently left her husband for belatedly accepting a minor Government post, decided to sum up what appeared to be the prevailing opinion. 'I think the agreement is that no one should be turned away. But I also think the students should pledge to observe certain codes of conduct as part of being admitted. I'm sure Kobby and Obo can help with this. Actually, it will make a lot of sense if their university union members were made to assume the role of monitoring the formation of these secondary school groups, as well as coordinating their involvement within the parameters of our general resistance strategy. Kobby, what do you and Obo think of this? Also, have there been any reactions in the female high schools?'

It was the charismatic student union President, Kobby, who answered. 'It should be no problem for us to get involved with Saga's Orphans, starting with his school. Many of our people have brothers there to start with, and the entire incident has already generated a lot of interest within our ranks. Some chaps even approached Obo about forming an Orphan chapter on campus as a solidarity move. Nothing from the girls' schools as yet, though. Some of our female activists are talking about moving in there to find out what their reactions are but they don't expect much, for obvious reasons.'

Raba bristled at this and appeared more than a little annoyed with the latter part of Kobby's reply, and reacted accordingly. 'It's good you guys can help, but tell me, Kobby, what *obvious reasons* are we talking about here? You think because they are girls and it has to do with politics, they are incapable of any meaningful reactions? Being girls means the concept of freedom is alien to them? Come on! I'm surprised at you. I thought you were a progressive leader. I'm the one who is obviously mistaken here, for *obvious reasons*!'

Some laughter broke out at Raba's taunt. Another female member added encouragingly, 'Give it to them, Raba. Girl power all the way.'

Kobby merely smiled at the taunt. Raba was noted for always keeping the predominantly male membership of their group on their toes when it came to female-related issues. She wanted to make sure that none of them ever reverted to the traditional upbringing, which held women to be subservient to men.

'Raba, I know you are familiar with my progressive credentials, so I will take it you're merely taunting me. But on a more serious note, you know how it is with the young ladies in the secondary schools. At that stage, it's not that they don't care or don't have opinions or feelings. It's just that they're under so much scrutiny from their conservative teachers, parents and even brothers, to the extent that they are not afforded the opportunity to express themselves. But I can assure you that many of them more than make up for it when they get onto the university campus. Sometimes, it's like letting a bird out of the cage. You should see the female firebrands we have in our midst. But you know all of this already, so why are you on my case?'

Raba smiled at him and replied, 'Just testing, Kobby. I need to be sure sometimes as one can never tell with you men!'

This was greeted with some laughter, which was good, as it helped to reduce the tension in the room. Obo, however, had another question. 'Are these to be secret groups or are they to function openly?'

Given the fact that it was starting off as a mass student reaction to Saga's stance against the authorities, the meeting concluded that it would be unrealistic at this stage to insist that membership of the Orphans be kept secret. However, few in the room had any doubts that there would soon come a time when the Orphans would be driven underground. They knew that with the increasing popularity of the Orphans, the Regime would soon move to outlaw it from all the schools. The meeting resolved to have a strategy in place for when that time came.

Saga was quite dazed, and struggled to comprehend that all that was being discussed by this august gathering was because of him. He felt really proud of himself. He nonetheless had some concerns. He was hesitant to start with, having to address this assembly, which boasted of living legends of the resistance struggles.

Seeing this, his Uncle Tiger sought to calm his nerves. 'Speak freely, my dear nephew. I know it is a lot to take in for one so young. But see it this way – today, we are here because of your bravery. All these famous people you see now are all here today because of you. So believe me when I say we are all very happy to hear what you have to say as Chief Orphan – even though your parents are still very much alive.'

This latter part sally of Uncle Tiger drew smiles and laughter from one and all, and buoyed on Saga to speak. 'Thank you, Uncle. I thank you all too for giving me a chance to speak. I will get straight to the issue. The main problem is what to do about a group of boys in our school called the Princes. Their fathers are very powerful – men like General Yalley – and they are forming a group to oppose and confront us.'

Saga went on to brief them about what happened with Yalley and his group in school, and the potential for violent confrontations initiated by them. He also drew their attention to the fact that the Princes were talking about forming their own chapters in other schools.

Uncle Tiger rose to address this issue. 'Saga, you and your young followers have to understand the mind-set of these so-called Princes. They have, for a while now, perceived that the opposition against their families who run this government is growing on a daily basis. For them, this ultimately means a complete loss of the privileges they have enjoyed for so long. While this opposition was not present in school, they did not feel the threat too directly. As a result of what you did, they are now running scared and are bound to react. But, at your level, they can never be truly strong because they are completely in the minority. They may initially get some of their lackeys to follow them, but that will not last in the face of the growing membership of your Orphan group.'

'It's not just that, Uncle Tiger, I think some of the teachers are on their side,' Saga admitted.

'Yes, they may enjoy the support of the authorities, but that will also not last, since the tide is turning against them. These Princes are nothing more than bullies who don't know any better. They were not born bad people. It is ignorance that makes them the way they are. And remember what your father taught you about bullies: though they can cause a lot of grief and damage, never forget that deep down, they are driven by fear. That is why they pick on those they perceive as being weaker than them. Also, they have had no proper examples set for them beyond what they see their parents doing to innocents in this country. They are all cowards and should never be feared by you or your group. Face them squarely when the need arises but never let them goad you into using your fists. Using violence against them is precisely what they will want you to do, as it will give their fathers the excuse to call in the troops. Do you understand all I've said?'

Saga understood clearly and said so. He marvelled that this was the longest string of sentences he had ever heard his quiet Uncle Tiger speak. Though he did not doubt his uncle's wise analysis, he knew that he and his group would be hard put not to engage in fisticuffs with the likes of Yalley and his followers, given the levels of provocation they were capable of. He would do his best to follow his Uncle Tiger's advice, but it was easier said than achieved.

Finally, Saga was again warned by his father in front of everyone that under no circumstances was anyone at all to know that he was in touch with this group, and that they would summon him from time to time to give him guidelines as to how to proceed. They also assured him that in various ways, the resistance would do all in their power to protect the Orphans!

He was then discharged and asked to go home, using circuitous routes, and to ensure he was not followed. Saga left, remembering then that in his excitement, he had even forgotten to tell them about his experience with Bayou. Anyway, that could wait till later.

Obo and Kobby were also dispatched shortly after, with a stern admonition to keep a very close watch on Orphan issues in the secondary schools and to draw up immediate strategic guidelines for the formation and monitoring of their chapters. They were to employ as many of their members as possible in this exercise to prevent things getting out of control.

The rest remained to discuss this truly thorny issue of secondary school involvement in their necessary but dangerous struggle. For the umpteenth time, they yearned for a much different legacy for their children! Why had fate dealt their children such an unpleasant card in the bloom of their youth? However, no amount of yearning, no amount of wishful thinking, could ease away this awful reality. The only way their children would be ultimately protected was for them, the parents, to intensify their struggle to create a free society based on equality, social justice and economic development. They had serious work to do.

Nana and his fellow activists also knew only too well that their entreaty to the Orphans to adopt a pacifist approach by rejecting violence, no matter the provocation, was a very tall order indeed! It almost bordered on the unrealistic, given the lengths to which they knew these pampered Princes could go to in the arts of goading.

Over the past few years, stories had reached them as to some of the dastardly acts committed by these Princes against their fellow students, and even against some teachers who would not kowtow to their imperious demands. Despite their youth, many of them could prove sinister indeed. There had been, for instance, an incident in the very same elitist Brewman High in which some of these Princes, led by the 16-year-old-son of the Justice Minister, had constituted themselves into a kind of kangaroo court, tried, and 'accidentally' hanged, an innocent student, falsely accused of stealing a pen from one of them. The victim had actually dangled at the end of a thick rope latched to the rafters of the carpentry shed in the school until rescued by a group of passing non-Princes!

Their victim was in a coma for two weeks. Also, although the 'stolen' pen in question was later discovered by its owner in a side pocket of his many-pocketed school bag, those responsible had gotten off with very light sanctions. They were each given a one-day suspension from school!

And to add grave insult to ample injury, the incident was hushed up by the school authorities under great pressure from the Minister of Justice himself. The headmaster of the school was forced to release a misinformation circular to shocked and worried parents, explaining that the victim had brought his misfortune on himself by way of a practical joke gone awry. As to how this bogus explanation tied in with the suspension of the Princes was never answered. This was the Justice Minister's notion of justice.

This was what their children had to face from the Princes, who were essentially an extension of the Regime in the schools. This was what they had to live with. For these not-so-young veterans of the struggle, the late singer Bob Marley's reggae-inspired admonition that 'he who fights and runs away lives to fight another day' had frightfully realistic implications for their children. They had little choice but to stand and fight now or would certainly live to fight another day soon.

CHAPTER FIFTEEN

Louis Vuitton to the Rescue

The Minister for Public Education, Mr Huma, was someone who thoroughly enjoyed the perquisites of his job. To his mind, his job primarily consisted of travelling abroad to every conceivable conference related to education anywhere in the world. Even when not invited – which was not infrequent – he still made it a point to invite himself, as travelling and shopping were the twin passions of his existence. As to actually running the ministry he was in charge of, well, that was a matter for his subordinates to worry about while he globetrotted. He was very good at delegating.

That he spent vast sums of taxpayers' money every year to cover his first-class tickets, lavish per diems and five-star hotel bills while dining in the most expensive restaurants around the globe during these almost wholly unnecessary trips did not bother him in the least. He believed he was most deserving of such an expensive, jet-setting lifestyle as a minister in a government that was not accountable to the citizens they ruled over. Why else be a minister if you could not do just as you pleased?

He had just arrived the previous evening from a wonderful epicurean trip around the Scandinavian countries when news of the Orphan incident finally reached his ears the very next day. And Minister Huma was far from happy about it. The manner in which the news had reached him infuriated him immensely, though he had been insufficiently courageous to hit back at the news-bearer. He had just received a very rude call from General Yalley, Minister for Presidential Affairs.

Without ceremony, Yalley Senior had angrily demanded to know what he and his Ministry were doing about this unsettling business of these Orphans in a school that bore the President's revered name. Without waiting for an answer, Yalley Senior had rudely muttered something about good-for-nothing ministers who though they greedily enjoyed the perks of their positions, did not have a clue about how to do their jobs properly. The General had then proceeded to drop the phone handset with a bang – not even offering a goodbye to boot!

'Who the hell does General Yalley think he is?' fumed Minister Huma out loud. 'Are we all not Cabinet Ministers? How dare he speak to me so rudely?' But in reality, the Minister knew that there was very little he could do about General Yalley's rudeness. His angry thoughts were just about as far as he could proceed with the matter. Minister Yalley's closeness to the President had made him immensely powerful. This had led him to develop a commensurate amount of arrogance.

To add to that, Yalley was a military man, whereas most of the other ministers were civilians, appointed as window dressing in an attempt to disguise the fact that the President was in fact, running a military dictatorship. Every minister knew that the President favoured his military lackeys and henchmen over his civilian appointees. Consequently, no civilian minister would be foolhardy enough to go to him with complaints about his rude generals. It was simply a no-go area. He would have to quietly swallow these insults and thank his lucky stars that the rudeness was not accompanied by a summons to the Presidential Palace.

A summons to the Presidential Palace was a nightmare come to life. Apart from members of the President's inner kitchen-cabinet, no Minister of State relished that particular privilege in the least. Every Minister lived in fear of a summons to President Brewman, whose dangerous mood swings and erratic behaviour was something that bordered on the extremely unpleasant, and were indeed not a fine sight to behold.

Minister Huma came out of his reverie completely mystified. It had just dawned on him that he truly did not have a clue as to what the General was raving about. Who in heaven's name were these Orphans? Whose parents could have died to generate such interest from on high?

The Minister did not even know where to start, having decided that he was certainly not going to phone Yalley Senior back to seek some form of clarification. Furthermore, if it were something that truly concerned his Ministry then he would look all the more silly and incompetent by revealing his ignorance to the likes of General Yalley. But he still had no idea where to start. He hit the buzzer on his desk to summon his personal assistant. He needed her to get cracking and mobilise his senior advisors at the Ministry to brief him as to what was really amiss.

She sauntered in. She was a tall, slim, dark-skinned, amply-breasted, sleek, lissom female whose main asset in life was the ability to completely turn the heads of heterosexual men, including that of the Minister himself, whose neck had still not recovered from one such very costly turn he had regretfully made a while back.

However, Minister Huma's personal assistant, Ayesha, did not have the foggiest notion as to what went on in the Ministry, or a clue as to the concept of personally assisting in anything there. She therefore assisted not a jot in the Ministry. The young lady, somewhere in her mid-to-late 20s and clad in an obviously expensive designer business suit, perched herself against the filing cabinet in his office and, with one hand on her hip, glared at her Minister, before screeching at him, 'I have told you I don't like you calling me with that bell of yours! When will you get it into your head that I am not one of your messengers? I am your wife-to-be-in-waiting after you divorce that ignorant woman you keep in your house – okay? What do you want, anyway? I was busy!'

'Busy? What do you mean busy when all you do is paint and file your nails and read magazines all day long?' he wanted to scream back, but dared not.

The Minister sighed inwardly. How had he gotten himself involved with this vile-tempered young girl, who would be the death of him if he were not careful? What had possessed him to reveal so many State secrets and make so many irrational promises to this awful creature in an angel's body, just to be able to gain her favour? He had been blindly in love, he thought to

143

himself. No, in truth, he had been wildly and blindly in lust, and was still paying the price for it. Now he was totally in the power of this little harpy, and was daily dismayed that she still had the power to make him go almost berserk with desire. When was he ever going to be rid of her? Never – because if I do, I'm damned, though if I don't, I'm still damned, he thought, in a fog of misery.

'Oh sorry, my dear. Terribly sorry. I was not thinking. My mind was preoccupied. Oh you must forgive me. Ah – we must order a Louis Vuitton bag for you as compensation. How could I be so silly?' he replied, his voice all honey.

Her eyes crossed, as she remained far from placated. 'Yes – every day, you talk Louis Vuitton. Every day, it's Louis this and Louis that – yet it never comes! You call yourself a Minister, yet where is my bag you've been promising forever? How can you do this to me, who has given you all my youth? You want me to go in tatters before you are happy? Do you know how many other ministers are trying to lure me, though I have sacrificed myself to you? Where is all the money you have stolen from this government anyway that you can't buy a simple designer bag? My patience is running out! Don't let me do something you will regret!' she screeched to a halt.

Mr Huma knew he had to calm her down quickly. She did not know when to stop once her rage flew beyond a certain level. He spent a fortune on her, but he knew it would never be enough. She had a money-counter, a veritable abacus in her chest instead of a heart. In a fit of pure lustful passion, he had foolishly promised her he would leave his wife and make her his new missus. Now the idea was firmly stuck in her head and she had recently been harassing him to make good his promise. Two months ago, he had tried reasoning with her gently, telling her that these things take time, appealing for her patience and buying her off in the meantime.

Unfortunately, it didn't have the soothing effect desired. In fact, Mr Huma was trapped into an ultimatum. He would either leave his wife now, or his young paramour would work for him as his PA until he did so.

Now, he was hostage to this deadly affair. In yet another terribly unguarded moment, he had told her ghastly secrets about the President and some of his closest and most powerful aides. Thus, he could not in any way risk getting her angry, for fear of his own life should she decide to spill it all. She had since planted herself firmly in his front office and was hell-bent on making him fulfil his promise to her. He was in very deep trouble.

Today, the situation was brightening. He had finally managed to placate her with promises of more designer gear: Versace perfume and Gucci shoes, along with the Louis Vuitton bag, which would accompany the next arrival of the diplomatic bag from their Embassy Mission in either Washington or London or even Paris. Slightly mollified, she went back to her busy schedule of reading recent issues of the chic *Cosmopolitan* magazine.

Shaken by the incident with his abacus-hearted mistress, as well as a sharp recollection of the menace in General Yalley's voice, the Minister hastily summoned his Chief Director at the Ministry. The Chief Director quickly briefed him on the incident at Brewman High involving the Deputy Minister, and expressed dismay that Deputy Minister Com had not seen it fit to inform Minister Huma of this potentially disastrous development.

This was an opportunity for the Chief Director to subtly poison Huma's mind against his deputy, whom he disliked, and secretly coveted his job as well. He felt he would do much better as Deputy Minister and was delighted at the opportunity to bring his rival down a peg or two!

'I was coming to brief you straightaway when you arrived yesterday, but your deputy insisted I should leave that to him, and you know how he is... hmm!' His voice trailed off, having managed to instil what he knew to be just the right amount of disapprobation in the Minister's mind toward his deputy.

He noticed the Minister's face mottle with anger at this, and was secretly delighted his words had hit their mark, despite the fact they were all lies. The Minister, though steeped in a personal crisis of his own making with his mistress-cum-wife-to-be-in-waiting, was nonetheless alive to the harm that the Orphan incident could cause him. He knew that if the matter were not contained soon, he would be held accountable, as Yalley had already insinuated. But how was he to contain it?

A frontal attack would serve to attract the kind of attention and publicity that had to be avoided at all costs. Indeed, it was one thing sending military tanks and security goons to assault university students when they took to the streets, but quite another matter to roll huge military tanks with their mounted lethal guns into an elite, peaceful secondary school, where many of the students were literally babies. To do nothing would also mean a quick summons to the Presidential Palace, where his fate would be undoubtedly sealed. He needed advice and he needed it quickly. He curtly told his Chief Director to organise an emergency meeting of all senior officials in the Ministry within the hour, and savagely added that he wanted no absentees.

Saga was very busy the day after his uplifting meeting with the adult resistance group. School was still in a state of general excitement and confusion. The teachers had not yet managed to resume normal academic classes and were themselves constantly being summoned here and there, to and fro, by a hysterical headmaster who had been receiving ominous calls from highly displeased, powerful personages. It was impossible for anyone to pretend that all was normal.

Consequently, the students, in turn, were practically left to their own devices that day, though cautioned to remain within their classrooms, apart from break-times. Saga had sent Ibrahim around earlier on to arrange a meeting of the core membership of the Orphans around the isolated hockey pitch behind the main science block during the noon break-time. He had then spent much of the morning jotting down the thoughts he wanted to share with his group members, as well as writing down names of potential recruits to their cause.

As planned, the meeting took place near the hockey pitch under the welcome shade of sweet-smelling, tall orange trees in a large grove, which the students had dubbed 'Orange

Free State'. And forewarned by Ibrahim, the members came individually and not in groups, in order not to attract too much attention. Lookouts were posted and the meeting called to order.

Saga explained to them that he had had the benefit of seeking advice from his brother, Obo, and the immensely popular university student leader, Kobby. The Orphans were impressed. Their main task for now was to recruit as many into their club as possible. Though they did not intend to hide, he suggested that it was better if it was done on the quiet, as he had read somewhere that it was always better to let your opponents overestimate your weaknesses and underestimate your strengths. Thus, he did not think it wise, for example, to place tables in the assembly hall with a long line of students queuing to register. All recruiting was to be done quietly, outside the classrooms and during break-times.

Saga then imparted some of the wisdom he had learned from his brother and the resistance meeting. He told them that though what they had started promised great adventure, they only needed to look around them to understand the danger of what they were getting involved in. Many of the younger students who wanted to get involved would not fully understand this but it was important that they, as the leaders, were completely aware.

It was also important that they realised they were part of a historical movement to help make their country a freer and better place to live in. There were to be no individual wildcat actions without reference to the group, and violence was to be avoided. They were to be each other's keepers, and loyalty to themselves was crucial to their success in positively contributing to the struggle.

As to what their tasks were going to be, Saga assured them that they were not alone in this matter and that they would be receiving guidance from the National Students' Union. He finally cautioned them not to discuss with anyone outside the group what their plans were, apart from the university students who were sent to assist them. Not even their parents, he sternly admonished. It was not that many of their parents were not to be trusted, he explained. It was just that they might do something to hinder their cause without realising, but simply out of concern for the safety of their children.

Sablon, who was still very grateful to Saga for his single-handed attempt to foil his father's brutal arrest, had now joined the front ranks of the Orphans. He asked for the benefit of them all, 'What are we going to do about Yalley and his Princes, Saga? Are we simply going to allow them to provoke us, harass and bully our supporters in the lower forms without doing anything about it? What if they try to beat up some of us, as they did with those other students and even Ibrahim? Don't also forget that the teachers are afraid to punish them. We have no one to protect us when they come at us, apart from ourselves. So what do we do?'

They all looked to Saga for an answer to this very pressing problem.

Saga had anticipated this question and was ready for it. 'We've got to realise that the situation has changed for everybody since I did what I did. Before then, Yalley and his Princes could do whatever they wanted without any of us doing anything about it. But look at what happened the other day when Yalley and his idiots tried to beat up those small boys. We went to their defence and the Princes backed down. True, we had to use our fists a little, but they still backed down. That foolish headmaster of ours will not hesitate to bring in the Zombies to shut down the school if fights are breaking out all over the place and it starts to look like the school cannot be managed. I realise that it is not going to be easy, but I have to again plead with you guys not to allow us to be provoked into fights.

'The Princes themselves know the situation is not what it used to be. They will hesitate before they seriously provoke us. They are mainly cowards, though I know that some like Yalley are very rash and full of their own importance. I also know that we cannot control the actions of every single Orphan, for that matter. Some fights will no doubt break out, but our job is to contain them, rather than allow them to spread. Yalley and his Princes will never be truly strong because they will always be in the minority. We are in the majority. Never forget also that

Yalley and others are not the true enemies. It is the Regime and their collaborating fathers who need to be unseated. Yalley and others are just ignorant mini-me's, terrified of losing their privileges. When the time comes, and we have no choice but to fight, we will not run away. It is true we are young, but we have to be very wise. Children much younger than us have been involved in harder struggles around the globe to fight off their oppressors. It is now time for us to prove that we are also equal to the task.'

The meeting broke up with Saga's words ringing in their ears. They got the message. This was no joking matter. They would prove equal to the task of helping the resistance to make their country free. After all, they were young and idealistic and ready to take on the world! They would soon have the chance to prove themselves.

* * *

The next week saw no visible reduction of tensions within the school. On the surface of it, all was calm, but in reality, the Orphans and Princes were feverishly trying to sign on new members. The school had the atmosphere of an armed camp without the presence of arms.

The headmaster and his staff were still on tenterhooks, and were also frantically trying to get the school back to its normal mode of academic pursuits, with some minor success. They had been briefed by Ministry officials as to the outcome of the meeting held recently at the Minister's insistence. The official line was to adopt a 'wait and see' attitude to see if the issue of the Orphans would die a natural death out of fear of reprisals, while the school was placed under close scrutiny. Little did they know what minute chance there was of that happening!

Meanwhile, things were growing from bad to very bad within the wider society. The oppressiveness of the Regime's rule was becoming unbearable. The President was also suffering major losses in his unjustified war of blame against the neighbouring country, and as such, was forced to ship an increasing number of soldiers to the war front.

In actual fact, the President was running out of soldiers for the war effort. He thus decided to introduce a forced conscription programme of National Service to enable him to secure much-needed troops. This programme was to include all males between the ages of 18 to 25. The decree issued by him to put this into effect was accompanied by a dire warning that any resistance to this initiative would be met with swift reprisals, as the country was on an emergency war footing.

For the citizenry, this was an outrage! This was intolerable! What of the numerous elitist troops milling about the cities, having been designated by the President as his very own Presidential Guard? Could some of them not go and fight in this war, which no one knew the reason for? What did those good-for-nothing soldiers do, apart from terrorise and oppress innocent citizens? There seemed to be no purpose for their existence. After all, couldn't some special units from within the regular army and police guard the President, as was done in so many countries?

But what the citizenry did not know was that the President lived in mortal fear of assassination due to his own misdeeds. Thus, he felt completely dependent on his Presidential Guard – the infamous Zombies – for his personal security, as well as the survival of his unpopular Regime. He felt could not do without them. Thus, to send them to the war front could prove suicidal for him, and he had absolutely no intention of contemplating or committing suicide.

Another critical reason for establishing the Presidential Guard in the first place was to deliberately create another military force in the country that was loyal to him alone and no one else. Privilege upon privilege was heaped on this personal regiment to ensure their complete and undying loyalty. This was also necessary to prevent the regular army from having any ideas of trying to depose him through a coup. He needed to offset their power with his Presidential Guard, which had become a counterbalancing force.

The President also knew that his war of blame was not very popular with the regular Army, which had thus become a potential threat. This was yet another reason why he had to continue this war at all costs, since he needed to keep the army distracted. They may not like the war, but as professionals, they had no choice but to fight in the face of external aggression! Such was the cynical and treacherous workings of the mind of a tyrant who would do anything to perpetuate himself and his bloody rule. The loss of human lives meant nothing, in so far as they were sacrificed for his personal glory and to keep him in power. The world had unfortunately seen many such leaders.

A sinister and barely-concealed aspect of the new National Service decree was that to all intents and purposes, many of the recruits or victims would be the troublesome students populating the universities. It was thus a very serious matter indeed. It also meant that those in the secondary schools who were 18 could also be forcibly recruited.

Those such as Saga, at 18, could thus technically be uprooted from school and rushed off to the war front without much ado! For the general populace, this was much too disturbing a development.

Thus, was this also a not-so-subtle move on the part of the Regime to rid itself of the vocal and irrepressible student opposition? There was no question about this in the minds of the student leadership. To them, the President was determined to forcibly send them to their deaths, and was in line to become a latter-day Pol Pot, who had supervised the annihilation of millions of his countrymen to keep himself and his deadly Khmer Rouge Party in power in Cambodia!

The student leadership under Kobby and Obo vowed to resist this bloodthirsty decree with everything they could muster. They would not permit an African Pol Pot to flourish in their country. They cautioned that the country should thus prepare itself for a mother of all showdowns between them and the Government.

The vile decree was to take effect within a few months, at the start of the Easter holidays. This way, most of the students would be at home and not at their schools and university campuses, making it much more difficult for them to organise any meaningful resistance. The ruling elite thought themselves very clever with the timing of the start of the exercise. By the time the students were ready to report to campus for the next term, all their radical leaders would safely be away, fighting for dear life in the war.

Indeed, had his stocky arms been long enough, Public Education Minister Huma would have complacently patted himself on the back. In actual fact, a confluence of circumstances had aligned in recent times to place Mr Huma in a very good mood. He was feeling somewhat fulfilled – at least in the short-term, until his crisis-oriented existence re-asserted itself yet again. To start with, the designer items he had ordered for his mistress-cum-wife-to-be-in-waiting-cum-personal-assistant had finally arrived, and that brought him great peace. The diplomatic bag from their Embassy in Paris had delivered the goods, and indeed, Louis Vuitton, Versace and Gucci – bless them – had saved the day. Furthermore, the National Service decree that had suddenly been 'decreed' by the President-For-Life-Until-Further-Notice seemed destined to resolve his chronic problems of student unrest, and the new but potentially destabilising matter of the Orphans, who had suddenly appeared out of nowhere in secondary schools.

Mr Huma had just happily extricated himself from the warm embrace of his grateful mistress, Ayesha, and was now contentedly sipping expensive Remy Martin XO cognac in her equally expensive apartment in the affluent Airport Grove residential area, which he of course paid for.

'I can see you are happy today,' Ayesha commented, as the man was practically purring.

'Well, who can blame me? You make me happy, and it seems God is solving most of my pressing problems for me with this National Service decree. I am, in fact, thinking of going to church more often to thank Him,' replied Mr Huma, who was now vainly attempting to look pious.

'But why are you so happy about this decree that everyone else seems to hate? And what's the decree about anyway? How does it help you and your problems?'

Mr Huma studied his mistress-cum-wife-to-be-in-waiting and was awed by her sheer sensuality and his inability to control his desire for her. He just could not resist her.

'Come over and give me a hug and a kiss and I will answer you with a short lecture on the importance of this decree, my dear.'

Ayesha, who was momentarily grateful for her recently-acquired designer goodies, was not about to deny her paramour a hug and a kiss, though she had not planned for a lecture on some decree that she felt had absolutely zero to do with her. She had asked the question about the decree simply out of politeness. 'Good grief,' she silently muttered to herself, but nonetheless, smiled coyly and, feigning enthusiasm, replied, 'A kiss and a hug you shall have, my dear, and I am all ears for your lecture.'

Her reply delighted the Minister so much. He proceeded to instruct her after receiving his wonderful hug and kiss. 'You see, Ayesha, our President needs troops for his war, which he is not winning. Please don't repeat this anywhere. So basically, the National Service decree is nothing but disguised conscription. He is forcing young men between the ages of 18 to 25 into the army to fight the war, and there is nothing they can do about it.'

'I know all that, but how does that help you?' she asked, somewhat impatiently, now anxious for the boring mini-lecture to be over.

'It helps me because it is an important tool that can be used to put an end to all the student demonstrations that are causing so much trouble in the country. All the radical university students and their leaders can be identified, immediately conscripted, and sent to the war front. Hallelujah.'

'Oh, so then you, as Education Minister in charge of the universities, will now have some peace. Okay. Good lecture. Thank you,' replied Ayesha, trying to halt the lecture, but the Minister had not quite finished.

'And now, we can ship off those new, awful Orphans in the secondary schools as well. The records show that the Saga boy who started it all at Brewman High is 18, and so are many of his supporters in those second-cycle schools. So you see, that is another problem solved for me, and now I won't have that dreadful bully, General Yalley, breathing down my neck. *Laus Deo* – Praise God for these important victories...'

Ayesha quickly jumped in to finally curtail the 'lecture'. 'Oh yes, praise God. You have done so well, my darling. You have killed a bird and a stone. And you speak French too. You are so clever, and that's why I love you so much. I am even thinking of going with you on some of your many trips abroad so I can always be close to you, my darling. Oh you are so wonderful. I think it's now time to do a diplomatic passport for me.'

Minister Huma felt himself so deserving of such praise that he did not even bother to correct her that *Laus Deo* was Latin and not French, and that he was killing two birds with one stone, and not that he had killed a bird and stone. He did not even show his apprehension at the thought of her trailing after him from continent to continent, as she had suggested. Why spoil the mood? He happily concluded to himself.

But Minister Huma and his like-minded colleagues in Government were probably quite naive if they truly believed that Kobby, Obo and the general student body leadership could not read through the Regime's infantile though macabre political ploy. The radicalised students were certainly not going to sit back with their arms folded and wait meekly till the axe descended on them while they were dispersed around the country during the holidays. Their aim was to render the decree stillborn!

The President's decree was certainly ill-timed and completely counter-productive for himself and his Regime. That was the price that those drunk with unfettered power sometimes paid with their complacency. What the decree actually served to do was to hugely swell the ranks of those now implacably opposed to the Regime. For example, parents who had been sitting on the fence in the hope that Regime would simply disappear soon enough were now coming off those fences in grim determination to protect the lives of their children. They were not going to simply sit back and watch their children led to the slaughter for absolutely no purpose. Enough was enough! They would back the students all the way!

The President and his ministers had gravely miscalculated!

The announcement of the decree represented a massive seismic shift between the Regime and the citizenry.

Thus, the coalition against the Regime grew.

Various bodies and associations entered into the fray and started coordinating their efforts with Nana's resistance group and the student leadership. Everyone had a role to play.

A Joint Action Committee (JAC) was established to bring most of the opposition strands together to fight this inimical decree. It was decided at the initial coordinating meeting of the JAC that there would be a showdown with the Government in an attempt to force the withdrawal of the decree.

Nana was present at this meeting and had forcefully argued in favour of non-confrontational resistance as opposed to any form of violent confrontation. He nonetheless met with stiff opposition on this issue. Mr Kamson, a seasoned and well-respected workers leader, argued forcefully, 'We are not prepared to hit the streets like meek lambs to the slaughter. We all know the Regime is bound to unleash the Zombies on us, as has always been the case in the past when salvo after salvo of deadly rubber bullets have been hurled into our ranks, with fatal consequences for some.'

But Nana, backed by his pacifist supporters, would still not budge. He pointed out to them the foolhardiness of trying to fight 'fire with fire'.

'First of all, the opposition is mainly civilian, and we are generally not in possession of any so-called fire. Secondly, the President's Zombies are trained professional killers, and untrained civilians are certainly no match for them. Finally, violence on the part of the opposition would give the Zombies an excuse to shift from already lethal rubber bullets and truncheons to even more fatal live ammunition.'

'Fighting fire with fire is not always a foolhardy proposition, Mr Nana,' Mr Kamson shot back, quite irritated with Nana's response. 'I may not be an intellectual such as you, Mr Nana, but even I know that those who fail to learn the lessons of history are condemned to repeating them. Also, do we not have many instances in history where those with very little firepower have defeated seemingly invincible regimes with overwhelming firepower? Ultimately, did Fidel Castro and Che Guevara not start their armed resistance with just 12 men, after the rest of their group were captured when they landed in Cuba on the Granma? Indeed, though I respect Mr Nana a lot, I think our point of view must be given sufficient consideration. Consequently, I suggest that we put this issue to a vote.'

When put to a vote, most voted in favour of Nana's pacifist reasoning. Despite having won the argument, Nana knew that those such as Mr Kamson, who favoured some form of retaliatory violence against the troops if attacked, were not simply rash. Their reaction was based on years of frustration at their own impotence in the face of the wanton brutality that had been visited on their kith and kin, if not they themselves over the past years. They were also mightily enraged at the Government's dastardly move to have their children annihilated on fields of dubious battle.

Nana understood all of this very well, and was not convinced that those in favour of some violence had actually bought into his pacifist approach, despite the favourable outcome of the vote. For a start, the margin had been rather narrow, which was testimony enough that a sizeable number of them still favoured some use of violence.

He knew he had to find some middle ground to placate this 'fighting fire with fire' group, if they were not to go off on their own to engage in acts that might prove costly for them all. He suddenly had a flash of inspiration; inspiration born of desperation; a veritable 'eureka' moment.

'I have an idea. I'd like to concede that it may be impossible for us not to engage in certain acts of violence ourselves if this struggle is to be successful. But first, allow me to caution that we do not become unrealistic in our expectations of outcomes. Though it is the general wish of the majority of the people of this country to unseat the Regime, we must understand that that is rather unlikely at this juncture.

'Our main goal at this moment is to get the Regime to nullify the forced recruitment decree and also to sue for peace in this foolish war. Of course, many of us do not wish to be mowed down by these brutes without having a chance to hit back. However, we have voted on that and our non-confrontational approach is binding on us all without exception. My idea is simply this: why don't we rather take out those instruments of violence that could be used against us? Why don't we limit their ability to inflict violence by destroying the weapons themselves instead of attacking the people who carry them? Ladies and gentlemen – I am talking about sabotage!'

The Joint Action Committee greeted Nana's message with enthusiasm.

'I thank you for your approval by acclamation. To conclude, let me however stress that it will not at all be an easy task. It will involve considerable and careful planning, together with tons of luck. Our strike must be comprehensive and thorough. Once we are initially successful, the Regime will be on its guard, hence the need to do as much damage as possible in just a few well-coordinated and simultaneous attacks. Finally, I propose that a sub-committee be formed to specifically handle these sabotage operations. We will be wise to include some of you who have knowledge of weaponry as our advisors. Thank you.'

Nana was selected as the convener of the sub-committee charged with destroying weapons used by the Zombies against unarmed civilians. Though his middle-ground solution appeared accepted by the wider committee, Nana had no doubt that many were quite sceptical as to their ability to actually pull it off. Indeed, it was truly a Herculean task, and Nana himself did not have a clue at the time of his brainwave as to how it was going to be done. At a glance, it was also quite obvious to him that the opposition did not have the kind of intelligence and allied wherewithal needed to carry out such a major operation. Though this could prove to be very tricky, Nana, however, refused to be daunted. He and his sub-committee would somehow find a way, he quietly assured himself.

CHAPTER SIXTEEN

All Glorious Within

Zara had the face and grace of an angel. She was an exquisite young lady whom many found a joy to behold. Though it was often said that beauty lay in the eyes of a given beholder, in Zara's case, her beauty appeared to firmly lie in the eyes of all beholders!

She also had the temperament of an angel. Intelligent, generous, patient and respectful – she was truly one of a kind. And as her headmistress at school put it, she was 'all glorious within and without'.

Zara was 18. She was also mixed-race and a twin.

Her mother, who was an English lady of noble birth, had died when Zara was only 16. Zara missed her mother considerably. She had been the light of her mother's life and Zara was forever thankful to her for imparting those attributes that made her all glorious within before she passed away. Zara was not particularly concerned with being all glorious without and was generally quite oblivious to the stunning effect she had on people. Her deeply ingrained tender sensibilities prevented her from flaunting her good looks. Vanity was an alien concept to her.

Zara was not a happy girl.

She was a deeply troubled person and the source of her woes was her family. Her father was the notorious Minister of Presidential Affairs and her twin brother was the aspiring Chief of the Princes in Saga's school. Her father and her brother were the bane of her existence.

Zara had long nursed the belief that her mother's premature death was mainly due to the dramatic and brutal changes that occurred in her father when he decided to devote himself to the government's New Patriotism a while back. Zara believed that her mother had been completely heart-broken when her father had moved to betray every single principle and ideal she had ever held. From the little she had garnered from her late mum's diaries, she was also secretly convinced that her mother committed a form of suicide by taking slow-acting poison. She later surmised that her father had probably used his considerable power to hush it up at the time of her death. Her mum had chosen to take her own life rather than to live in the shadow of a husband who had gradually turned into a monster, and a son who showed eager propensities to become a mini-monster himself.

Zara wore a mournful look about her. Happiness had long since fled from her inner being and thus from her demeanour as well. Her only source of some joy was when she found herself in a position to help other people.

Thus, against her father's wishes, she snuck out of their heavily-guarded fortress of a mansion three times a week after school to do charity work at a small orphanage in the city centre, using a false name. She was the exact opposite of her twin brother and took extra pains outside of school to prevent people from associating her with him and their father.

Prior to the Orphan incident, Saga had developed a blinding crush on Zara, and it was becoming quite a serious matter. Such had been the case for months now. He had first seen her at his school gates a year ago when she came with their driver to pick up her brother, Yalley Junior. Though she made quite an impression on his 16-going-on-17-year-old mind at the time, he had soon pushed her into his subconscious mind. Unfortunately for him, this initial impression resurfaced with a vengeance when he saw her in action at the market, where she bravely sought to protect the beggars from the brutal policemen. He had since seen her quite a number of times.

Zara simply took Saga's breath away, quite literally. His heart went into a fierce flutter, his palms actually started to leak with nervous sweat, and a host of very robust butterflies caused total chaos in his stomach when she so much as gently acknowledged his unguarded stares with demure yet lovely smiles.

He had heard stories of her kindness at school and how she had led some campaign against bullying, which the older girls inflicted on newcomers or greenhorns, as they were called. He recalled being rather shocked at the time, since he had not been aware that girls were also into bullying. For some reason, he had foolishly assumed it was a male thing. Now, if this was a person who disliked such things then surely she could not be like the arch-bully Yalley Junior or the diabolical General Yalley himself! How could such exquisiteness be related to such brutes? Why could she not have been born into some other brute-free family?

Of course, he had done his own research among his female friends in Brewman Girls to ascertain whether or not she was in any way like the brutes she dwelled with. He had also indirectly elicited information from his younger sister, who was a junior at that school. Much to his delight, his research findings had given her what he thought of as a clean bill of health.

Under normal circumstances, Saga would have at least tried to communicate his feelings to Zara. He was not particularly shy of girls and had many female friends. He had even, at certain periods, thoroughly enjoyed the thrills of teenage romance. But with Zara, it all felt very different. He instinctively knew that to be with her would guarantee the maximum delights to be derived from pure, unadulterated love. He truly believed himself to be in love and would have been very cross if anyone had dared to refer to it as puppy love!

Saga's dilemma, which he saw as an unusual circumstance, was that she was the sister of someone who was universally loathed in their school. What would his friends think of him if it were ever known he harboured a secret crush on Yalley's sister? Even though his crush preceded the Orphan incident, he would still not be seen in a favourable light by his peers for daring to have feelings for a girl whose brother and father were 24-carat examples of all that was wrong with their society.

Consequently, Saga suffered in grim silence from the pangs of unrequited love. Deep down, however, he felt that it was wrong for him and his friends to ostracise the likes of Zara for the simple reason that she was in possession of an awful brother and odious father.

He decided to run this scenario by his father. He would omit the true names of those involved. He knew his father was a fair man and was interested in finding out his views on such a matter. Nana, as usual, did not disappoint when the matter was placed before him.

He quickly pointed out to Saga that this was in a sense tantamount to visiting the sins of the father unto the children, which he regarded as a very unfair and unjust proposition.

'Saga, supposing I got up each morning and went into town to cause mischief – do you think it would be right for the authorities to appear here every evening to flog you for the mischief I caused earlier on? Certainly not! So please understand that it is important to assess people on their own merits or demerits. How can people assume, for example, that you are a robber because your brother is one and punish you for things you did not steal? No, Saga, please don't judge people by what their parents or sibling do. They could be very different from them! We don't exactly choose our family, you know! We are born into them.'

Saga was glad of his father's reassurance. He knew his instincts had been right all along. Though reassured, it did not exactly get him out of his dilemma and his crush, which was relentlessly growing by the minute. He wondered again whether his friends would relent if they were also privy to the deeds of kindliness he had heard of her. Or would their feelings run too deep on the matter and not budge? What of his own parents? Saga was not exactly apprehensive with respect to his father, since he knew him to practice what he preached.

But what of his mother? Though she broadly thought along the same lines as her husband, she was, as she herself put it, more in touch with reality. She would be very sceptical indeed.

Saga knew, for example, that she had disagreed with Nana when he first ventured to embrace President Brewman's Regime with some fervour. Not one to mince words, she said she found Brewman too fishy and his eyes too shifty. She simply maintained that one had to be more circumspect in embracing a Regime that came to power through the barrel of a gun. Killing even just a handful of people to get to power was, for her, tantamount to wading in blood to the throne.

'Why make a coup in the first place? No coup, no casualties! I do not trust that man!' she had said.

How right had she been! Now they were all casualties of the coup!

Given her tendency towards pragmatism, Saga also knew that although his mother would in principle not oppose a 'friendship' between him and Zara, she was nonetheless bound to question the wisdom of it. For her, it would no doubt be akin to setting a cat among pigeons in their neighbourhood, and among some of their friends and relatives, who were not simply just hostile to the Government but had suffered at its hands. What was he to do?

His heart was bursting with what he believed to be pure love. He needed to be with this girl. He needed to talk to her. He needed to share with her. He needed to touch her and inhale what he no doubt knew would be the fresh fragrance of her scent, and the world was conspiring to deny him these much life-affirming delights!

There were periods during which Saga could think of nothing but Zara.

There was another problem that needed to be addressed. Hierarchically, Saga did not consider himself an exulted Prince by virtue of the new social order that had come into existence with Brewman's Regime. Though he was from what could be loosely referred to as an upper-middle-class background with prominent and well-educated parents, he did not see his family as part of the new aristocracy. His family was pre-eminent prior to the military take-over and also aristocratic in the traditional sense, since his maternal grandfather was a prominent paramount Chief of an important area. They were, however, not part of the 'newly very rich'. And these days, 'very rich' was the only thing that seemed to matter in Africa!

Would Zara thus look down on him because he was not as newly 'exulted' as she was? Certainly, her brother, Yalley, would haemorrhage at the mere thought that he, a self-declared non-Prince, should have the nerve to even dream of taking a fancy to his sister, who by all rights was a Princess as well! Yalley would no doubt organise a thorough beating for him for his amorous intent! Their father would probably even go so far as having him shot for such dastardly impertinence! One could surely not put anything past that odious duo when provoked!

In this particular case, however, love was to prove a powerful lure, which neither the possibility of beatings or bullets could offset. Though the hurdles in his way appeared formidable enough, Saga was determined to make the lady's acquaintance – come hell or high water or both! He was absolutely resolved. All he needed was a strategy, since his initial contact had to be away from the prying eyes of friends, family, his would-be beaters and potential shooters!

Saga usually passed the Yalley mansion on his way from school after he'd parted with Ibrahim. He had noticed on a number of occasions, when he had been late, a rather furtive-looking Zara wheeling her bicycle out of the side gate in their wall and pedalling off at high speed, as though she were being pursued by a horde of banshees. He had often wondered where she went, and thought her stealthy manner a touch out of character from what he had surmised of her so far.

Saga decided to follow Zara to see what this business of stealth and peddling away for dear life was all about. He was profoundly perplexed by it all. He knew that the exulted Princes and Princesses hardly ever went anywhere without being chauffeured in the back of some posh automobile with bodyguards thrown into the equation most times. For Zara to zoom off like that on her own was certainly unusual. Curiosity and desire got the better of him. Who knew? Maybe his self-imposed surveillance mission could very well provide the opportunity he so desperately needed to make one-on-one contact with her away from ubiquitous prying eyes. He nonetheless hesitated when he remembered the adage about how 'curiosity killed the cat'. He instantly dismissed it with a responsive adage of his own, which was 'but satisfaction brought it back'. Nothing was going to stop him from satisfying his love-inspired curiosity about the adorable Zara Yalley!

For two consecutive days, Saga rushed home after school, wolfed down his lunch, grabbed his bike, and rushed off to conceal himself behind some tall shrubbery not too far from the side gate of the Yalley Fortress. There he remained, with the hope of catching Zara sneaking off. For those two days, nothing happened. On the third day, Saga was rewarded. A few minutes after he had parked himself and his bike behind the bushes, Zara appeared, wearing a wide-brimmed hat pulled low to cover her face, and hurtled off on her bike. Saga waited a few seconds and zoomed off after her. Though he did not wish to be seen, it was imperative that he did not lose sight of her. He followed her to a familiar building in the city centre, watched her park her bicycle and slip inside. The place was an orphanage. Saga was puzzled. What in the name of heavens could she possibly be doing in an orphanage? It was mind-boggling. Did she have some relative there who was an orphan child? If yes then why the secrecy and attempted disguise? Or did she have a secret child whom her father had 'donated' to the orphanage to spite her? At 18? He doubted that very much, but did not know what else to think. He decided to peer over the wall, still feeling rather mystified.

Saga was nowhere near solving this mystery when Zara came out of the white, freshly-painted building into the garden with about ten children, ranging from probably six to seven years old, following her. What was going on? Did she have a part-time job as a teacher in an orphanage? What did she need the money for, since her family was literally rolling in cash from her father's ill-gotten wealth?

Zara and the children sat in a semi-circle under the shade of a huge avocado tree and started playing a game to the sound of joyous laughter. Soon, all the children went quiet and Zara began talking to them in her unhurried manner. Saga could not hear too well what she was saying and assumed that she was probably telling them a story. He could hear peals of laughter from time to time and clapping at whatever story was being told to them.

After about an hour later, Zara got up and led them back into the building in an orderly line, after giving each of them a hug and a peck on the cheek. How Saga wished he were one of those true orphans that day, even for a fleeting moment, just so as to have a hug and kiss bestowed on him as well.

By this time, Saga's feet were aching from all the tiptoeing he had been doing to enable him to carry on with his peering and straining. He decided to sit on the cement blocks he was standing on to rest his agonised toes and ball-joints. He had barely sat down for a few minutes when Zara appeared in front of him like an apparition.

Saga was startled.

This was not part of the plan!

He was supposed to have seen her coming and scamper off around the side of the building to discreetly follow her back when she set off. This was definitely not in the plan at all!

'Hello Saga, what are you doing here?' she asked in a gentle, lilting voice. And there was a slight hint of an English accent. The posh type.

'You… you… you… know my name?' he stammered in response.

'Yes Saga, I know your name and I know who you are. But please answer my question: what are you doing here?'

'I… I… I err… err…' He was at a loss for words and started casting his eyes at the passing cars as if in search of support from them.

She gave him a smile, which he felt right through to his aching toes.

'You followed me here, didn't you, Saga? You thought I was up to no good and you were curious. Am I right, Saga?'

Saga recovered slowly. 'Yes, yes, you are right. I didn't mean to be nosy. Sorry. But please tell me also, what are you doing here yourself with all those children? Is it a job or what?'

'No Saga, it's not a proper job. I'm only a volunteer in my free time. That is, when I can escape from home without being missed. I read in the papers that they were short-staffed, so I volunteered to come in thrice each week to help out, and I love children, Saga, so I'm having fun.'

Saga was dumbstruck! Of all the possibilities, he had not thought of her being a volunteer. This was no joke. He was, in reality, beholding an angel in his presence. He did not know what to say. Her nearness, the genuineness of her smile, and the way she kept mentioning his name so often in every question or statement, was making his head swim. He felt unwell. Heaven must be truly missing an angel and he had found her!

'Saga, are you all right?' she asked, totally unaware of the havoc she was creating within the young man.

Saga stumbled to his feet. 'I'm okay. I'm okay. Just a bit tired from all that fast cycling. How come you don't appear tired in any way?'

'It's because I'm used to it, Saga, and now that you've discovered my secret, why don't we walk our bikes home together? We can always cycle a bit when you feel less tired, though I'd have thought you'd have had enough rest by now.'

Saga accepted this invitation from the heavens with alacrity, and a journey that should have taken them just about an hour on foot took them over two-and-a-half hours.

They talked.

They joked.

They laughed.

They lingered.

Saga had never known such happiness, and Zara shed her mournful look, revealing a radiance that had Saga dazzled to his very marrow. There was no awkwardness between them, and it was as though they had been talking all their lives and not just that very afternoon.

Finally, they got to the side gate of the Yalley Mansion and reluctantly had to part. Just as he was leaving, she placed her hand gently on his arm and asked, 'Saga, why don't you come with me the next time I'm going to the orphanage? I like your company and you could also help me with the children. I'm sure they will love you. It'll be awfully nice of you. They could use some extra help there as well.'

Saga loved her directness and could hardly believe his luck. He told her he would very much love to come and agreed to meet further down the road in a couple of days so they could go together. Thus began a friendship that Saga fervently hoped would turn into something more intimate such as proper dating, which would then last forever.

* * *

Under Zara's influence, and without his parent's knowledge, Saga soon became a volunteer at the orphanage, though he could only manage two afternoons a week due to his other extra-curricular activities. They became very close and soon started giving each other warm hugs and dainty pecks on the cheeks. Saga was thoroughly enjoying himself and was living life as though in a dream.

But given whom they were and their honesty in approaching things, the dreaded issue of their reality soon came up. Zara confided in Saga and told him how she was permanently haunted by the prominent role her father was playing in spreading the misery that had engulfed their country. She simply could not come to terms with it and spent half the time crying and wishing she were dead. She often found it so hard to get out of bed in the mornings and felt herself burning with shame the moment she stepped out of her house each day. It was only when she was at the orphanage that she felt her life had some purpose to it. She had loved her father very much when she was much younger but could not bring herself to love him anymore now that she was older and her eyes were now open.

What baffled her most was her twin brother's agreement with what their father and his people were doing to the country. How could one so young accept such atrocities against fellow human beings as though such were the normal course of events? How could someone who came from the same womb as her almost at the same time condone such evil?

Zara, it appeared, felt her brother's perceived betrayal in condoning such injustice just as acutely as her father's. Many times, she thought of running away and changing her name, but she simply did not know where to go. Worse than that was her powerlessness at being unable to do anything about what her father did and her brother condoned. She lived with them as a stranger in the house and they laughed at her whenever she tried to register her protest at some of the sad things that were happening all around them. Her father had even gone to the extent of slapping her very hard on the face when she once dared to call Brewman an evil dictator, and had cut her allowance in half at the time.

Her ultimate plan was to leave the country the moment she finished high school. She was saving towards that and there was also a little bit of money in England her mother had left to her, which she would inherit when she turned 19. She did not want her father's blood-drenched money! She planned on using that money to pay for her tuition fees at Manchester University in England to study medicine, and fervently hoped that it would be enough. Up until that time, all she wanted to do was to stay out of everyone's way, get good results for her A-levels and work at the orphanage.

All these issues came out in spurts and bursts over a period of time, and much of the story was told to Saga amidst heart-rending tears. Saga was touched to the core. No one meeting Zara on the street with her lovely smile and gentle ways would ever in a thousand years imagine the agonies that plagued her youthful mind and tormented her lovely soul. Given the way her feelings ran so deep, Saga felt it was a mystery that she had not actually taken her young life already.

The only other person Zara had confided in was the comely, generous and wise Matron of the orphanage. When once she mentioned her thoughts of suicide, the Matron had firmly chided her thus: 'My child, taking one's own life in the face of what may appear as intractable problems that confront us can never be an option for us to even consider. It is not a solution but rather an addition to the overall problems of the world in which we live. It is a coward's way out and must never be contemplated. Never forget that once we breathe, have good health and remain alive, there is always hope. And hope is one of the true joys of life. Also, remember that what is true of today may not be true of tomorrow, and our own problems, when weighed against the problems that others go through in this world, are like a drop of water in the ocean. It is a form of vanity that allows us to believe that our problems are so unique that we must think of killing ourselves.

'Look at these children we work with. You know the stories that follow some of them and the horrors they have been through since their parents departed this world. Some of them have been victims all their lives and have had to endure needless suffering because their parents were not brave enough to face the world for what it is and selfishly abandoned them to their fate by taking their own lives. Look at how many of them love you so dearly and are daily begging that you stay with them permanently. Do you wish to add to their agonies by having them find out that you took your life rather than be with them? Of course, they know that you will one day be gone from here, but would they not be much happier knowing you were somewhere thinking nice things about them instead? I think I have said enough my child, and I know deep down that you are one of those sent to Earth to bring happiness. Let these foolish thoughts of yours go as quickly as they come.'

Zara confessed that since the Matron's telling-off, she had thought less and less of death, but was still forever cringing in shame, embarrassment and disgust at her father's misdeeds. She was truly not a happy person.

Saga, for the most times, had listened to these outpourings without much comment. He nonetheless felt her pain very deeply in a manner that absolutely rekindled his rage against the Brewman Regime. He knew it had taken a lot of courage on her part to come out so strongly in expressing her feelings to someone who was a relative stranger. He also knew she was very brave to have taken an uncompromising stand against her father and brother, and sought to spread love and joy in direct opposition to their bid to spread only hatred and sadness.

In his own way, he tried to comfort her by reasoning that it was wrong for people to visit the sins of the father unto the children or to think along such lines. She was touched and told him so, but also reminded him, 'What you are saying, Saga, is very true and should be the case in a normal world. But it isn't because our world is not normal. People are often judged by their associations, whether we like it or not. There's even a saying that says "show me your friends – I'll show you your character", how much more "show me your family" in my case? It is true that I do not go around ordering troops to pull the trigger on innocents or bombard university hostels. And neither do I go around bullying and beating up people in my school and creating divisiveness – but the people who go around doing such things are my own flesh and blood. I live in the same house with them; I eat the same food as them! Do you think I am not going to be painted with the same brush as them? Do you think people will not see me as tainted as they are? They will, Saga. They will, and that is a burden I have to bear for now. But I thank you for your support and you are so cute when you look worried!'

What she had said was true. There was nothing more to say other than to believe in her.

* * *

Zara almost jumped out of her skin when news reached her of Saga's confrontation with Deputy Minister Com at Brewman High. She was terribly frightened for him and was beside herself with worry. And yet, there was nothing she could do then. She knew now that she loved him endlessly and that he was one of the few and far between sources of pure joy in her life. She would simply die if anything happened to him.

Zara marvelled at Saga's bravery and the irony of his use of the word Orphan. It was as though, among other things, he had done it for both of them. She also quickly grasped the implications of what Saga had done, and knew enough to realise what her father and his security thugs could also do by way of retribution. She needed to speak to Saga as soon as possible. She dropped him an urgent note that very afternoon at their pre-arranged mail drop, asking him to meet her as soon as possible at yet another pre-arranged spot.

She rushed into his arms the moment he appeared and started kissing him fiercely on the lips for the first time ever. 'Oh you fool, Saga! I love you so much. I love you so very much,' she moaned over and over again in between all the kissing. Saga felt his heart was about to burst with sheer joy. He was stunned. All his anxiety over his impulsiveness in school deserted him in an instant. He returned her kisses with unambiguous eagerness and abandonment. He was in heaven.

Was this his reward for what he had done? If that was the case, he probably ought to rush off and confront a few more ministers to ensure a never-ending flow of these lovely, life-giving kisses!

'What have you gone and done, my love? What have you done, Saga?' she asked once the kisses had temporarily ceased, as they both needed to surface for air. 'Oh Saga, oh Saga, so brave, my darling, yet so foolish. Now you have really gone and put your foot in it, and I love you for it though I'm terrified for you! What are we going to do?' She was now very serious.

'Don't worry, Zara, nothing is going to happen. At least, not now. They may punish me in school later but who cares? I really don't know what made me do it, beyond the fact that I'd just had enough of this stinking New Patriotism rubbish and what it is doing to all of us. Somewhere in the back of my mind was also you. It's as if I needed to do something for you or rather for us. I don't know how it all ties in, as it all came out in a rush! I don't know, but what's done is done. Please don't worry about me. I will be fine, okay. And I love you too, okay? Forever, okay? Now, can we go back to kissing? It's much nicer than talking about this!'

Zara was almost fuming.

'Be serious, Saga! This is not a joke. I would die if something happened to you. Please go home and talk to your father as soon as you can. From what I've heard, he is very wise and brave. That is why my father's goons hate him. Please, okay? He will know what to do. Forget about kissing for now. As for my lips, they belong to you alone forever. They won't run away or dissolve overnight so leave them alone for now. Just go. I also need to think of what to do to help you out of this mess!'

Saga saw she was not joking. He knew what she was suggesting was the right thing to do. He left after securing a promise that they would meet at the same time and place the next day. He was in need of more kissing.

Zara watched him leave. He was her hero. She knew, however, that despite his making light of the entire matter, nothing was ever going to be the same for them. She surmised his public defiance of the New Patriotism would take root in other schools if the excitement generated in her own school was anything to go by. She also knew that the Regime could not tolerate such defiance for long. The Regime thrived on fear. Thus, to allow such defiance to go unpunished once it ceased to be an isolated incident was to create serious chinks in its own armour. The Regime could not afford that. She knew her father very well and was positive he would most likely be at the centre of the planning for reprisals. She also knew her brother, Yalley Junior, would react precipitously. He would be mortally affronted that such a thing should happen in his school, which also bore his idol Brewman's name. His ignorance, arrogance and sheer stupidity would make him attempt some form of retribution of his own brand.

He was his father's son.

'Well, they are not the only ones capable of reacting! I can also react and I will!' she vowed loudly to herself, unafraid.

She resolved that she was not going to let anything happen to Saga. She would do everything she could to protect him. She had never gone against her father directly, due to filial duty, or against her brother out of sibling loyalty. But enough of that! They had abused it all and she had also abused her own conscience by keeping mute for so long. Not this time. If Saga's destiny was to help the cause that existed against Brewman in the schools, then she would serve the cause by protecting him. All she needed to do now was figure out how best to execute her resolve in practical terms.

CHAPTER SEVENTEEN

Never a Pariah

The mood in the country was one of simmering rage and defiance.

President Brewman, the citizenry felt, had irretrievably crossed the line with his forced recruitment decree, targeted at the youth of the country. There were secret meetings taking place everywhere, as people in their various associations and groupings wanted to know how best to contribute towards fighting this infamous decree.

The decree had one positive impact, which the Regime, in its complacent arrogance, did not foresee. The divisiveness that the Regime had sought to encourage by promoting the North/South Muslim/Christian divide among the population had in the main evaporated in the face of this new threat of a decree. What the Regime had forgotten was that both the North and South alike, Muslims and Christians alike, had children they did not wish to see senselessly slaughtered. The age group that was affected by the decree was not confined to one geographical section of the country; it was also not confined to any one particular religious persuasion. It was a universal threat and was to be treated as such.

The likes of Nana had their hands full with matters relating to the coordination of the strategy that was being put together by the opposition to defeat the decree. The main thrust of the strategy was to be a series of sit down strikes across the length and breadth of the nation, aimed at bringing the country to a standstill. These were to involve professional bodies and formal sector workers acting through their trade and professional unions. Informal sector non-unionised workers such as traders, farmers, market-women and hawkers had also signalled their intention to fully participate. University students were of course at the forefront. Even the vast pool of the unemployed was eager to join in the battle to have the vile decree repealed. Workers of every conceivable profession be they doctors, nurses, bus drivers, teachers, industrial sector workers, etc. were all resolved in their majority to take part in these strikes.

Peaceful mass demonstrations were also to take place simultaneously in all major cities of the country, demanding a repeal of the decree, a cessation of hostilities in the insane border war, as well as a considerable relaxation of the censorship imposed on the media by the Regime.

One aspect of this process, which Nana welcomed, was the relative freedom with which they were able to coordinate their affairs. There was a simple explanation for this. The decree had so inflamed people that anyone suspected of being an informant now seriously risked the possibility of a lynching. Though Nana was an advocate of non-violence, he felt that in this case, the mere threat of lynching spies and informants was acting as a splendid deterrent. The fact of the matter was that most informants were opportunists who had thrown in their lot with what they perceived to be the winning side. They were not however prepared to risk a lynching and consequent loss of life or limb, or both, on a matter that so blatantly affected them as well. Though they would not take to the streets to demonstrate against the Regime, many would suspend their treacherous ways for now as a matter of self-preservation.

That did not mean, however, that there were absolutely no informants on the prowl. Of course, there were the embittered die-hards, such as Bayou, who were in too deep and had their fate tied irrevocably to that of the Regime's. Thus, they did not have a choice in the matter. Do or don't; they were damned either way.

What was bothering Nana was the business regarding the destruction of the Zombie armouries. His sub-committee had been charged with coming up with a strategy, and three meetings on, they were still floundering, with no plan in sight. They simply did not have the intelligence to start putting together a strategy, and time was seriously running out. Though the coordinating bodies had yet not agreed on the exact dates of the strikes and demonstrations, he knew it would have to happen before the decree was to take effect, which meant they barely had six weeks to go. One did not plan such things hastily, and he was sorely tempted to go back and report that it could not be done. But he could not do that. He could not cede the initiative to those who favoured the use of aggressive means. That would be too dangerous. He had to find a solution and it had to be fast.

The forced recruitment decree had also served to heighten the tension in Brewman Boys High School. The Orphans had recruited over half the student population. The decree would affect many of the seniors who had already turned 18 and were thus anxious to throw in their lot with anyone who was organising against it. The decree had prompted many of those who initially joined the Princes to defect to the side of the Orphans. It appeared that the decree was universally hated within the secondary schools and that many students were now saying that they would prefer to die alongside their friends fighting for the opposition against Brewman and his Zombies than to die in some lonely far-off place, fighting for nothing. Their mood was turning ugly and had to be contained and temporarily diffused until the time the opposition was ready to move. Saga knew that it was important to find an outlet for the Orphans before they turned their pent-up energies on Yalley and his Princes, who had less than a tenth of the students behind them, although they enjoyed the unwavering support of headmaster Money and some of his staff.

Unsure as to what to do about the building pressure, Saga sought Obo's advice. Obo said that since it was a matter that was beyond him, he would ask permission from Nana for Saga to attend the next meeting of the resistance movement, where he could seek permission at the coordinating level.

The request was granted, and after ensuring the necessary precautions and keeping a strenuous eye out for the likes of the inimical Bayou, Saga soon found himself once again in Uncle Tiger's hallowed Masonic Temple basement, in the midst of those whom were fast becoming living legends in their society. Saga was promptly asked to explain the problem in his school. He did so quickly and succinctly. He pointed out that things could no longer remain calm as a result of the decree, and that some form of guidance for the secondary schools was immediately necessary to prevent a wave of student unrest from that quarter.

Obo and Kobby also reported that other Orphan chapters had been formed in 12 other secondary schools in the city, and that some of their colleagues from the university had been dispatched to meet with their leaders and explain the broad objectives of the movement. They confirmed that they had also come under increased pressure for guidance and for more active participation from these new formations in the wake of the National Service decree.

The lines were clearly drawn.

The resistance had no option but to assign a role for the secondary schools in the upcoming struggles. But they did not want them on the streets where things could get very hairy.

'With all due respect,' Saga began, 'I would like this meeting to take the secondary schools issue a bit more seriously. I know you are all very busy with matters of national importance and are fighting very hard for us. But it is not enough to just tell the students that they cannot take part in the demonstrations, and that all they can do is boycott lessons. Who is going to stop them if they decide to join one of the marches on that day? Already, we have heard that there will be virtually no teachers around during that period for most schools, as many of them will be going on the demonstrations as well. There has to be a way in which we can participate while avoiding the front lines where most of the troubles might occur. We could be confined to a section and monitored. Please think about this. I am humbly and respectfully asking that you reconsider. It will be too difficult to go back and tell them they are not welcome to participate though it affects them so directly. Please excuse me for speaking so directly and taking up your precious time.'

Saga had scored an important telling point.

Uncle Tiger agreed. 'You can't keep these students off the streets even if you wanted to. Those who have turned 18 are legally adults and deserve to be treated as such. Furthermore, they are directly in the line of fire where the decree is concerned. It would make a lot more sense for us to rope them in and monitor them, rather than leaving them to their own potentially unruly devices.'

The rest of the group agreed. Saga, Obo and Kobby were thus given the mandate to tell the Orphan leaders that a proper participatory role would be found for them during both the strikes and demonstrations, and that they were to sit tight until then.

The meeting was soon progressing too intensely for anyone to think of dismissing Saga after they had finished with his business, and he was not about to remind them to do so. He simply made himself as inconspicuous as possible to listen intently to all that was being said. Indeed, Saga was truly amazed that he was yet again sitting amongst this august national gathering, made up of resistance representatives and leaders from all over the country. When did he go from a happy-go-lucky teenager, listening to his rap music, to becoming a veritable dissident, fighting against a brutal dictator and his Zombies to better things in his country? When and how did this transition occur with such rapidity in which political action had virtually taken over his life? He simply shook his head in wonder and reminded himself to focus on what was being said. He had much to ponder about later on.

Saga's interest perked up a few more notches when he heard Nana telling the meeting that his sub-committee was yet to come up with a plan to neutralise some of the military hardware used by the Zombies. He explained that without insider assistance and intelligence, it was proving very tough. They needed to know, for example, which weapons were stored in which dumps or bases, their quantities, the schedules of the security personnel guarding them, etc. He nonetheless assured that they were working diligently on the matter.

Something about this particular problem kept nagging at the back of Saga's mind long after he had left the meeting. For some reason, the problem appeared not as difficult as Nana had made out. But he simply could not for the life of him fathom why he thought it ought to be easier than it appeared to be. Saga felt that he was definitely onto something here. He had for a while now been racking his brain for some heroic role for the Orphans, which while having a considerable impact on the struggle, would not prove too dangerous in its execution. This business of destroying the very physical instruments of brutality had an alluring appeal for him. In addition, the Orphans would be helping the sub-committee in charge to do their job. Something his father had said about not having the necessary intelligence kept coming back to him. He felt this was the key to solving this particular problem.

Saga had heard it said many times that President Brewman was a very paranoid leader, who was virtually afraid of his own shadow. Consequently, apart from issuing a few regulation pistols and rifles to some of the soldiers who patrolled the streets, and aside from what was being used on the war front, it appeared that a considerable amount of the armaments he spent much of the country's wealth purchasing were kept under lock and key in carefully selected munitions dumps within the capital city. Only his Presidential Guard were truly well armed for special assignments – such as beating up unarmed, defenceless students.

Brewman, in his paranoia, was not about to allow a proliferation of arms that could be turned against him. He simply did not trust anybody. Rather, he relied on the psychology of fear and terror, including arbitrary arrests and beatings, and the not infrequent display of fearsome-looking military hardware to keep the population cowed. It was only when he perceived a real threat of mass civil disorder, such as the university riots, that he allowed the Zombies to be issued with these menacing instruments.

Saga was formulating a plan. Destroying the weaponry would be an ideal operation for a few handpicked, carefully instructed Orphans to carry out as a great adventure, which would, in turn, help the struggle against Brewman's hated decree. The first issue would be the location of the weapons.

The second would involve how to destroy these weapons, since neither he nor his Orphans nor the civilian opposition were in possession of grenades, Semtex, C4, or allied military explosives needed to blow whatever weaponry was found to smithereens. In fact, the opposition movement strictly forbade the possession of any form of arms or incendiary devices by any of its members. This was quite apart from the fact that none of them had the expertise to handle such lethal explosives.

However, Saga was a perennial optimist. He knew that there had to be a way to employ non-violent means to destroy violent instruments. Something came to him that suddenly gave him hope. He remembered a funny Eddie Murphy movie he watched a long time ago, *Beverly Hills Cop*. He remembered how Eddie Murphy, after proving himself a nuisance to the Beverly Hills Police Department in Los Angeles, had been placed under surveillance by the Police Chief of the city. Murphy, in the role of Axel Foley, a detective from Detroit, bent on finding those who had murdered a friend of his, was not very happy about this surveillance, which restricted his movements. He thus decided to immobilise the vehicle assigned to follow him. Murphy was able to achieve this by stuffing a couple of bananas down the tailpipe of the surveillance car, thus rendering it immobile. How simple! In truth, Saga and Ibrahim had tried it at a later point on a neighbour's car and it had worked! However, he managed to get his ears subsequently tweaked by his mother for his experimental efforts. She also had to placate the seriously irate neighbour in question. This was the non-combustible kind of solution Saga was looking for, though he did not think bananas would work in this case.

He needed to lay his hands on the relevant intelligence, since the locations of the dumps were obviously well-guarded State secrets. He now had an idea as to how to lay his hands on this intelligence. It could prove a long shot, but given the circumstances, it was worth a try.

For the first time in many years, Yalley Junior was having niggling doubts about what he believed to be the unparalleled and inexhaustible wisdom of his idol, President Brewman. His initial reaction to the announcement of the National Service decree had been one of unadulterated glee. 'Serves those university morons right! Now, they'll all be shipped off and leave us in peace,' he had smirked.

His first realisation that all was not well was when he surmised that his own fellow Princes were far from enthused about it all. He was quite baffled by the cool reception he received from them when he approached them to jubilate.

'What is your problem, you guys? Why are you not excited that some lousy troublemakers are going to be shipped off and probably be permanently out of our hair? Why, are you afraid it will affect us because some of us are 18? Rubbish – do you think our fathers will sit back and watch us get shipped off just like that? Wake up, you morons! Don't you understand anything about privilege and connections and influence? Don't be foolish. We are in the clear. It is the Sagas of this world who will be shipped off pronto when the time comes. You get my meaning?'

One of the Princes faced up to him. 'It's not that simple, Yalley. Though we may be Princes, not all our parents have your father's power and influence. My dad told me, for example, that President Brewman is thinking that it would be good PR and a morale booster to send off some of the sons of highly-placed officials to stop some of the unpleasant rumours about what he is trying to do. You, Yalley, may not go, but the axe could fall on some of us, and who wants to go and die in some lonely, stinky place?'

Yalley was appalled. He had not thought of it this way. He had not seen this coming. But he needed time to verify what he had just been told. He would ask his father. For now, he simply retorted that it could never happen that way and that he would confirm it with his father, whom they all knew was very close to the President.

Yalley asked his father that evening whether it was true that the forced recruitment under the decree would be across the board and would include the sons of the Regime's elite.

'That's how President Brewman wants it. It's good for PR. I agree with him. But don't worry, my son, you will not be going anywhere. I am thinking of sending you to school in America so you can enjoy yourself. So, don't worry at all.'

'But Daddy—' he started to protest, but was cut short.

'I said that is the way the President wants it so there is no argument. The President's wishes are law. You know that, so leave me alone because I'm busy. Why are you worried anyway? Just try and make sure you don't fail all your papers at school, so we can find you a school in America.'

Yalley knew the score. If he was not careful, this decree was going to cost him his most crucial support base. He had to stretch the truth a little, take the sting out of it. Already, things were looking rather grim for him, with the bulk of the student population defecting to those awful Orphans instead of following their natural leaders like himself. He had also heard rumours about new Orphan formations in other schools – even his sister's. It certainly did not look good.

Thus, Yalley went back to his mates with his own invented, sugar-coated amendment. 'I told you chaps it was not really that bad. My dad said that for people like us, it would only be for about three months instead of the two years for everyone else. It's only to set an example. Surely that can't be so bad, so let's just forget this whole business and try and see how we can stop these Orphans from doing anything crazy about this decree, which favours us!'

The Princes were not so easily mollified. This was not a joke!

'What do you mean by "us", Yalley? You think we don't know that your father will never let you go to the war front? Why are you trying to deceive us? How can we just forget about it when many of us are 18 already or will get there very soon?' one of them retorted.

Another of them had even more pertinent questions. 'What I don't understand is why we have to be examples for showing other people how to die? Why can't they just go and die without the benefit of us having to show them how? You think three months is not enough to get killed? From what I hear, we would be lucky to live three days! And, Yalley, how do you show others how to die by way of example if not by having to die yourself first? I don't care what you say but this is rubbish and I don't understand it at all!'

Yalley was in serious trouble and was soon faced with a lot more defections to the Orphan camp. But Yalley was a die-hard. He was not about to concede that the National Service decree was a bad one. He would not even think it. He employed the perverted logic that kept him secure in his beliefs: if Big Daddy Brewman thought that it was good then it must be good. If his father thought it was also good then it had to be good. Case closed! Those who wanted to defect should just go. They were all rabble after all. He would just cut his losses and only allow die-hards like himself to remain with the Princes. All he needed was a few spies in the Orphan camp to know exactly what they were planning so he could thwart them. The time had also come for him to goad his father into doing something about the Orphan menace! He would show them all. He would show them who the true masters were! TIA – This Is Africa – or did they not know?

Saga went to see Zara at a pre-arranged spot near her house. He had become worried about being followed, even though he had heard that some informers had thrown in their towels in the face of the public's uncompromising mood. He did not want to get Zara in any unnecessary trouble.

Saga was overjoyed that he and Zara were now officially dating. They had decided to live 'in the moment' and enjoy every minute while it lasted, due to the uncertainties, which were now a daily feature of their existence. Circumstances had forced them into a secret relationship, which all things being equal, was certainly an unwelcome strain, despite the joy of being together. But things were not equal, and since that was all they could have for now, they were determined to see it through.

Zara came up with a daring idea.

'Saga, I think the best place for us to meet over the next week is in my bedroom!'

Saga was confused. 'Are you out of your mind? Have you been drinking your father's booze? This is no time for games!' he gushed.

'Hear me out. You say you want to be a leader, yet you have no patience. My idea is simple and simple things always win the day! My father has gone with that "brute" of a President to visit the troops on the war front. He will be away for a week. My brother is never in when my father is away. He'll be with his fellow Princes, causing trouble somewhere, or at that new club in Victoria Town, chasing girls. The number of guards have also been reduced until he comes back, and those that are left are always drunk and asleep. I have also given most of the house-help some time off – so tell me, am I not wise or what? Out here, anybody can see us and report us. We are safer inside, and even a wannabe brute like my silly brother won't dare to come into my room uninvited. He doesn't even come there at all. What business has he got in my room? Come, let's go. I have a key to the side gate!'

She had made perfect sense and they were soon in her bedroom, rolling around on the soft carpet in each other's arms, and kissing as though the act of kissing was about to be outlawed by decree the very next day. Theirs was a precarious and dangerous world. They had to make the best of every second they had available. Even a budding revolutionary such as himself could be forgiven for letting that beautiful angel take his mind off the Regime, for an hour or two. Drunk on teenage lust, Saga felt emboldened.

'Zara, what I need to ask of you is a very serious favour. If you can't do it, I'll understand, and it will not affect my love for you in any way. It is to do with the opposition cause and it would mean going against your family. Let me explain what it is and I'll give you time to think about it. You've been bugging me about allowing you to help us Orphans, and with what I'm about to ask, you'll be helping us, and the entire opposition cause. It's even likely that you'll be helping to save lives. My father keeps saying that we are young and should not be doing this. Instead, he says we should be thinking about schoolwork, movies, parties and our friends and girlfriends. But the Regime does not want that for us. They want us to fight their wars and die. So we have no choice but to become adults in our thinking and actions and fight them off. Are you ready to listen?'

Zara did not bat an eyelid. She said she was ready.

Saga quickly explained what he needed and why. He told her about the planned demonstrations and strikes against the decree, and that it was very broad-based, with participants from all walks of life, including many secondary school students.

'Anybody from my camp who hears me telling you all this will call me a traitor; a young informant who has betrayed his people and the cause. But I've faith in what I'm doing because I've faith in you. I am trusting you with my life, the lives of my family, as well as those of many who are involved. No one knows you like I do and I'm the only one who realises at this stage that you can help us a lot. The point, Zara, is that as far as is possible, we must prevent the Regime from wholesale brutalising of the marchers during the demonstrations.

'We have to try and limit the violence, and one key way we can do that is to destroy the guns and whatever military hardware they will use. We understand that most of them and their ammunition as well are kept in a few dumps somewhere in the city. We need to know where these dumps are so we can strike. Your father is one of the few people who will know the location of these dumps and we need that info. It will no doubt be in his documents somewhere in his office or in his office at home. Like I said, it is a difficult and dangerous task. Can you help? Will you help? I will understand if you can't, and no one on Earth knows that I'm asking this of you. I have not told anybody. It's entirely my own idea.'

Zara looked at him with sad eyes before replying. 'Saga, you've made me both sad and happy. Sad that you can even think of the possibility of me not wanting to help if ever I could. You of all people know how I hate what my daddy and brother stand for. There are times when I've even had evil thoughts of poisoning them, but I know that's not a solution and I'm certainly not a murderess. Of course I'll help, Saga. Of course, I'll do anything I can to stop this stupid violence. This is the chance I've been looking for to contribute and now you've given it to me and I love you even more for that! I'm also happy because you have trusted me above all else. I love you, Saga. It's guys like you who give me hope, despite everything.

I'll never betray you. We're only 18 Saga, but even now, I know I'll always love you and I will always stand by you!'

Saga was touched. He knew now that asking Zara was not even what one would call a good gamble. She was a sure bet! He believed in her absolutely. Though what she was going to do was completely dangerous and also meant going against her family, it had not drawn even the slightest hesitation from her. Her logic was pure and simple – she hated violence and she loved Saga, and would thus do everything in her power to further these twin causes of her own, come what may. Zara said she would take advantage of her father's absence and start working on securing the information from that very night.

Zara's agreement to help placed Saga in yet another dilemma. Was there no end to dilemmas? The problem was that Saga wanted this to be a unique and solo Orphan operation. He wanted to present his father and the resistance movement with a *fait accompli*; a done and dusted deal. There was some vanity in this, he knew, but he still wanted it so badly for himself and those who had stood by him. He hoped the Orphans would have the wherewithal to plan and execute such a critical and potentially dangerous operation.

Saga knew that it would be wise of him to approach his father with the information on the munitions dumps once he got it from Zara. That is if Zara could get the vital information in the first place. But taking the info to Nana or to the movement posed even greater problems. They would no doubt insist on knowing the source of the information for corroboration purposes or whatever, and therein lay the crux of the problem. How on earth could he tell them that he had revealed all to the 'enemy' just to secure this information? Not that the information was not critical; it was just that in the present circumstances, they would not go for any explanation along the lines of ends justifying means! Never in a thousand years! They would be appalled. They would most likely even call off the strikes and demonstrations, citing infiltration and betrayal! Infiltration and betrayal caused by him, Saga? Never! That could never ever happen!

The more he thought of the matter, the more he realised he could never tell them, and the more he became troubled and confused! Not even Obo or Kobby would understand if he tried to explain! He had truly boxed himself into a corner!

He would become a pariah!

He would be branded a traitor!

He would be doomed!

Saga tremblingly acknowledged that in all honesty, he had only two options, which were to see Zara and ask her to stop her search, leaving Nana and his sub-committee to ponder their non-solutions, or to take the proverbial bull by the horns and make it a solo Orphan operation! These were certainly not the best options – but they were the only ones available.

Saga knew enough of contemporary history to know that people much younger than him had actually led military units into battle. He had read about some of the liberation movements in other parts of the Third World where even 16-year-olds had served as military commanders in the field. The Viet Cong in Vietnam, the Fretilin of East Timor, the Farabundo Marti National Liberation Front of El Salvador, and the Sandinista National Liberation Front of Nicaragua – which he had read about recently since the Orphan incident – all boasted of routinely using teenagers as field commanders. What of the Child Soldiers in Liberia, Sierra Leone and the Congo in their own Africa? What of the dying children of the Intifada in Gaza and the West Bank in Palestine, who daily faced occupying Israeli guns?

Of course, he did not wish to emulate these young warriors per se, as he was not about to engage in actual warfare. He only thought about them to draw inspiration from their youthful involvement in such weighty matters. If people younger than him could be military commanders then what stopped him and his mates from planning and executing an operation that would limit the Regime's capabilities of inflicting violence, thereby saving lives in the process?

Saga surmised that it would be criminal not to do anything about this problem once he was in possession of the information/intelligence from Zara. Thus, he did not really have a choice

– he was going to have to go with the solo Orphan operation. But this was nobody's idea of a joke. It was an extremely serious matter, which could go horribly wrong. His planning had to be impeccable. He had to select the best and the bravest of the Orphans. He knew he would have an endless supply of eager volunteers who were looking for adventure, and who would pour total scorn on the dangers involved. Everyone wanted to be a hero. But it was not as simple as that. He needed cool heads, closed mouths, lion hearts and steady hands, as his friend, Major Kata, was wont to say!

Furthermore, he also had to come up with some non-combustible modus operandi to destroy the Regime's weapons of destruction. Worse than all that, he also realised that he and those whom he selected for the mission may not come out of it alive. This was seriously getting out of hand! But Saga knew that he would rather face death than be branded a traitor! Once the mission was successfully accomplished, he would tell his family and the opposition people the truth and he would ultimately be exonerated. He had long learned in his youthful life that unqualified success had a way of tampering with people's memories and opinions. He would certainly be forgiven for his indiscretions, his solo wildcat operation, and what would be viewed as his potentially lethal recklessness! Success was his only option!

Finally, Saga knew he could not plan this operation alone. However, it was absolutely crucial that he kept his cards very close to his chest for as long as was possible and feasible. Who could he plan this with? His closest pal, Ibrahim? No, Ibrahim may not be able to hold on to the secret for so long. It was not that he was a blabber mouth. Never! He would simply not be able to handle the pressure of keeping such a weighty secret. There was only one person it could be: Zara.

Another matter that was plaguing him was the fact that he had been compelled by circumstances and stern admonitions to keep so much from his bosom friend, Ibrahim. They always did everything together since they were kids and practically had no secrets between them. Ibrahim had also proved to be his most ardent supporter and ally in the entire Orphan business at their school. He felt he should at least tell him about Zara, which was a matter that was very dear to his heart. Thus, Saga decided to tell Ibrahim about Zara, but not about her helping the opposition cause. How could he? It would also mean revealing his limited participation with the resistance steering committee, which he was absolutely forbidden to do.

* * *

Saga and Ibrahim were walking home from their school library when Saga nervously said, 'Ibrahim, I need to discuss something important with you. It's to do with a woman.'

Ibrahim answered smugly. 'Ah Saga, my boy, look no further afield for advice pertaining to the fair sex, for here stands before you a master of the game in these matters. Unburden your soul and let this master guide you. And yes, woman matters are always important.'

Ibrahim was surprised when Saga did not smile or laugh at his light-hearted response. Instead, he got a stern, 'Stop messing around, Ibrahim, this is serious. And it's top secret. It can't get out.' Abruptly, Saga switched to Pidgin English as if to emphasise the conspiratorial nature of what he was about to reveal. 'It's dat Zara girl. I de love her too much. When I see her, I de confuse.'

Ibrahim automatically replied, also in Pidgin. 'Eii, you mean dat Zara Yalley? De one and only Zara Yalley? And you love her so much dat you confuse if you see her?'

'Yes, de same beautiful Zara Yalley.'

'Eii na dis one is too big a matter for even woman expert like me, Saga.' Ibrahim was indeed so shocked that he quickly resorted to English language proper. 'Saga, are you out of your mind? Oh Allah save us, but what the hell is this about? Zara Yalley, of all people? Of course, she is soooo fine, but this is serious can of worms we are talking about here.'

Saga, however, persisted in Pidgin. 'Worms or no worms, I de love dis girl too much. She now enter for my soul and notin' in dis world can stop dis true love I get for ma heart. If I leave her, I go die. Dis one bigger than Romeo na Juliet, for real.'

Ibrahim persisted in English language proper as this was too serious a matter to trifle with in Pidgin. 'Saga, stop with this Pidgin nonsense. You sound like you are already seeing her and you did not tell me, your mainest man? *Wallahi*, but if this gets out, it'll be a nuclear megaton bomb. The Chief Orphan dating the twin sister of his arch rival, Prince Junior Yalley, who is hated so much by all your followers? The Chief Orphan dating the daughter of the monstrous, murdering and universally loathed General Yalley? So what were you thinking, Saga, and why did you not consult with me before making this disastrous move?'

Saga switched to English proper. 'Ibrahim, let's stop walking for a minute. I want you to hear me properly. I could have continued hiding this from you but you're my bosom friend and it wouldn't be right. Your own reaction right now answers your own question as to why I did not consult you. You know in your heart, this girl is kosher. You told me yourself after the market scene that she was not like her brother. You even said this one didn't even need "Botox for bums", remember? Why must we visit the sins of her father and foolish Yalley Junior on her? And I seriously love her with all my being.'

Ibrahim looked at his best friend for some time and said, 'I see you really love her and yes, I have heard she is very kind. Saga, everything you have said about not visiting this sin and that Yalley sin on her is true, but so what? I love you man, but I can't pretend everyone is gonna understand like I am trying to do here. Everyone will say either you have betrayed us or you will eventually betray us by hanging out with her, and you also bloody well know I am right!'

'Yeah, you're right. So, what do I do, Ibrahim?'

'Bottom line is you can't tell anyone on our side for now. Not even your parents. The situation in this country now is too tense for even them to understand you dating Zara. Wrong timing. Officially, even I can't know about this. In fact, officially, no one can know about this. I am glad you have found true love so early, but you got to keep it a secret like you yourself said. Wow, but you have really nabbed a true beauty. She is the best there is, despite the trouble that is bound to follow her and the serious family baggage she has.'

'You don't think even my open-minded dad will understand?'

'Saga, Zara is not just Yalley's sister, she is his twin sister. The emphasis here is twin. Already, people think twins are weird and there's all kind of superstition surrounding them in Africa and right here in Zimgania. There is all that stuff we've all learnt about mystical bonding and heightened telepathy between twins. Many people will not believe she is not like Yalley Junior deep down or that she will not tell him whatever she learns from you. Many will believe that ultimately, she will betray you and side with her blood.'

This was fast turning out to be the most serious discussion the two friends had ever had.

'But she is not like that, Ibrahim. I can vouch for her'!

'Again, so what Saga? Look at me, Saga, and hear me well. Be practical. Like your mom. They don't know her and they just won't trust her. Her father represents all that is evil in this country. Her father represents all the pain, horror and death associated with Brewman's Regime, so how can you expect our people and their friends and families who have suffered so much to understand? You think Sablon, our own friend, will understand after what they did to his dad, despite your heroics that day? Come on! Think man! Do you get me now?'

This was definitely that serious side of Ibrahim that he rarely showed. Saga marvelled at his friend's shrewdness and analytical mind. Ibrahim was right. His love for Zara and their budding relationship had to remain very secret. The grim reality of their existence heavily militated again flaunting such a relationship amongst their peers and families.

Saga tapped his friend on the shoulder and simply said, 'you're right, Ibrahim. Let's continue walking.' He was glad he had finally discussed this critically important matter with Ibrahim. He was also both glad and heavily disappointed that Ibrahim had arrived at the same unpalatable conclusions that he, Saga, had also arrived at. It proved he was right in keeping Zara a secret from both his peers and family. He wished he was not.

CHAPTER EIGHTEEN

'Eyes Only'

'Why are you walking around looking as though you have impregnated a woman and are terrified that you are going to become a young father?' Saga's mother screeched at him. 'Well, have you?' she persisted.

'Have I what?'

'Impregnated a girl? Why else would you be walking around like that? What is that matter with you anyway? Why won't you eat my peanut soup anymore? You barely eat at my table!'

'I'm fine, Mama. Nothing is the matter. Just some pressing school work I need to finish.'

'I see. Well you could have fooled me,' she retorted, not at all fooled for even one second. Not one to be bested, she resolved to make her husband get to the bottom of it.

So Nana had spoken to Saga, but try as he may, the boy insisted that all was fine. Nana could see this was patently untrue.

'Saga, are you worried about this Orphan business? Are you afraid something may go terribly wrong with the demonstrations we are planning? Are those Princes bullying you in school? But how can that be with all your support in school? What is going on, my son? Since when did you start hiding things from me? What is it? You know you can talk to me, please!'

Worrying about Saga had taken on the dimensions of a full-time occupation, and his words were desperate as he really needed to know why the boy was suddenly so morose!

But Saga remained unmoved. How on earth could he offload his burden onto his father? How could he tell him that he had revealed their most secret plans to the despised General

Yalley's daughter, and that he may soon be leading some of his mates to their death as well as his own?

Saga persisted that all was well.

Nana was forced to give up in frustration. Saga's answers, or rather lack of them, made him even more worried. He needed to keep a close watch on the boy, but how was he to do that with all that was going on and his own extremely demanding central role in the upcoming showdown with the Regime? What was he going to do?

In truth, Saga's burdens were crushing him. But he knew that they were his alone to bear. He was plagued with doubts about whether he was doing the right thing or otherwise in deciding to plan and execute this potentially fatal solo mission. He didn't want to die or cause the death of his friends. He could not sleep at night; he could not eat and was frantic with worry at all times. He even found himself secretly hoping Zara would not come up with the information he needed to act on.

He needed to confide in someone. He needed some reassurance. He needed to know he was not such a terrible person who was about to invite disaster on everyone around him.

There was only Zara.

He would confide in her.

He left home and went in search of her.

Nana had come home a bit earlier than usual, which was a treat for him indeed. His plan was to place a reclining chair under his favourite mango tree in the back garden and indulge in some much-needed rest.

His wife, Aba, was sitting alone at the dining table when he entered. She had done her silky hair in the popular 'corn-roll' fashion and was wearing a brown and muted yellow tie-dye blouse that matched her fair complexion nicely. She was looking very pretty indeed, Nana observed, even though he was exhausted.

She asked him with a welcoming smile, 'How was your day, my husband? You're a bit early. Anyway, how did it go last night at the resistance meeting? Has the Joint Action Committee agreed on a date for the demonstrations?'

Nana replied without much enthusiasm. 'Yes, my dear – it seems the plan is to launch the demonstration around three weeks before the Easter break.'

'So how is your sub-committee doing? Have you found the location of the Zombie weapons dumps? You must be under a lot of pressure to deliver on the front.'

'Yes, you're right. There's no aspect of this entire business that does not involve strident pressure, but I guess that's what we signed up for. As for the sub-committee, we are doing our best.'

Aba's eyes suddenly flashed and her face became very straight, which was an unmistakable giveaway that her temperature was soaring. She was becoming very annoyed with her husband. 'Nana – who do you think you're talking to here? Why do you keep answering my questions with meaningless generalities? What am I? Suddenly, I am some clueless bimbo in your eyes who has to be fobbed off with rubbish answers?'

'Aba, please, not now. This is no time for anger. Emma is upstairs and please don't start. Not with all that is going on.'

Aba, however, ignored her husband and continued, 'Nana, you have been my husband for a quarter of a century and I respect and love you very much, and I always will. But this nonsense must stop now. You walk on eggshells around me. You no longer discuss anything substantive with me pertaining to the resistance. You never go into details as to the progress being made in fighting this decree and my question is WHY? What have I done to deserve such disrespect? And it is worse coming from you of all people; someone as enlightened and progressive as you! How dare you? How dare you treat me this way when my husband and both my sons are at the forefront of this madness we all find ourselves in? Or you think Obo and Saga belong to you alone? Every time any of you step out of this house, waves of fear go through me to the point of near paralysis because I know what can happen at any moment and that none of you are safe in any way!'

Nana knew he had to stop her then before her anger escalated further. 'Aba – enough! You have said your piece. Now calm down and listen, okay? Are you ready to hear me out?'

Aba calmed a bit and nodded to her husband to continue.

Looking somewhat contrite, Nana decided to say it as it was, as it was not in his nature to be disingenuous. 'Aba – I am ashamed of myself because you are right. Keeping things from you when you have been my backbone and the glue that has kept this marriage and family together for 25 years is insulting indeed and I am deeply sorry. Please understand that maybe I don't always do this consciously. I believe that probably because I know of the terror embedded in your heart for the safety of your family and friends, I may have subconsciously been keeping things away from you in an effort to lessen your burdens. But like I said – unconsciously or not – that is not the right way and you have my word that henceforth, I will keep you fully in the loop.'

'Yes Nana, please do. Being kept in the dark and knowing that important issues are deliberately being withheld from you in this volatile situation only increases the terror you mentioned. Yes, I am worried. Yes, I yearn for a less turbulent life. And yes, I wish my family members were not at risk every day, fighting against a brutal dictatorship. But I can handle it. I know my own family. I know what I also signed up for. Ultimately, never forget that the fact that because I do not attend your meetings now does not mean this is also not my struggle. Come here and give me a hug before I go upstairs to see what Emma is doing. I am in need of a warm hug from my overprotective husband,' she ended with a smile.

Nana hugged his wife whom he deeply loved and respected so much. How could he have forgotten how tough she was?

Zara was shocked at Saga's appearance when he arrived at her house. It was as though he had aged overnight. He looked dreadful.

Saga laid bare his soul to Zara. He told her everything. He told her why he could not confide in his father or even his brother, Obo; his criminal negligence if he did nothing about the information once it came; his incapacity to plan and execute the operation if it came to that; and his belief that his attempt would lead to certain death for himself and his mates!

Zara heard him out. She did not speak for a while. And then she was ready. 'Saga, my love, your problem is a very big one. Sorry. My mistake. I meant *our* problem. There is no easy way out for us. We cannot sit back and let the Zombies mow down the people, and you cannot go to your father with what I get to help the movement. You also can't go to your brother. They'd never understand. You're right about that. We don't have a choice. We've got to act. In the books, they call it having the courage of one's convictions. Not to act will be the worst thing we can do. The greater sin will be for us not to try. I'll help. I'll think of a way, and we will not die. No one will die – I promise you this. You are brave, Saga. And I am also brave. Being a woman does not mean I should be afraid. Some of us are braver than you men. We will succeed, Saga. You must have faith in us. I give you my word – we will succeed.'

All this was said with such quiet conviction that Saga sat up in amazement. Where did this girl get her guts? Why was she not afraid? She was really something else! Her unwavering conviction had instantly infected Saga. Somehow, he believed her. Somehow, they would win! Together, they were unbeatable!

He told her all this. She was happy. They were happy. But first she wanted him to sleep. She was not taking no for an answer. His protests were feeble enough. She lay by him and placed his head on her bosom.

He slept while she thought.

Their courage and determination were admirable, even though their circumstances were exceedingly distressful. They were practically children who were being forced to grow up ahead of their time; they were being frog-marched into an uncertain adulthood while leaving plenty of their youth behind on the way. Would they ever have the opportunity to be young again? Or would they become cynical and world-weary before they had even had the chance to grow up? The Regime had much to answer for.

* * *

A week later, Zara was still in search of actionable intelligence for Saga and the opposition.

It had not been an easy assignment for her. The General kept his study locked at all times and always had the key on his person. How was she to gain access, short of breaking the door? She soon remembered, however, that while her mother was alive, she always kept a bunch of housekeeping keys, which had the spares of all the keys to every door in the house. She had to locate those keys. Her mother's belongings were in storage in the basement, so she spent an entire night looking through the assortment of knick-knacks her mother had accumulated during her lifetime. Eventually, she found the bunch and thus, the spare key to the study. The General, who was also a Security Czar in their country, had been singularly lax in this matter!

Night after night, she waited for Yalley Junior to go to bed before locking herself up in the study to conduct her search. She painstakingly went through her father's innumerable and at times voluminous files up until the early hours of the morning. She barely had any sleep during the period of her search. Some of what she read made her recoil in anger and revulsion, and made her even more determined to help Saga and his resistance people. She also filed away in her mind a lot of useful information that she was sure could help them at some point. The information she so desperately needed to find was, however, proving elusive. She was starting to panic, as her father was due back from his travels any day soon.

She hit pay dirt the very morning he was due to arrive. She was by then quite frustrated and saddened by the prospect of failure. She had looked everywhere and the information was just not there! What was she going to tell Saga? How were they going to sabotage the weaponry of the Zombies without this information? She was frantic. Her brother would be waking up soon and her father could arrive any minute. She was wildly looking around the large room, lined with shelves with multitudes of files and books on them, praying for a last-minute miracle of sorts, when she spotted something behind the curtains that hung behind her father's officious-looking swivel chair.

She walked around his desk, came behind the chair, and carefully prised the curtains apart. Perched there unobtrusively was a tan leather briefcase. Would she have time to look through all its contents, as it appeared to be rather bulky and heavy? Yet to stay any longer in the study was too dangerous. She decided to gamble. She let herself out quickly, locked the door and took the briefcase to her bedroom. She had just locked her own door when she heard Yalley Junior emerging from his room and rudely shouting to one of the housemaids to bring him his tea tray followed by some breakfast. He was shouting that he was to be served the proper Twining's Earl Grey tea from England and not common Lipton Tea, which was for peasants.

Zara knew she was going to have to skip school that day in order to rifle through the briefcase to see what it had to offer. She was quite beside herself with anguish when she heard the crunching of her father's car tyres on the gravel that covered the driveway. She prayed, as she had never done before, that he did not venture into his study or that he did not notice the missing briefcase even if he went in. She put her ear to her bedroom door, listening to the comings and goings of both Yalley Senior and Junior. Soon, she heard her brother shouting out for her.

'Hey Zara – where are you? We are getting late and the driver is ready to take us! Where are you? I'll leave you behind at this rate! Aren't you the one who is always going on about early birds and early this and early that? Hurry up and come out now! What is it with you women anyway?'

Zara stuck her head out of her door. 'I'm not going to school today. I'm not well. Just go and stop shouting like some uncivilised maniac! Earl Grey tea indeed! Just leave me alone, you bully!'

Yalley, however, did not stop shouting. 'Daddy, Zara is trying to play truant and she has the nerve to call me uncivilised and a bully. A goody-goody like her missing school? What next?'

It was the General's turn to shout. 'Hey Zara – what is this nonsense about not going to school? Nobody has told me you

197

have been unwell since I got back – so why are you not going? What is the matter with you? Hurry up and get down here!'

Zara could not help but join in this uncivilised shouting match to get her point across. 'Female problems, Daddy! I don't feel well at all. It's that time – when it's not supposed to be. Something is wrong!'

The General was most certainly not about to enmesh himself in what he perceived to be unsavoury female plumbing problems. He did not need that this morning.

'Ah, I see. Okay then. Junior, just go on without her. Let her stay in her room. Off you go! Zara, call the people downstairs if you need anything. I'm late for the office.'

The General took off without entering his study. Zara used up a considerable part of the entire morning to painstakingly sift through the contents of the case and finally found what she was looking for in a file that was marked 'Top Secret – STRICTLY Eyes Only'. She had actually come across many files marked 'Secret' and 'Top Secret' but 'STRICTLY Eyes Only' was something quite new. She wondered as to whose 'Strict Eyes' alone. Probably the General's. Though exhausted from the emotions and exertions she had undergone, and despite her lack of sleep, she was nonetheless quite ecstatic that 'Eyes Only' had delivered what she was looking for at long last! Now, all she had to do was return the briefcase after she had made copious notes.

She slipped back into the study and carefully placed the briefcase exactly where she had found it. It was now approaching lunchtime. She quickly exited and had just finished locking the study door when she beheld her father's most trusted bodyguard, Warrant Officer Rockson, climbing the stairs towards her! She was too dumbfounded to move. What was this stroke of bad luck?

Had he seen her leave the study? This was not good. She kept the bunch of keys tightly in her fist behind her back and fervently hoped that they would not jingle. 'Err, err... W.O., what are you doing here? May I help you?' she queried politely.

'Good day, young madam. Please, Minister General has sent me with his key to pick up his briefcase. Are you from your father's study? He told me it was locked. Maybe he forgot!'

She needed to think fast. And she did. 'No, no – it's always locked. I was just looking at all the doors. It's these helpers. They never clean the doors. I keep telling them that Daddy does not like dirt in any form. Please send one of them up on your way down to come up and clean. That is what they are paid to do – no?'

'You are right, young madam. They are all lazy. Don't worry, I shall go and give them a blasting! Your father is lucky to have you. Don't mind those useless maids and steward boys at all. Left to me, we would take them all to the barracks and give them a good dose of military drilling. There, they will smell hot pepper and that should make them see sense!'

She thanked him and left him to go about his business of retrieving the briefcase, shouting at servants and fantasising about drilling them at the barracks. What a brute, she thought. They were all the same, these Zombies! But that was close! She hated the way she had had to feign disapprobation towards the maids and steward boys, as she was always kindly and considerate towards the help. But that had been her only way out. She dropped those thoughts and, lying on her bed, gave in to the much-needed sleep that soon engulfed her.

* * *

The intelligence community that serviced the Regime was worried. Something was afoot and they did not know what it was. The uneasy calm that had gripped the main cities was unusual. Too many things were unusual. For example, there had been hardly any of the anticipated public reaction against the National Service decree from the university student bodies that were usually very vocal and quite unafraid. The workers had also not reacted. Neither had the professional associations reacted. This was too much of a coincidence and everyone knew that one of the fundamentals of intelligence gathering or spying for that matter was never to trust in coincidence.

Commander Musu was indeed becoming very nervous. He presided over the intelligence community as boss of the notorious Bureau of National Research (BNR). This benignly pompous name fooled nobody. Every man, woman and child knew that the BNR was made up of official spies and brutal para-military types whose fundamental responsibility was to use any means necessary to keep the Regime in power. They were practically unaccountable to anyone and had been given wide-ranging powers by the paranoid President. Many who had been guests in their cells had simply vanished. To the general population, BNR stood for Bureau of No Return!

No aspect of government interested Field Marshal Brewman more than security. He was known to doze off during cabinet meetings held to discuss issues such as the economy, education etc., punctuating said meetings with his loud, unfettered snoring. He had neither an interest nor much of a clue about such matters. Security was all-important, his security for that matter – end of story! And that was also why General Yalley was profoundly powerful as Minister for Presidential Affairs. After all, the only 'Presidential Affair' that really mattered to the President was security and security alone!

Commander Musu knew very well what his Master's priorities were, which was why he was so nervous. He had recently been appointed to this position and was desperate to please and show his worth. The previous boss of the intelligence community, his predecessor, though a thoroughly oppressive and mean character, was less complacent and more discerning than most members of the Regime's top brass. He had therefore cautioned against the introduction of the National Service decree. He advised it was counter-productive and tantamount to shooting one's self in the foot! He had been promptly hurled out of his office and banished to some remote corner in the Northern Territories, and placed under house arrest for his efforts. Musu did not want to share his ex-boss' fate by under-performing, or telling too much of the truth for that matter.

But he was still in trouble. The Minister for Presidential Affairs, the feared General Yalley, acting on the direct orders of President Brewman, was demanding an immediate up-to-date intelligence report on the state of the country's internal security. They also wanted intelligence reports on what the opposition had been up to since the announcement of the National Service decree. The problem was that the Commander had nothing to report. He was himself quite mystified as to the silence that had engulfed the communities. It was as though the opposition had successfully cast a blanket over the flow of information in the communities. He was facing what could only be termed as 'information blackout'.

It was also as though many of the informants the BNR relied on had taken a lengthy sabbatical from spying and informing. He had personally pressured a few of them without results. They all seemed terrified of talking but he did not know why. All the 'tails' he had put on suspected leaders of the opposition had been somehow flushed out and beaten quite soundly by the opposition's own counter-intelligence operatives. Some had since retired from being 'tails'. They claimed it did not seem to augur well for life and limb these days, despite the seemingly appreciable levels of remuneration. It was just not worth the associated woe!

Commander Musu had some serious thinking to do and a report to write. Maybe he would get lucky. Just maybe…

Commander Musu was not the only one struggling with lack of intelligence,

Nana's team was still bereft of the vital intelligence needed to fashion a credible plan to destroy the armouries. There were practically no sympathisers left within the core of the Regime or in Government to come to their assistance. All those suspected of having sympathetic leanings towards the opposition had long since been purged from the circles of power and influence. Many had fled the country or had been hounded out of it and were now living in exile.

This posed a serious problem indeed.

Already, some of the leaders led by Pappy and the workers' leader, Mr Kamson, had called for a debate to consider the possibility of calling off the entire mass action until such a time as the necessary intelligence could be obtained. At the meeting of the Joint Action Committee to debate the matter, they argued that the possible casualties that could result from a full-scale attack on the demonstrators by the Regime were too horrific to contemplate. They simply did not wish to lead their people to the slaughter!

'Although I sympathise with what our veteran, Pappy, and Mr Kamson are saying, the issue of halting the action is not really an option, since any delay would see the enforcement of the forced conscription of our children into Brewman's wars. Once the conscription commences, these youthful victims would be given very minimal training and shipped to the war front to meet their death. The casualties in such a case would be even more unacceptable. Also, once the enforcement starts, it would be all the more difficult to halt,' Nana forcibly argued.

The group was mixed in their opinions. Nana's team argued further that since they still had a few more weeks before the 'action' began, it was probably premature to talk about calling off the entire operation.

'I assure you, my team is still working on the problem. I'm sure the situation will change in our favour very soon,' he appealed to Pappy and his followers.

Nana reckoned he needed to give them something positive and so shared his committee's latest idea.

'We are thinking of contacting some of our more influential sympathisers in Europe and America and asking them to place the international media on alert regarding what we are planning here. Of course, the timing of it is crucial, since we don't wish the Regime to have sufficient notice to plan a counter operation against us. Once the international media is primed and we become a focus of attention, Brewman will hesitate in employing all the force at his disposal in full glare of international cameras. Of course, he'll block reporters from the major channels, but those that slip through the net will be enough for us. It's about time we drew increasing attention to the horrors we are facing here.'

This was met with nods of approval from the crowded room.

'To internationalise our struggle is to attract more sympathisers to our cause, while attracting more outside opposition to this brute of a president who has usurped power! Another factor, which could very well work in our favour, is the anticipated presence of these Orphans during the march. You see – it is one thing to send troops charging into the midst of demonstrating university students-cum-workers, and quite another matter to brutalise schoolchildren. The Regime could never play it down if they launched a full-frontal attack on these kids. Never! But please don't misunderstand me. Surely, I know it's better to be safe than sorry. I also know that Brewman is an unpredictable paranoid maniac – international cameras or none. As such, please rest assured that we will do all in our power to come up with a way to destroy those weapons.'

Even Pappy nodded his head in approval. Trust Nana to get to the heart of the matter without being showy. He knew why he admired this man so much.

The group in the main agreed with Nana's international dimension analysis. Brewman was getting away with murder because of insufficient international focus on their country and the true nature of their problems. Brewman had to be made to feel the heat from outside as well as inside. They had to force the issue of their country onto the international stage! Nana's sub-committee was authorised to lose no time in bringing their sympathisers overseas up to speed and to seek their necessary assistance to globalise their dire internal oppression at the hands of a frenzied and remorseless dictator!

CHAPTER NINETEEN

Spider Vibrations

Now that Zara was in possession of the vital intelligence needed to destroy the weapons of destruction, she knew they had very little time to put a plan into effect. Too much depended on it. They could not fail, and thus, they would not fail! But where to start? She needed to get together with Saga immediately so they could begin. She sent him a text message from her mobile phone.

Saga had been having a particular problem at home for the past couple of weeks. Zara had given him a mobile phone to use so they could be in touch at all times. She had insisted it was necessary, given the critically important nature of the job in hand. She also maintained that constant communication was one of the key fundamentals of sustaining true love. Due to her father's position, expensive gadgetry such as mobile phones were easy for her to come by.

Saga was not in the least averse to having a mobile phone. It was one of his dreams to own a new one, and Nana had promised to get him one for his next birthday. He didn't want one simply because it was a status symbol. The Princes, for example, were constantly brandishing their mobile phones about the place whenever the opportunity presented, showing off their exulted lifestyles! He wanted it because he was fascinated by wireless technology and often marvelled as to how these phones kept getting smaller and smaller with the passing years. The early mobile handsets were rather fearsome-looking with their bulkiness, and had at times reminded him of truncheons that one put to one's ear. He also thought that they were most convenient to have.

Though he agreed with Zara as to the necessity of having one for the operation and its added utility for their blossoming love, he nonetheless knew he would have major problems at home trying to explain the existence of a mobile phone among his possessions! He explained this to Zara, who remained unmoved and persisted adamantly, 'Extraordinary times call for extraordinary measures, Saga. All you have to do is keep it out of sight and put in on vibration alert mode.'

'Vibration what? What is that?' he asked, rather dazed at this new terminology.

'Oh Saga, you are really quite retro. All you have to do is turn off the ringer and activate the function that makes the phone vibrate when you have a call or text message instead of it ringing noisily. If it's in your pocket and I call, you'll feel the vibration and then you can either move away from your parents to answer the call or wait and call me back as soon as convenient. Never mind, I'll show you how it's done. Mind you, I'm not asking you to deceive your parents. I would never do that. It's just that this operation is too important for us not to always be in touch. One day, they will understand when you explain it to them. Don't forget that if we succeed, they will also forgive you for coming to ask me for help and letting me into some of your resistance secrets!'

Saga yet again succumbed to her flawless reasoning. He consoled himself with the thought that presently, the cause was certainly more important than just making his parents unaware that he had a mobile phone. She was right again. What was it she said? Yes – extraordinary times! Bring on the mobile!

Saga's agreement to hold on to the mobile phone was what engendered his 'jerky' phase, which caused his parents to believe that either their son was either possessed of some rare ailment or was actually 'possessed' in spiritual terms!

Being quite unaccustomed to the sensations produced by the vibrations of the hidden phone in his pocket and also being of a very ticklish disposition, Saga inadvertently took to breaking into startling jerks whenever Zara called. His mother was deeply disturbed when she first beheld this unsavoury sight of her son breaking into a series of rather disturbing body spasms for no apparent reason. She was as alarmed, as any caring mother would be!

'Whatever is the matter with you, Saga?' she asked with grave concern. 'Are you having an epileptic fit or what? How can this be – when there is no epilepsy in this family? Is it not hereditary or something like that?' she wondered aloud.

Not expecting his mother to walk into the room when she did, just as the call came through, and being startled a whole lot more by the shrillness in her voice, Saga reflexively accomplished a few more spasmodic jerks before summoning his wits to reply. 'Oh, it's nothing, Mama. I think a spider or something may be crawling under my shirt. Nothing to worry about!'

'Spider? What spider? Since when did we get spiders in this house? Come here and let me find this spider myself and dispose of it! Take off your shirt and come here!'

Luckily, Saga was able to resist her 'spider search and destroy mission' at the time, much to his relief.

But his relief did not last long. Through some diabolical twist of fate, Zara often called when he was in his mother's presence. After witnessing a few more of Saga's sudden and most distressing spasmodic, jerky break-dancing, she was compelled to flee to her husband in a state of panic. Moreover, Saga's excuses, which had graduated from spiders and now covered a range of insect species crawling over his body at odd times and with alarming frequency, had utterly convinced her of her son's urgent need of medical attention! To add to this was the equally disturbing phenomenon of having heard him a few times ostensibly talking to someone in a room, only to find him very much alone upon entering! Something was hopelessly wrong with her younger son! Something had to be done!

'Nana – our son is not well! You must do something. He has become jerky and is suffering from some kind of epileptic fit. He's also been conversing with himself and sees himself fighting with all kinds of different insects, some of which I didn't even know existed in this country! He needs help, Nana. Please do something. Today! It's all this pressure! How can they put a young boy through all this? Oh how I hate this

Government for what they are doing to our babies! The boy can't take the pressure. He must be examined straight away. They should check both his head and body, okay! Should I go and bring him? Don't forget that I said both head and body!'

Nana was quite puzzled to see his usually calm and practical wife enter into this state of frenzied hysteria over a rather normal-looking Saga. He could barely understand what she was saying, given the speed at which her words tumbling out. He finally caught on fully. He was nonetheless still puzzled. Surely, if there were something wrong with the boy, he, Nana, would have certainly noticed by now – or…

Anyhow, he needed to calm his wife down all the same. 'Please calm down, Aba. Our son is quite normal, as far as normal goes. As a teenager, with his hormones all over the place, how can he not jerk a bit from time to time? Boys of his age are fidgety. Maybe it's a growth spurt. As for this talking to himself, he may be learning some lines for school. I must admit that I'm quite baffled about this armada of insects coming out of nowhere, but I'm sure I'll soon find a rational enough explanation for that.

'Please leave it for now while I observe him a bit more closely myself. You need to rest a bit yourself. As a loving wife and devoted mother, I know you are terribly worried about your sons and husband and our involvement with all that is going on – though you try very hard not to show it for our children's sake. I too am beside myself with worry. But what can we do? Leave it to me – okay? Saga will be fine.'

Though not fully convinced of her son's normalcy, Saga's mother decided to give it a rest for now, though she promised herself to be extra vigilant on her poor son and his mysteriously acquired body gyrations!

As for Saga, he quickly fled the moment he heard his mother deliver her verdict on the necessity of having his head and body examined. He had absolutely no plans to participate in any such unpalatable project with him as guinea pig! But he knew he had to come clean about the phone very soon, before he caused his mother to either faint or before she forcibly had him dragged off to some unsavoury mental asylum!

He went off to the underground press, which had been set up on Uncle Tiger's land for the purpose of publishing resistance leaflets and posters, where the prospect of hauling and packaging vast quantities of 'illicit' literature had a lot more appeal than what his mother had in mind for him!

Such was the saga of Saga's mobile phone-induced domestic tribulations.

As they had arranged via text message, Saga went to see Zara soon after a hectic jerky afternoon at the underground presses, sorting out the clandestine literature that was to be soon circulated. He was very tired but said that tiredness was a luxury he could not afford at this moment.

Zara disagreed.

Tired people made avoidable mistakes. That was even more of an unaffordable luxury! She was not having it. She insisted he sleep for an hour at least.

He slept.

She gently shook him after an hour.

He slowly came back.

'Now go into my bathroom and wash your face with cold water. That should do the trick. I need you alert. We've much to do.'

He obediently did as he was told. Zara did not look like she was in a mood to be trifled with. She was all business. As such, his hopeful thoughts of rolling around with her on the bed and kissing and fondling for a few minutes to get him in the mood had to be regretfully abandoned for now. She was looking rather stern as she quickly scanned her notes.

'I've got the information, Saga. It wasn't easy to get, but that's not important. There are two major dumps in this city – one is Fort Id in Sandy Town, the other is Fort Brewman on Brewman Boulevard. They are on opposite sides of the city. But we all know those areas. Everyone's been there. They are not so heavily guarded because they believe no one knows about them, apart from a few ministers and security chiefs. That is good for us. Now we need to plan. I have some ideas. Are you ready?'

Saga looked at her with his mouth agape! He could not believe what he was hearing! This girl was the real deal. Look at her, sitting there delivering such vital information so coolly as if it was normal, everyday, mundane info! And look at how she had so confidently taken over! This beautiful, almost shy girl was something else!

In response to her question as to whether he was ready, Saga jumped off the bed, yanked her off the table she was perched on, and gave her a huge bear hug and started doing a now voluntary break-dance! 'Are you great or what? Zara, you are unbelievable. You're awesome! You're the bomb!' he bellowed.

'Be serious, Saga. And stop shouting. You know my father is back. We're dead if he catches us here! You really think I'm the bomb? Sounds good but who's a bomb? Not someone who blows up things, I hope!'

'No, you silly girl! Who's retro now? Bomb means you're "it"! As in, you are the best! Wow girl, I just love you! Thanks ever so much, Miss Life-Saver!'

'Okay Saga, I'm the bomb, so please settle and let's get this thing done before this bomb detonates all over you!'

She became serious again. Saga composed himself becomingly to match her mood switch. She explained what had to be done initially. Firstly, they had to 'recce' the sites – which was military lingo for having to do some reconnaissance to ascertain what went on there, exactly how many guards etc. It was like a sneaky fact-finding mission. They could not just go in blind. That was senseless. It was only when they knew what went on in those places could they fashion a plan. But the two of them could probably not do it alone – so it meant they also had to start recruiting those who would be on the mission with them. This had to be done now. There was absolutely no time! She wanted to know if Saga already had some people in mind for the operation.

Saga suddenly jerked. He had imagined a vibration from his phone.

'Saga – you really have to try and get used to this vibrating thing. From what you told me, your mother already thinks you are going mad from all the pressure and your imaginary insects!

Soon, you'll be getting a lot more calls when you hear what I've done for the team you're putting together. Are you going to be jerking all over the place during your mission to give your position away when you get a call? Try and get used to it, Saga, and stop break-dancing all over the place.'

Saga said he would apply himself with all the diligence he could muster to divest himself of these rather embarrassing jerks that, among other things, was causing his beloved mother needless anxiety!

Zara told him what she had done for their team once it was operational! She had told her father that she needed about ten mobile phones for a school telecommunications project. Her father, who appeared to equate whatever he understood of affection with giving her material things, had simply ordered his personal assistant to 'get on with it' and procure the phones from his office petty-cash funds. That she had told her father a lie of sorts did not bother her very much, as she had come to the conclusion that one either stood for what was right or what was wrong and in this case, her father clearly stood for wrong! After all, she was helping to save lives, she reasoned.

Zara explained to Saga that without the ability to stay in touch, the dangers inherent in their mission increased exponentially, and since it was their aim to come out alive, they were obligated to do all in their power to minimise their risks.

Saga had already given some thought to who the members of the operation ought to be. Though he already had a list of names, there was not much point in discussing the individuals with Zara, as she did not really know them. Saga assured her that these were guys who could be trusted to keep their mouths firmly shut, were unafraid, intelligent, and not prone to rash actions. He would meet them the next day in school to recruit them and brief them as to what needed to be done.

Saga suggested to Zara that, if possible, the first surveillance mission should be done by the two of them that very night, so he would be better informed when briefing the team. Even a drive-by would suffice to give them a better picture of what they would be dealing with. Zara agreed and said she would borrow one of the cars in the house, as she was permitted to drive. It was also too far to cycle. She knew she would not be missed as she was very much left to her own devices. Both her father and brother would definitely be home much later than her. They agreed she would pick him up at one of their old rendezvous points.

Saga left to get ready.

They first went to Fort Brewman. It was easy to locate, as it was an isolated, walled structure on a large tract of land at the end of the town's main thoroughfare towards the sea. They parked some distance away, and initially strolled past the front gate like two young lovers out on an innocent walkabout, away from prying eyes.

The general area looked rather deserted, with a just a handful of guard soldiers milling around the entrance of the fort and chatting with a group of young ladies, who were hawking some snacks. The guards were smoking, and appeared to be laughing at their own sallies, while the ladies giggled in encouragement. The guards appeared to be much more interested in the ladies than in their guard duties. They did not even bother to look at the two young lovers strolling by.

Saga and Zara then walked around the side of the walled compound, away from the guards' line of vision. The side of the Fort was bordered by a weedy patch of land that stretched for about 200 metres towards a rather insecure-looking bridge that crossed one of the insignificant streams that lazily meandered their way across township towards their rendezvous with the sea.

Both Saga and Zara were confident that at that distance, no one in the rickety cars and mini-buses crossing the bridge would be able to recognise them at that time of night. In fact, given the dilapidated state of the bridge, both drivers and passengers were bound to be far more gainfully employed in hoping and praying that they managed to cross the bridge in one piece, rather than in wasting time idly gazing at others on less shaky ground.

The concrete side-wall of the Fort was not very high, though quite thick and solid-looking. Saga knew he had to risk climbing up to peer at what was within the compound. He had become rather seasoned at peering.

He climbed the wall and immediately laid flat on it while he surveyed the compound. What he beheld left him almost breathless. Parked in neat rows were all kinds of military vehicles and other mobile vehicles of oppression – all new-looking and gleaming malevolently in the relatively well-lit compound. The vehicles stretched across the length and breadth of the enormous compound and were far too many for Saga to even attempt counting.

From what he had seen on TV, in real life and also in magazines, he was able to identify some of the vehicles. They ranged from Armoured Personnel Carriers (APCs), MOWAGS, state-of-the-art armoured tanks with their caterpillar-like wheels and lethal-looking mounted guns, riot-control water cannon vehicles, ambulances decked in olive green military colours and red crosses, PINZGUARS, Mobile Command Vehicles and a few others he simply did not recognise.

'Saga, hurry. You are spending too much time on the wall,' Zara whispered urgently.

He looked around quickly to see if there were any other guards in the compound and, seeing none, hopped off the wall. He landed silently. Hurriedly, they made their way back to the main road, where they paused to assume their original nonchalant lovers' pose as they walked past the guards, who were still too preoccupied with their female audience to take any notice of them.

They got to the car and decided to go back home because Zara thought it best to have the car parked before her father and tattling brother got home. They would do the other weapons dump site on the other side of town the next day. Saga briefed Zara in the car on everything he saw.

'So this is what the taxpayers' hard-earned currency is spent on! Not to educate more people or build more hospitals to combat growing mortality rates from preventable diseases, but rather to acquire such vast arrays of vehicular instruments of violence to hold the people down.' Zara was appalled.

'Yes, and so scantily guarded!' added Saga.

'It's a glaring manifestation of the Regime's arrogance and complacency. Brewman and his henchmen like my dad are so sure that they have the general population so thoroughly cowed by their brutality that none would dare venture near such equipment!'

'Well, like many a totalitarian regime before them, they feel truly indestructible, which gives us an advantage,' Saga said smugly.

Before dropping Saga at the corner of his street to go home, Zara told him to hold off on telling the boys he intended to recruit about the exact nature of the operation.

'Tell them that though it'll be dangerous, they'll be saving lives and they'll also become heroes eventually. Tell them you'll soon reveal what the targets are. I think we can do this "recce" business by ourselves. I've an idea I want us to discuss with you once we've also seen the other place tomorrow. And we both know that it's best to reveal as little as possible for now, to prevent any unintended leaks. I read a little military history last night from my father's collection and found out that all the great generals, such as Julius Caesar and Napoleon, always kept their true plans to themselves until the last possible moment. Consider yourself General Saga for this operation!'

* * *

The next day was very hectic for Saga. He was fully charged on adrenaline and set to work the moment he arrived at school. He knew he had a long day ahead, as he had decided to meet those he had selected individually. As far as he could manage, Saga did not want the members of the mission to know about each other until the last possible moment. This was a security measure Zara told him to adopt, which she had picked from a spy-thriller. It made a lot of sense to him, for obvious reasons. He looked at his list again. They were all section leaders of the Orphan club. He decided to leave his best friend, Ibrahim, for later, as they always walked home together, and meet all the others first. He had nine clandestine meetings in all to accomplish!

The school was still in an unsettled state. The announcement of the National Service decree, with its forced conscription agenda bound to affect many students, had not helped matters since the precipitating Orphan incident. Most of the students were instinctively aware that something quite serious and imminent was about to happen sooner rather than later, though they did not know exactly what it was. They knew from the tension in the wider society and from the little they gathered from their parents that the opposition was not going to give in to the decree without a fight.

Most of the students were now firmly in the camp of the Orphans. All those who had been forced or pretended to support Yalley and his Princes had come to their senses and defected in the wake of the decree announcement. Those who had also been bribed by the Princes for their support had also deserted camp, as their deal with the Princes had not included being shipped to some remote war front to be shot at and probably killed!

The hard-core Princes, having lost the little ground they had initially captured and losing a whole lot of face in the process, were now keeping to themselves. They were nonetheless secretly comforted by the knowledge that if and when it came to a showdown, the Regime would always send in the Zombies. They were thus not too worried, beyond being irked about the loss of face.

The Orphans for their part knew that they would somehow be directly involved in the troubles that were brewing and were thus in a pent-up state of excitement. They were just waiting for it all to explode so they could take off and participate in helping to reverse this decree they had come to hate.

Though the school could not be said to be ungovernable, the headmaster, Mr Money, and his underlings, soon gave up the pretence of trying to bring the routine academic life of the school back on its normal footing. It was of no use. The children had gathered from their friends that it was a similar situation in many of the secondary schools since the decree announcement, and that not much was being done anywhere else either. The focus as far as Money and his staff were concerned was just to keep the students in the classrooms and out of mischief until all the current societal tension exacerbated by the decree played itself out. They were powerless to do more.

In their secret hearts, many of the teachers felt the Regime had gone too far with this forced conscription business. It was a grievous mistake. Yet, many were too scared and spineless to dare say what their true feelings were. Even the sycophantic Money was in a constant state of lamentation these days. Though regretting the Orphan incident, which had brought his school under the spotlight, he knew that it would have all died naturally but for this decree he secretly loathed. Why did the Government have to go and do that? Now, they were all caught up in a scenario that was fast unsettling the cosy world he had built for himself, as well as his having to disgracefully comply with sending children he was training to become lawyers, doctors and PhDs onto the battlefield as mere conscripts. Enmeshed in his own fear, Mr Money shuddered at his subversive thoughts and decided to hold his fear-inspired peace and say nothing of what he truly thought!

Saga met his key Orphans individually as planned. He told them that there was serious work to be done to aid the planned strikes and demonstrations. The work was to take the form of a very secret and dangerous mission, which he was not at liberty to reveal now. But it involved saving lots of innocent lives, and they would become heroes the moment their selfless deeds came to light at the appropriate time.

He explained that there would be 10 of them in all, and also the reasons for individual meetings at this stage. He assured that before the mission, he would meet all who were involved a few more times to go over and perfect whatever plans that were being drawn up as they spoke. They would all have communication equipment in the form of mobile phones. They would all have to dress in black for the mission.

Saga further explained that the mission would be for only one night, though he emphasised again the potential dangers. They could be shot at, they could be arrested, and they could die. He gave them the option of backing out now. It was not compulsory. It was purely voluntary. Charged by the talk of danger, subsequent popularity as heroes, and mobile phones, which they even got to keep afterwards, no one was backing out of anything. They all firmly told Saga so in more or less the same words at their individual meetings. They would wait for his next summons. They would also maintain strict secrecy, as was required.

Saga knew he had achieved a lot in a day and was modestly pleased with himself. He felt even better later on that afternoon when a call from Zara in the presence of his mother had not resulted in any form of break-dancing! He was gradually getting there! All he now needed to do for the day was to help out for a couple of hours at Uncle Tiger's clandestine press before going off to meet Zara for the second night of surveillance.

Zara was already waiting in the car when he got to their appointed place. Saga briefed her about his meetings as they drove along, and he assured her that they had a solid team.

'Saga, you are a true General after all. But a General with a difference – one who is out to save lives and not out to order his troops to kill others. Not like my father,' she had sullenly added.

Fort Id in Sandy Town was an isolated compound, similar to that of Fort Brewman, though not quite as large. It was also walled. To their amazement, there were absolutely no visible guards at the front gate, although they knew there would be some within the compound. Saga again decided to peer from the side-wall.

Inside the compound was very different from the other Fort. There were just a couple of guards smoking and lounging in a wooden security kiosk near the main gate. They appeared to be involved in a discussion, though how they could hear each other above the din of the transistor radio that was blaring out the latest 'Highlife' song with all the atmospheric static it could muster was beyond Saga's comprehension. The compound basically consisted of a series of uniform warehouses, whose doors were secured with some not very secure-looking padlocks, which reminded Saga of the one he used on his school locker.

Also, there were many large barrels of what he presumed to be some type of fuel, arranged on some sturdy-looking sawhorses. Just like in Fort Brewman, there were also vast quantities of sandbags strewn about the place.

This time, Zara wanted to see whatever was there for herself. With Saga's help, she climbed up as soon as Saga got down and also had a look.

They left soon after and were not long in getting back to her place, as Sandy Town was not far off as Fort Brewman. She parked the car and quietly admitted Saga through the side gate, taking care not to alert the dozing guards.

Soon, they were settled in her room.

'Saga, I want you to carefully pay attention to the plan I've thought of. I can tell you straight away that you'll not approve, but we'll come to that later. What you've got to understand is that although we've seen something of the dumps so far, it's simply not enough. There could be more guards in there that we know nothing about, and endlessly peering over those walls may not increase what we know now and we just don't have the time.'

'So I've decided to enter the forts myself as the daughter of General Yalley, in need of some assistance with a flat tyre or some such thing. I can easily identify myself with one of the special passes issued by the Regime to close family members of senior ministers and security chiefs. It gives us access to almost anywhere, and given that my father is one of those who are much feared, those guards on duty will be falling over themselves to help me out. I could act interested in their work, give them big cash tips, and innocently ask them about what goes on there, how many guards etc. Don't say anything now, Saga. Let me finish, please. I know what you are going to say, which is that if we are successful, when they do their post-mortem, they'll know I've been to both places and how would I explain that?'

Saga sighed.

'Not to mention the trouble I'll get into, which we both know will be terrible – but I really don't care about that. What can they do? Shoot me? You can say what you want, Saga, but there is no better plan! Also, I can dress in a very sexy way that will make those silly guards at Fort Brewman drool. Mind you, I am not saying that I'm sexy. I just know what it is that lecherous men look out for!'

Much to her surprise, Saga did not say anything for a while. He just sat there, looking at her. He did not even offer a single protest. It was a good plan, though it guaranteed getting Zara into a boat-load of very serious trouble indeed someday. But somehow, that was not the main focus of his thoughts. Though he knew Zara was completely committed to helping the cause and was generally a very selfless person, he now finally understood that she also had a hidden agenda. This was also a personal crusade for her. He decided to confront her with this new-found insight.

'Zara, you say you love me and I believe you. You are really going out of your way to help the resistance through me, and I'm very grateful for that. But you are hiding something from me and it's about time you came clean. So what is it?'

She knew that despite his youth, Saga was highly intelligent and unusually perceptive. He was certainly no fool. She had always known it was just a matter of time before she would have to confess. Saga was on to her, so it was now time. She did not mince her words.

'If we are successful and I'm caught at the end of it all, my father will be forced to resign. You've figured that out, haven't you? Saga, please understand that my father practically killed my mother, whether he likes it or not. I have never told you this but it was what he turned into after becoming one of Brewman's favourites that drove her to the grave. I know in my heart that she took her life because she could not believe she had married and had children with someone who turned out to be nothing more than an evil, murdering monster.

'Look at the number of people who have vanished so far! Look at those who have been brutalised by the Zombies and are now disabled for life. You think my father is not directly involved? He is not one of those civilian ministers who have little say in such matters. He's a military man who has no regard for the lives of others. Do you know the kind of things

I saw in those files when I went looking? It's even worse than you think! Saga – I beg you not to try and stop me. I have to do this for my mother. I have to. She said something to me on her deathbed that I never fully understood until I met you. Sometimes, when I'm feeling a little superstitious and I'm missing her terribly, I start to think that maybe she sent you to me.'

'What did she say?' he asked quietly.

'She said, "*I know that somehow you will make it all become right.*" And this has puzzled me forever. I came to understand her meaning after I met you and decided to help. I must take the family out of this murdering business, even if it costs me my life. I have to do this, Saga, or she would have died in vain!'

Saga understood. It was the kind of understanding that came from oneness of the soul. This was often described more loosely in popular parlance as 'soul mates'. But what they had he felt transcended that. It ran far deeper than just being soul mates. It was as though some deep, mystical bonding was occurring between them and fusing their souls together in the process. He truly knew that she had to do it and would do it, and he, Saga, would help in any possible way. He told her exactly that. Her depth of feeling for him, coupled with her dread at what needed to be done, simply burst forth in a gush of silent yet shoulder-shaking tears.

Saga knew enough to say nothing.

He simply drew her to him and held her closely for a long time.

CHAPTER TWENTY

Hard-Working Duties

Nana noticed that Saga's earlier depression had left him, but suspected something was nonetheless still amiss. The boy now appeared to be animated but in a subdued sort of way. It was obvious to him that Saga was trying very hard to suppress a great deal of tension borne of impending excitement. Nana knew, without a doubt, that his son was hiding something significant from him. Yet, try as he may, he could not figure out what it could possibly be.

He had noticed Saga did all he was asked to do with diligence and exactitude, but had taken to disappearing from home for lengthy periods of time. Though, of course, he knew that both his sons were very excited about the imminent mass action and were contributing significantly to its ultimate success, he was equally aware that whatever Saga was experiencing was much more than that. However, Nana knew it would be wrong to force whatever it was out of Saga. That could easily backfire and create other tensions. He was nevertheless still uneasy about it all.

For reasons he could not logically fathom, Nana intuitively suspected a direct link between Saga's jerky phase and whatever it was that was causing the current pent-up excitement. Since these were uncertain times, he questioned whether he was being unduly lax in his parental duty by not forcing the issue. How could he, for example, protect him in these extremely turbulent times if he did not know what the child was up to?

He came to the conclusion that Saga had the kind of determination that could resist all degrees of parental interrogation and coercion if it came to it. He knew his son only too well. This conclusion did not ease his distress in any way.

Nana was in despair. He felt the powerlessness of parents when confronted with a potentially intransigent adolescent offspring. Nonetheless, he had to admit that so far, he had been lucky with his children. They were smart, courageous, and yet very respectful of their elders and peers and everyone else. They had not given him serious cause for concern, beyond their recent involvement in the turbulent drama that was unfolding and threatening to swallow them all up. He knew he had to hold his horses, not pester his son, and hope that the young man was sufficiently wise to avoid doing anything rash.

Nana could not help but continue to wonder about this criminal regime that was disrupting their lives in a most destructive manner. He did not even know whether he or any of his sons would be alive in a month or two. How could anyone live their lives this way? This flouted every notion of decent living. It even flouted all fundamental human rights that people aspired to. How could a nation's army be turned against its own peaceful citizens in this day and age in 2004? It was not as though there was some bloody civil war raging across the country!

Were armies not established to defend countries against external aggressors and also to guarantee the territorial borders of a nation? Were he, his sons, their neighbours, families and friends, and all the peaceful citizens in the country, external aggressors by virtue of simply not agreeing with the Government? Were they undermining the nation's territorial integrity or tampering with its borders in some way or another? This was not just becoming unbecoming! It was already horribly unbecoming!

Nana had certainly much to ponder, but for now, he needed to focus on their own situation vis-à-vis their impending opposition action. Well, in that regard, Nana, had come to agree with the dictum that if the mountain would not come to them then they would go to the mountain! With this thought, he resolved to intensify his efforts to place his country's problems firmly on the international agenda. That way, they could hopefully get these self-appointed 'globocops' to finally take out their global-truncheons they had been wielding and bring the likes of Brewman to heel! It was long overdue!

With Saga's blessing, Zara dressed very carefully for her rendezvous with the hopefully lecherous guards at Fort Brewman. She had actually gone out and bought new, sexy clothes. She had been blessed with kind of face and body that could turn any head, and for once, she had no choice but to flaunt her attributes for the cause. She showed just enough cleavage and legs to hold many a heterosexual man literally spellbound.

She picked up Saga at the corner of his street and drove off with him. He was amazed at her stunning beauty and sheer sexiness, and told her so, causing her to blush deeply, though happy to hear such compliments from him in particular. They parked a couple of hundred metres away from the Fort gates, while Saga got down and drove a long nail into the back left tyre of her car. The tyre quickly deflated without too audible a hiss. She left Saga on the street and drove off slowly, with her now rattling tyre. She parked right in front of the gates of the Fort and, as she had hoped, the guards were milling around, as usual, with some lady hawkers they were yet again hosting.

'Hey young woman, you cannot park here! This is a restricted area. And what is that noise coming from your car? Just move away. You can't park here. Go now!' one of the soldiers wearing sergeant stripes barked at her.

She got down and walked a few paces towards them. The effect was instant and their consequent speechlessness gave her the opening she needed.

'Good evening to you all. I'm sorry, sergeant, but I just had a flat tyre and I'm looking for help to change it. Sorry to disturb you. I am Minister General Yalley's daughter. My name is Zara. Please, here is my special ID. I would be very grateful if you could help me.'

They just continued to stare at her. Even the hawkers stared unabashedly with unmasked admiration. *Is this apparition of a stunning angel also the fearsome General Yalley's daughter to boot?*

A fog of confusion enveloped the sergeant's mind. All he could think of for no particular reason was 'action stations!' He knew he had to do something quickly if he was to avoid losing his job, as well as being subjected to other unpalatable rigours. He saw his colleagues were also in shock, if their agape mouths were anything to go by.

He reacted instinctively, stood at attention, and threw her a brisk salute. His other two colleagues recovered to follow their sergeant's example and flourished salutes in unison. They could think of nothing else to do.

'Sorry madam. Very sorry. I did not recognise you at first. Of course, we can help you. Anything for you, madam. Anything at all. We are hardworking guards, madam, and we will show you. We just came out to drive away these hawkers who are disturbing our duties. Of course, this is not a restricted area for you. Would you like to come in? Please do. Hey – you there, open the gate and call the private inside to help you push madam's car into the yard. In fact, call everybody inside. Also, replace the punctured tyre and wash the car. In fact, polish it as well. And you, over there, escort madam inside. On the double, I say! I am coming myself to see to her. As for you women – what do you want here? Go away before I put you in the guardroom. If I catch you here again coming to disturb our hardworking duties, you'll see what I'll do to you! On the double to you as well! Off you go! Sorry madam. Don't mind those hawkers. They have nothing better to do. Please follow me.'

All this was said in a frightful gush. The sergeant was terrified. He did not even bother to look at the ID. Of course she was who she said she was. He had seen her picture in the papers some time ago with her dreaded father. What if she went to report him for being rude or standing outside chatting up those women? He would be finished! Woe, woe and woe! He would surely see the inside of a cell and that would be the mildest of the punishments! *What evil wind has brought this girl here at this time? What at all, eh?* Although he had to admit that she did not look evil at all.

Zara quickly caught on to the sergeant's thinking. She clearly understood why they were terrified. She had them exactly where she wanted! *Hardworking duties indeed!* This was probably going to be a lot easier than she thought. But she knew she also had to keep them a little sweet to make them not clam up.

'Don't worry at all, sergeant. You don't know how lucky I am to have developed this flat tyre in front of your gate. What would I have done if it had happened in the middle of nowhere? Let's go. I'll follow you.'

She followed him through the gate while the others stood gawking at her, totally oblivious to the commands they had been issued.

What she beheld the moment she stepped through the gates took her breath away. It was exactly as Saga had described, though much more overpowering at ground level with the mean-looking machines right in your face! It took a lot of control for Zara not to whistle. But she was savvy enough to know that she should offer some exclamation of surprise, which she did gently, yet noticeably.

After barking fresh orders at the still gawking trio of guardsmen, the sergeant led her into a well-furnished reception room, dominated by a huge, formidable picture of President Brewman. He was in full military regalia, adorned with endless arrays of medals for some inexhaustible 'in the line of duty' achievements he must have dreamt up. The sergeant put on the air-conditioning and stood at attention, very uncertain as to what to do next.

Zara took over. She had to do that or remain there forever. She asked him to sit – which he did quite awkwardly at the edge of one of the chairs. If there had been a way for him to sit at military attention, he would have gladly done it. She expressed her gratitude yet again for his help and gradually drew him into a conversation. He was soon under her charm and was spilling out his guts to all her gentle enquiries. He gratefully told her the number guards on duty at any given time, when their shifts were changed, what went on during the day. He even told her they had been warned that they would soon be put on a 'state of high alert', as the Government was sure that there would be some bad disturbances soon. He repeatedly added that he was a very hard worker, and finally praised her father copiously for good measure.

Zara herself was equally effusive in praise of their assistance to her. She assured that she would let her father know of their help in her hour of need, as well as how hardworking they were. Indeed, it was people like them who were the backbone of the Regime, and she would return, with her father's permission, to reward them well. She collected their names, the phone number at the guard post, and promised to call them soon with her father's undoubted pleasant reaction. She gave the sergeant a healthy wad of bank notes to share among themselves as an initial token of her appreciation. She made to leave as her tyre had been changed, and her now gleaming car polished within an inch of its mechanical existence!

Just as she was leaving, she got lucky yet again. On a hunch that came from nowhere, she simply said in passing that she had heard from her father that there was a similar military depot in Sandy Town. That was enough to get the grateful sergeant to spill it all out again. Oh yes, Fort Id had been his previous posting. In fact, all who were on duty here had at various times worked there. He described the similar patterns of guard duty and shifts, told her what was stored in the warehouse-looking structures and everything else she needed to know.

Bingo!

She again thanked him effusively and thanked the others as well. She mentioned again her soon-to-materialise phone call to them and took off to pick up Saga, amidst a flourishing of eager salutes and cheers from the newly-enriched guards. And as she was leaving, a new plan started forming in her head.

Once in the car, Zara told a suitably astonished Saga everything. He could not believe her sheer bravado and amazing luck. More than that, she had been spared a similar mission at the other weapons dump, where any number of things could have gone wrong! They agreed to go back to Zara's to discuss the matter fully and consider whatever plan was brewing in her mind. The one thing that was haunting them though, which neither mentioned, was the million-dollar question: how on earth were they going to be able to disable those mobile instruments of violence?

General Yalley sat in his study, staring thoughtfully at the curtains his wife had made him so many years ago when he was a struggling captain in the military. Such pretty patterns, he thought, and remembered the hours she had spent on the delicate embroidery and hand stitches at the time. She had been everything to him then, and now she was dead. And he had killed her! He had betrayed her, betrayed his family, and practically killed her in the process. She had poisoned herself because of this betrayal and he had used all his power at the time of her death to hush-up her suicide. He had done this by bribing and forbidding the pathologists at the Military Hospital never to mention what had actually taken place, on pain of a fate far *'worse than death'* – he had viciously assured them personally.

There were times, such as now, when the General felt that his head was about to split open, and that he would soon be destined for the lunatic asylum. Away from his ministerial colleagues, his security operatives, and from the public (including his own children), he was a man in extreme torment. He was filled with such self-revulsion at that moment that he actually started to retch!

How could he have done the things he had done? How could he be sitting here today as a pivotal part of an inhuman regime with blood on his hands? How had he risen to become a top henchman of one of the most brutal dictators on a continent renowned for brutal dictators, such as Idi Amin and the 'Emperor' Bokassa? What had it been for? Had it been for power? For wealth? For glory?

He was a haunted man, who had dangerously forgotten that when you sup with the devil, you should use a very long spoon. He had used a short spoon and was now doomed for all eternity! He had metamorphosed into a demon himself!

General Yalley knew exactly what had driven him to become the monster he now was: FEAR! Fear of being seen as a failure, fear of poverty, fear of failing like his father before him, fear of ignominy!

He had lived a terrible childhood.

His first-class brain had landed him in a top school, filled with rich children, while he was very poor. They had teased him mercilessly. They scorned him and shunned him. They had flung his poverty in his face, made him feel worthless, and had lorded it over him with as much cruelty as children are capable of. How he had hated his father and his own background for having caused him to endure such humiliation! He had never forgotten the treatment he had received at the hands of these exulted kids. It festered into a blind hatred of them and a deeply ingrained pathological fear of 'not making it to the top'. Never ever! And he would get them back. Oh yes, he would!

And his chance had come with the assumption of power by his colleague, Captain Brewman!

Fear was what had engineered his meteoric rise by Brewman's side, which had guaranteed his own rise to eminence. But it had been a bloody rise and a bloody eminence indeed! He had been by Brewman's side as they waded in blood to the throne! He had achieved wealth and power beyond what he had dreamed of – but at what price?

He had tracked down many of those who had humiliated him during his childhood, and had destroyed them one way or another. He had instigated their arrests on trumped-up charges, destroyed their businesses, and generally generated mayhem for them! He had lost his soul in the process, betrayed all his inner beliefs, and 'killed' his wife! Even the wealth he had achieved was heavily tainted with corruption. He was truly lost and was now in too deep to back out. He had known for a while, with utter certainty, that to back out of what he was involved in meant certain death! He was a bedfellow with the devil and there was no way out.

The General was privately filled with remorse and had become paranoid to the extent that he sometimes felt his deceased wife was haunting him as revenge for his murderous betrayal. There were many times he had thought of taking his own life to go out into the great void to seek his wife's forgiveness. But he did not have the courage. He wanted to tell her that to atone for his crimes by cutting his ties with the Regime at any point would have meant instant death. He, of all people, knew that Brewman was a brute beyond belief. He knew too many of the Regime's secrets to be kept alive if he bailed. He also knew that taking his own life was too easy a way out for him. His wife would banish him from her sight, even in the great void!

A sad part of it all was that he had rarely given a direct order that had resulted in anyone's demise. He had carefully avoided that. His reputation as a hangman was less real than was imagined. But he also knew that perception was 90 per cent of it all! And he had done nothing to disabuse that perception, since it had served him well! He also knew that the fact of his direct non-involvement, together with the fear factor that drove him, were absolutely no excuses for the evil he had helped sustain in other forms. He was tainted. He had deservedly been painted with the same brush. It was called the principle of collective responsibility – and he was right smack in the centre of the murdering collective!

He knew there was no atonement for him. He had also spawned a beastly male child who was on his way to becoming a monster after his own image. The only saving grace in his life at the moment was a daughter, who was almost an exact replica of her mother.

But his daughter loathed him.

He could see it in her eyes and mannerisms in unguarded moments, and the mere sight of her deepened his torment. That was why he took pains to avoid her whenever he could. He knew in his heart that Zara suspected the true circumstances surrounding her mother's death, and despite her outward gentility even towards him, he had always known that she blamed him without reservation and would never forgive him. She was ashamed of him. Ashamed of her involuntary association with him by blood-ties! Ashamed to be a Yalley!

She was home now. She had just come back. *And the boy is with her.* He had known about that for a while now. He knew exactly who the boy was, as well as his associations! He knew he was the original Orphan. He knew they had been secretly seeing each other for a while now, but he had done nothing about it. He had not even had them followed on the nights they had been out in the car. He knew they were up to something but he chose not to know what.

The fact of the matter was that he could never do anything against his daughter. He had some time ago impulsively slapped her in front of her brother and had not slept for days after that, out of sheer mortification. If the truth were told, it was as though he knew in his innermost soul that if there was any redemption for him at all in what was left of his miserable existence, it was to be found through this angel of a daughter. He had often wondered whether this was an actual belief of his or a desperate hope or simply uncanny insight. He did not know how this redemption, if ever it came, would pan out. All he knew was that she was the remaining light and salvation for both himself and his replica son, and that he had to protect her, no matter the cost, even if it meant losing his life.

But it was easier said than done. The slightest deviation from his reputation could result in disaster for him. Another reason he had not taken his own life was also because of her. Unless she was absolutely safe, he could not die. What was she up to with this boy? Was he right to turn a blind eye? What if what they were doing was dangerous and was part of what the boy's father was planning with other members of the opposition? Oh yes – he knew about that too, but had quietly sat on that intelligence, mainly because of her. But he was also weary to the death of his government's relentless brutality and confrontational approach.

And if it ever came to light that he had buried this particular crucial piece of intelligence about what his daughter's boyfriend and his father were up to, which he had acquired through an elite cadre of carefully-selected operatives who were absolutely loyal to him and no one else, he would be finished and so would his children. How could he openly protect her if she was involved with the boy's people without exposing himself? Should he use his loyal core group to find out what she was up to so he could protect her? How far could he even trust them

– knowing the limitless extent of treachery and malice that humans were capable of?

General Yalley knew more than anyone that he was walking a very tight rope, and to trip or slip in any way spelt his annihilation, which would be engineered by his own peers. He had to find a way of protecting her at all costs. He would find a way, he hoped.

CHAPTER TWENTY-ONE

Do Something Before You Die

Oblivious of the General's awareness that they were together, Zara and Saga were animatedly going over the fortuitous events of the evening. Their unbelievable luck had increased their confidence about accessing the Forts when the time came. Zara outlined her new plan, which was simplicity itself.

'It's easy, Saga, I will call the sergeant soon and tell him that my father is very grateful for the help they gave me and will be sending me to them shortly with some token of his appreciation. Once you and I agree on a date, which must be a day or so before the opposition action, I will call again to make sure they are on duty and give them the specific time I will come. The point I am making is, if whatever we are going to do is not noisy and won't take too long, I will be able to distract them for the period. I will take drinks and food and lots of cash, and insist that we all sit together and have a small party before they go back to their duties. They will agree and I will pour them large quantities of whisky or brandy or whatever booze they fancy to get them drunk. Have you known any of these Zombies to refuse free booze? I even smelt alcohol on the sergeant's breath. I hope the others drink as well. What do you think?'

'Not bad, not bad. You have missed your true calling. You should have been a spy like Jennifer Garner in *Alias*. I'm gradually getting used to your outrageous plans, which seem to work. It's all good but let's think through this properly. First, it depends on how we are going to disable those things and that is seriously bothering me now. Secondly, it may work for where we went, but what of the other place? You see my point? If what we are going to do is something quiet and fast then the plan is good, otherwise, I don't know. Again, given the number of vehicles there, do you think 10 people will be enough? Even more crucially, it is looking now as though the Orphans I chose may see you there, and that's pretty dangerous for us both, unless there's a way to avoid that. What do you think?'

It was obvious that their plans so far held too many imponderables, which could prove very dicey. Like all those involved in the unfolding drama, there was still a lot more for them to contemplate and iron out. In their case, the most crucial issue was how to quietly sabotage the vehicles the Zombies needed for their movement to the trouble spots on the appointed day.

* * *

The next day, Saga decided to pay his father's auto-mechanic, Mr Balu, a visit. He had known the engineer since he was a child and was on very friendly terms with him. In actual fact, it was Mr Balu who had ultimately saved the day by removing the tailpipe and fixing the car for the irate neighbour when Saga and Ibrahim had rendered his car immobile with their banana experiment. Yes, if anyone could help, it was Mr Balu, as time was running out for them. He had to be nonetheless careful not to arouse any suspicions in the man with his questions. He decided on an approach.

As expected, Saga's reception was warm, especially since the Mr Balu had heard of his exploits in school. 'Come on in, Saga. How are your parents? I've heard all about you. One day, you'll make a great politician. But be careful of those Government people though, and that fool of a headmaster in your school. So no more Formula One driving for you now, eh? That's what you wanted to be when you were 10. Now, where did I go and sleep last night that I'm being honoured with a visit from a future leader today? Maybe I should sleep at that same place tonight and my luck will again change for the better. How can I help you, my boy?'

Saga explained it was to do with a school project. He needed to write a mini spy story and was looking for ideas, and hoped Mr Balu could help. His hero in the story was a secret agent who needed to noiselessly disable the vehicles of some baddies who were up to no good. He wanted to know what uncomplicated methods could be used, since noisily blowing up the cars was not an option.

Mr Balu loved the sound of his own voice and proceeded to instruct Saga. This is what he lived for – cars! And what a joy to impart some of his knowledge to an interested youngster! He told him all the possible methods he could think of and Saga departed from him in a state of euphoria! He now had the information he wanted. He could not wait to tell Zara. And to think it could be so easy! His confidence was rising in leaps and bounds. Fort Brewman was not going to be such a problem after all!

Saga wasted no time and went straight to tell Zara all he had learnt from the mechanic. The easiest and quickest way to noiselessly destabilise the vehicles was by contaminating their fuel, be it petrol or diesel. All it involved was locating the fuel tank and giving the fuel a dose of contaminants! And surely, this could probably be done without causing much disturbance, which made Zara's diversionary plan for Fort Brewman even more feasible!

'Sounds great, Saga, but what if the fuel tanks are locked? Where will we find the individual keys to unlock scores of fuel tanks?'

'Relax. If you were the driver of a military vehicle in action and you needed to refuel quickly to re-engage in battle, would you want to get down with a bunch of keys, walk over to the side of the tank, figure out which key you need from your bunch, and unlock it before refuelling and re-locking afterwards? It does not make sense, Zara, for them to be locked.'

'Also, Mr Balu told me the buttons you need to push to open fuel tanks are usually located in very visible areas in or around the dashboard or gear lever, so we shouldn't have a problem there.'

'Okay, but make sure you open and close the vehicle doors with minimum noise. I'll insist the soldiers play their radio to drown out any inadvertent noise during the operation.'

'Great idea. All we need to do now is decide on the contaminants, and with that, I vote for sand.'

Sand was the easy solution as it was already in abundant supply in the Fort. Mounds of sand were heaped all over the place at Fort Brewman, as it was used to fill sandbags. There were even the sandbags themselves, from which the raw material could be liberated. This was truly heaven sent, as it would mean minimum expense and the fact that those involved could travel lighter on mission day!

Saga, however, wanted something else to be mixed with the sand. Something that would generate an instant chemical reaction with the fuel, just in case the sand particles settled and took their own sweet time to rise and clog up the injectors or carburettors or whatever it was that needed clogging up to render the vehicles instantly immobile or soon after they took off. He suggested a mixture of salt and sugar to be added to the healthy doses of sand they were going to administer. He knew instinctively that somehow, a mixture of those seemingly harmless food substances would generate the requisite disenabling chemical reaction that was bound to cause chaos, one way or another, to the internal mechanical organs of those vehicular monstrosities. Some vague recollection of his younger days as a somewhat avid student of chemistry in school gave him the assurance that a combination of sugar and salt added to inert, combustible hydrocarbons would certainly get his much-needed instant chemical reaction without a doubt!

What was left for them to do regarding Fort Brewman was now looking like just routine stuff. Zara would phone the sergeant and arrange the time. This of course would depend on the date the opposition gave as the day of 'action'. She would also go the shops to get some sugar and salt in sizeable quantities. She was to get enough 10-kilo cloth bags and 10 large knapsacks, all black. She would mix the salt and sugar, re-bag them, and place the mixture in the cloth bags.

The Orphans on the operation would place their contaminants in the knapsacks. She was to get 10 pairs of thin but strong surgical rubber gloves for the operatives to wear once inside the Fort. She knew what to do about the food and drinks. The cook would be told to put a nice assortment of dishes together for an evening picnic, and she would simply help herself to the vast cache of drinks that were in the lounge bar for her father's visitors. Finally, she would also deliver the mobile phones, which had been promised for the next day. Zara would borrow money from her father to fund the mission. He was not in the habit of refusing her. It's just that she almost never asked! This time, she would ask for plenty!

Saga was to brief the Orphans two days before the operation, which would be three days before the march. He was to outline the plan to them, the objectives, and what their role was. They would strike on the night before the march. They had to assume that the Regime did not know exactly when the mass action was to take place. He would assure them that someone would distract the guards, but would reveal no name for security reasons. He would remind them of the dress code, which was black throughout, including the footwear.

Zara also needed to get five pairs of opaque black female stockings that could stretch very well. Saga would cut holes through them to use as balaclavas. Saga, who was a good driver, would pick up his team members individually from pre-arranged isolated spots in a van he would borrow from the family mechanic, Mr Balu. He would hand out the mobile phones and numbers so he could communicate with them up until the time he picked them up. There would be strictly no talking amongst them once they got into the back of the van. He did not want them to recognise each other in case anyone was caught. For himself, he was in too deep to care. Some may recognise each other's build but they could never be a hundred per cent certain in the dark, behind makeshift balaclavas. Finally, they needed beach buckets with their little kiddie shovels to scoop, mix and shovel the contaminants and sand neatly down the fuel tanks. Would Zara get those as well?

They marvelled at each other. They were not bad at all for amateurs. Saga recalled a proverb from a book he'd read called *Things Fall Apart*, written by the famous Nigerian author, Chinua Achebe. "The lizard that fell from the high iroko tree said that if no one would praise him, he would praise himself."

They truly felt like a pair of Achebe's lizards that evening. They resolved to go over the plan every time they met until they had it perfected. If anything else came up in the interim, they would talk on their mobiles. Saga would also find out from his handpicked operatives if they had anything to add to the plan.

The problem now was Fort Id in Sandy Town. There was absolutely no time to go through the exertions that Zara had undergone at Fort Brewman. Furthermore, there was no guarantee that she would be twice lucky if she attempted the same strategy at Fort Id. Though the sergeant had described the layout, nothing could really be done unless they themselves had ventured onto the premises. They could not fashion a plan on hearsay! And there was already so much to do to ensure that the Fort Brewman operation there went without a hitch. Saga also had other very pressing responsibilities at the underground press, running resistance-related errands for his father, as well as going over plans regarding the Orphans' involvement in the mass action.

After a lengthy discussion on the matter, Saga and Zara decided to focus solely on Fort Brewman. They would be over-reaching themselves if they took on Fort Id as well. They would be dangerously pushing their luck. But their reasoning was sound. They did not know the place well to start with. There was no time. The sergeant had told Zara that it was mostly armaments such as surface to air missiles, missile launchers, rocket-propelled grenade launchers, actual grenades, live ammunition such as bullets, riot-control rubber bullets and Kalashnikov AK47 assault rifles and heavy duty Karl Gustav machine guns.

Despite its propensity to wantonly use force against opposition demonstrators, they did not think that the Regime was about to use rocket-propelled grenades or missile launchers at them. Neither would they find any demonstrators in the skies if they decided to deploy their surface to air missiles. Both Zara and Saga also knew of the efforts to co-opt the international media into the impending fray, which would make the Regime hesitate before using live ammunition on unarmed women and children. The problem was with the rubber bullets, which had often proved lethal. But there was nothing they could do about that, apart from the fact they didn't even know exactly where they were stored within the Fort. They could not presume, even in their wildest fantasies, that they could cover all bases.

The military vehicles were quite another matter. The sergeant had explained to them that most of the military vehicles around the country had been deployed to the war front. Consequently, the depleted collection they were guarding was currently the largest concentration of military vehicles in the country. Thus, if a huge part of the Zombies' means of mobility was already tied-up in war, then what they had at the Fort became even more crucial for quelling demonstrations and bamboozling innocent citizens. Fort Brewman had thus become exceedingly important in the scheme of things. They would simply focus on the all-important vehicles and, having arrived at this decision, were relieved of a huge weight on their already over-burdened shoulders!

In the wider society, the stage was now set for the mass action! Everyone involved had been primed. The opposition had worked tirelessly to ensure that all the organisations involved would move on cue. They would not seek police permits, which would be automatically refused and render the demonstrations illegal from the word go. They also needed to keep the Government guessing as to when they would actually move. To seek police permits meant stating dates, times and venues, which would be akin to giving the game away, and thus could not be even considered on any serious basis by even those who were pedantic sticklers to the letter of the law.

Posters would go up at the crack of dawn on the day in question, while the leaflets were to be distributed just before and during the march. It was to be the biggest show of defiance in the history of the country, where for the first time ever, all the various opposition streams and strands would have come together in common cause. This was solidarity indeed.

Sections of the international media had also been primed. They had acquiesced to keep mute until the event actually begun. Many international journalists had already slipped into the country unobtrusively. Some, with their equipment, had been smuggled in through neighbouring countries. To the main protagonists, the only problem was the inability to sabotage the Regime's weaponry. But they had unanimously agreed to go ahead with the plan nonetheless. Pappy, Kamson and others had finally relented for the common good. The University Student Union, led by the likes of Kobby and Obo, had dispatched many of their members into the secondary schools to organise the students for the action and place them on standby. They were told that things could happen any moment without telling them exactly when.

General Yalley now knew all of this. But he still had not acted. He was now almost certain that his daughter was somehow involved. He thought of ways in which he could limit the Regime's inevitably brutal response. He had to do something. He had been having terrible dreams of late, in which he always saw his deceased wife covered in blood, pointing an accusatory finger at him, while screaming, *'Do something before you die!'* repeatedly. It was always the same dream. He was frightened and exhausted. He had once even woken up in the middle of the night, screaming in terror. Luckily, his bedroom was sound-proof, so no one had heard. All he knew was that he would never be rid of the nightmares until he did 'something'.

As luck would have it, confidential military intelligence reports from the war front suggested serious setbacks that required urgent attention. Of course, such damaging reports were kept from the general public by Brewman's information blackout. The President was frantic with worry, and had charged General Yalley to get together with the security chiefs to do something about this or there would be grave repercussions!

This was the opportunity he needed.

He decided on a plan, which he hoped his wife's ghost or whatever it was that was 'visiting' him in his dreams would approve of, and thus cease to haunt him. His incessant, hellish nightmares had made him suddenly very superstitious. He did not know that what plagued him were his own misdeeds.

He had decided to deploy as many troops as possible outside of the capital city. He started shipping as many as he could to the war front on the pretext that he was merely following the President's orders that he should employ 'any means necessary' to reverse the war losses. He knew the opposition mass action was to happen any day now, and was frantically trying to get the troops out to Cape Cove and other regional capitals. His aim was to drastically reduce the number of Zombies available to clash with the marchers, but they were not moving out fast enough! He went to the extent of commandeering commercial airlines operating in the country to fly the troops out. Those airlines that had the temerity to protest that their schedules would be disrupted were threatened with an immediate withdrawal of their licence to operate within the country, with their expatriate staff deported as well. The airlines thus beat a hasty retreat from their original positions, declaring now that they would be overjoyed to assist the Minister in any way possible!

General Yalley's next move was to also ship out as much ordnance and allied munitions to the war front as possible. He virtually emptied places like Fort Id, all in the name of the war effort. He had vast stocks of the crowd-control rubber bullets 'accidentally mis-shipped' to the war front. He would later put the blame on some underling if it came to that. But he did not think it would even be necessary, given the sheer extent of bureaucratic inefficiency that characterised the Regime's rule.

He could however not deploy all the military vehicles that were concentrated in Fort Brewman. He could deploy only some of them. To deploy all the vehicles there would undoubtedly raise eyebrows. He commandeered as many of the vehicles as he could to the war front, but knew that it would take some serious stretching of the imagination to justify, for example, sending an anti-riot water cannon to the war front. How would he explain it? That he thought to make the enemy wet? Or to dampen their powder and shot by spraying them and their firepower with highly pressurised water? That would indeed take some doing, and he doubted if he was up to it! For now, he would concentrate on internally sabotaging the Government's response capability in confronting internal disturbances, citing the escalating external threat as justification. After that, there were other things he had to do as part of his atonement!

* * *

The Joint Action Committee finally handed down the date for the mass action to all the coordinating bodies.

Thus, the day before the mass action had arrived.

Thus, the day of the secret 'Orphan Mission' was at hand.

The Orphans were set.

Over the past few days, Saga had been very busy indeed. He had briefed the mission crew individually, visited them at their homes at various times to inspect their very dark clothing, agreed where each would be picked up, and had issued all of them with their mobile phones, knapsacks and balaclavas. Later, he had had to call a few of them on their mobile phones to alter some of the various rendezvous points.

Zara had also done her part with near manic efficiency. The sergeant at Fort Brewman had been informed of the General's vast pleasure and his wish to show his gratitude. He was given the time he was to expect Zara at the Fort. The sugar and salt contaminants had been purchased, mixed, bagged and also delivered.

Her mother's bunch of keys, which had not been returned to their resting place, had been used to quietly enter the General's bedroom to avail herself of or rather 'borrow' vast sums of cash she knew he would not miss. The General simply had stacks of them in his bedroom. She had decided on this course of action instead in order not to evoke any suspicions by asking the General for too large a sum. He had been looking at her rather strangely these days, which had made her a touch uncomfortable. She would have ignored those looks completely at any other time, but now, she knew she had to tread carefully. 'Borrowing' made a lot more sense in this case! She would gladly tell him where she got the money from the moment her involvement came to light.

The cook had been instructed to have the food – made up of spicy mutton kebabs on skewers, chunky portions of deep-fried chicken, pita bread or what was locally referred to as Lebanese bread, succulent grilled king prawn on skewers, as well as grilled, imported, thick Cumberland and Lincolnshire sausages – ready and packaged by 8p.m. that evening. This was not to be a cumbersome traditional rice and stew affair. Five bottles of expensive liquor, made up of extra-fine Remy Martin XO cognac, Johnnie Walker Blue Label whisky, Glenlivet single malt whisky, Bombay Sapphire dry gin and Grey Goose vodka, were safely resting in the boot of the car she intended to use that night. The beach shovels and allied accoutrements had also been delivered to Saga, together with a large wad of cash for 'just in case' purposes.

They were truly ready but for one major unforeseen setback. It appeared that, worried by the rumours of a definite impending clash between Government troops and the opposition, Mr Balu, the mechanic, had decided on the spur of the moment to evacuate himself and his family to safety at some unknown location! In the process of flight, he had completely forgotten he had promised Saga a van for his use!

Consequently, Saga, on the eve of the mission, found himself without the all-important vehicle! He communicated this most debilitating development to Zara, and they both had not come up with a solution by mission morning. What were they going to do? Where could they avail themselves of a van at this eleventh-plus hour? This was worse than bad! Their luck to date, coupled with the smoothness of their preparations, had been too good to be true. Now this!

Desperate situations called for desperate solutions. Zara placed a call to her father's personal assistant, Mrs Tutu. She knew her father was out of the office for most of the day, meeting with security chiefs about the war effort. She had heard him on the phone that morning but had not ventured into his presence to say her usual 'good morning' greeting because of the unusual and unsettling looks he had been giving her lately.

'Good morning, Mrs Tutu. Madam, this is Zara Yalley. I hope all is well with you?'

'Zara? Oh, as for you, I am always happy to hear your voice, though you hardly ever call us and you never come here! And why are you calling me madam? I should be calling you that. Anyway, I'm fine and what can I do for you, my dear? Are you looking for your daddy?'

The PA was genuinely happy to hear Zara's voice. Unlike her pompous, arrogant brother, who was secretly loathed by all at the office and was constantly phoning them with some imperious request or other, Zara was universally liked; thought of as charmingly polite and respectful, and never made any demands on them. For her to call was most unusual, and to be able to assist her in any way would be purely delightful.

'No, I'm not looking for my father and I'm ever so sorry to disturb your busy schedule, but I really do need an urgent favour. I would have asked Daddy this morning but I could see he was very busy and left in a hurry. I have a bit of a crisis on my hands. We have this school picnic this evening and we don't have a mini-van to convey my classmates and the food. A friend's father was to have provided one but it suddenly broke down and we are stranded. I was hoping the office could rent one for us. And I would prefer it to be a self-drive, as I will get one of our teachers to drive. I would be really grateful for your help. Thank you.'

'Ah Zara, this is what you call a problem? Don't even spend one minute worrying about it. Leave it with me. I will arrange everything and ring you when it is ready. Are you sure you don't want a driver from our office at least? They will be only too happy to drive you. They all like you very much. Just let me know later where you want it delivered and at what time. It was good you did not bother the Minister General with this small matter. It's no problem at all. I will also make sure there is a full tank of petrol. Don't bother to fill the tank when you finish. We will take care of that here. Please call us more often and have a nice picnic.'

Zara assured her that the driver was not necessary, thanked her politely and hung up. Her only problem now was where to have the van delivered. That could prove tricky. She could not exactly have it delivered at her home.

She quickly rang Saga to let him rest assured that the problem was mainly solved, once she could come up with a delivery spot. Saga did not see this as a problem.

'Just tell them to leave it by your school gates around 6p.m. No one will steal it and I'll be lying in wait. They should just leave the keys on the visor on the driver's side. We'll be fine. You can always let them pick it up from the same place tomorrow or whenever!'

Zara agreed. They would not be seeing each other till after the mission. Hopefully. Fingers and toes as well for good measure were in need of sustained crossing! They reaffirmed their undying love for each other, wished each other luck, and resolved to speak a few more times to ensure all was well until the time Saga was in possession of the van.

CHAPTER TWENTY-TWO

Salt, Sugar, Sand

The van was delivered by 5.45p.m.

Saga was in possession by 5.53p.m. He needed all of two hours to round up his crew. Escaping from home, however, had been a nightmare. Nana had made an unscheduled appearance at home during the daytime and requested Saga to come with him to the final opposition meeting before the mass action the next day.

For once in his recent lifetime, Saga was in no mood for this particular honour. He couldn't risk a delay. He asked his father if it was absolutely necessary, as he had a lot of work to do at the underground press, as well as having to meet up with the Orphan leaders later about the next day's events. His father said it was. Saga assured him that he would be there, without fail. His father said the venue had changed and that they would be leaving home together. The meeting was at 6p.m.

6p.m?!

It was even worse than he had imagined. He did not have an option. He knew exactly what he had to do. It would soon be time for them to leave. He simply went to his room, donned his black mission attire, walked through the back door in their kitchen, went by the side of the house, and calmly jumped over the wall. He picked up his items for the mission, which he had earlier on hidden under some nearby shrubbery, and made his way towards Zara's school. He would face the consequences of defying his father later.

By 8.05p.m., he had rounded all the Orphans up from various points within the city. They were suitably attired as agreed, had their opaque balaclavas on, and were in possession of all their required accoutrements. They observed agreed protocol and sat without speaking in the back of the van. Saga remained alone in front at the wheel. Saga knew that Zara would leave home at 7.50p.m. and should be at the Fort Brewman by 8.40p.m. She believed she would have the party with the guards going by 9p.m., which was when the team was to start making its way over the wall. She would send a text message to confirm.

Saga decided to cruise towards the mission venue. He did not want to attract attention by driving fast. He knew they were safe from security checkpoints, as he and Zara had carefully chosen this route, based on a document she had liberated from her father's study, listing all the current checkpoint locations around the city. Unfortunately, what he and Zara had not known was that some of these checkpoints were sometimes relocated on a random ad hoc mid-weekly basis, and that the document they had seen was not as current as they thought! Thus, Saga went into shock when, without warning, he found himself a few metres away from a military checkpoint!

'Get a grip, get a grip,' he kept repeating to himself, as he tried not to think about what else they could have been wrong about.

But how was he to get a grip when he saw what the soldiers at the checkpoint were doing? They were inspecting the trunks of the cars that had queued up, and there were only four cars ahead of him! How in the name of heaven was he going to explain nine youngsters in the back of the van, clad in all-black attire, wearing improvised balaclavas, toting knapsacks of mixed salt and sugar, as well as holding kiddie mini beach buckets and mini shovels to boot? To behold such a sight would be too bizarre for these soldiers, and there was absolutely no sane explanation that would sway them! They would detain the lot of them on the spot until they got to the bottom of such an inexplicable sight. The stress level involved in this business was becoming way too high. The option of doing a simple U-turn to bolt away was fast becoming non-existent. He was too close to the soldiers now. His van had already been spotted!

The impending disaster was now only a couple of minutes ahead of him. All the doubts and misgivings that had initially beset him but which he was later able to put aside in the face of Zara's contagious confidence, their unbelievable luck, and the smoothness of their preparations now suddenly descended on him with a vengeance. He needed to act very quickly or all was hopelessly lost!

There was only one conceivable thing he could do, short of bolting off, which would place him in a far worse predicament than what he was currently facing. He calmly leaned over and took out a huge high-denomination wad of the 'just in case' money Zara had given him from the glove compartment, placed it on the passenger seat, and waited for his turn in the queue. He used his right hand to loosen up the wad and spread some of the notes on the seat to make them hard to miss. Not once did his eyes leave the roadblock ahead of him.

It got to Saga's turn.

A soldier approached and stuck his head through the passenger-side window, which Saga had rolled down.

'Young man, get down and open the back of your van. What have you got in there? Hurry up, okay? I have many cars to inspect!'

Saga said nothing. He simply looked at the soldier's face then moved his eyes downwards to the money on the seat. Whether it was some telepathy at play or whether he simply felt a powerful urge to follow the direction of Saga's eyes, the soldier's eyes were involuntarily drawn to the cash on the seat.

The soldier gasped. He could not take his eyes off the cash. Avarice had taken a firm hold of him. At a glance, this was more than a couple of years' salary at the very least!

Saga knew it was time to act. Literally thinking on his feet, he said, with a combination of urgency and deference, 'Officer, I'm in a terrible hurry. I have an emergency on my hands. My mother is very ill and must get to the hospital, and as you know, there are not many ambulances these days. I need to rush. My mother has no one but me. For your kindness, why don't you let me give you something little? But only out of respect, please. My mother says you soldiers work very hard. Please take some of this money. It is no problem at all. Help yourself, sir.'

The astonished guard could not believe his luck. He could barely contain himself. With scarcely concealed haste, he clawed more than half the wad into his beefy fist, bent over a bit more through the window, raised his elbows, as though creating a protective screen, and stuffed the cash in his olive-green army shirt. All this was done with considerable speed, to avoid being seen by his colleagues, with whom he would then have to share his incredibly good fortune! He stepped back and briskly waved Saga through, urging him to hurry before any of his colleagues could saunter over.

Zara's vision had saved the day yet again. Was there no end to his amazing girlfriend's brilliance?

That was all he could think about, with relief coursing through his body as he sped away!

By 9p.m., Saga had parked the van near the rickety bridge by Fort Brewman. He and his team were crouched beside the same side-wall he had previously climbed during his 'recce' assignment with Zara. In their dark clothes and fake balaclavas, the team was safe from prying eyes. They waited apprehensively for Zara's signal to move.

The signal came.

They were over the wall in a flash like a band of modern-day, well-coordinated ninjas. They knew the potential danger they were facing, and this somehow lent them added efficiency and stealth. No one tripped. No one stumbled. No one spoke.

Their sugars-cum-salt contaminants were quickly mixed with sand in the mini buckets.

The vehicles had somewhat reduced in number. That was even better for them.

Fuel tanks were opened noiselessly.

The new mixture effortlessly shovelled into the tanks with marked efficiency.

Fuel tanks were noiselessly closed.

The process was repeated several times.

The mission was accomplished in just over an hour, thanks to the depleted number of vehicles.

No hiccups.

By 10.15p.m., they were driving off.
Bravo!

Zara's diversionary party also went without a hitch.

She made the guards replete with food and drunk on fine, expensive alcohol.

She stuffed their pockets with her cash gratitude.

They adored her.

They now believed in the existence of angels on Earth.

They lavished drunken praise on her.

They called her a mother of the nation.

She left.

They slept.

Mission accomplished.

Bravo!

Zara parked her car at home and went through the side gate to meet Saga. They hugged. They were triumphant. They were for now, at least.

Zara wept. Saga held her close and tasted her salty tears. There was one more thing to do. Further tears had to wait. They got into the van. Zara drove. They disposed of any remaining evidence in the van on their way and left the vehicle by her school gates. The guard on duty there was asleep. They walked towards the main Independence Road and hailed a taxi. They sat arm in arm in the back seat all the way back to Zara's place. There was not much to say. A huge burden had been lifted; a vast amount of tension dispelled. But only momentarily.

They were back in each other's arms in Zara's room. Zara pushed Saga away and became very quiet and started to unzip her dress. Saga was unsure what to do; he was in unchartered territory.

'Listen carefully, Saga. We don't know what will happen out there tomorrow. Maybe the Zombies will shoot. Maybe they won't. Maybe I will see you soon after tomorrow. Maybe I won't. But there is one thing I am sure of and that is I cannot take the chance of never having been with the man who I know is, and forever will be, the greatest love of my life; the man who brought me out of mourning and gave me a renewed sense of purpose in life. That man is you, Saga, and I love you with all my heart. Don't say anything, my love. Just come to me. I am yours tonight. I have never been with anyone before. I wanted it to be special and you are the most special thing in the world to me. Come my love and make me your woman tonight.'

Saga was overwhelmed and profoundly touched to his core. He was a young man, completely in love the woman before him, with raging hormones to boot. He desired his beloved Zara and this was the best 'invitation' he had so far received in his young life.

But raging, lustful hormones or not, Saga knew better.

He calmly got up from the bed and drew Zara to him.

'I love you with all my heart, my dearest, and your words tonight have touched my soul. There is nothing more in the world I wish for than to be with you. But I want us to be together, not from fear or from a sense that we might not see each other again, not from a sense of possible loss. It must always be from hope; it must be positive and not brought on by the negatives in our lives. I hope you fully understand me, my dear, because I love you so much as to only want you under a bright aura of joy and happiness.'

Zara just stared at him and burst into tears. She understood that this was not a rejection but rather a definitive affirmation of love.

She wept uncontrollably. Saga wept as well. They fell asleep in each other's arms. But only briefly.

Soon, Saga had to go and their reality dawned once again. They had succeeded tonight in their mission, but they had also opened a deadly can of worms.

The repercussions would come.

The retribution would come.

It would be brutal, horrible.

They had absolutely no control of what was to come.

These were the thoughts that now hurtled through their minds like huge, crushing boulders. And they were powerless to do anything about it. Their world was literally crashing about their feet, despite their success. In a manner of speaking, their respective families would be facing each other on opposing sides of the 'battlefield' the next day, with the commencement of the mass action. The battle lines were irrevocably drawn. Zara had done her bit for the opposition cause. A huge bit at that, but it was time for her to sit back and wait for the inevitable backlash against her.

Saga, on the other hand, had to soldier on. He had to lead his Orphans into 'battle' the next day. There was much to say between them. But they were at that place where words were superfluous. They had said all they had to say to each other previously. If they lived, they would find each other. They would be together. They would find a way. What more was there to say? They had to part now. They went to the side gate, wearing their bravest faces.

'I love you, Zara. Always!'

'I love you, Saga. Forever!'

'Goodbye!'

'Goodbye!'

And he was gone!

Just like that.

CHAPTER TWENTY-THREE
Bedlam in the Eyes

The city woke up to a deluge of posters and fliers as a result of a section of the Orphans and university students having worked all night to achieve this. The likes of Saga, Ibrahim, Obo and Kobby were sporting seriously red-rimmed eyes in the morning from their prodigious all-night efforts. By all standards, they should have been hardly able to stand on their feet, let alone function at full throttle on such an important and extremely active day. But they were captive to the adrenaline, which had taken over their bodies, in anticipation of what was to take place. In actual fact, they were raring to go!

By 10a.m., the capital city, Cape Cove, was in an advanced state of paralysis. Almost all business establishments and Government offices had shut down. Water and electricity supplies were suspended, as workers in these key utility sectors took to the street in support of the opposition. Almost every factory and industry had shut down. The airport had become inoperable, as airline and civil aviation staff vacated their posts to register their protest by joining the march. Incoming aircraft were diverted to neighbouring countries, and flights scheduled for take-off were grounded.

Public transport, or what little there was of it, had also ground to a halt. Many private vehicles in the form of haulage trucks, fuel tankers, buses and mini-buses had been parked and abandoned in pre-arranged strategic locations around the city, aimed at blocking certain major roads and arteries that would severely limit troop movement around the capital city. Other vehicles had been mobilised to carry medical personnel and supplies to attend any of the marchers who were hurt by the anticipated police brutality. An armada of taxis had also been stocked with vast quantities of bottled water for many of the marchers.

Vital areas such as the hospitals had been left with a skeleton staff of doctors and nurses to attend the seriously infirm, as most medics had left to join the protest.

All schools had shut down. Younger secondary school pupils, along with all primary and nursery school children, were made to stay at home. Several pirate radio stations, which had suddenly sprung to life in aid of the protest, had been advising parents since the early hours of the morning to keep their children at home.

Older secondary school students, mainly under the aegis of the Orphans and their university minders, had joined the march in specially designated areas. Most teachers and support staff also left the schools to join the march, though certainly not the likes of Mr Money and his sycophantic staff, who were feverishly preparing to flee the city – should the need arise!

Hordes of protesters had been pouring into the city since the crack of dawn. They were literally coming from all the points on the compass.

They came by the busload.

They came in private cars.

They came in taxis.

They came on bicycles.

They came on foot.

They came to protect the lives of their children!

Government security personnel manning the checkpoints at the various entry points of the city were in an unprecedented state of bewilderment. Something was obviously going down, as thousands and thousands were descending on the capital city from every possible entry point. They did not know what to do about this sudden avalanche of people. They had received no orders to halt this deluge of humanity on the city, and thus could not do so. They had also not been alerted as to any impending Government-sponsored mass rally, which the Regime tended to orchestrate from time to time. Repeated radio messages sent through dispatch centres to the various unit and section commanders informing them of these highly unusual developments and to seek instructions on the matter were met with even more confusing silence. They simply had no choice but to sit back and allow the multitudes to stream into the city!

There was a reason for this silence. The security chiefs charged with the protection and orderly running of the capital city were in a state of panic, right up to the BNR offices of Commander Musu, where fear and pandemonium reigned unabated! Their phone lines were jammed with repeated calls from frightened senior commanders, seeking urgent instructions as to how to proceed in the face of such unprecedented phenomena! The airwaves assigned for wireless security communications were equally jammed with frantic calls and appeals from those junior commanders who were not having their phone calls answered as well as lower level personnel, who were equally at a loss as to the absence of direction from their superiors.

Commander Musu sat in gloomy silence in his office, contemplating his fate. He had forbidden his agitated staff from disturbing him. He would summon them when he was ready. He knew he had to act in the face of this sudden internal threat. The only problem was that he was virtually paralysed with fear! It would not be good for his staff to witness his extreme state of nervousness.

'Consider the facts… consider the facts,' he kept repeating to himself. *What are the facts?*

The opposition had faked him out.

His intelligence had failed him miserably.

The opposition had taken over the city.

President Brewman was on holiday outside of the city, hosting his latest mistress, after having sent his wife on a prolonged holiday-cum-shopping-spree in Europe.

And the President was not to be disturbed unless it was a national emergency and, even then, only through General Yalley. Those had been his exact orders. And though it was undoubtedly a national emergency, bloody General Yalley was not answering his any of his phones or walkie-talkie.

And General Yalley, on the orders of the President, had shipped out most of the troops in the city to the war front. Reports from the Zombie commanders indicated that their response capabilities had been seriously sabotaged, as their principal means of mobility within the city had been mysteriously neutralised. All the riot-control vehicles stationed at Fort Brewman had suddenly and inexplicably broken down. They simply would not start. Their engines were unusually refusing to crank up. Every single one of them!

The security forces in the city were in a state of disarray and were all desperately seeking urgent guidance.

This was the manner in which the immediately discernible facts presented themselves to Commander Musu and they cascaded into his mind in no particular order. He was in *huge* trouble, and his punishment would undoubtedly be severe. It would make his predecessors' plight look like a walk in the park. Or should he shoot himself first?

His executive personal assistant, Grace Abbey, suddenly bursting into the room and shouting at him that General Yalley was on the line, however, disturbed his dismal, suicidal thoughts. She had shouted as this was no time for observing protocol and other normal niceties. If nothing at all, these times were certainly as far from normal as could be imagined. He scrambled for his phone extension – sweeping away everything on his desk to get to the phones, as notebooks, pens, papers, teacups, cigarettes, mobile phones, walkie-talkies and ashtrays were sent flying. He did not even wait for the General to begin. His words came tumbling out. He had lost control. He was not even aware that he was wailing in the presence of his personal staff members that were massed at the door to his office, observing him with a mixture of alarm and disbelief!

'General, we're in trouble! General, it is not my fault! General, I did my best! I have never failed before! I don't know what went wrong! What are we going to tell the President? What shall we do? I have been trying to reach you for some time. We don't even have vehicles to transport the remaining troops. None of our vehicles at Fort Brewman work! How is that possible? I have no aerial reports. We have only two helicopters left in the capital. The President left in one of them and we sent the other to pick his new madam. What are we going to do? General, you have to help me please! Please help me! Tell me what to do!'

The General was deliberately contemptuous in his reply. 'Shut up, Musu! Stop screaming into my ear! Are you a child? It is your incompetence that has brought us to this point. I will deal with you and your staff later. This is what you will do. Send word to the commanders to round up all available troops to form a perimeter around the protesters. They should commandeer all vehicles they come across. I will look into the Fort Brewman sabotage business myself later. For now, it's spilt milk. There should be no confrontation with the marchers – do you hear me? I said NO CONFRONTATION whatsoever! If I hear of any such thing, you will be the first person to be arrested today. We are not in strength today. Even an incompetent like you should realise that. Also, my own intelligence tells me that there are many foreign journalists around, so use your head and make sure those commanders use theirs as well. You are in charge for now! And don't dare make any mistakes! Now get off the phone so I can talk to the President!'

'Eh, thank you, General, but please, it was not my fault. I will do all you ask. Please tell the President I am not to blame. They beat up my informants. You said something about doing something with some milk! Is it a plan? Or a code? I didn't get it? What do you want me to do with the milk, sir?'

'Musu, you are truly an idiot! How did you get this job? I must have been sleeping at the time it was offered to you. Spilt milk means we can't do anything about that now. Jesus Christ, but did you not go to school at all? Now get off the phone. Now!'

General Yalley leaned back in his leather swivel chair in his office. So far so good, he thought. He knew he was in vast danger of being swallowed because of the game he was playing. He wanted to protect the marchers for the sake of his wife's ghost and his daughter, and also as part of his atonement. His children were both at home. He had forbidden them to leave the house and had placed extra guards inside his home to ensure this.

He had deliberately not answered the calls that had been pouring in since dawn. He wanted the security apparatus to descend into a sufficient state of bewilderment to desperately need his guidance. That way, they would jump to obey the firm hand that stepped into the vacuum to assume control! That had been achieved. Now, he needed to deal with the devil himself.

He was quickly patched through to the President. He deferentially yet quickly and concisely explained the situation. He explained that though the protest was undoubtedly broad-based and probably involved more than a million people, it was not as bad as it looked from a security standpoint. He told him what he knew of the opposition's demands. He explained the presence of the foreign journalists who were already on air around the globe. He assured him that he could contain the situation. However, for security reasons, he wanted the President to stay put. He was dispatching additional security for the President's protection. He further assured him that no foreign power was behind the mass action. He wanted the President not to be worried but to remain on standby to receive hourly reports from him. He asked if he had the President's consent to assume sole command for now.

The President was stunned! He was in shock! He had been serenely oblivious until a few moments ago. What happened to his intelligence apparatus that consumed hundreds of millions of US dollars each year to make sure that disturbances on such a scale never happen? In his bewildered state, he booted his 'new madam' out of their bed (presumably to aid his thinking)! The equally stunned and belatedly-booted mistress knew better than to complain. She fled his presence in quiet alarm.

The President was livid! How dare the people turn against him? How dare his very own Southern people join the opposition? Broad-based, indeed! After all he had done for his country? What was wrong with neutralising a few destabilising youngsters by sending them off to the war front? Did they want him to lose the war? Why were his troops not shooting these insurgents? Why was Yalley calling him instead of ordering the troops to shoot? Was Yalley going soft or what?

Where were his ministers and generals? Had he not given them all positions and wealth beyond their dreams? Was it not their collective duty to protect him and make him look good in the eyes of the citizenry and the rest of the world? He would show them all that he, President Brewman, was made of sterner stuff. He would shoot everybody. He would declare himself President-For-Life-Forever and no more Until-Further-Notice! He would shoot all the foreign journalists as well for meddling in his affairs! The country belonged to him. He could do just as he pleased! He would order the troops himself! They would see! They would all see!

All this was manically screamed into the General's distressed eardrums. The General had anticipated all this and knew that fear and disbelief had brought this on. He had witnessed various versions of this display over the years, and sought to carefully bring the dictator around to the reality. He needed to calm him down very quickly as he knew exactly the kind of mindless and impulsive damage the man was capable of. The man had no heart and had lost touch with reality. The man was a maniac! His late wife had been right in saying, *'That man has bedlam in his eyes'*. Now the 'bedlam' seemed to have migrated to his brain. Only one with 'bedlam in his brain' could speak as the President was doing now.

The General repeatedly crooned soothingly into the phone, assuring the rabid dictator that it was not that bad, and yes, he, the President, had done a lot for his people, and yes, he was the best ruler ever, and yes, he was quite right to be angry, and continued to agree to all the irrational points that were being hurled at him in rapid succession. After almost half an hour, he finally prevailed.

The dictator was now spent, so the General moved into the offensive. He persuasively explained why it was in their interest not to shoot either the protesters or foreign journalists, which, among other things, could very well attract some serious aerial bombing from the West in the near future, as had been known to happen elsewhere. He even managed to sell the idea of how this could be an opportunity to show the whole world that their view of the Regime was unfounded. He assured the spent despot that he could turn the entire thing around to make him look good and even more famous!

'Yalley, you are the only one I'm going to trust. You are in charge. You are responsible. I will instruct my ADC to issue a dispatch that you alone are in charge. Keep me posted. After this is over, I will launch my own offensive. Do whatever you must to send the ungrateful people home and the workers back into their factories. Deport those nosy journalists as well. Also, I want a list of all our people who allowed this to happen. Make sure you include that fool Musu's name. I will order his punishment personally. I am going to order a cabinet reshuffle of all those fools who call themselves ministers. And I want those who sabotaged my vehicles in my Fort! Do not fail me, Yalley, or you will no longer be on my side! I repeat – you are responsible! Call me soon.'

The General agreed to all of this and deferentially rang off. Even he, the all-powerful and notorious General Yalley, had broken out in a nervous sweat. He understood exactly what Brewman was saying, and he knew the man meant every word. Retribution would be swift and merciless, and he could not be seen to have slipped up! But for now, things were going as planned.

CHAPTER TWENTY-FOUR
'The People Must Love Me'

From the opposition's standpoint, things were progressing very well. Their leaders, such as Nana and the likes of Pappy, would have been ecstatic if they had the time to entertain such an emotion. They were worked off their feet directing affairs. But they, nonetheless, could not help marvelling at the enormity of the turnout! By midday, they practically had an over one-million-man-march on their hands! And an orderly one at that! Incredible!

Nana soon came in for a major surprise. A journalist approached him and told him that he had overheard on the police band that the anti-riot and allied military vehicles based at Fort Brewman had been sabotaged! Every single one of them! Did Nana and his team know anything about it? Did they play a part in this sabotage? He wanted to know so he could report it.

Nana had gasped in disbelief. Was the journalist pulling his leg or what? Was he serious? Was he sure? Of course he was serious, the journalist protested, quite offended. He took his work very seriously! What more, others had also heard it if Nana wished to seek verification! It was the journalist's turn to become startled when Nana let out an enormous bellow of joy and gave him a crushing bear hug, to the wonderment of all who were in the immediate vicinity. Which guardian angel had come to their rescue? This was too good to be true! Providence certainly appeared to be on the side of right!

The masses of humanity that had converged to disavow and end the Regime's hateful National Service decree in no uncertain terms made their way towards the city's enormous

Independence Plaza. It was a massive concrete clearing constructed to commemorate independence from the colonial masters, as well as a venue to hold huge ceremonial functions of State, as well as rallies and huge bible conventions.

Thousands of opposition chaperones dressed in black T-shirts emblazoned with 'SECURITY' in bright scarlet, both on the back and front, efficiently shepherded the teeming multitudes towards the square, where they would be addressed by their leaders and representatives. 'March stewards' were also everywhere, handing out plastic bottles of water to prevent dehydration. Everything was proceeding as orderly as possible, save one moment of serious tension when the flowing mass of humanity suddenly stumbled to a halt as a number of armed policemen and soldiers suddenly appeared from the opposite direction in a motley collection of vehicles, including taxis, and started to disembark. The opposition leaders had anticipated this and had warned over and over again that in such an eventuality, the 'lines were to hold' at all costs. Panic and pandemonium had to be avoided or things could turn out very badly.

The lines held.

The outrage that was so deeply felt against the Regime lent the marchers inordinate doses of bravery. They were not about to run away. Secondly, they were quite surprised at the relatively small number of troops and the mishmash assortment of vehicles they had arrived in. In a sense, it was more comical than scary. Much to their increasing amazement, the troops showed absolutely no signs of aggression and simply took up positions on the periphery of the marchers. Their guns were not even raised, but hung almost meekly by their sides. The marchers stared at them briefly with noticeable collective contempt, if such a thing was possible, and resumed their forward movement!

The marchers eventually congregated at the Plaza, which was overflowing with people. There were people as far as the eyes could see! The huge bench-lined stalls were also packed to the brim. The opposition had rigged the place with a very clear and good quality public address system. The leaders were to address the crowd from a makeshift podium that had been erected for the occasion. They did not wish to use the same elevated podium used by the likes of the President during state functions. They could very well do without the association! A tight cordon of bodyguards surrounded the opposition leaders.

Nana took to the podium.

'Fellow citizens, my brothers, sisters and our children, we will not stand up here on this podium and thank you all for coming. This is a collective effort, and we must all congratulate each other for the turnout we have achieved here today, so I want you all to turn to whoever is standing by you and let's all shake each other's hands and congratulate ourselves!'

A roar of approval and loud cheers greeted this suggestion, as people turned, shook hands and even hugged! They had done very well indeed! Those on the podium also followed suit and shook each other's hands. Nana also hugged several of the leaders on the dais before resuming.

'I have seen many things in my life but never have I seen so many people gathered in one place. We all heard of the million-man march some time ago in America. We have beaten them hands down! The presence of so many people here demonstrates the depth of our concern for what is happening in our beloved country today. We are not a poor nation. We are endowed with significant natural resources. We have gold and coal. We have diamonds and abundant crude oil. We have virgin forests. We have agriculture and some industry. We have golden beaches and our sea is rich in fish. Yet, despite all this, most of us are poor. There are shortages everywhere. There are queues everywhere for basic commodities such as sugar, rice, cooking oil and even toilet paper. Many people have been forced to abandon their cars because there are no spare parts.

'The majority of our children do not have books in their schools. They have no computers. Our roads are in a serious state of disrepair, and potholes frequently cause accidents and deaths. Our hospitals have no equipment or medicine. Doctors and nurses are leaving to seek their fortune in neighbouring countries or in the West. Other professionals are leaving as well, and in droves. Why should it be so? Why? We all work very hard. We are not a nation of lazy people. Foreigners who come and work here are amazed at our diligence. Things have become this way because the present government has failed! It has betrayed us. The State, which is being run by the Brewman Regime and their gangs, is dysfunctional and has been chronically malfunctioning for a while. They are running a failed state. And to add to their horrific list of failures, they have amassed incredible personal fortunes at our expense and used the rest of our money to buy instruments of oppression to brutalise us.

'Vast sums are also being spent to purchase armaments to wage a useless and bloody border war against innocents in a neighbouring country in an attempt to divert our attention from the real problems that plague us. Not only are members of our families being slaughtered in this useless war, but the money generated by all of us that could be used to purchase drugs for our hospitals and books for our children is being diverted into this unholy war of blame! Huge sums are also being spent on equipping Brewman's useless and wholly unnecessary Presidential Guard Regiment with all the latest weaponry to visit terror on us! Enough is enough! Shall we allow this to continue any further? SHALL WE?'

A missive roar of 'NO' greeted this question. 'NO! NO! NO!'

'You are right, my fellow countrymen – we cannot allow this to continue any further! Now, to add serious injury to a string of horrific insults against us, Brewman says he is going to conscript our children, the youth of this country, who are also the future of this country, into his army to fight his dubious, illegal war! How dare he? The time has come for us to put our foot down and ask Brewman to withdraw this inimical National Service decree or this country will come to a standstill. We shall shut down every factory, every school, every office and every farm; in fact, we will close down everything in this country if this decree is not annulled within the next six hours. That is our deadline. That is our ultimatum. We shall all remain here today until those who were criminal enough to commission it, abolish this hateful decree! We are not going anywhere today till this is done!'

Massive roars of approval resonated across the entire city. The shouting and chants of 'ENOUGH IS ENOUGH! KILL THE DECREE, NOT OUR CHILDREN! BREWMAN MUST GO!' could be heard everywhere.

Nana continued as the roaring abated.

'Those of us who had the courage to protest against the Regime's excesses have been horribly brutalised by these worthless soldiers who follow Brewman, like the mindless Zombies they are! Many of our people have disappeared. They have been placed in jails around the country and their whereabouts kept secret. Some may have even been tortured to death, as has been known to happen within the dungeons of the Bureau of No Return! All this evil will cease henceforth. It stops today! We have a list of demands we are presenting. These include a return to rule by a democratically-elected, civilian government within a year, the need for strict laws banning the military from operating internally, the lifting of all media censorship, the outlawing of all forms of police brutality, and an immediate cessation of hostilities in this useless war! Finally, the Government must render accounts for all those who are missing! We demand to know the whereabouts of the students who were arrested during the last student demonstrations! The Regime has truly run this country into the ground and oppressed us daily and we are fed up!

'The most glaring and undeniable evidence we have as to how bad things have become is when the Head of State himself refuses to deal in a currency that has his own head printed on it! Is Brewman's personal and illegally-amassed fortune in our local currency that bears own his head? No, it is not! He amasses his wealth in foreign currencies such as US dollars, euros and British pounds, while he is constantly devaluing our local currency at the behest of the IMF and World Bank, and what does that tell us?

'We appeal to all foreign journalists present here today to go back and highlight our problems to the wider world. They should put pressure on their respective governments to impose sanctions on the Regime till our legitimate demands are met. We do not care that those sanctions will negatively affect us initially! That is an unavoidable price we may have to pay. We are also not asking that they fight our battles for us. We are simply asking that they cease to look on unconcerned while important sections of the global community are being terrorised by illegal regimes. We are simply asking them to extend their global war on terrorism to include State Terrorism visited on innocents around the globe by their own governments! That is all we ask! It is time for me to step aside for others to address you. I thank you for listening and remember, we are staying put till the decree is rescinded!'

A tumultuous roar of cheering greeted Nana as he ceded the platform to another leader. What he had said was sadly true. Things were truly bad if the likes of Brewman did not respect the value of the banknotes that bore their own portraits. And it was also true that the international community had woefully failed many a country with similar plights.

The other leaders that spoke touched on nefarious deals struck between luminaries within the Regime and unscrupulous foreign multi-national companies, and their hugely negative impact on the economy and society.

They talked about the brutal and dehumanising effects of the Third World indebtedness to the Western countries and their multinational banks.

They spoke of the unfair global world economic order being dictated and orchestrated by the IMF and World Bank that relegated countries such as theirs to the status of 'hewers of wood and drawers of water'.

They spoke some more of the West's cynical condoning of State Terrorism and their unyielding adherence to global double standards.

They condemned the vast sums of money spent on armaments worldwide, while millions were dying of hunger and related diseases.

They illustrated how all of this affected them very directly, and the need for the World Community to take concrete steps to rectify these global injustices!

General Yalley was abreast with what was happening. So far, there had been no incident that could trigger off any violence. The security commanders were strictly adhering to his strict 'no confrontation' orders, and all requests to rush troops into the city had been firmly denied by him. The only problem he had not foreseen, and which could have the effect of causing a major violent showdown, was the deadline issued by the opposition! Six hours? He had anticipated the usual twenty-four hours, but six was quite another matter. It was simply not enough time to persuade the President, who was now seething with rage at the unfolding events he was viewing live on television! His last phone conversation with him had very gone badly.

'See here, Yalley, I am running out of patience. These people are insulting me on television. I am being made to look weak. How dare they say I do not accept my own money? Is it my fault that it has no value? These people are supposed to love me. Communist, anarchist, Islamic terrorists are trying to poison their minds to destabilise me. I won't have it, Yalley! What are you doing about these insults to me? What of this rubbish that I should withdraw my own decree? Are they mad? It is a good decree and I am not withdrawing anything! Whatever I do is good for this country! They think I'm a punk? I'll have them all punked! Where are all my troops? Why are they not attacking these insurgents? I see their guns are not even raised? How can they send my troops in taxis? Yalley, I'm not having any of this. The people must love me – do you hear me? They must love me! I insist on this. Yalley are you with me?'

This kind of irrational raving and ranting was extreme, even for Brewman. The man had simply lost the plot! He had no conception of what was going on out there. Yalley had to guide him while there was still time.

Something had to be done about the decree, as he had absolutely no doubt that the marchers would not disperse till that was done, and the more restless they grew, the greater the danger of violence. He knew that had it not been for the stern, uncompromising discipline imposed by the opposition leaders, all hell would have broken loose by now! Many of the marchers, given the chance, would have mercilessly lynched the few Zombies that were out there. General Yalley knew his analysis was correct, and that under no circumstances must the marchers be allowed to stay put without dispersing. The decree had to be repealed. He had to go to work on 'Brewman the Brute', as the students called their President.

'Mr President, please understand that the people love you. We all love you. How can we not love our revered leader? How can you even doubt that? As for the people you see out there, they are all victims of opposition propaganda. These are ignorant city labourers and farm peasants who don't know any better. The reason they are all out there is because of the National Service decree. Mind you, Mr President, I am not saying your decree is bad. How could I? What is happening is not your fault. It is the fault of our own ministers and officials who failed to explain the decree properly to those people on the streets. It is a failure of our own propaganda machinery. Had they done their job well, these ignorant people out there on the streets today would not have been swayed by opposition lies and fabrications. It is not your fault, Mr President. The people truly love you and you are without peer in this, sir. I know this as a fact!'

General Yalley paused for effect. He needed the man to lap it all up, and very quickly. He continued only after he was certain that the President was convinced that he was indeed peerlessly loved by all and sundry.

'And this is why we cannot shoot them, Mr President. They are like your children, whose only crime is that they have been misinformed. There are also real children in the crowd. We cannot shoot them in the full glare of international cameras. Whenever we have sent our troops to teach the university hooligans a lesson, these cameras have never been around. It is different now, Mr President. As for the opposition leaders, don't worry about them. They have played into our hands. They have exposed themselves on television. We now know who the secret ones are. When this matter settles, we will deal with them one by one. Also, shooting the journalists may not be in our own interest at the moment, Mr President. They are mainly from the countries who supply us with our much-needed armaments under our secret Defence Pacts, and who also supply your Special Regiment with a lot of their modern equipment as gifts to you personally for signing those deals. We cannot lose these Defence Pacts, Mr President. We need those arms and special equipment for your glory and protection, Mr President.'

The General paused again. He knew he now had the President's undivided attention, since anything to do with his security and Regime survival was of overwhelming importance to him.

The President replied. 'Hmm. Maybe you are right, Yalley. Yes, the people do love me, and we certainly do need the arms. Let the white people know we need more, Yalley. And Yalley, you are a good man. Only you understand me. Maybe I should make you Vice President. What do you think? But what should we then do about this immediate problem? If we can't shoot anybody, how do we get them to disperse, eh? And Yalley, I need the names of all those idiots who did not use "propaganda" as they should have done! They are responsible. Of course, you are right – all my decrees are good. So what do we do, Yalley?'

'The thing to do, Mr President, is to show the whole world that you are generous by rescinding the National Service decree. Let us make it look as though you are someone who listens to the pleas of his children when they cry out to you. In fact, we don't even have to rescind it. We can simply announce that we are suspending it with the aim of reviewing it with stakeholders and also to sensitise the people. Yes, that is the language the foreign white people like, and it will also make you look democratic in this matter. That should do the trick for now. It will give the opposition the impression they have won today's battle, forgetting that we still control the war! You see, Mr President, we don't want these troublesome foreign journalists to put too much pressure on their governments to stop dealing with us. That would be a disaster for your security. So what I further suggest is that we concede to a few of their other demands as well when making the announcement. We can also add that we are going to review the war situation with the aim of eventual cessation. The only thing that truly matters is that you are still President and that the people be made to love you even more by making these minor concessions!'

General Yalley knew that he had won! He exhaled with vast relief! He now had the President's ear to the exclusion of all else. Manipulating the megalomaniac was indeed tricky, since there were no guarantees as to which way he would ultimately jump. The man was disturbingly unpredictable and prone to prolonged bouts of stark irrationality. But he had to admit that though the President had generally lost the plot with all the sycophancy and fear-induced obsequiousness that surrounded him and had the effect of shielding him from reality, he nonetheless had moments when his need for self-preservation forced him to acknowledge aspects of what was truly real.

Yalley knew he had to bring matters to a close. He barely had two hours to meet the opposition deadline. He did not wish for things to get out of hand.

'Mr President, with your permission, my next move will be to go on air and announce the things you have just agreed to. That will make them disperse and buy us time to see how best we can neutralise the opposition. I will present it in such a way as to make you look very good. In fact, I will draft something and act as though I am reading it out on your behalf. Do I have your permission to proceed, sir?'

'Anything you do is fine, Yalley. Go right ahead. I have already told them you are in charge. Make sure the people continue to love me. Keep me posted afterwards. I will be coming back to the capital in a few days after this nonsense has died down. We must meet to celebrate, and don't forget to bring the names I want. Thanks for the extra troops you sent for my protection. Also, I need more security gadgets for my guards. I saw some new gadgets in the most recent James Bond movie. The one with the pretty Halle Berry girl. I want them all, if they exist, Yalley. We must keep abreast with technology. My ADC will show you the movie so you know which definite ones to get in case you can't get all. Tell our secret defence partners that I need them after we have placated their journalists. I suppose you won't be deporting them anymore. Never mind, just get on with it, Yalley. And don't forget to watch the movie. We must be abreast, I say! Over and out!'

General Yalley had very little time left, with the opposition deadline rushing relentlessly towards all the major protagonists in this potentially deadly real-life drama.

'Call Broadcasting House and tell them to bring their cameras and radio crew here post haste. They should set up in the conference room. Tell the Director General that if he knows what's good for him, he should absolutely make sure he wastes no time at all. I want national and international coverage, and I want to be hooked into the system rigged up by the opposition at the Independence Plaza so each one of those demonstrators can hear me clearly. The foreign press people and all other networks should all be plugged in. Finally, they should go on air every 10 minutes with the announcement that I will be making a statement on behalf of the President at exactly 30 minutes before the opposition deadline. Call my house and see that my children are all right. Monitor the 10-minute interval announcements and let me know. Now get moving,' he said to his PA, Mrs Tutu, as soon as she entered his office upon being summoned.

General Yalley leaned back in his chair and closed his eyes. He felt drained from his session with Brewman. What had just transpired between them was not new. In fact, although it was as far removed from public knowledge as possible, Yalley had, over the years, acted as a restraining influence on Brewman. And without that influence exercised by him to curb some of the dictator's ghastly excesses, the suffering being endured by the citizenry today would be 10 times worse! This awareness of his private role in literally protecting the people of the country from Brewman's true murderous impulses added to his overall anguish, mortification and confusion. Part of him felt this was why he had not abandoned the Regime earlier. But try as he may, he knew he could never escape his reputation as a hangman for the Regime.

Why had he not explained this private role to his wife, instead of keeping mute, while she became anguished over his perceived misdeeds to the point of taking her own life? What at all had possessed him then? Did he think at the time that he had enough time to come clean with her? What of his own actual transgression of persecuting those who had made his life a misery as a child? Why had he been so unforgiving towards those who really did not know any better or know what they were doing as children? Why had his hatred of them festered? Did he, Yalley, have defective genes? Were his genes inherently sinister? But then, how could sinister genes produce a Zara? What of the good things he had done by restraining Brewman the Brute? Did Zara get only the very few good ones he had and the rest from her mother? Would his wife stop haunting him if he told her of his good deeds? But as a ghost or spirit of sorts, should she not already know this without being formally informed?

Yalley knew he had to put these confused thoughts aside if he was to maintain his sanity. His own very private hell had to be placed on hold while he dealt with the immediate problem that would not keep for much longer. The crowd of demonstrators had to disperse before violence broke out. He knew he was treading a fine line, as it was also important that whatever he said looked as though it was President Brewman's own words, with all his marked idiosyncrasies! He had to come down to the man's level.

He needed an uncluttered mind to address the nation.

He attempted some meditation to achieve this.

He was partially successful.

He jotted down some notes.

He was as ready as he could possibly be, under the circumstances.

The State Broadcasting people had finished setting up their equipment in the conference room and were ready for him.

He soon went on air.

'Fellow citizens, this is General Yalley speaking to you today on behalf of our President-for-Life-Until-Further-Notice, His Supreme Excellency Field Marshall Brewman. Consequently, what I say to you is, in truth, the President's own words so kindly bear that in mind.

'My fellow countrymen, sons and daughters, I salute you all. I am heartbroken that many of you have been misled by subversive malcontents into taking to the streets against my recent decree that is aimed solely at guaranteeing the security and territorial integrity of our beloved nation. All I have ever done for this country is to create the stability that you all currently enjoy. Nonetheless, I am like a father who cannot ignore the pleas of his children, even when those pleas are misguided. In my generosity, I have decided to suspend the National Service decree indefinitely, pending discussions between stakeholders and other sensitisation programmes. Also, I give my assurance to approach the neighbouring country warring on us to consider a negotiated temporary ceasefire. I am also going to ask the Minister of Information to begin consultations with the press houses and media representatives to consider relaxing our media regulations, but within a context where national security considerations remain paramount. Government will also hold meetings with the Students' Union about those university students who were detained.

'Fellow countrymen, countrywomen and country children, I, President Brewman, have never sent my troops against innocents. Only against communist, anarchist, Islamic terrorists who hide behind students and workers to destabilise me! If you do not want my troops to come to you then you also have to weed out the anarchist, communist, Islamic terrorist agitators in your midst who spread rancour and bitterness for their own evil end. Even then, I am willing to confine most of my troops to the barracks, apart from those fighting our glorious war, and leave the street patrolling and security checkpoints to the regular police. In fact, those military troops currently on the perimeter of your march are ordered away forthwith. Return to barracks now! Stand down! You are dismissed!

'Fellow country people, in effect, I am doing all that you are asking of me and thus, you must also do what I, your President and Father of the Nation, asks of you my children: I want you all to immediately disperse and go back to your homes. The demonstration is over as I, in my generosity, have granted all your requests. I am requesting police commanders to take over from the dismissed military troops and ensure an orderly dispersal of our citizens. Also, I ask in the name of national security that you are all vigilant in your communities to smoke out those anarchist, communist, Islamic terrorists and evil malcontents I have mentioned so we can continue to enjoy the stability I have created for you! I wish you all a good evening!'

What an arrogant, egotistical man! Can this brute really see beyond his own nose? If this man really believes the things he says then the country is in even more serious trouble than I have imagined! But never mind – we have won! For now, at least. We have actually WON, WOW, UNBELIEVABLE, thought Nana, amidst the tumultuous din that had engulfed them all.

'WE'VE WON!! WE'VE WON!! WE'VE WON!!' was the chant taken up by all and sundry. The marchers literally roared their heads off with pure joy and sheer disbelief at the immensity of their immediate victory over the Regime.

'Brewman backing down?!'

'Unheard of!'

'Whenever in recent living memory has such a thing occurred? Truly it is *Vox Populi, Vox Dei!* Yes, the "voice of the people truly is the voice of God".'

Now they could go home.

Now their children were safe.

Now they would stay in school and get an education – all things being equal.

Now their sons and daughters at the war front may also come home.

They had won!

The people had won this round.

CHAPTER TWENTY-FIVE

CCTV 'Juju'

Basking in their victory, the people were making their way to their various homes in an orderly manner. The opposition organisers had not left even this aspect of events to chance. Saga's Uncle Tiger, who was enormously wealthy, had volunteered to pay scores of private bus drivers, as well as truck and taxi drivers, at going commercial rates to transport as many people as possible, including the students, back to their various domiciles or prior congregation points, both in and around the capital city. This was not randomly done but placed under the supervision of a transportation sub-committee of the opposition's Joint Action Committee.

Saga was sitting, grinning from ear to ear, in one of the buses paid for by his Uncle Tiger to cart some of the students back to Brewman High School. Like his fellow schoolmates, he was in a state of ecstatic triumph. They had all managed to shout themselves hoarse from unbridled jubilation. Saga was truly proud of himself, as well as his fellow Orphans and other schoolmates.

The din in the bus was such that conversation with his best friend, Ibrahim, who sat by him, was almost impossible. Thus, they sat grinning broadly and left the shouting and caterwauling to their fellow student compatriots. They were now passing the area where Fort Brewman was located, and Saga's mind drifted towards his brave, beloved and so exquisite Zara. In actual fact, Zara had not been far from Saga's unconscious mind all day. It was as though his soul was fused with hers, and that she was with him at all times.

He suddenly remembered their mission the night before, which gave him a hollow feeling in the pit of his stomach, and immediately wiped the jubilant grin off his face. He turned from Ibrahim so as to avoid having to answer any questions about his sudden and probably visible mood swing.

God Almighty, but how could he have forgotten about that? And now that the demonstrations were over, there was bound to be some serious post-mortem analysis by the authorities of key events such as the sudden demobilisation and undoubted sabotaging of the military vehicles at Fort Brewman! Saga began to fear for Zara. Somehow, the thought of fearing for himself and his own central role in their mission simply did not occur to him. Where Zara was concerned, Saga had actually become the very epitome of selflessness.

He would call Zara when he disembarked from the bus at Brewman High. He would simply have to find a way to escape from the impromptu victory celebrations his Orphan compatriots had just decreed were to happen when they got back to the campus.

Zara's thoughts mirrored Saga's in a most uncanny fashion. The focus of her concern was Saga's safety. She knew that the Regime's retrospective analysis in the aftermath of the demonstrations would be swift and clinical, and the consequent reprisals, merciless. In fact, her father had just come home in a foul, aggressive mood. She could hear him in the living room, barking orders and hurling stern reprimands to underlings over his mobile phone and walkie-talkie. Zara carefully tiptoed almost half the length of the stairs leading to their fashionable and nicely-appointed main living room, in which her father now grimly sat. She bent cautiously to espy him through the banister, taking care not to be seen.

The General had finished his tirades for now and irritably banged his mobile handset on the polished oak side table next to the high ornately-carved armchair in which he sat. Thinking himself unobserved, he bent forward and placed his face in both his hands, and let out a huge sigh, which caused his shoulders to droop.

Observing this, Zara was perplexed. Was the great despotic General himself about to cry? Why? Was it because the

Government had been forced to back down in the face of the opposition's undoubted victory? Zara was still pondering this when she heard and then espied her brother, Yalley Junior, enter the living room through the sliding French glass doors that opened onto the outside porch and led to their vast, well-groomed, landscaped gardens. Hearing someone enter the living room, the General quickly sat upright from his hunched position and resumed his usual stern, erect, commanding demeanour.

'Daddy, Daddy, I'm glad you're home. I'm a bit confused. I saw you on TV. How could you make us back down? How could you agree to their demands? And why did you send the soldiers away? Daddy, what is going on?' asked his son in a rush, as he sat down in the chair opposite the General.

Junior was obviously distressed by what he could only view as an intolerable opposition victory, which he considered a huge affront to himself and all he stood for.

'Shut up and stop whining, Junior. What do you know about running a country? What do you know about war? Or don't you know that this is a war? Don't you ever learn anything? Sometimes, when you are fighting your enemies, it is wise to concede or pretend to lose a battle in order to win the overall war! Do you understand?'

Undeterred by his father's harshly-spoken reply, and still incensed by the humiliation he felt they had suffered at the hands of his hated rival, Saga's father, he shot back at his father, 'But Dad, why concede a battle when there is no need to do that? Why deliberately lose when you can win? This doesn't make sense to me!'

'It does not make sense to you because you are a fool. I have raised a fool in this house. You are a twin and yet, you do not have half the brains of your sister, whom you are always foolishly insulting and belittling. Why, but did you want us to shoot unarmed women and children in the full glare of international news cameras? Do you want us to shoot your own schoolmates? Are you really that stupid? Now that we have conceded and pretended to give in, we know the faces of the true opposition leaders. Did that Orphan boy's father not show himself as one of their senior leaders? Now we know them all, is it not much easier to hunt them down and punish them so they wish they had never been born? Now get out of my sight and do something useful with yourself before I ground you forever! Get out!'

It appeared as though the only thing the receptors in Junior's tunnel-vision brain were capable of receiving from his father's outburst was that the opposition would be punished and Saga's father and family, in particular, would suffer significantly, as they had been singled out! This warmed the cockles of Junior's heart nicely and made him almost effusive in his thanks as he made his way out of his father's presence, as he had been ordered.

Having heard the entire exchange between father and son, Zara was in a state of panic. The General had actually singled out Saga's father, and that also meant their entire family would suffer terrible retribution! Watching her brother make his way towards her hidden position, she quickly tiptoed back up the stairs and once on the landing, silently made her way to her bedroom and, with trembling hands, closed the door.

Having been repeatedly cheered, carried shoulder-high, and patted and thumped on the back by crowds of adoring demonstrators from which he had eventually escaped, Nana now sat grim-faced in the basement of his brother's Masonic Temple with a relatively small group of people who had gathered there in the aftermath of their victory against the Brewman Regime. He had been joined by his brother, Pappy, Raba, the women's representative, Mr Kamson, the workers leader, Obo, and his friend, Kobby, of the National Students' Union, as well as a few other trusted members of their core leadership cadre.

The sullen, grim visages that they each wore could not be attributed to a failure to recognise the enormity and importance of the incredible gains they had made on that very day in securing critical concessions from the heavy-handed, despotic Brewman Regime. It certainly was a resounding victory insofar as it guaranteed at the very least that their children would not be summarily shipped off and dumped onto the killing fields of a dubious war to meet their premature and inglorious demise. Tiger was the first to speak, addressing the small group. A hush fell on them, as they had been murmuring among themselves while sipping mugs of steaming hot coffee, brought to them courtesy of Tiger's devoted factotum.

'We look like mourners at a wake, instead of the victors that we truly are, and we all know why. Brewman and his sadistic cohorts now know who we all are and they are coming for us and will show us no mercy. We have seriously compromised their aura of invincibility and the only way they can repair it is by making examples out of us. This is not a formal meeting and we must keep it very short. Let's hear what you all have to say about this. We have to let the wider Joint Action Committee know our decisions soon.'

There were appreciative murmurs for Tiger's directness. It was Nana who spoke after his brother. He was equally direct.

'Our victory is a fantastic one. The National Service decree is essentially dead. They'll convene some meaningless committee and give the impression of democratic involvement, but in the end, they'll kill the decree. They'll ease a few censorship rules and also release some of our colleagues and students from the jails and black sites where they've been kept. They'll also make some overtures towards a cease-fire agreement to halt the war for now. However, this is no time to pat ourselves on our back. We knew this moment was coming. There are three main questions we need to address, and they are: How do we limit the Government's fury about to be unleashed on us? How do we protect our families from this unpleasantness? And finally, how do we advance the gains we've made today, despite this inevitable backlash we are facing?'

'Here's my perspective,' Raba started. 'This backlash, though inevitable, will not be immediate. Even dictators must sometimes appear to have a judicious sense of timing. Public opinion against them at the moment is too intense for them to ignore. For now, the international community is also watching. So yes, they will lick their wounds for a while and plan. When they attack, they will round all of us up in one fell swoop. However, we can't allow the opposition to be without leaders.

As such, some of us will have to go underground while some of us will have to stay and face the grim music. Obo and Kobby and their top people will be safe for now because the students are perceived as too vociferous for the Regime to pick up their leaders so brazenly this time around. Saga and his Orphans should also be safe. Thousands of secondary school students were part of the demonstration and I don't think the Regime will risk singling them out, despite the central role that Saga and his group played.'

Raba had succinctly summarised much of what was on everyone's mind. She was neither blowing hard nor soft. She was merely telling it as it was. Members of the gathering could only nod sullenly in reply. Tiger then decided that it was time to bring the meeting to a close and also move them away from their unbecoming despondency.

'Both Raba and my brother are right. Who stays to face the music? Who deserts his family and lives a life on the run underground? What happens to these deserted families? How do they cope? How do we deepen the gains made today? These are important questions we must answer quickly, but for now, many of those who came from the other regions and cities around the country and cannot return tonight are waiting to meet with some of us here. I hear Kobby and Obo have a national meeting of student representatives tonight, so we must break this up now. Let us go and attend to our responsibilities, and reconvene as soon as possible to answer these thorny questions and many more. One very important reason for this brief meeting is for you to inform those from the regions you will be meeting tonight that we will need safe houses all over the country for those who will have to go on the run. We will also need the help of our regional colleagues in extending our underground "railway" network to smuggle our people out of the cities. This is critical. Kobby and Obo should also inform their regional branches. Meanwhile, remove those lousy, mournful looks you are all wearing before you go and meet anyone. What a group we make! We are the only people who mourn in victory! Now, come on and wear your smiling, victorious faces and get out of here. All those with long faces will be sanctioned! Out you go now!'

Tiger's last remarks drew smiles and subdued laughter from almost all present. Yes, it was time to laugh again and postpone the incongruous 'mourning in victory' session until later. For now, leadership duties still beckoned. The mourning would just have to wait.

'Saga, we need big words, Saga, give us some of your big words!' his friends chimed in unison now that they were back on their school campus. The students had hijacked the main assembly hall and were making merry and jubilating with boundless energy and genuine enthusiasm. They were shouting, singing, drumming on makeshift drums, and dancing simultaneously. It was as though huge millstones hanging from their necks had mercifully been removed; 'swords of Damocles' ominously positioned at the nape of their necks now removed as well.

Saga decided to give them a few big words as a treat for their bravery and success. He stood on a chair to speak and a hush fell on the room.

'All I can do is thank you all so much for your participation. We are all heroes. We went out to crush the horrible National Service decree and yes, we crushed it. You were all there so there is no more need for me to elaborate or pontificate. That would be the epitome of tautology itself. Are "elaborate, pontificate, epitome and tautology" big enough words for you guys?' Saga asked playfully.

'No, we want bigger words, Saga, from our biggest Orphan here,' shouted his friend, Ibrahim, to cheering from all.

Saga responded, 'Okay, then let me leave you with this string of P's by saying that we students finally refused to permit the persistent plethora of pernicious ploys perpetrated by a perfidious, parasitic government and their pestilential Praetorian protectors.'

This brought on another resounding cheer from the students, with clapping and catcalls of 'Encore, encore, and encore!' It was doubtful if most of them understood even half the words, but that was far from the point. They still wanted more!

But Saga had said enough. Indeed, it was time for him to sneak out and find a way to see Zara, whose house would have no doubt been turned into an impregnable fortress in the wake of the public disturbances.

Zara and Saga could not rendezvous in her room as usual, given the sheer number of armed security personnel her father had deployed to guard their mansion in the wake of the opposition action. Indeed, it would be near impossible for Saga to enter the premises without being spotted, apprehended, and most likely, manhandled. She decided she would go to him.

Eventually, after some cajoling and employing much of her considerable charm, she managed to get the guards stationed at the side gate to drop their stern posturing. In addition, she was forced to give them hefty cash tips to allow her out of the gate. Even then, she had to literally swear to them that she would be no more than 200 metres from the gate, and that she would be away for only half an hour.

Zara rushed into Saga's arms the moment he walked round the bend, onto the corner of the side street, where she'd been waiting for him. She kissed him passionately on the lips before he could utter a word, and clung to him as if for dear life.

Saga gently pushed her away and smiled. 'I've missed these lovely kisses of yours, my dear. But maybe we should talk first. How are your father and his Zombie mob? They must be pretty angry about what happened today.'

'Hmm Saga, I am so proud of you. I am so proud of what you and your family and all the opposition did. I am also proud of you and me and your Orphans as well. Come, let me kiss you again before I continue,' she said in a breathless rush, as she sought his lips again in the rapidly darkening night-time.

Saga wholeheartedly obliged and then gently held her at arm's length so they could discuss what was pressing on their minds. For them, the opposition victory opened up a whole new can of problematic and potentially lethal worms they had to address without delay. Saga looked expectantly at Zara, who smilingly continued as promised, 'We're in a heap of trouble. At least, I'm in serious trouble. I heard my father discussing with one of his special men about secret CCTV cameras they have in places like Fort Brewman. I heard him issue instructions that they should bring him the footage. Need I say more? As for me, I will be seen plain as day on those recordings. He will see you guys too, but you all had your faces covered. Dad will know straightaway that I am part of the sabotaging of the vehicles. This is serious, Saga. But I am so happy you are safe and that there was no violence today at the march.'

Saga looked at Zara in unabashed wonderment. The calmness and serenity with which she had just described what could only be viewed as an unmitigated disastrous development was unbelievable. Here they were, having been caught on camera performing acts that could only be described as high treason, and here she was, as cool as a cucumber and as right as rain. This girl is something else, he marvelled to himself.

'Zara, have you suddenly lost all your wits?' Here you are telling me we have an "end of days", doomsday scenario on our hands once these tapes get to your father, and you don't even appear to be bothered?' he asked in some amazement.

Zara retorted with uncharacteristic heat, 'Saga, what's done is done. We can't unspill the milk. My father will come at me to tell him who the other people on the tapes are. He will be mad as hell but I will face him squarely. I will never give him your name, Saga. I will protect you at all costs, so please don't worry. I will protect you, come what may!'

The girl in front of him was what could only be described as the real deal; the genuine article, or what Americans referred to as the 'Real McCoy'. How could one so young be so selfless and so brave? Saga just stared at her in admiration.

But how could he also just sit back and allow her to bear the brunt of what would no doubt be a swift and clinical investigation, with fierce repercussions to boot, once the culprits were unmasked? No, he could not do that. In fact, that he would not do!

With great effort, General Yalley hoisted himself up from the high chair he was sitting in within his spacious, luxuriously-decorated sitting room. He was groggy on his feet but managed to make his way into his private den, which also served as his office at home. 'No time to be weak,' he muttered to himself, as he forced himself to consider what must be done.

The President was livid and spoiling for a brutal offensive against the opposition leaders, as well as those within his own Government, whom he perceived as having failed him by allowing this humiliation of an opposition victory. Though General Yalley himself, as High Minister for Presidential Affairs, was effectively in charge of all security in the country, the President curiously did not hold him responsible. Rather, he had been given the very important task of smashing the opposition leadership and punishing his own colleagues who had been remiss in this humiliating affair.

General Yalley, using his extraordinary powers of persuasion and the sobering effect he sometimes had on his rabid boss, had persuaded the President that though his wishes would ultimately be carried out to the letter, it was nonetheless imperative that they proceed with some caution and patience. He explained that they virtually had the eyes of the world glued on them as a result of the demonstrations, and that it would not augur well for the Regime to strike back immediately. Consequently, it was better to wait for global eyes to be averted and for the opposition to feel complacent enough to lower their guard. And all this seemingly sensible reasoning added to massive amounts of subtle cajoling and hyperbolic flattering, which his boss lapped up, had thus bought the General a bit of time from the President to enable him to contemplate what must be done.

The General, however, was currently not as focused as his President would wish on planning his 'search and destroy' orders. He was more concerned with assessing the depth of his daughter's suspected involvement in helping the opposition. He was also plagued with worries as to how to protect the resistance leaders from the carnage that he had been ordered to visit upon them, without revealing his hand.

Sitting at his desk in his private office, he stared glassy-eyed at his wife's embroidered curtains that adorned his office windows. Looking at his deceased wife's curtains sometimes had a cathartic effect on him and allowed him to think carefully. Thus, he sat, virtually unblinking for an hour, having muted all his phones and walkie-talkie as he contemplated his next moves. One thought persisted in his mind above all else: 'My daughter and the Saga Orphan boy must be saved, no matter the cost.'

General Yalley then lapsed into reminiscing. His thoughts went back to his wife, whom he missed so much, and yet had also come to dread so seriously since her untimely, self-induced demise, and her recent visitations and apparitions in his dreams. He remembered the genesis of their romance so many years ago in England.

His wife came from Bowden in Cheshire, within the Greater Manchester area of England. Bowden, during the 1970s, 1980s and 1990s, was renowned for being a residential area with one of the largest concentration of millionaires in Europe. Thus, in contrast to his poverty-stricken upbringing, his wife had certainly been born with a sterling silver spoon firmly ensconced in her oral cavity.

He had met her while he was training as a cadet officer at the eminently prestigious and renowned Sandhurst Military Academy in Camberley, England. The colonial origin of the armed forces in his country dictated that would-be army officers in Zimgania train in British military institutions, even after the attainment of political independence in the mid-1960s. Such crucial military defence ties with the Mother country were not to be severed but rather preserved and nurtured.

After a particularly brutal, month of training, young cadet officer-to-be Yalley had welcomed a much-needed bank holiday weekend break. He decided at the time that he was in ample need of recuperation in a distinctly serene environment, and thus decided to visit the famed Lake District in Cumbria for his short rest and recreation, popularly termed by soldiers as R and R.

It was during the second evening of his salubrious stay at the Lake District that he met his gorgeous wife-to-be in the Goat in Boots pub near Lake Windermere. He had been relaxing with a large whisky and soda, which he was quietly nursing on his own. It was the first of many a nightcap planned for the evening. He wanted to get tolerably inebriated so he could sleep all morning the next day without the fuss or usual screaming expletives from his drill sergeant back at Sandhurst, urging him to haul his worthless, sorry arse out of bed at some ungodly daybreak hour.

It was a classic moment of love at first sight, and what followed over the next few weeks was a flourishing romance that encompassed ever-growing love and unbridled desire whenever he beheld her or even just thought of her. To him, she was the absolute embodiment of a 'pure English rose'.

It was, however, not what could be described as a fairy tale romance in any shape or form. From her quarter soon arose the ugly head of racism, when her parents sternly admonished her to cease and desist from cavorting with a 'darkie' or 'native' from the dark hinterlands of an equally dark continent. Indeed, she was made to feel a race traitor by even daring to suggest marriage to a black man, which would undoubtedly land her family of noble origins in unimaginable disgrace.

Love, however, did prevail, as no strenuous suggestions (or even threats) of dis-inheritance could dissuade the pure-hearted English rose to abandon her true love, despite his 'native' origins and rather dark hue. Thrown into this mix was also her quasi-liberal training at the equally prestigious Cheltenham Ladies College, which would not permit her to stoop so low as to acquiesce in any enterprise that required one to make decisions based on illiberal, backward and antiquated notions such as racism.

From his quarter also came the lamentation of his soon to be abandoned betrothed back at home in Africa, whom he had previously promised to marry immediately upon his return. The soon to be discarded betrothed had unceremoniously been informed by a blue air mail letter, 'par Avon', that their anticipated arranged marriage was now permanently off the books.

This, in turn, generated an even greater howl from his parents and other key extended family members, who, by return blue air mail post 'par Avon', threatened to cut him out of the family line if he dared discard a bride they had so painstakingly chosen for him, in favour of a pale-faced, white daughter from the land of their colonial oppressors.

General Yalley's wife's grandfather indeed happened to be an illegitimate son of a duke, whose name and noble antecedents were firmly enshrined within the hallowed sheaves of both Burke's Peerage and the Almanac de Gotha. These were both seminal, authoritative works in which the true nobility and aristocracy of Britain could be found, among others. However, being of illegitimate ilk meant that her fraternal grandfather, despite his very noble blood, could not aspire to any dukedom or baronetcy or peerage, for that matter, via inheritance. That did not, however, prevent her great-grandfather, the Grand Old Duke himself, who, by all accounts, was enormously wealthy, from giving his illegitimate son, whom was a cherished 'love child', a handsome start in life by setting aside a huge fortune for his living. As to how this doting, loving old Duke managed to manoeuvre around the strictures of the entail and primogeniture, which at the time legally prevented the division of inheritances in England, no one knew. It was nevertheless acknowledged by those in the know that it was a masterful feat indeed, to say the least.

As such, it was the besotted young lady's initial inheritance of a small part of this fortune, already received at the age of 19, that further enabled her to cast aside her family's severe disapprobation and embark on an elopement into the heart of the Dark Continent with young cadet Yalley.

Of course, she was promptly disinherited after the elopement and prematurely divorced from the remainder of her fortune by her family. Nonetheless, what she had thus far received as her initial inheritance was just about enough to see them through the most difficult times when they had returned to Zimgania, after the young, equally besotted Lieutenant Yalley had finished his training at Sandhurst.

All this General Yalley recalled with both fondness and sadness. His mind then focussed on some of the 'good' things he felt he had accomplished in recent times, despite his reputation as the ruthless henchman of a brutal dictator. He had over the years taken people into protective custody, banished others, and even hidden some to keep them away from the President's erratic and murderous whims. He had done so much on the quiet to protect many people from the brutal excesses that would have otherwise been visited on them, but could never own up to these good deeds for obvious reasons.

He knew one of the key demands from the opposition was for the Government to account for the whereabouts of the missing university students who had been arrested during the last riots. 'Missing indeed,' he scoffed. It was General Yalley who had been keeping them safe and under house arrest in isolated safe-houses scattered across the country after a Presidential Order had gone out that they were to be tortured and made to disappear as enemies of the state. And what did he get for all this? Vilification upon vilification as the chief villain of the Regime after his boss!

* * *

The very next day, General Yalley sat in his study again and quietly watched the footage from Fort Brewman on the night of the debilitating sabotage. Yes, it's my daughter alright. My brave, beautiful daughter with an obvious death wish, he thought grimly.

Unbeknown to anyone but himself (and a select few of his own ultra-elitist military intelligence officers who were loyal to only him), General Yalley had secretly installed undetectable CCTV, at his own expense, in certain key security areas within the capital city, and a few other strategic places around the country, including both Fort Brewman and Fort Id.

He had thus garnered from this secret enterprise a wealth of information he used to keep many of his colleagues and minions in line. Having absolutely no knowledge of these secret cameras, many of his colleagues thought he had superhuman or African magical juju powers. They thus dreaded him accordingly. They would never dare cross someone who, with the aid of juju, 'magically' knew so much. CCTV, at the time, was not yet a common feature in Zimgania.

He had seen the shadowy figures leaping from the walls, shoving some indeterminate stuff into the fuel tanks of the vehicles, and running off the same way as they had come in.

He saw the soldiers, who were supposed to be guarding the Fort, helping his daughter to bring in several covered baskets, as well as bottles of liquor, with their clearly distinguishable and expensive labels, which most likely came from his own stock at home! The nerve of this girl, he thought, almost laughing at the sheer audacity of it all, even though this was far from being a laughing matter.

The General was certainly security-savvy enough to immediately realise that whatever his daughter was up to at the Fort was essentially diversionary tactics. She had so effectively drawn the guards away from their guarding and patrolling duties to 'party' with her in the main mess hall, while her co-conspirators wreaked havoc on the engines of the extremely expensive military vehicles sitting quietly at the Fort. It was classic misdirection. Despite his horror, he could not help but secretly admire his daughter's courage and undoubted intelligence.

The General indeed believed that he had now pieced it all together. From the sheer agility, sprightliness and speed of the shadowy, masked saboteurs, he concluded that this was the crew of the Orphan boy, Saga, who was dating his daughter. If that boy planned this with my daughter alone then the kid is equally gutsy and terribly brave, he thought again, in what was ostensibly unbecoming admiration from his official standpoint as a victim of the sabotage.

The only issue that he still could not determine for certain was whether the opposition leaders had put his daughter up to this or whether this was a wildcat solo scheme cooked up by her and the Orphan boy. He suspected the latter to be the most likely scenario.

He would know soon enough, he assured himself with quiet confidence, but what was truly important here was how to prevent Zara's involvement from ever becoming known. Under no conceivable circumstances could he allow his daughter to be charged with treason. In actual fact, the repercussions of such a development on himself as the person effectively in charge of overall National Security would also be irretrievably damaging. He would certainly have no choice but to resign his high office as Minister for Presidential Affairs with Oversight for National Security. And he would certainly not be permitted to live much longer after that, unless he found a way to run away and go into exile.

General Yalley swung into action.

He decided to execute a minor 'black-op' to enable him to reach out to one of the key leaders of the opposition in furtherance of his quest.

Also on that very next day after the opposition victory, General Yalley dispatched some members of his elite squad to forcibly coerce the guards at Fort Brewman to significantly amend their recollections of that fateful night of the sabotage to permanently exclude ever setting eyes on Zara Yalley. They were assured in no uncertain terms of a terrible fate if they ever mentioned to any living creature about having ever laid eyes on Zara Yalley. They were also given very substantial cash bonuses equivalent to five full years of their salaries each to keep them completely mute. This was accepted with alacrity, amidst undying pledges to delete the visage of Zara from their memories forever.

Now, what was he to do about the Orphan boy and the now nationally exposed opposition leaders, including the Orphan boy's father, whom he was to make examples of in the most punitive manner possible? The General pondered this question, as he had received new, explicit instructions from the President-for-Life-Until-Further-Notice to severely punish the opposition leaders sooner than later, and to stop putting too much store on the timing of it.

CHAPTER TWENTY-SIX

'Mummy Comes at Night'

Three days after the opposition's victory, Uncle Tiger was driving home very late after leaving Nana's home in Ridge Heights. He had gone there for some 'proper' home-cooked food, as his own assistant-cum-cook-cum-factotum was not too adept in the culinary arts. This generally suited Tiger most of the time as he was usually of an abstemious disposition. However, there were times when he missed good, home-cooked food with the warm presence of family to share it with, hence his occasional trips to his brother's home for this particular culinary and familial indulgence.

Tiger was just about to turn onto the street on which his house was situated when he was suddenly blocked by two large cars, which seemed to appear out of nowhere. He quickly jammed on his brakes to avoid a collision and instinctively looked in the rear-view mirror as well. Much to his chagrin, two other large vehicles had also moved to block his retreat. Uncle Tiger was many things but he was certainly not a fool. He knew there and then that he had walked into an ambush from which there was little or no escape! They had been lying in wait for him.

The vehicles, both in front and behind him were hefty, dark SUVs, though he could not ascertain their exact make and models in the dark, unlit street. Eight men in all emerged from the SUVs and surrounded his modest Toyota Camry saloon car. Their bearing and holstered side arms suggested to him they were Government security personnel.

'Rational apprehension of danger and not fear is our situation here,' he whispered to himself, for he was truly a fearless soul. Tiger quickly pondered his options. He knew without a doubt that this was part of the crackdown on opposition leaders he and his colleagues had correctly anticipated. However, they didn't think it would be so soon, given the preponderance of deep anti-Government sentiments prevailing in the country in the immediate aftermath of their victory. Clearly, it now seemed that they had gravely miscalculated, since he was no doubt about to be taken into custody to await his Government-ordered unsavoury fate.

'What was that saying again?' he asked himself, and then remembered. 'One does not take a knife to a gunfight.' However, in this case, he did not even possess a knife, or any implement resembling such. Surely the logical extension of such a sagacious adage would certainly militate against him bringing just his fists – which were all he had – to a fight with eight undoubtedly trained military or paramilitary goons wielding guns!

'Well it seems there is nothing to do but to cooperate for now,' he thought to himself, as two of the men approached his driver side window. Uncle Tiger rolled down his window and politely asked, 'What can I do for you gentlemen on this fine night?'

To his amazement, the reply he got was quite polite, even if a bit gruff, and certainly a far cry from the heaping of opprobrium on him and the shouting of expletives with him being dragged out of the car that he had expected.

Instead, the one who responded simply said, 'We are with the Government and you are not under arrest, sir, and we apologise to you for stopping you in the street in this manner. However, it was necessary. You are to come with us. One of my men will drive your car and follow us. You will have to be blindfolded, but you are not in any danger. We appeal to you to step out of your car and not resist or we will be forced to restrain you. Again, we apologise for having to do things this way but these are our orders.'

Tiger was indeed amazed at this clipped, seemingly polite and obviously rehearsed mini-speech, as he stepped out of his car to cooperate.

Tiger was driven blindfold for about 30 minutes before the car come to a stop. The driver took so many turns on the journey that he soon gave up his spirited effort to memorise the route. He wondered whether the zigzagging pattern of driving was purposely done to prevent him from doing exactly that.

Tiger had his blindfold removed the moment they arrived at their destination. He noticed they had stopped in what appeared to be a rather large, dimly-lit garage with neatly-arranged car tyres and sandbags against the walls. There were also guns and allied boxes of ammunition and military gear of an indeterminate nature stacked on shelves built into the garage walls. There were two seemingly new Toyota Land Cruiser vehicles also parked there.

Tiger was then led through a side door and traversed a long corridor into an average-sized room with just a medium-sized kitchen table in the middle of it. Two unadorned, straight-backed wooden chairs had been placed on opposite sides of the square table. Tiger was made to sit on one of the chairs and politely asked to wait.

General Yalley briskly entered the room and sat opposite Uncle Tiger. He was unarmed and in mufti. He said nothing as he sat down and simply stared at his guest. Tiger stared back, unfazed.

They sized each other up from across the table. Both men were unafraid, though thoroughly distrustful of each other. Both were driven by different yet equally compelling motives. The General was driven by guilt and the absolute need to protect his daughter as a form of absolution or penance in the eyes of his dead wife, and Uncle Tiger was driven by the unshakeable righteousness of his cause to create *ordo ab chao* – 'order out of chaos' – within his country.

General Yalley finally spoke. 'I apologise for the ignominious manner in which I dragged you here, but you and I must talk. I chose you because you are less publicly visible than your brother, Nana, who addressed your demonstration. I know you hate me and everything I stand for. I know about you. I have read your file. You are a reasonable man, so let us reason. What we do here tonight affects not just our respective families, but our country as well. Do you have anything to say before I continue?'

Uncle Tiger quietly pondered the General's words for a few moments before replying, 'Bringing me here in this fashion is a bit dramatic, is it not? I thought this is the stuff of movies. I am honoured though, that you have a file on me. Why, but you don't have anything better to do? I do not hate you. I do not hate anyone. Your President and what you stand for are bad for this country and opposed to any notion of reasonableness and progress, so I must strive to end you and your obnoxious government. That is all. It is not personal. As to why you brought me here, I guess you will have to enlighten me.'

'Okay, as you wish. I'll get straight to the point. Whatever I say here can never be traced back to me. I know you are an honourable man. I know about your principled fight with our Masonic Orders. I know you don't think me honourable, but that's of no consequence, so let's cut to the chase. You know I must punish the opposition leadership. I must make public examples of all of you. I am talking about harsh punishment. President Brewman has ordered this. I need your help in this matter.'

Though managing to keep a straight face, Uncle Tiger was quite puzzled and surprised at these opening remarks of this known enemy of the people.

'General Yalley, are you normal in the head, or as they say, have you eaten of the insane root that holds reason prisoner? You kidnap me in the dead of night and ask me to betray my people. I thought you said you knew me? Hellfire will freeze over and exhibit truly arctic features before I betray my own brother and allies, so maybe we should stop this foolishness now and send me to your torture chambers at the BNR. I am ready.'

All this, Uncle Tiger said with determined calmness. He was unafraid. He was indeed ready to deal with anything they could throw at him, including torture. He had strenuously prepared himself for such a possibility through his constant meditation and communion with Providence.

The General looked at the fearless man opposite him and his respect for him went up a few rungs. He then proceeded to elaborate. He explained that he was, in reality, not the enemy they thought he was. He told him of the things he had done, such as shipping troops and ammunition to the war front, which would have otherwise been used against the marchers; ensuring there were no open confrontations between the security forces and the marchers during the demonstration; persuading the President to desist from the use of force and to suspend the National Service decree, etc. In fact, he had done all he could to sabotage his own Government and seriously cripple their security response capabilities in order to protect the very opposition groups that viewed him as the most determined and implacable of enemies.

Uncle Tiger just sat there and stared at the General with mounting comprehension, as the pieces gradually started to fall into place in his mind. Uncle Tiger looked at the General, in wonder and shock at what he had just been told. The implications were huge.

'So that is why we got off so easily. That is why we succeeded that day without violence and bloodshed. We even joked amongst ourselves that we certainly had a guardian angel watching over us and clearing all obstacles in our path for us, and it appears we actually did have one in reality! General Yalley, so you have been our guardian angel and protector all along? Jesus Christ of Holy Nazareth! How can that even be possible?' Good Lord, but this was too much for him to comprehend in one go!

The General continued before Tiger could even muster the requisite clarity of mind to continue. 'I can see from your initial expression that you believe me. The main question you must be asking yourself is the big WHY! You are wondering why I did all this. We don't have time for elaborate answers so let me simply say I have much to atone for and this was part of my penance. What I'm also about to do now for your opposition group is part of my penance too. But I have an even more critical selfish interest in all this.' The General paused for a few moments and continued.

'Though you don't know it, my own child is one of you. My own child supports you and has aided and abetted you enormously in your campaign. Not my boy. Not the notorious, troublesome one in Brewman High School you may have heard of. I mean my gentle daughter, Zara, is one of you, and she has committed high treason to support you, and I must protect her at all costs. And she committed these acts of treason with your own famous nephew, Saga the Orphan boy. I bet you don't know they have been secretly dating for many months now and are very much in love. Come on, Mr Tiger, but who do you think sabotaged the military vehicles at Fort Brewman? Yes, it was my brave daughter and your equally brave nephew, Saga, who accomplished that mighty feat!'

Uncle Tiger's mouth involuntarily opened wide at these new and completely unexpected revelations. The sabotaging of those military vehicles that aided the opposition immensely was a mystery that had baffled them since the march, and to find out that it was their own young Saga and this man's daughter was just too bizarre to contemplate!

'What in God's name are you talking about? Our Saga and your daughter sabotaged millions of dollars of the Zombie military vehicles? Are you off your head or what?' was all a thoroughly bewildered Uncle Tiger could manage by way of an answer. His usual cool and calm demeanour had been considerably ruffled by the amazing revelations.

The General pointedly ignored his question and proceeded to instruct Tiger as to how he thought Saga, Zara and their so-far anonymous friends managed such a feat, from the evidence he had garnered to date. The General continued, 'When I say I need your help with the punishments, what I mean is that you and your brother must help me figure out how to play this. There must be a semblance of me having followed the President's directives, while allowing most of you to escape or go unpunished. I am trying to help you some more. And you must also help me to figure out how to protect my daughter and to fully cover up her involvement and your nephew's. They did not do it alone. There were nine other people and they must never be made to talk. By the way, your brother, Nana, is the only person on Earth you can discuss this with. No one else. Do I have your word on this? If any of your people know we are talking, there will be huge misunderstandings and you might even be branded a traitor to your people, my boss will put me in front of a firing squad post-haste as well. We must also find untraceable means to communicate without meeting like this unless extremely necessary. What do you say?'

Uncle Tiger had regained his composure and renowned mental acuity, and was thinking clearly now. 'There are many questions that need answering. Suffice it to say, nonetheless, that I believe you for now. The situation is extremely dicey for all of us. I will not thank you for what you have done so far for us. Like you said, you have much to atone for. However, be comforted by the fact that some of your recent actions may have saved many lives, and for that, I am grateful to you. I will consult with my brother and revert. As to how we will communicate, leave that with me. You'll soon find out and it will be safe. Just give me an initial mobile number to reach you on. It should be untraceable. Be careful. You are playing a dangerous game with an unforgiving, maniacal boss. Let me go now.'

'Okay Mr Tiger – I will trust you. You can go. Your car is here. No more blindfolding as proof that I am trusting you completely. Very few people know of this secret base of mine but now you know, as one of my men will give you directions home. I will wait to hear from you. My daughter must be protected at all costs. You may not believe it but I am honoured to meet you. Here is the number. We can only use it once. Goodbye,' replied the General, who, as if having anticipated the request for a phone number, took out a small piece of paper from his breast pocket and gave it to Tiger. One of his operatives suddenly appeared in the room and quietly led Uncle Tiger out. General Yalley simply sat and stared at the back of his adversary. That was enough for one day.

* * *

The next morning, General Yalley felt it was time to confront his daughter about her involvement in the sabotage of the military vehicles. There was no way out of this. Also, the more he knew, the more he would better be able to protect her and the Orphan boy. The showdown with his daughter could thus wait no longer.

The General summoned Zara into his study. She stood in front of him, slightly uncomfortable but decidedly unafraid. She did not sit when he waved his hand to gesture that she should. In fact, before he could even utter a word, Zara pre-empted him by going first. She spoke in very measured, serious tones.

'Mummy comes to me at night. Sometimes. She keeps telling me to make all of this right, all this murderous mess. Because of you, she cannot even find peace in death. I am ashamed to be your daughter. I am ashamed you are my father. Yes, I helped them. Yes, I helped them to disable those killing machines and I am proud of it. Lock me up if you want. Let your murdering goons torture me. I don't care anymore. I did this for Mummy and for all those people you and that Brewman brute have been oppressing for so long. I do not fear your notorious firing squads. Kill me, Daddy, and I will be at last free of your shame and I will be with Mummy.'

The General was dumbstruck. He did not know what to say to this revelation, which bordered on an epiphany! Was he himself not partly driven in recent times by epiphanies in the form of blood-besmirched, ghostly apparitions of his dear departed wife? He simply looked at his daughter and, heaving a sigh, told her she could go and that he would speak to her later.

'But Daddy—' Zara started, but was cut off mid-sentence.

'Just go, Zara. Please go. I just hope that one day, you will find it in your heart to forgive me. Please go, my dear, and know that no matter what has happened and no matter what will happen, I love you very much and I understand why you did what you did with your Orphan boyfriend.'

It was Zara's turn to be dumbstruck. She could not believe what she was hearing and she had never seen her father look so sad and even somewhat defeated. And how in God's name did he know about Saga? Her father never spoke like that, never uttered the 'love' word! She involuntarily stifled a sob, ran out of his study, and made for the sanctuary of her room, where she could cry freely and in peace.

After Zara had left, the General kept his head down with his chin on his chest for several minutes, trying to quieten his turmoil and get back control of his emotions. He achieved partial success in this and then swung into action.

He attacked his phones and walkie-talkie like a man possessed and proceeded to spew forth stern instructions to his underlings and commanders at the various Government security agencies.

Through military directives, he transferred all the guards stationed at Fort Brewman on the night of the sabotage and deliberately arranged for the paperwork on the transfers to be 'misplaced' or at least buried for a while to come. He had already paid them handsomely to forget they ever laid eyes on this daughter.

He also arranged it so that all the 'post-mortem' reports in the aftermath of the opposition action by the various security agencies were routed through him before they were sent to the President. This way, he would be able to engender some damage control and eliminate all suspicion or evidence that could implicate his daughter.

An unfettered avalanche of emotions cascaded through Zara's entire being. Her brief confrontation with her father had fuelled the high state of anxiety she was perpetually living in these days. She lay on her bed, sobbing uncontrollably, for over half an hour, before sitting up to examine her own feelings clinically.

What in the name of heaven was wrong with her father? How come this brash, dictatorial excuse for a father was suddenly sounding so contrite? And, more importantly, what business did she have feeling sorry for her father when she was fully aware of all he had done to help bring their country to this pitiful point? And what did he mean by 'I understand why you did what you did with your Orphan boyfriend'? And why were they being let off so easily without any fuss whatsoever, despite the enormously problematic nature of what they had done?

For once, Zara could not think clearly enough to answer any of the questions tumbling through her mind. A cluttered mind was a rare occurrence for her indeed. She desperately needed to speak to Saga. Who else in the world could she discuss such grave matters with, apart from her one true love, Saga? She prayed he would soon be able to tear himself away from his jubilant friends and family and come to her quickly. She simply needed to be with him.

Nana had been summoned by his brother, Tiger, for what he said was an urgent meeting. It was unlike his very calm and collected brother to ask for 'urgent meetings', and had thus arrived post-haste at Tiger's sprawling compound in Uso Town.

They were sitting in an austere room in the basement of the Masonic Temple. It was adjacent to their usual meeting venue. The room sported just a desk with a few chairs around it and two brown, plain-looking armchairs on which they sat. A grey wall to wall industrial carpet on the floor did nothing to offset the decidedly spartan hue.

'Tiger, what is so urgent that you asked me to drop everything and come. What could possibly be the matter? I thought we had covered all bases for now,' Nana asked his brother, still a little flustered over the suddenness of the summons.

Tiger looked at his brother calmly and replied, 'Nana, even as children, you were the most patient one amongst us. Today, I need you to summon endless reserves of that patience to fortify yourself, as I am about to drop quite a few bombshells.'

Nana could see his brother was quite serious. He was now quite recovered and had regained his composure. 'But who is more patient than you these days, Tiger? You who speaks only a few sentences per month? When did you become such a non-talking person, my brother? I am even surprised you speak at our meetings. You should see some of our people staring at you in shock whenever you make any statement that is more than two sentences. I guess they're more used to your usual monosyllabic grunts,' Nana ended with a light laugh.

'Nana, please be serious. That I have grown up to be a silent man of few words in my middle age is my destiny. It is borne out of meditation and reflection. Are you ready to listen?'

Nana nodded in the affirmative and Tiger began his narration, sternly asking Nana not to interrupt him until he had finished.

Uncle Tiger began his briefing from the moment he was stopped by General Yalley's security men when he left Nana's home that night. Even though Uncle Tiger spoke very softly, he could see his brother's increasing concern and agitation as his story developed.

Nana grew wide-eyed with wonder at what he was hearing about General Yalley's immense but secret assistance to their opposition cause. He then became bewildered and very confused when he heard about Saga's amazing but outrageously dangerous actions with the help of General Yalley's own daughter.

He could no longer remain quiet. 'Tiger, please stop. Stop. Just stop for now. Are you seriously telling me that my son, our very own Saga, and his girlfriend, who somehow happens to be Yalley's daughter, planned and executed such an extremely dangerous mission successfully with just a few friends? A mission that the entire united opposition in this country could not make head or tail of? And have you thought of the implications? What if they had been killed? What if they had been arrested? And Yalley did not know of this sabotage with all the spying he does?'

Without realising it, Nana was now standing and had raised his voice. Image upon image of what could have gone wrong kept tumbling through his mind like floundering items of clothing in a washing machine that just wouldn't stop spinning. He suddenly stopped mid-sentence, coughing uncontrollably from talking too fast in his now thoroughly agitated state.

Tiger stood up as well and gently thumped his brother on the back a few times. 'Nana, please sit down. You have to get a grip. This is classic locking of stable doors after horses have bolted and that's not you. You probably have the most powerful mind for reasoning amongst us all. Now use that, together with the patience I asked you to summon, and calm down. Think, my brother. Think. What's done is done. Yes Saga is your son and my nephew, and things could have gone badly, but they didn't. Not yet at least. What's important is what we do now. So get a handle on your emotions, please?'

Uncle Tiger then paused and observed his brother, who now appeared to be calm. They both sat down again. As if he had anticipated his brother's reaction, he reached out to the side of his chair and produced a bottle of Glenfiddich single malt whisky and two medium-sized glasses. He filled both glasses almost to the top, handed one to his brother and kept one for himself.

'Take a big gulp and sip the rest,' he said to his brother, who quietly obeyed.

They sat silently for a few minutes before Nana spoke. 'You must forgive my reaction. I'm still trying to get my head around it all. Tell me something, did Obo know about this and say nothing? Don't worry, my head is straight now. Your whisky has helped. Good thinking. I just want to know.'

'No, I don't think Obo knew. From what Yalley told me, it seems it was just the two sweethearts and their Orphan buddies – I'm sure Ibrahim was among them. We have much to discuss. How you react to Saga is very important. Try to imagine what the child must have gone through. Try to imagine the terrors he is probably facing now. Saga is very brave, even if a bit impulsive, and that Yalley's daughter must be quite brilliant and courageous too. In truth, they are both heroic. I hear she looks like a movie star.'

With that, they huddled closer and began to consider and analyse everything General Yalley had told Tiger step by step and stage by stage. Between the two brothers, there was the sufficiency of intellectual capacity, compassion and common sense to guide them in determining possible solutions that would affect their families as well as many others. They certainly had much to discuss, including General Yalley's request that they 'assist' him with managing the President's directive to hunt down the opposition and destroy its leading lights, such as their own very persons!

CHAPTER TWENTY-SEVEN
Paul Please, Not Saul

It was now time for Nana to talk to Saga about what he knew regarding the Orphan mission the night before the opposition action. He thought long and hard on the subject until he fully imbibed the notion that he had to tread as cautiously and as delicately on this matter as he could. After all, Saga was still a child, albeit a wilful one, and had undoubtedly undertaken the operation to immobilise the Regime's military vehicles from selfless and altruistic motives, even if there was a hint of adventurism involved. He truly marvelled at his son's bravery and undoubted tactical brilliance. The simplicity of the operation he carried out with his girlfriend and Orphan chums with stunningly effective outcomes was a truly laudable feat.

But now, his son had a massive target on his back, even though, according to his brother, Tiger, their ostensible 'enemy', General Yalley, had vowed to protect the boy. And there was the very pressing issue of the others who took part in the mission, apart from Yalley's daughter, Zara. What if they spoke? What if they spilled the beans? That would be a very expensive and lethal spillage of leguminous products indeed, and had to be prevented at all costs! That is, if no such spillage had already occurred.

Nana toyed with telling his beloved, long-suffering wife about what Saga had done and decided against it. It was not simply that she would hit the roof in an apoplectic rage. Yes, she would initially be sufficiently stunned enough for her rage to soar. But ultimately, she was a wise and very level-headed woman, who had the gift of being able to place things in their proper perspectives. It was just that she had suffered for far too long on a roller-coaster ride of unalloyed anxiety and it would just not be fair to extend that unpalatable, debilitating ride, which in truth, was very far from over, as things currently stood.

And since he, Nana, was not in a habit of withholding secrets from his wife, he knew he would have to tell her someday, and soon. However, he would do that when things were less tense and their lives were back on a more even and steady keel. It was a judgment call and it was his to make. Period!

He also considered telling Obo about Saga's immense bravery and bravado in planning and almost flawlessly executing the mission. Again, he decided to hold off on that. Obo was neck-deep in both national and student politics, and this was also not the time to add to his already overloaded plate.

Again, Nana needed what he termed as a 'fine balance'. 'Fine balancing a conundrum,' he mused to himself. Talking to Saga on this issue was going to be a tricky one, but there was no avoiding it. The time had come.

It was Uncle Tiger who telephoned Saga at home and asked him to come over to his home in Uso Town. Always pleased to see his strong, silent uncle, Saga did not hesitate in racing to his home on his bike straightaway. The security men at the gate assured him he was expected and was to proceed directly to the basement of the Masonic Temple.

Saga was surprised to see no one but his father in the large meeting room that the opposition had been using. He coughed ever so slightly to announce his presence. His father, who had been sitting quietly in an armchair, staring at the wall, turned to look when he heard Saga's cough. He beckoned Saga to come over and waved him into a brown leather armchair opposite him.

Saga was puzzled. Where was his uncle? Why was his father here? For them not to meet and talk at home, as they had done all his life, meant there was something seriously out of kilter.

'Saga, your uncle telling you to come here and you finding me here instead is not to mislead you. It is for a good reason. And for now, our discussion must be very private. You cannot tell your mother or your brother about what we are about to discuss. You cannot discuss it with anyone apart from your Uncle Tiger. He is the only other person who knows about this meeting and what we are about to discuss. Are we clear?'

Saga was nobody's fool. He simply stared at his dad and nodded. Somehow, some way, his father knew about his wildcat solo action with Zara and Ibrahim and his other Orphan buddies. And yet, his father did not appear angry or distressed.

Lieutenant Commander Musu was a very well-trained spy. He was also reasonably well educated. Though his antecedents lay in the Navy, his brilliance and perceptiveness as a Naval Intelligence Officer is what ultimately brought him into mainstream intelligence work concerned with the overall security of the State. Currently, he had risen to the apex of it all as Chief of the dreaded and amply-resourced Bureau of National Research, euphemistically known to the general public of Zimgania as the Bureau of No Return!

He had studied under the famed Mossad in Israel and had taken lengthy courses in spy-craft at the CIA's headquarters in Langley, Virginia. He had also done a spell with the British MI6 at their headquarters on Vauxhall Bridge Road in London.

And yet, despite all this, despite such excellent pedigree, he was currently facing doom! Only six months as Chief of the BNR, his dream job, and now he faced disgrace and severe punishment at the hands of a merciless, unforgiving dictator – his very own boss!

And what was he to do? Was it his fault that the President's own foolish National Service decree had incensed the populace and caused them to rise up against him? Was it his fault that with the decree being so draconian and so hated, many of his spies and eyes within the civilian population had decided to abandon spying for some time now?

At least the President still had his job and power, while he, Musu, was about to be made a scapegoat for the Regime's own foolishness and inimical arrogance for attempting to ram such an insidious decree down the throats of a long-suffering population. Musu knew his thoughts were taboo in the current political environment, but he simply could not help himself.

He continued with his taboo musings. He also wondered why he – known by some as the 'bright and fearless one' – turned into such a bumbling idiot whenever he dealt with General Yalley. What was it about Yalley that terrified him so? Yes, he was in awe and certainly shook a little in front of the President-for-Life-Until-Further-Notice, but with Yalley, it was as though he literally became intellectually and verbally incontinent, with very little control! Indeed, it was as though Yalley could see into his very soul!

Anyway, he was not about to sit meekly like a lamb waiting to go to the slaughter. No way! Had he not trained with the foremost intelligence agencies in the world? Was he not known for his brilliance? Yes, he would act. He would fashion a plan that would make his boss hesitate and probably even desist from hanging the scapegoat noose around his neck!

Musu now had the makings of a plan. After all, until the axe fell on his rather thick neck, was he still not head of the BNR – the premier intelligence agency in the country? Did he still not have swarms of both official and unofficial spies within his employ? And finally, was he still not in charge of official para-military security agents who did his bidding?

His plan began to take shape. It was no longer lingering foreshadows of what was possible. He would pacify the President by embarking on a mission to apprehend the opposition leaders who had humiliated him so much, and offer them to him on a silver platter. He would also find out who was responsible for sabotaging the President's beloved military vehicles. He would make this a solo BNR operation. He would not even tell the Security Czar, General Yalley, about this. He would present his triumph as a *fait accompli*, and be lauded by all as a hero of the times. Surely, with such a triumph, he ought to be allowed to keep his powerful job. He certainly would!

'So Saga, sit down and let's talk. I can see from your face that intuitively, you seem to know what the subject matter is, so I won't beat about the bush. Anything you want to say before I continue?'

Saga sat down and faced his dad. Even though he was generally unafraid, he was certainly a little apprehensive. What was actually baffling him was how his father and obviously his Uncle Tiger had found out about it. To the best of his knowledge, only twelve people in the world knew about it: himself, the nine members of his crew of Orphans, Zara, and more recently, General Yalley, through his CCTV shenanigans. So who amongst this 12 could have leaked this to his father? Try as he may, Saga could not place his finger on where the leak emanated from. Had they been betrayed by one of his own Orphans? That was nigh impossible!

'Thanks Dad. I knew we would one day have this discussion, but I didn't expect it to be so soon. Before we continue, however, may I please ask how you found out about what I did and those I did it with?'

'I know what you're wondering about, Saga. Don't worry. None of your Orphans have betrayed you. And I know you don't think your secret girlfriend spilt the beans either. We'll come to all that. Anything else?'

'No Dada. I am ready to listen,' replied a visibly relieved Saga.

'Saga, I am not here to condemn what you did. Neither am I here to heap praises on you for your bravery or for the successful outcome of your operation and how it greatly helped our cause. I know what you've been through already. I know the doubts, fear and uncertainties that must have plagued you. I know the sheer anguish you have been through. We will deal with all that as well.' Nana paused and then continued. 'Correct me if I am wrong, but this is how it must have all gone down. You fell in love with Yalley's daughter but you could not tell us about it because of who she was. You heard about the opposition's quest to destroy the armaments and vehicles of the Regime at one of the resistance meetings. Your girlfriend got you the information about where the vehicles were. You could not bring it to us because of the source. You thought you might be branded a traitor. You also felt you had to act on the information to help save lives. Somehow, you and the girl and Ibrahim, no doubt, planned it all and successfully accomplished what you set out to do. Am I correct so far?'

'In a nutshell you are, Dad. I tried to come to you many times but I was scared. I knew you would insist on knowing where the information came from. I knew I could not tell you that. Even Ibrahim does not know about Zara's involvement, though he knows about her. Nobody knows. I am so sorry, Dada. I know 100 per cent what could have happened if all had gone wrong. But it didn't go wrong, Dad. Anyway, please continue. And thanks for understanding the sheer hell I went through because of all this.'

Nana looked thoughtfully at his son for some time. He was, in truth, proud of him in his innermost heart. But at the same time, in some other corner of the same heart, he was truly upset with him. But all that again had to wait for now. The boy seems to have matured overnight. Look how calmly he is even answering my questions. Hmm. Maybe this new girl must be good for him, he mused.

Nana continued. 'Saga, though you were successful, you must understand that there are always repercussions. In this case, we have to anticipate them in order to thwart them. There have also been some developments I must tell you about. Again, it is only your Uncle Tiger and me who know what I am about to tell you. For now, just listen very carefully.'

Saul Azo was a bright, young lad who always achieved excellent grades in school. He was a naturally gifted thinker. Saul was in Saga's form at school and, though his father was an authoritarian military officer working for the Regime, he was one of the first people to identify with Saga after the Orphan incident at their school, Brewman High.

Saul had two pet peeves in life. Firstly, he was totally opposed to everything that his father stood for as a military officer who supported President Brewman and his dastardly Regime. Secondly, in his mind, he was forever at loggerheads with his father for naming him Saul instead of Paul. Why, but had his father never heard of the Pauline conversion on the road to Damascus that even every child in kindergarten knew about? Why did his father choose to name him after the obnoxious, New Testament-persecuting Saul, when this same Saul later became the venerated St Paul who is essentially credited with building the Church of the Lord Jesus Christ? Was it any wonder his father supported that 'Brute' of a persecuting President?

Young Saul Azo had indeed resolved to legally change his name to Paul once he was no longer dependent on his father and no longer under his authoritarian roof. Come to think of it, he might as well change his surname in the process to fully divorce himself from all the wretchedness that his father represented

Saul Azo was also one of the nine Orphans Saga had chosen for their immensely successful mission in demobilising and destabilising the military vehicles. Saga indeed knew that Saul was one of the most dependable people he could rely on within his school, which was why he had selected him for the mission. Apart from his intelligence, Saul was also both very brave and very discrete.

Young, modern-day Saul, however, had one defect that was to prove very costly to both himself and his Orphan compatriots. Unfortunately, no one knew about it. In a sense, not even Saul Azo realised he was in possession of such a defect that would soon prove so debilitating, with far-reaching consequences.

Indeed, having turned 18, Saul had discovered the wholly pleasurable delights associated with imbibing alcohol. Alcohol gave him a sense of euphoria like none other. It warmed his heart when he drank and it made him feel gloriously at one with the universe. Most importantly, it liberated him from his natural shyness towards women, and for that, he was eternally grateful towards whomever it was that invented alcoholic beverages during mankind's evolutionary march towards progress. Saul felt that if this peerless, industrious inventor could ever be found then that extraordinary person ought to be exhumed and given a boat-load of posthumous awards and accolades for bringing so much delightfulness into the world.

Alcohol, however, did, in fact, have seriously debilitating effects on him, which he did not realise. Firstly, it significantly compromised his memory. He could not remember much of what he had done whenever he recovered from one of his occasional alcoholic hazes. Secondly, it also created huge holes, huge chinks in his armour of discretion and reserve. His natural inclination towards discretion took flight the moment he had imbibed as little as two bottles of ice-cold Star Lite beer or half a bottle of chilled Mouton Cadet white wine, which was his favourite. Consequently, uncharacteristic verbosity and equally uncharacteristic indiscretion usually resulted whenever young Saul occasionally sought to pursue the delights to be derived from entering an alcoholic haze.

In this particular instance, the 'occasion' happened to be his father Colonel Azo's barbecue lunch party for some middle-level functionaries of the Brewman Regime.

Colonel Azo was a military man through and through. He was ramrod erect and had been gifted with the ability to follow orders *par excellence*. The 'order' he was fulfilling at the time was a directive, emanating from the Presidency, for its functionaries to celebrate the 'defeat' of the opposition when it attempted to 'destabilise' the Regime and sow seeds of 'rancour and bitterness' with their 'Over Million Man March'. That the Regime acknowledged that over one million people took to the streets against them while forcing them to rescind a major decree and make other serious concessions, and yet still chose to see it as a victory in their favour, was something that the likes of Colonel Azo would never ever question. For him, the directive was to celebrate victory and thus, he would, and without compunction. To his son, Saul Azo, his father was the epitome of what a Zombie truly was. A man who never questioned an order – no matter how appalling and ridiculous – truly exemplified the embodiment of unadulterated Zombie-ism.

He was a young man who was secretly disgusted with his father and all he stood for, but did not dare voice out such sentiments in his authoritarian household, where their father brooked no opposition in any form to what he did or what he stood for.

To this victory barbecue lunch party came many middle-level stalwarts of the Regime. Into the mix came a smattering of party 'foot soldiers', as well as those associated in diverse ways with the Regime. Among these was none other than the notorious Bayou.

Bayou was a man in total agony. He was utterly and inconsolably incensed that the planning and execution of the opposition's redoubtable 'Over Million Man March' had virtually been carried out under his very own nose. Of course, it had now come to light that leading luminaries of the opposition who had so skilfully planned the enormous event included people in his very own backyard, such as Nana and his children, Obo and Saga, the Orphan boy.

Indeed, his snitching instincts had been spot on that day, not so long ago, when he decided to follow that young punk, only to be sabotaged by none other than his dreaded wife. He secretly cursed her for the umpteenth time for stopping him that day from apprehending that youthful miscreant, Saga.

What made him shiver the most with fear and was causing him prolonged sleeplessness was the strong rumour that the President was about to vent his considerable fury on all those civilian spies who had miserably failed to adequately spy and snitch on their neighbours in order to have prevented such a huge embarrassment to the President himself.

Indeed, chief amongst those who were bound to feel the President's formidable displeasure and vindictive punishment would of course be those like Bayou, who failed to root out such pernicious dissent within their own 'constituencies'. They were seen to have sat down 'apparently unconcerned', while high treason flourished under their very noses. Bayou was of course under no illusions as to what would be done to him when they eventually called on him to account for his woeful inability to do his job in his own neighbourhood.

His own evil tattling and spying had landed many a man in the dreaded Traitors' Jail, and he was very much aware of the torture and macabre degradation that was visited on the inmates there. Oh, oh, oh, but how am I going to evade such a dreadful fate of ending up in there if I don't come up with something to make up for my failure, he thought through his fog of misery, as he entered the Colonel's home for the barbecue lunch 'celebration'.

Indeed, though Bayou was perceived by many to be a thoroughly odious fellow, the same, however, could not at all be said of his very handsome daughter, Aden. Anyone seeing his daughter could not at first believe that such an angelic-looking person could have in actual fact been fathered by so unprepossessing an entity such as Bayou. But as to whether the apple fell far enough from the tree in this particular instance was something that most could not readily ascertain from mere looks.

Young Saul, who desperately wanted to become Paul, was sitting very much alone at the far corner of his father's reasonably large back garden in their home at Ridge Heights. He sat under a huge avocado tree, in a state of self-imposed alienation. He was trying very hard to make himself as inconspicuous as possible, as his father's guests began arriving for their so-called victory celebratory party. He was very annoyed that he had been compelled to partake of this charade, which made no sense to him whatsoever. He had thus commandeered an ice-cold bottle of Mouton Cadet white wine to keep him company, and was already halfway through it.

His earlier gloom at having been forcibly made to participate in the fake celebratory get-together was fast lifting and dissipating into the balmy air, as the Mouton Cadet began to warm his innards. Young Saul was completely grateful for the euphoria that the wine was bestowing upon him, as he now felt delightfully at one with the universe.

In his alcoholic haze, Saul beheld a most inviting apparition; the resplendent features of Bayou's very good-looking daughter. Much to his delight, it was not an apparition at all, but an actual three-dimensional person heading his way. Under normal circumstances, Saul would have been in a state of panic but now, he had ample Dutch courage.

'Hey Saul. It's Aden. Don't you recognise me? You're looking at me as though I'm some stranger. Hmm, so much for a nice welcome.'

Far from being his usual naturally tongue-tied self around women, especially extraordinarily pretty ones, young Saul was now virtually waxing lyrical in the art of conversation, being thoroughly aided and abetted by the booze flowing through his bloodstream.

'Good heavens Aden, but how can you blame me when I am merely blinded by such exotic beauty? Your appearance dazzled me and proved a touch too bright for my eyes,' was his confident, booze-inspired reply. They had both grown up in the same neighbourhood.

'Aw. That's nice of you, Saul. Didn't quite peg you as a flatterer. Listen, mind if I sit with you? Too many fuddy-duddies out there, talking nothing but boring politics.'

Saul could not believe his luck. His euphoria soared. 'Of course you can sit by me. I'll be honoured. But don't blame me if I can't take my eyes off you. You're just so amazing to look at.'

So started an afternoon of joyous, euphoric banter between young Saul and the notoriously odious Bayou's very good-looking daughter.

Unfortunately for young Saul, one of the problematic effects alcohol tended to have on his behaviour was soon to become manifest. And this was the tendency to abandon his natural reserve and become quite indiscreet whenever he drank.

Unbeknown to him, the angelic-looking Aden Bayou was not so angelic after all. Ms Aden was in actual fact someone who absolutely did not disapprove of her father's role as one of the chief civilian spies for the Regime. Neither was it of any consequence to her that her father's betrayals and tattling tended to cause untold sorrow and ruination in the lives of so many.

Ms Aden operated on a simple code of ethics, which for her, was beyond reproach. The 'ethical' logic she subscribed was simple: her father's association with the Regime's intelligence apparatus meant increasing wealth and position for her family. This also translated into a lot of the finer things in life for

312

her, which she absolutely believed was becoming of her status. Thus, all her clothes were now from major international and very expensive designer labels: Gucci, Versace, Christian Dior, Fendi, Donna Karan, Vera Wang, to name but a few. And what of her shoes and handbags? Now, she sported only the best: Louis Vuitton, Salvatore Ferragamo, Jimmy Choo, Bally, also to name but a few.

In fact, being the only one within her family who supported her father's nefarious activities, she had become very close to him, much to the chagrin and staunch disapproval of her mother. Mrs Bayou suspected that her daughter had been secretly spying on her mates at the university where she was a student and reporting their so-called 'subversive' activities to her father. As a result, her mother was no longer on talking terms with her, and had taken to locking herself up in the bedroom whenever her daughter came home from the university campus to visit.

Ms Aden, however, cared not a jot for her mother's disapprobation, and dismissed her protestations as the ramblings of an ignorant village woman, which was how she actually perceived her own mother. To her mind, her mother lacked the sophistication and good sense to understand that in this life, one had to take absolute advantage of the blessings that came one's way. She had been blessed with indisputable good looks, which she constantly milked to the fullest. She had also been blessed with a father whose association with the Regime had led to her being in possession of the finest apparel and accessories that money could buy. As such, why on God's good Earth would she give up such divine blessings?

What did her mother know of Vera Wang? Or Gucci? Or Versace? That ignorant woman, a veritable philistine, ought to just keep herself locked up in her room or go back to the dusty, backward village she hailed from, and leave her and the father in peace to serve President Brewman and acquire more wealth. Such was Ms Aden's *raison d'être*, and she made no bones about it.

A few days prior to the victory barbecue party at Saul Azo's house, Aden Bayou had become very concerned about her father. She had come home from campus in the aftermath of the opposition victory only to find her father a shell of his former self. He was living a terrified existence. The fact that key protagonists of the opposition action lived and had flourished within his 'constituency' meant certain wholly unpalatable reprisals from an unforgiving and merciless Regime against his person. He was not eating or sleeping, and was almost always retching from fear-related nausea. He spent a considerable part of his days indoors, vigorously inviting pestilence and perdition on Nana and his family, as well as on all those opposition folks who lived and thrived within the catchment area he perceived to be his domain.

Ms Aden was indeed shocked at her father's wretched state. How could someone disintegrate so quickly simply in anticipation of that which 'might' happen? To her practical mind, this was becoming unbecoming. She quickly took charge of affairs at home, as her mother proceeded to lock herself up in her bedroom in protest of her presence in the house.

She quickly reasoned with her father that it was foolish and weak to sit around and wait for the axe to fall when one ought to be out there, finding ways and means to mitigate his failures in the eyes of the Regime. Maybe an 'information coup', a priceless piece of intelligence, could help absolve him of his crime of insufficient spying, which had led to unmitigated embarrassment for the President. But how could such redeeming intelligence ever be acquired if they all chose to lock themselves up at home and sulk and moan to no end? Whatever redeeming intelligence that existed was out there, and one had to step back out into the real world to acquire it.

The thought of losing all the perquisites that came with her father's petty power made her stomach churn. She simply could not go back to being a 'nobody' and clothe herself in common, non-designer apparel. What was she going to wear then? Clothes from J C Penny? Walmart? Marks and Spencer? *God in Heaven but that must never happen.* She squirmed at the thought and developed goosebumps for good measure as well, in contemplation of such an unbecoming 'common' existence. As for the thought or possibility of acquiring her clothes and accessories from local seamstresses and designers, such did not even occur to her. It was an absolute 'no go' area in the world she had manufactured for herself.

Indeed, never in a thousand years would she permit such a comedown for herself or her father. Consequently, she resolved to do all in her power to prop up her father and find a way to help him hold on to his petty power for as long as he drew breath.

CHAPTER TWENTY-EIGHT
Spilt Legumes

Ms Aden was inordinately incensed at all the opposition members in her neighbourhood who had rendered her father into a hidebound mass of quivering, frightened jelly. Her father had become a shadow of himself.

It was in this fear-induced state that Bayou initially summarily dismissed the 'celebratory' invitation sent to him by Colonel Azo to come and join in the 'victory' barbecue party. But his daughter would not hear of it. She had astutely learnt at a very early age that 'perception' was a very important aspect of the game. How people perceived you was essentially all that mattered, since, in her world, people tended to live their lives as a mirror of what their peers thought.

For her father to barricade himself at home and desist from socialising was, to her mind, an unsupportable admission of defeat. Now, that could only be permitted to happen over her dead body. She wasted no time in berating her father and aggressively taunting him with offensive names, designed to jolt him out of his state of slothful ennui. She called him a coward; a man who lacked the courage of his convictions; a has-been; and veritable loser in every sense of the word. And was that how he wanted the whole neighbourhood to perceive him? A broken man who deserves to be thrown into the dreaded Traitors' Jail to face the very souls he himself had helped place there and were literally out there, baying for his blood?

And then, she was all honey. 'Dad – I think it's important for you to understand that you are a man amongst men. Look at all the good things you have done to strengthen this Regime. Look at the traitors you have put away. Surely, you deserve a medal for your unparalleled services. I think so. Don't you? After all the good things you've done?'

With such praises being heaped on him, Bayou was beginning to emerge from his depressive, lethargic state. 'Yes, I am a great spy. Yes, I have done a lot for this Regime. Yes, I deserve a medal,' he replied with gathering confidence. Indeed, his confidence seemed to increasingly assert itself with each sentence he said in recognition of his own peerlessness.

'Then Dad, don't you think it's about time you stopped feeling sorry for yourself and went out there to show everyone that you are still in charge?' His daughter continued to both simultaneously goad and butter him up.

'Yes, yes. It's about time. It's about time I showed them that I am still Bayou the great. Our President is for life so my power must also be for life. Yes, I will hunt down and punish all those who tried to bring us down. I will make them wish they had never been born!' replied the now seemingly recovered Bayou, with his signature vindictiveness and very necessary need to hurt others for his own advancement and gratification.

His daughter smiled secretly to herself. '*Mission accomplished.*' Now, all she had to do was convince him to go to the barbecue victory party. She had heard a rumour that their host Colonel Azo's son had thrown in his lot with the terrible Orphans in the prestigious Brewman High. She could work on him to elicit any relevant information pertaining to that troublesome Orphan Saga and his family once she got there, accompanying her father. No one was going to stand in her way of restoring her father to his position of petty power! That was how come she had landed at the party and went straight into the company of young Saul Azo.

In the far corner of the garden, as the party was underway, Miss Aden soon realised that despite having remembered her name, Saul did not remember that she was in actual fact Bayou's daughter. This was what she had prayed for. She knew exactly what to do.

She went to work on him as planned. She plied him with the Mouton Cadet wine. She called for another bottle. She kept filling up his glass, while she sipped hers sparingly. Oftentimes, she surreptitiously poured hers onto the lawn, giving her the requisite excuse to keep refilling their glasses. She praised him for being so handsome. She praised his ramrod athletic posture. And she regaled him with anecdotes of some of her romances in college, saying she had rather those silly boys been more like Saul.

Saul was in heaven. He could not believe that such an alluring woman would choose to spend so much time with him and nobody else. He was totally overwhelmed when she made to feed him with lamb kebabs from her plate, and then proceeded to delicately dab his lips with her own wonderfully-scented handkerchief. In his inebriated state of complete euphoria, and being of the enraptured view that he was experiencing unbridled love, there was nothing in the world he would not do for her at that material moment.

And didn't Ms Aden just know this only too well? After all, was it not unfolding just as she planned it? Skilfully, she soon steered him in the direction of the very politics she initially claimed to loathe. She lowered her deliberately honeyed voice, which she had been using on him with such great effect, and whispered conspiratorially to him, 'Saul I am so happy about the opposition triumph the other day. Look at these clowns celebrating their so-called victory. Disgusting lot – the whole lot of them. They are so ignorant, they can't even see the writing on the wall. They will all soon follow that Brewman brute of a President into the grave!'

Saul was elated. This woman was truly a rarity. She even shared his secret yet acute hatred for all that his father and his cohorts stood for.

Ms Aden Bayou knew she had hit a home run with Saul, with her jabs aimed at the Regime and its supporters. She had astutely observed his surging elation when she ventured her criticism. This was going just too well for her. Her own emotions also soared at her success. She continued. 'I have heard a lot of good things about your school and those brave, young Orphans. Oh how I wish I was one of them. I heard their leader, Saga, is so brave and handsome too. But I doubt he can ever be as handsome as you. Is he your friend? Oh, please tell me about those Orphans...' she finished off quite breathlessly.

This was Saul's chance to shine. This was his chance to elevate himself in the eyes of his new-found, seemingly all-encompassing love.

So Saul began his own drunken yet accurate tale about the Orphans, his own involvement with them and their recent oh so secret heroic achievements. Oh how she listened... and how he rambled on...

* * *

He was manacled, hands and feet, and thrashing about with every ounce of energy he could muster. The tight restraints were cutting into his flesh and causing his ankles and wrists to bleed profusely. He just could not free himself, and kept shouting to the darkened room repeatedly, 'I didn't do it on purpose, I didn't do it on purpose!' He then felt himself sinking into an inexplicable bottomless hole, which made no sense to his fevered brain, as he was supposed to be firmly chained to the walls. He then felt his whole body awash with sweat and pain, and that was when he woke up.

He had been having a vivid nightmare of epic dimensions. Saul sat up and looked around him. His bed sheets and cover cloth were in complete disarray. And they were wet with his still gushing sweat. He completely recalled the nightmare and his heart kept thumping in his chest, which he could feel all the way up in his ears. He was very afraid.

After taking many deep breaths and calming himself down a bit, he wondered why he had experienced such a dreadful nightmare. And then it hit him with full force, causing him to jump off the bed and groan loudly. Something deep within the recesses of his brain had broken through the thick fog and haze of his drunken hangover and concomitant memory loss, jolting him to remember what he had told Bayou's beautiful daughter the evening before!

'Jesus Christ of Judea, Jerusalem and Bethlehem, but what have I done? God in heaven and on Earth but what did I do? Oh, oh, oh,' he piteously lamented to himself.

He had shown himself to be a true Saul and not a Paul. A traitor and not the hero he fancied himself to be. With uncharacteristic clarity that was most unusual after keeping company with the bottle, Saul completely recollected everything he had told Ms Aden Bayou. In his alcoholic haze and desire to impress the seemingly angelic lady, who seemed to be fascinated with his company, he had told her – lock stock and barrel – about the successful Orphan mission in destabilising and destroying the military vehicles stationed at Fort Brewman.

He had given her detail upon detail. He told her of Saga's undoubted brilliance, as could be witnessed in his impeccable planning and subsequent exemplary execution of the operation. He told her about the still unknown mystery lady who had helped them and provided them with cash and mobile phones. He told her of his deep-seated hatred for all that his father stood for. And finally, he told her about his obsession with becoming a Paul and abandoning his baptismal name of Saul.

He remembered yet again, much to his utter dismay, that his father had asked him after the visitors had left about why he had not mingled with the guests and only spent time with Bayou's daughter. Bayou's what? Oh no! But how could he have not recognised her, as they all grew up in the same neighbourhood? How could he have been so foolish? How could he have betrayed his own beliefs and compatriot Orphans thus?

Saul felt like dying. He felt like committing suicide. He felt like disappearing into that huge, bottomless hole in his dream. However, that was all fleeting. It was stark naked desperation engendered by unalloyed guilt. In the end, good sense prevailed as he calmed down. His natural inclination to be logical took hold. He knew what must be done. He had to drop everything in the world and go in search of Saga. There was nothing else he could do.

Back in the Masonic Temple, Nana was telling Saga about everything his brother, Tiger, had told him from his abduction on the night he left their home until his release a few hours later. Nana also told Saga about General Yalley's secret but extremely effective assistance he had given the opposition.

Thus, it became clearer to Saga how his father and uncle had found out about his solo Orphan mission with Zara as his chief co-conspirator. General Yalley's knowledge of his involvement, however, did not come as a surprise to him, having already been prompted by Zara about his secret CCTV cameras. He was nonetheless shocked to his very marrow when he heard about the details and immensity of General Yalley's clandestine assistance to the opposition movement in their country.

'Saga, it is obvious that we cannot immediately address all the issues arising out of your actions. In our own way, despite the enormous implications, we are grateful to you, your girlfriend and your Orphan friends. It also appears that all of us in this country have misjudged General Yalley for what he truly is. It is as though he is one part monster and one part saint. Whichever it is, the man has helped us a great deal and plans to help us a lot more. Consequently, we have to help him protect his daughter, who also happens to be your girlfriend. Of course, there is no doubt that you wish to protect her too. So the question is: what do we do? It seems that General Yalley's paramount concern is to do with Ibrahim and the other eight boys who assisted you. He is afraid that one of them may talk or somehow spill the beans. That is an important issue we have to address now. What do you say to this, Saga?'

Saga attempted to order his thoughts before replying. Inwardly, he was still reeling from all that he had heard and its implications, not only for him, but for his one true love, Zara, as well. Who could also have imagined just a week ago that he would be sitting here today with his father, discussing issues that had Zara as the chief topic of discussion?

'Dad, I don't think we have to worry too much about my fellow Orphans who helped in the mission. They will never talk. Ibrahim will never talk. I hand-picked them myself. I can assure you that we are wasting time focusing on them.

Apart from all that, I planned it in such a way that none of them ever saw Zara. And I never mentioned her to anyone, apart from Ibrahim, but as I said, even he does not know of her involvement. Dad, please let's not focus on the Orphans spilling any beans. Please trust me on this.'

His father sat there, looking at him while he spoke. Yes, he was proud of the way he stood up for his friends. However, he was too seasoned, too aware of the ways of the world, to know that life was not as simple as young folk such as Saga thought it to be. It was much more complicated.

'Saga, I like the way you are defending your mates, but I am not sure you fully understand the entire matter. But before we get into that, tell me something: your friends must have wondered where you got all those expensive mobile phones from and huge sums of money for the operation. What did you tell them when they asked?'

Again, Saga was careful in his reply. 'Yes, some of them asked me, and others were not particularly concerned. Ibrahim, in particular, wanted very much to know. All I told them was that we had a mystery lady supporter who was helping us with resources. I explained that the lady wished to remain anonymous for now, and that I could not break my promise to her by revealing her name. So you see what I mean by nobody knowing who she is?'

'Ah, so they all know there was someone else involved and that the person is a woman. Saga, please understand that in protecting her, we are protecting you as well and, in protecting you, we are also protecting your friends. Also, though I know you have complete faith in your friends, again, you must understand that our concern is that all it takes is for a single one of them to be careless with some loose talk and this whole thing will blow up in our faces like an atomic bomb. What you did is high treason and the penalty for high treason is death!' Nana's voice wavered with worry.

Saga involuntarily shivered a little at this revelation. It was not that he didn't know that what they did was certainly serious and that, if caught, the punishment would be severe. But raw

DEATH, just like that? Yes, they had considered getting shot if they had been caught in the process of sabotaging the vehicles, but death after they had been completely successful? No, no, no!!!

His father noticed that Saga was now properly shocked, but he continued nonetheless. 'So Saga, this is a lot more serious than you may have fully worked out. And make no mistake, this President is merciless. In fact, we have only just learnt that it has been General Yalley who has been quietly blocking the President from doing even more unspeakable things, while protecting a whole lot of people from the President's wrath. Even the university students who went missing are under Yalley's secret protection and have been hidden somewhere without the President knowing. However, in this case, if it ever comes to light that General Yalley's own daughter was involved, Yalley himself will be arrested and probably shot, so who will protect you, your Zara and your Orphan mates?'

Saga was visibly quite shaken, causing his father to stop talking, as he was very much concerned for his son. The two of them sat silently for a while before Nana decided to bring the discussions to a close for now.

'Saga, I know you trust your friends, but there has to be a way for us to ensure that they don't speak to anyone about what happened. Also, NOBODY should know we are in touch with General Yalley. Nobody apart from his daughter. With her, I think you must tell her about these developments, but please do so very gently. I can help you in this if you want. I am happy to meet with her. Please keep this from your mother for now. If she knows of your involvement in the sabotage, she will immediately understand what's at stake and she'll never sleep another wink thereafter.'

It was indeed truly sad that unbeknownst to the pair of them, Saga's very trusted student compatriot, Saul Azo, had, during the previous night, already spilt all the costly legumes there was to spill by revealing all the details of their Fort Brewman mission to the beautiful but not very angelic Aden Bayou in a drunken and amorous haze. Unbeknownst to them as well, Saul Azo, having realised his disastrous, albeit inadvertent mistake, had been all over the place that very next morning, looking for Saga, but simply could not find him, as he was holed up with his father.

CHAPTER TWENTY-NINE

Intelligence Manna

Commander Musu sat in a deep, leather burgundy chair in his plush office on the fourth floor of the Bureau for National Research Headquarters. He was concentrating on the various security reports he had received so far on the humiliating opposition action that continued to threaten both his job and the safety of his person. He had asked his staff not to disturb him under any circumstances. Only calls from the President or General Yalley were to be put through.

So far, the reports told him nothing he did not already know. What a bunch of hogwash, he thought to himself. And what atrocious English. People simply have no right to mutilate the English language in this fashion at all, he thought, appalled at the quality of the reports before him. That is what you get from promoting unqualified sycophants instead of well-trained and properly educated professionals to do the job, he concluded, as he pushed away the uninspiring reports.

What was he to do now? Where was he to get the much-needed crucial intelligence to act on in order to restore his credibility in the eyes of his maniacal President? 'I need manna from heaven. I need the gift of manna,' he said aloud. Intelligence manna, he thought, and burst out laughing at his own sally. Intelligence manna indeed. At least he could still laugh, and he was very proud of that.

His intercom telephone buzzed.

'What is it Grace? Did I not warn you not to disturb me? Am I not dealing with matters of national security? This had better be good or you will pack up your things and leave this office this very day. Talk woman! What is it, I say?'

His executive personal assistant at the other end of the intercom was not in the least intimidated or impressed with her boss's outburst. Apart from being used to it, she had discerned that the man was essentially driven by fear these days and nothing else. She replied evenly, 'There is someone here to see you. A lady. One Ms Bayou. Her father works for some of your agents. I think you should see her.'

'And why should I see her?' Commander Musu retorted. 'And who is this Bayou fellow who works for me? He can't be that important if I don't recognise his name! So why should I see her, Grace? Do you now decide for me whom I shall see or not see? You really want to get the sack today, don't you?'

Grace, the executive PA, was still not fazed in any way. She knew her boss through and through. The man had an incurable weakness for pretty women, and seeing Ms Bayou was probably what was needed to get him out of his foul humour. Also, the Bayou woman claimed to have solid intelligence, which she knew her boss was desperate for. How could it hurt to listen? As such, all she said in her unflappable reply was, 'I am sending her in, sir. I hope you are presentable,' and then she cut off the intercom and pressed the buzzer under her table to unlock the electronic locks on his door.

Commander Musu had just grabbed the intercom phone and was about to give his assistant an earful when Aden Bayou walked gracefully into his huge office. The Commander simply froze with the phone receiver in his hand mid-air and gawked unashamedly at the unparalleled beauty of Ms Bayou.

Jesus Christ of Holy Nazareth, but this is simply God's finest work. Where has this woman been all my life? Young, tall, fair-skinned, curvy hourglass figure, yet slim and sleek, perfect smile, perfect teeth, perfect face, unbelievable hips, and the right age too. Probably early to mid-twenties... I can go on and on, was all Commander Musu could think about when he beheld Ms Bayou. He then recovered and forced himself to act normally, as though unperturbed by the overwhelming beauty before him.

'Err, err, Ms Bazou – is it? You're welcome. Please have a seat opposite me. My assistant tells me you wish to see me. What is it about, my dear? But wait first. Is there anything I can get you to drink? Anything?' ventured Commander Musu, in what he thought to be the clipped tones of an English gentleman; something he thought he had picked up from his short spell with the Oxbridge fellows he had worked with at the MI6 in London. In actual fact, it was what was locally termed as LAFA – Locally Acquired Foreign Accent.

'Commander, it is Bayou and not Bazou. And thank you. Perrier water will do nicely. That is if you have any,' she replied gaily.

Commander Musu could not believe his good fortune in having insisted to his staff that there must always be imported, bottled Perrier water at the office for himself and his more discerning guests.

'Of course I have some, Ms Bazou. Perrier water it is then,' he replied without missing a beat, while confidently mispronouncing her surname again. He now had a use for the intercom receiver he still held in mid-air. He pressed a button. 'Grace – please get one of the waiters to bring young madam here some Perrier water. Now please.'

Soon, a waiter dressed typically in a white shirt, black trousers and a thin black tie brought the water and served the young madam efficiently and left.

Commander Musu took advantage of the brief interlude needed to serve the Perrier water to compose himself. He sat down behind his cluttered desk and forced himself not to gawk. He gave her time to partake of a few sips of the Perrier water before properly engaging her.

'Ms Bazou, again, you are welcome. I hope the water is to your taste. Yes, your surname, Bazou, strikes a bell. So tell me how I may be of assistance to you?'

Ms Bayou took her time to reply. She needed to quickly assess the man. He was obviously powerful and fairly well-spoken, despite his pretentious LAFA. Most importantly, he was impressed with her, which was critical to her game plan. Yes, she surmised that she had indeed come to the right place. She could sense that despite his initial friendliness, there was a touch of impatience about the man. She decided to delve straight into the reason why she had come. But only after correcting his persistent mispronunciation of her surname.

'Again, it is Bayou with a Y, sir. Bayou and not Bazou with a Z,' she gently chided.

'Of course it is. Y and not Z. Bayou with a Y. I have it now,' he remarked with good humour. Pretty women always put him in a good mood.

'Thanks Commander for receiving me so nicely. I have information. I have what people in your area of expertise will call "crucial intelligence". I will give it to you. But I have conditions. I will give you the information if you will meet my conditions. Otherwise, I will go elsewhere.'

Jesus, this pretty, young thing does not mince words at all, Musu thought to himself. Who the hell does she think she is, sauntering into my office and laying down conditions for me? Does she know who I am? Does she not know I can have her interrogated and tortured for the information she claims she has, under the President's National Security Assurance Decree? Musu could barely keep up with his racing thoughts. He was starting to get himself worked up at the sheer effrontery of the woman, when a sudden, warm smile from her – as if especially for him alone – dissipated all the ire he was building up.

He decided then to play along for a while to see where all this was going. He was not quite ready to let such a pretty thing out of his sight as yet.

'Ms Bayou, or maybe I'll call you Aden. Nice name. I see you don't beat about the bush at all. But we are in a bit of a quandary here. How do I agree to your conditions when I don't know the nature of the intelligence you claim to have? How do I know your information is worth my agreeing to whatever conditions you have? Here's what we should do: first, give me the information you claim to have, then let me know your conditions and I will decide. Sounds fair, doesn't it?'

Aden Bayou now had some measure of the man in front of her. He was wily for sure, and hid it behind practiced charm. Yes, he was impressed with her looks and would not mind dating her. It was in his eyes. But she had to make him take her seriously. She measured him some more.

Despite his cluttered desk, the man was fastidious. Apart from the desk, his office was very neat and functional. His burgundy carpet and curtains were of the highest quality and matched the leather chairs. His office furniture was Italian; none of that pedestrian IKEA-like stuff. Her trained eye noticed he was wearing a Brioni suit. High thread count, quality fabric –$10,000 at least. This was a man who looked after himself. They had similar tastes. She knew exactly how to handle him. She was a highly intelligent and motivated woman. She decided to continue being very direct.

'You are an impressive man, Commander. You are handsome and very well dressed. Your Brioni suit shows your sophistication and is very finely cut. And you are nobody's fool. You have to be at the very top of your game to have landed such an extraordinarily powerful job. I will thus show you the respect that is your due by being very open with you.'

She paused for effect. The man was hooked. He was watching her with undoubted admiration. She continued. 'With all due respect, you suffered a massive intelligence failure that allowed the opposition to win and strike down your National Service decree, among other things. I have it on authority that President Brewman is very angry and is looking for scapegoats. I can help you. I can help you regain favour in his eyes. I know who sabotaged the military vehicles at Fort Brewman, costing you hundreds of millions of dollars. And I know how it was done. I also know how valuable this information is. So Commander, are you now ready to hear my conditions?' She stopped and then crossed her shapely, long legs while arranging the edges of her Christian Dior skirt into a pretty pattern around her lovely, fair knees.

None of that was lost on Musu, as he persisted in his gawking at this wonderful phenomenon before him.

Commander Musu was gob-smacked. *I need a divorce, I need a divorce! This is the woman I am supposed to be with. This is the woman of my destiny. This is the woman who will make me the second most powerful man in Zimgania. I love her. I just love her. She has just made 'love at first sight' a truly believable concept. And a doable one too.* Such were Commander Musu's thoughts upon realising the all-important nature of the information the woman held. This was the 'intelligence manna' he had been dreaming of. And guess what? It had actually come to him as though it was manna directly dropping from heaven! Oh, and what a delectable vehicle of delivery in the form of the beautiful Ms Aden Bayou!

Commander Musu could barely contain his excitement. He responded with unfettered magnanimity, maintaining his 'clipped' LAFA tone. 'Ms Aden – you are indeed a bearer of capital news. You are the bearer of salvation. And you shall name your price. Give me your conditions, my dear, and I will meet all of them. You and I are destined to do great things together. You and I are cut from the same cloth. I am all ears, young lady. Fire away!'

Inwardly, Ms Aden heaved a sigh of relief. Yes, again, she had won. And yes, she was going places with this middle-aged, powerful man in front of her. They were truly of the same ilk.

Aden Bayou wasted no time in stating her conditions. She wanted her father retained as a top informant for the Government. She wanted his position formalised with the BNR. She wanted him on BNR's list of most favoured and valued spies with commensurate remuneration.

For herself, she wanted a lump sum cash reward and an ALL-EXPENSES PAID shopping trip to Paris and London. First-class tickets only, please. Five-star hotels only, please. No stingy parsimony, please. Finally, she also wanted to be on the BNR's payroll as a highly-valued informant. Now, what did Commander Musu say to that?

Musu was delighted. *Is that all she wants? With my unlimited security budget – this is peanuts! Oh heavenly Father, thank you for being so good to me!*

'Ms Bayou, I can meet all your conditions and more. I will put it in writing before you leave here today. I will order your airline tickets today. I will pay you today. I will formalise your father's role today and promote him as well. I will employ you today as well as an informant on a generous monthly stipend. So now, tell me everything. After that, we will drink champagne while we wait for your paperwork and cash.'

Ms Aden smiled to herself once more. She was deeply gratified. The deal was sealed. Long live President Brewman. Long live his reign!

Major Kata was not a vain man. In fact, he was the opposite of vain. He was unassuming and very conscientious in his treatment of people. He knew he was a man of vast knowledge and vast experience, but he kept all of that to himself like closely guarded secrets. However, despite his unassuming nature, Major Kata knew that a time would come when his country would need his services, despite his disability, despite his limp. And that time was fast approaching.

Unbeknown to even his beloved Zara, Major Kata knew everything about what Saga had been up to since his rise to relative fame as an Orphan and even before. He had in fact been secretly tutoring and guiding Saga for quite some time now. This was the only thing Saga had kept from his beloved Zara and this, he did on strict instructions from Major Kata himself. Saga had solemnly promised Major Kata that he would never reveal the depth of their connection to anyone, and Saga had never broken the promise.

Indeed, after meeting with his father in the Masonic Temple, during which he was informed of General Yalley's secret assistance to the opposition, Saga had gone back and faithfully reported everything to Major Kata.

When it came to Major Kata, Saga was a hundred per cent convinced that he was not betraying anyone by revealing things to him. After all, was it not Major Kata who had secretly guided him and also encouraged him during moments of acute despair, prior to his Orphan mission? He knew without a doubt that Major Kata was a very kind, decent and excellent human being who ultimately wanted nothing but for his country and the people within it to thrive and prosper. He was a truly selfless person.

Major Kata sat in his sparsely-decorated living room in his very modest bungalow in Uso Town. He had dimmed the lights to enable him to think clearly. He had just received a visit from Grace Abbey, and the revelations arising out of that visit were literally giving him a headache. But under no circumstances could he permit a headache or anything for that matter to compromise the clarity of thought he needed at the moment.

He was, as always, happy to see Grace Abbey. But today, she had put him in a very sombre mood. She had forced upon him a situation that required his immediate attention and action. The matter at hand was grave indeed.

Grace Abbey was a pretty, well-preserved woman of 50. She was a mother of two, a girl and a boy, and was devoted to them. Her husband, one Captain Abbey, had fallen in battle at the side of his comrade in arms, Major Kata. Being of an idealistic disposition and wanting what was best for Mother Africa, Captain Abbey had joined the cause to fight for freedom in some of the more troubled spots on the African continent, where some of the natives were then still attempting to liberate themselves from the yolk of oppressive Foreign Colonisers.

Captain Abbey had fallen in South Africa, fighting alongside Major Kata and the fighters of the Umkhonto we Sizwe, which was the military wing of the then proscribed African National Congress, the party of Nelson Mandela. They had been fighting an urban guerrilla battle against the Apartheid State of South Africa at the time.

Having made it safely back home after the retrenchment of Apartheid and the release of Nelson Mandela from prison, Major Kata had taken it upon himself at the time to fully support the now near destitute Grace Abbey and her two young children. Major Kata had been unstinting in his support and was happy that both his comrade's children were now at the university, pursuing degrees in law and medicine respectively. Captain Abbey would have been proud indeed.

As a result of his caring, selfless and very generous support of herself and her beloved children for over a decade, Grace Abbey had become a committed and irreversible disciple of Major Kata. She simply had never met such a giving and faithful person in all of her life. And what baffled her most was the fact that the kind Major never asked for anything, nothing at all in return. In actual fact, he had even gone a step further and made her promise to keep all he did for her family between themselves and nobody else. There was nothing in the world that Grace Abbey would not do for Major Kata. All he had to do was ask.

And ask he did, eventually.

Through her industriousness and her conscientious work ethic, Grace Abbey had risen high in the ranks within the civil service to become a top executive personal assistant. Consequently, it came as no surprise that chief directors and ministers were constantly attempting to head-hunt her to work for them.

When Commander Musu ascended to the apex of the BNR as Director and National Security Coordinator, he resolved to have only the best, and set out to lure Grace Abbey to come and work for him as his executive PA. He was very persistent and would not take 'no' for an answer. As head of the BNR, he was also an extremely powerful person whom few would dare to cross or refuse a favour. The head of the BNR automatically had the ear of the President, since matters of security were his greatest concern.

Grace Abbey, however, was seriously disinclined to work for Commander Musu or the notorious BNR. Though she was a civil servant and thus supposed to be apolitical, she was nevertheless sick of the brutal dictatorial Regime of President Brewman and his band of kleptomaniacs that populated his party of Southerners.

Furthermore, she had children at the university where the BNR and its other security appendages, as well as the President's Zombies, had unleashed wanton violence on the students. Nonetheless, to refuse to succumb to the wishes of the likes of Commander Musu could prove quite dangerous indeed. The man was known to never forgive a slight. She was in a dilemma. And it was this dilemma that she placed before Major Kata for guidance. (After all, it was also Major Kata who had secured a job for her within the civil service a while back.)

Major Kata had carefully weighed the matter and then asked her to accept the job as Commander Musu's executive personal assistant. For Grace Abbey, that was enough. Once the Major said she should accept it then she would do just that without further hesitation.

As such, many months later, she was sitting at her desk fielding calls for the Commander when the young Aden Bayou walked in and asked to see her boss without an appointment.

Previously, only two days after the opposition victory, Major Kata had telephoned Grace Abbey and asked to see her. She arrived with alacrity, always happy to see her taciturn yet kindly benefactor. After the usual pleasantries that were never much since the Major rarely spoke, he went straight to the point.

'Grace, the time has come for you to do something for me. I have decided it is time for me to take a greater interest in national matters. As such, I am going to ask you to spy on your boss, Commander Musu, for me. It is a dangerous assignment and hence, a dangerous request. If you are caught, you will be tried for treason and probably shot or certainly jailed. Will you do this for me?'

To Major Kata's amazement, the perennially grateful woman before him did not even blink. There was no hesitation whatsoever when she replied straightaway with utmost sincerity, 'I will do it, Major. There is nothing I will not do for you. The only thing is that you will have to show me how to do it.'

Major Kata was touched at her acceptance of such a dangerous mission without the slightest hesitation. 'But are you not afraid? What if you're caught? What about your children?'

Again, the woman did not bat an eyelid. 'My children and I are where we are because of you. You kept faith with your comrade, my late husband, and now, I keep faith with you. If anything happens to me, my children will still have you to protect them, for I will never betray you. This matter is closed, Major. Please tell me how to go about this spying.'

The matter was closed indeed. The woman wore a determined, implacable look. She would do his bidding. No questions asked. Period.

Major Kata had then proceeded to instruct her carefully. He had given her a tiny two-way parabolic microphone that was state of the art and hard to detect once installed. A day later, she came back to see him to report that she had successfully installed it in Commander Musu's office – under his table – and was now secretly monitoring her boss, as explicitly instructed.

Two paramount reasons prompted Major Kata to commence spying on the BNR through its boss, Commander Musu. Firstly, he had anticipated that many things would go wrong whenever the dust settled after the opposition victory. He knew the matter of the demobilised military vehicles would become a focus of serious attention, and that the Government would do all it could to apprehend and severely punish the culprits in quite the brutal manner, to serve as a deterrent. Thus, he needed to know what the paramount security agency was planning at all times. Major Kata knew that no matter the cost, he had to protect Saga and his family.

Secondly, his innate conviction that his country would one day soon need his services was growing stronger with each passing day. To be of service meant to be in the know, to be abreast, and to be informed. Providence had deemed it fit to place Grace right at the heart of the intelligence gathering security services. It was only thus right for him to ascertain, through her, what was going on within Government, for the greater good.

And now, all this had paid off with the disturbing information he had just received from Grace Abbey about the indomitable Ms Aden Bayou and her lethal, explosive intelligence!

Commander Musu was once again gob-smacked. He was stunned to his very core. What? A bunch of schoolboys and a mystery woman had breached the security of Fort Brewman and effortlessly demobilised and damaged hundreds of millions of dollars' worth of state of the art fighting military vehicles and machines? And they did this with nothing but sand, sugar and salt? He could not believe his ears. He had no choice but to grudgingly admire that Saga Orphan boy. The boy had guts. Recent engineering assessment reports even suggested that it would cost many more millions yet to fix those vehicles, as their mechanical innards had been severely corroded by the salt, sugar and sand mix!

Oh but what a coup this was! *'Intelligence manna' of the highest order.* He secretly praised his perceptiveness in deciding to listen to the young Ms Aden, instead of sending her away. That Ms Aden's exemplary beauty played a key part in his not dismissing her outright was something he had most conveniently forgotten.

He would build an airtight case against those perpetrators and their families, and present it as a done deal to the President himself. Surely, those Orphan boys, despite their obvious bravery, could not have planned and carried out such a huge operation so successfully without some serious mastermind behind them. And he was sure that the particular mastermind had either a military background or some advanced security training of sorts. He, Musu, was no fool.

And to think that such a reward from the heavens was accompanied by such an elegant specimen of the female species. *Oh, oh but my star is now surely on the rise,* he gloated to himself. No longer would he be in the politico-security doghouse. He was back in the main house!

Commander Musu had to put some brakes on his gloating. He had to get home and change into something more appropriate for his date with the delectable Ms Aden that very evening. He had a brand new Armani suit that was perfect for the occasion. He had promised her champagne, and champagne she would have. Cristal or Dom Pérignon? Ah, he would decide that later. He was to wine and dine her atop the only five-star hotel in Cape Cove. Oh, what a night this would be.

This whole matter with Ms Bayou was huge. It would restore him to pre-eminence in their intelligence community, as well as in the eyes of the dictator, whose goodwill was necessary to have in order to survive the murky, lethal and authoritarian political waters of Zimgania.

But he had to handle it well. He could not just rush in and hand this information to the likes of General Yalley, whom he was supposed to report to, and allow the General to build a case against the perpetrators and their families and then take all the credit. No way would he permit that.

CHAPTER THIRTY

Grace's Grand Prix

Saga and Zara were sitting under one of the deserted pavilions that adorned the Ridge Heights Children's Park near Saga's school. It was early evening and the moonlit night made the dimly-lit park not so dark. They sat on benches facing each other.

Zara was gently crying and Saga simply held her hand and stared at the top of her beautiful curly head as she cried. That they were together in the open and in public did not bother him tonight. There were much weightier matters to consider at the moment. Moreover, the park was virtually deserted at that time.

Saga had been open and told Zara everything his father had told him about her father and his enormous, albeit secret, support and contribution to the opposition cause. He told her about the protection he had given the students, who were thought to have disappeared, and his current single-minded obsession to protect his daughter and, by extension, all of them, from charges of high treason.

Zara had never in a million years thought that she would ever hear such a thing. She never thought she would hear of such good deeds from a man she had grown to loathe as part of an oppressive, murderous Regime. And here she was, being told that the Regime would have been far more oppressive, far more murderous, but for her despicable father!

Zara was tired and conflicted. How much more of this could she take? She was emotionally exhausted and for now, was content to just sit down and cry in the presence of the person she loved the most, while she collected her thoughts.

'Saga, I am very confused. Please help me here. If my father is capable of such goodness then why hide it? Why create such a brutal persona as the Regime's foremost hangman? Why allow my mother to die? Why not tell her about all these good deeds? Why Saga? Why? Please help me here. I have to understand this…' She trailed off in a fresh flurry of tears.

Saga was heartbroken. His heart went out to his beloved. He wished he had the answers she so desperately required. He wished he could hold her in his arms and wipe away the tears that were pouring out from her innermost being. But he knew her tears were a necessary part of the process of coming to terms with what she had just heard and trying to make some sense out of it.

'Zara, listen to me, if you can. Your father is obviously a very complex person. I cannot answer all your questions. But maybe he had to hide how he truly felt, and did so in order to stay exactly where he was to make things at least a bit better for so many and for the country. He had to stay in character like they teach us to do when acting in school plays. If he revealed who he truly was, he would have been in grave danger, which means your entire family would have also been in danger. Maybe he kept it quiet to protect all of you. And if people found out about his good deeds, he would have certainly also been booted out from his powerful position, which he needed to stay in to be able to help. Am I making any sense at all?'

'Yes Saga, you are making sense, but it's all so complicated. Where does his goodness start and where does his evil end or vice versa? And why could he not tell my mother? Why did she have to die? And how is it going to be between us now? And what of my brother, Junior? If he knew, he'd haemorrhage; maybe even betray him to Brewman, his idol. And why does he suddenly love me so much? Why Saga? Why?'

Saga truly had no answers, but wanted to be of use to her in her hour of need. But before he could say anything, she continued. 'So it means he has to stay where he is and remain in character, as you said, to protect us, and for the greater good? He just can't get out? Saga, I know what I saw and read when I went searching for the information we needed for the mission.

This Regime is worse than most people think. Brewman plans to rule until he dies. And he will stop at nothing – including murder, as we know – to achieve this. He even has a young son secretly training at the prestigious West Point Military Academy in the United States under a false name, to take over from him on his deathbed. The man wants to build a dynasty, and you are saying my father has to keep at it and help him achieve this sick ambition? My mind is choked, Saga. I can't think straight anymore!'

'Zara – I think the problem we have now is that we are all trying to digest everything at the same time. We are all emotional about this new information about your dad and how it affects so many things. There's even the pressing issue about his fear that one of my Orphans will accidentally tell someone about the mission and how that will destroy us all, including your father himself. We have to calm down now and let it all sink in gradually before we can also analyse it all correctly to know what to do next. And also remember, there's my dad, who can help us process all of this, and he'd love to meet you.'

He then pulled her up from the bench and held her closely.

* * *

Commander Musu was astonished! He was also elated. He sat down and whispered a silent and grateful prayer to God for bringing Aden Bayou into his life. The woman had been in his life for just a short period and yet his fortunes kept getting better and better and now, they were positively soaring. And what a night he'd had with her a few days ago when he had wined and dined her at the most fashionable hotel in the country. Now, he was seriously considering divorcing his wife and marrying Aden, since she brought him nothing but the best of luck and a tremendous feeling of self-worth.

What had finally convinced him to marry her was the astonishing information she had just uncovered. With her by his side, maybe he would one day soon become President-for-Life as well. Indeed, the critical information he had just uncovered meant he could now have General Yalley's job and become the second most powerful man in Zimgania.

Being someone who was very diligent when it came to his work, Commander Musu had made it his unalterable mission over the past few days to locate the guards who were on duty that night at Fort Brewman when the military vehicles were destroyed. This was all part of his process to build an airtight case against the perpetrators of such high treason. Commander Musu began to smell a rat when he was utterly thwarted in his initial attempts to locate said guards. What should have proved to be an exceptionally simple task was now proving to be nigh impossible. But how could that be?

He was like a dog with a juicy bone. He personally drove around in his three-car motorcade with police outriders and visited the commanding officers of the various guards on duty that night at their respective barracks. Together, with them, they painstakingly went through all recent military transfer records until they located them at surprisingly remote locations.

That very night, Musu deployed three teams of his most highly-trained operatives and sent them to various parts of the country to bring the guards back to him by morning. He issued high priority National Security mandates to his various teams to ensure they received maximum cooperation wherever they went.

By the time Commander Musu arrived at the office by 7a.m. the next morning, all the Fort Brewman guards had been rounded up and placed in various interrogation rooms, awaiting his directives. Again, he gathered together his best set of interrogators and tasked them with eliciting every single piece of information those guards could remember from that fateful night. He gave explicit instructions for them to use any means necessary to extract the information if they felt the guards were withholding or not being forthcoming.

By lunchtime, Commander Musu's interrogators had extracted some very revealing information, which was what had made him so buoyant and full of hope that day (and ready for new nuptials as well).

Commander Musu had carefully weighed the information and he knew he was, without a doubt, onto a complete winner. Zara Yalley had curiously been there on the night of the sabotage. And with strong alcoholic drinks and enough food to choke a donkey. And that she had been there again not so long before, on the pretext of having a punctured tyre, thus giving her the perfect excuse to enter the Fort Brewman premises. That she had specifically sought information on guard duties and rotation. That she took their phone numbers and called them to say she was coming back to visit on that very day of the sabotage at the exact time period that forensic analysis had determined the vehicles were destroyed.

God Almighty, but it does not take a genius to figure out what happened. This is not rocket science. This was what in the field we call classic misdirection. The girl was part of the operation, plain and simple! Commander Musu was elated at the discovery that Yalley's quiet and extraordinarily beautiful daughter was part of the terrible sabotage. She was the only girl he knew to be more beautiful than his own Ms Aden. Unbelievable! But the evidence said believable!!

With the information he had so far gathered, Musu knew that he was already in possession of Yalley's job. General Yalley could not wriggle out of this one. If the General claimed he did not know of his daughter's perfidy then how come he had set about to transfer all those guards to remote locations and bribe them with huge sums to forget they ever laid eyes on his daughter? Apart from that, even if he claimed ignorance, he would still be hugely culpable for permitting treason to flourish in his own home! The most likely scenario was that he was totally aware of her involvement and had been using his massive influence to cover it all up. Could it even be that he put her up to it for whatever diabolical motive he had?

Musu also knew he could lay hands on the boy Saul Azo, who had confessed to his 'intended' Aden Bayou, whenever he wanted and make him confess. There was also the Orphan Saga boy, who could be made to confess as well, and name Zara Yalley as a co-conspirator, if placed under extreme duress.

And placing people under extreme duress was his number one speciality.

So how was he to approach it? Option one: take the evidence to General Yalley and force him to resign while recommending that he, Commander Musu, become his successor in the process? Or option two, in which he would present the President with the information he had and cause Yalley and his children to be immediately arrested? Meanwhile, he would also arrest the Saga boy, his brother, uncle, mother and father as well as co-conspirators for better measure. Young Saul Azo would also be arrested, and soon after that, all the participants in that nefarious enterprise would be behind bars together, with their families to boot!

Oh what a coup that will be, with me as Minister for Presidential Affairs with Oversight for National Security and with beautiful Aden at my side as my new bride. Oh, why is life so good to me, Musu mused.

Commander Musu eventually decided to go with option two and cause the President to arrest Yalley and his family. Option one was indeed a bit dicey, given that his nerve tended to fail him whenever he had to deal directly with the dreaded General Yalley. Yes, it was better if he left that part to the Zombies directly under the President's command. The other arrests, he could of course handle himself, not to mention that it was also within his remit. He picked up his phone, which was a very secure line, and called his most trusted operative, who had supervised the interrogation of the Fort Brewman guys. He then gave the man explicit instructions as to how he wanted the arrests done. He wanted everything to be coordinated with scrupulous precision. All the people he had mentioned including Saga and his family members were to be picked up simultaneously, and there was to be an overwhelming show of force in this exercise.

'You have exactly one week to prepare. I want them all to be picked up the moment the President green-lights General Yalley's arrest. The President is back in Cape Cove in a week, so we must be very ready to move. I want confessions from all of them. Do you understand? I want them interrogated and tortured until they confess so we can legally have them executed for high treason. Hand-pick your teams and come and show the list to me for approval. I want the best of the best. I am waiting for you.'

Commander Musu had now set everything in motion for his own brilliant coup! All he had to do now was wait for the President's return to the capital. In the scheme of things, and given the enormity of the rewards, one week was a very short time indeed to wait for such peerless bounty!

Caught up in a reverie of all the wonderful things he would do and the new properties he would acquire for himself as the new Minister for Presidential Affairs, Commander Musu did not hear Grace Abbey enter the room.

Grace coughed ever so slightly to alert her boss to her presence.

Musu snapped out of his reverie, annoyed.

'What the hell do you want? Don't you people understand the concept of "do not disturb"? Jesus!'

As always, Grace remained unperturbed in his presence. 'Boss, you gave no directive not to be disturbed. Anyway, I am not feeling well. May I please have the rest of the day off?'

Commander Musu was about to bellow a decisive 'NO' to her request when he suddenly remembered that it was she who had insisted he saw Aden Bayou that day, which had, in turn, led to his tremendous good fortune. He decided to show concern and be magnanimous.

'Oh, what is it, my dear? Is it a headache? Maybe I can help? Should I send for some paracetamol?' he asked, feigning concern.

'It's all right, sir. Nothing major. Just acute pain from female issues. A bit of rest and painkillers should do the trick.'

'Then you shall have your rest. No worries. You can go but get that lazy assistant of yours to get her backside into your chair and hold the fort. Make sure I see you tomorrow. We have busy days ahead. You women must learn to control your female issues. Now off you go before I change my mind,' replied Musu, having now dropped his pretended concern.

Grace Abbey dashed out of the impressive glass and steel high-rise building of the BNR with such speed, as though she were being pursued by a flock of malevolent spirits who bode her no good. She had been given specific instructions by her revered Major Kata to let him know immediately if she overheard any significant developments concerning the mysterious Fort Brewman vehicle saga. And now, she had just overheard her boss say major arrests will be made just one week from now.

Grace Abbey drove as a woman possessed. She drove as if she were part of a Grand Prix tournament. She used her special BNR curfew pass to sail through the military roadblocks and police checkpoints that dotted the city. Within half an hour, she was at Major Kata's café.

Major Kata was going through his cash till to assess his sales so far that day when he saw a breathless and slightly dishevelled Grace Abbey arrive. That woman was never dishevelled. He immediately knew she was a bearer of urgent news, which of course could not be good. He met her before she could advance to the till and, gently taking her arm, led her to the back of the café where he sometimes sat with Saga. He pulled up two folding chairs for them to sit on.

Grace Abbey wasted no time in bringing the Major up to speed the moment she was seated. From the manner in which he received the news, she was gratified that she had done the right thing in dropping everything, feigning illness and coming to him immediately. He made her repeat a few more details of what she had overheard very carefully until he was certain he had the full picture.

Major Kata thanked Grace Abbey with heartfelt words. The woman had indeed done him a great service. In fact, though she didn't know it as yet, she had also done their nation an immense service. He then asked her to go and report back to work the next day. She was to keep her ears open for any more developments on that all-important matter of the Fort Brewman vehicles.

It was now time for Major Kata to move. He left his café immediately after Grace had gone. He went straight home as he needed total tranquillity to think. One week was just too soon and yet, there was nothing he could do about it. In a week, all the members of the family he loved most, Saga's family, were certain to be in the torture chambers of the dreaded BNR.

Once they were arrested, other mass arrests would follow. After all, no matter how strong a person was, everyone was bound to have a breaking point in the face of merciless, unrelenting torture. He had spent too many years in battle not to know this.

The Yalley family would also suffer a similar fate. Given Commander Musu's vaunted ambitions, General Yalley was probably his chief target. And yet, he knew as well that Yalley was the only man in the country who had a modicum of a sobering effect on their rabid, maniacal President.

What was the solution to all this? How was he, Major Kata, with the information he had, going to stop the disaster that was about to be unleashed on so many?

He sat quietly, virtually unmoving and unblinking for an hour, and finally arrived at what to his mind constituted as the only possible solution in curing the cancer that had taken root in their country and was presently threatening to end the lives of many patriots and innocents.

He picked up his mobile phone and called Saga at home. He asked him to meet him in an hour and a half at the café. After that, he took out a special notebook he kept hidden in the ceiling of his living room and started dialling. He was activating his clandestine network of old military colleagues who perceived him as their leader. It took him all of one hour to dial several numbers and recite the pre-arranged code words to activate his not insignificant network.

Saga was waiting behind the café by the time Major Kata got back. Major Kata was not his usual smiling self. Saga was perturbed by this and immediately on guard.

'Saga, I need to meet urgently with your father and his brother you call Tiger. I also want you to be at the meeting. Tell your father that I know it is an unusual request but tell him it is very urgent and that it concerns the safety of your entire family. Can you please do that for me?'

Despite trusting Major Kata completely, Saga agreed this was a highly unusual request. 'Major, what is all this about?'

Major Kata, despite his knowledge of how urgent the situation was, lost his stern demeanour and smiled at Saga. The boy was as sharp as a tack.

'Saga, are you worried that whatever it is that I need to discuss with your dad and his brother might reveal that you have been telling me things they told you never to tell anyone? Is that not correct?'

'Yes Major, you're right. I kept Zara from them. I kept the Fort Brewman mission from them. And now, they're going to find out that I've told you everything? They'll never trust me again, Major. Never!' Saga concluded, looking quite unsettled.

'Saga, we don't have much time to talk today so listen carefully. In this world, two things matter the most. One is the reason why people do the things they do; the intention. Two is the outcome of what people do; consequence. In this case, your intentions have always been good. And the outcome, as you will soon find out, is also very good. You told me these things because you believed you were doing a good thing, the right thing. Your father and your uncle are wise. Let me handle them. They will always trust you. Okay?'

Saga never doubted his older friend, Major Kata, and was thus quite relieved that the Major was going to 'handle' both his dad and his uncle. He believed in Major Kata, pure and simple.

'Oh thank you so much, Major, but before I leave, where is this meeting to take place?'

'You've described your uncle's place to me. The basement of his temple is fine. The meeting should be at 8p.m. That gives us all about four hours. Run along and arrange it. I repeat: tell them it is extremely urgent. Off you go, Saga.'

'Bye Major. See you at 8p.m.'

Saga then left to find his father, still quite perplexed as to what this was all about.

CHAPTER THIRTY-ONE

Stroke of State or FDI

Nana, Uncle Tiger, Major Kata and Saga were all seated in the main opposition meeting hall in the basement of Tiger's Temple in Uso Town. Four semi-comfortable-looking chairs had been arranged for them around a circular table. Uncle Tiger's factotum had just brought them all steaming mugs of sweet, milky coffee and had quietly disappeared thereafter.

Both Nana and Tiger looked at Major Kata with keen interest. Of course, they knew him pretty well. After all, was his business not situated within Nana's compound? And was Nana not a silent minority partner in the business? However, beyond their knowledge that Major Kata was a strong, silent and very decent man who adored Saga, he was to all intents and purposes an unknown quantity. And of course, there were all those rumours about his past. But they were not bad rumours. Rather, they tended to be of a heroic hue.

Major Kata went straight to the point. 'Thank you, Nana and Mr Tiger, for seeing me. I know a lot about what has been going on. Saga has kept me abreast. He has not broken faith with you. His intention, like his soul, is always pure. Soon, we may all very well go on our knees and thank him for keeping me abreast. Had he not done so, you would all be destroyed completely in the coming days.' Major Kata paused. He was not used to such long sentences. He was a bit like Uncle Tiger in this respect. But today, it was necessary to talk.

Major Kata spoke very softly though distinctly. He did not embellish. And it was his sincere directness that caused the two brothers and Saga to experience a chill.

'Major, what it this about please?' asked Nana, who was now a touch anxious.

'I have intelligence that your entire family will be arrested in a week and sent to the BNR. They will go for your other son at the university. Mr Tiger here will also be arrested. The entire Yalley family is also be arrested. You will be tortured and tried and eventually executed for treason. Your daughter, Emma, is the only one to be spared.'

'Jesus Christ, but what the hell is this, Major? What in God's name are you talking about? And where are you getting all this stuff from anyway? Are you even serious? What crazy talk is this? Some warped idea of a game?' exploded Nana in a fog of incomprehension.

'Please calm down, sir. Believe me when I say my source is completely reliable. I even have the exact times the arrests will be carried out. All you need to know now is this: while I am alive, this will never be permitted to happen.

'I know you each have a million questions. But we have absolutely no time to ask them now. Whatever I have to say, I can only say it once, and I want a couple more critical people to join us before I do that. And to do that, I need you all to trust me completely and do exactly as I say. I have to leave right now. I want us to reconvene here at midnight without fail. I cannot give any of you orders. You are not under my command. But if I have your complete trust then you will do as I say. Do I have your trust?'

The fog had cleared and Nana had calmed down a bit as well. His brother showed no emotion beyond carefully watching the Major. Saga was aghast at both the news and his father's outburst, but said nothing, as his heart was beating uncontrollably. Eventually, it was Nana who nodded in response, indicating that the Major had their trust. At least for now.

Indeed, there was a manner about Major Kata that inspired absolute confidence. They knew the man to be 24-carat genuine, despite not knowing too much about him. Also, the two brothers were both seasoned enough to know when someone was telling them the truth about such critical matters. Moreover, they were still quite shocked to the core about what the Major had just revealed.

Major Kata smiled his appreciation and continued, 'Nana, your son, Obo, must be here for the meeting at midnight. Please make sure he is. Mr Tiger, I know you are in direct contact with General Yalley. He must also be here. Whatever it takes, please get him here. Please tell them both nothing. Furthermore, you are going to allow me to take over the security of your compound here, Mr Tiger. This is going to be our headquarters for what we need to do to stop your arrests and deaths. I will have 30 armed men here within an hour. They will all report directly to you to introduce themselves. Saga should stay put. He should not leave this place. Saga, please supervise the storage of the provisions and water that will be brought in for the security people. Saga, if both your uncle and dad have to leave, you are in charge of the compound until they return. We all have a little over three hours each to complete our tasks. Are we all clear?'

They were all very clear.

The circular table had been replaced with a slightly larger one. The chairs were now six in number and were arranged as an outer circle around the table in Uncle Tiger's Masonic Temple basement. Outside, Major Kata's armed security men ringed the entire compound. Others were stationed outside the premises, patrolling the streets. There were even men with assault rifles strategically placed atop the Masonic Temple with night-vision goggles, surveying the entire area from their elevated positions.

Inside was an uneasy gathering of two youths and four much older men. Obo had come and was thoroughly at a loss to understand the presence of their arch-enemy, General Yalley, in their midst. However, his father had sternly cautioned him to say nothing but to trust him and his Uncle Tiger.

General Yalley had wisely come alone and unarmed. He was even sporting a slight disguise of dark glasses and a cap pulled low to conceal part of his face. He took them off when he entered the basement. He was also wondering what this was all about but had decided to trust Tiger and Nana, as he respected them both very much.

Major Kata again wasted no time in getting to the heart of the matter.

'It seems to me that the person who knows the least here is young Obo. He must be brought up to speed quickly so he understands the context. So for now, I will do that first. General Yalley, thank you for coming. I see you recognise me. Yes, we served together a while back, during the troubles in Liberia many years ago. Unfortunately, today is not for reminiscing. So young Mr Obo, here is the context...'

And with that, Major Kata succinctly and with complete precision brought Obo up to speed. He told of his younger brother's heroic exploits. He told of Zara Yalley's secret involvement. He told of General Yalley's secret and invaluable assistance to the overall opposition. He told of Yalley's secret assistance, even to the rebellious student movement of which he, Obo, was a prominent leader. He told of Yalley's secret sequestering of those students who could not be accounted for, as well as other perceived enemies of State from the murderous retribution of his boss, the President. Major Kata simply told it all.

Obo was a very tough young man who was also very astute and amazingly level-headed. He was a brilliant academic and had a lion heart to boot. However, despite having these qualities of sound character, he could not help but be utterly stunned and discombobulated at the sheer amount of astonishing information that he was being assailed with. And how on earth did Kata know all this? But all the others present had not contradicted a single word the man had said. He just couldn't grasp what was going on.

Nana was watching Obo carefully and could see that the young man was becoming increasingly bewildered. The boy could explode any minute. He waited for Major Kata to pause and then quickly intervened

'Obo, I know this is all too much to take it at once. Believe me when I say that even those of us much older and more experienced than you were completely floored by some of these revelations. For example, how could your younger brother have planned and successfully executed such a major operation with just a bunch of schoolboys and with only Zara Yalley as his sole confidant and chief accomplice? How can we, for example, accept without a struggle that General Yalley, a man we have all grown to hate so deeply, suddenly turning out to be a bona fide guardian angel? And how is it even possible for Major Kata, whom we all know never speaks more than a single sentence a week, to be suddenly transformed into a talkative lecturer?'

Nana deliberately added the last sentence about the Major to introduce a touch of levity, which he knew his son would appreciate.

Major Kata cast an appreciative look as well in Nana's direction. His intervention had been brilliantly timed to calm down his son. Major Kata looked around him. Neither Tiger nor Yalley had spoken. Both were very good listeners. Patient men. Saga, who was practically the central figure in all of this, was also listening intently without missing a word. His heart had now slowed down a bit.

Kata continued. 'Grace Abbey is a close friend of mine. She is the executive PA to Commander Musu of the BNR. She has recently been spying on Musu for me. She has been using a hidden microphone I gave her. And this is what she reported to me over the past few days, including today: a young beautiful lady by the name of Aden Bayou...'

And with that, Major Kata told them the full story without adornment. He told them of Saul Azo's drunken indiscretion up until the interrogation of the Fort Brewman guards at the BNR, and ending with Musu's plan to simultaneously have both Nana's family and Yalley's family arrested a week hence. He explained how Musu had planned it all to the last detail. BNR operatives were to effect the arrest of Nana's family members, while elite Zombie troops under the direct command of the President would effect Yalley's arrest, together with his son and daughter. BNR operatives would also arrest Saul Azo and all the other Orphans, such as Ibrahim, who were part of the mission, once their names had been obtained through the anticipated confessions. Many of their innocent family members would also be arrested and detained for good measure.

Musu had planned to torture confessions out of them and then have them all tried, convicted and executed for high treason. Musu was operating under the misapprehension that the members of the respective families colluded to back Saga, Zara and their Orphans in the destruction of the expensive military equipment at Fort Brewman. Thus, the families were all being perceived as being guilty of the highest treason.

Nobody said a word while Major Kata spoke. They were all visibly chilled to the marrow. Even Obo, who was new to all that had been transpiring suddenly, knew he was marked for certain death with his family. This was sobering indeed to say the very least.

For General Yalley, it was as if his worst nightmare was playing out exactly as he had feared. He had underestimated Musu and he was about to pay the ultimate price for his own foolishness. He came to the realisation that he was going to die and would thus be unable to save his beloved daughter. How was he to face his wife in the hereafter if he was unable to save his daughter? Even his son now needed saving! With great effort, Yalley pulled himself out of his reverie and spoke for the first time.

'Major Kata, you have done exemplary work. Everything you have said makes perfect sense. And yes, Musu is absolutely correct to calculate that he will have the President's full backing in all this. Certainly, we are all in the gravest danger. Who knows that better than myself? But Major, you have a solution, which is why you brought us here. Outside, I see you have not taken any chances. This place is like an armed fortress and the placement of the men is for maximum tactical advantage, which I assume is your doing. You are the only one here who is not in imminent danger, but yet you are here and obviously in charge. And you have taken charge because you have come up with a possible way out of this mess. Major, please tell us, what is your solution to all this? As I sit here, my heart is breaking. But maybe, just maybe, you may have a good plan. We are listening.'

'My solution is best expressed in the French language. I am talking of a *coup d'état*. A coup – with you, Yalley, as interim

Head of State in order to control the troops. With Tiger and Nana on the interim ruling council to be created. Either we all die, which is not an option since I won't sit down and let Saga and his family be arrested without fighting back, or we plan and execute a successful coup in one week. At least this way, we have a fighting chance. And most importantly, the people of this country need it. We must take power to give back power. Gentlemen – I say again, a *coup d'état*!'

Had a feather dropped in the room at the time, it would have been heard. Such was the resounding silence that greeted Major Kata's solution; a forcible overthrow of the current Regime, headed by President-for-Life Brewman.

Even someone as young as Saga fully understood the implications of a coup. By its very nature, a *coup d'état* – literally meaning a 'stroke of state' – was a violent act. Like a debilitating medical stroke that assaults the human body, causing untold chaos, *coup d'états* also tended to create severely pernicious political upheavals, oftentimes causing societal paralysis. Indeed, it was the ultimate political statement; usually a very violent one.

Coup d'états had bedevilled the African continent for decades, and sent many an African state spiralling downwards towards increasing poverty, political intolerance, dictatorships and failed nation states. The likes of Idi Amin and Joseph Mobutu were all products of *coup d'états*. It was probably the single most destabilising factor in Africa for many decades, following the achievement of independence by most African states. Even their own current woes as a nation with President-for-Life Brewman had its roots in a *coup d'état*. Coups had, to all intents and purposes, become taboo. In addition to this was a new world order that decidedly frowned upon coups. Military cabals that dared to perpetrate coups now faced severe disapprobation from powerful regional, continental and global multilateral agencies, such as the United Nations itself, the World Bank, the IMF, the Non-Aligned Movement, and the African Union, to name but a few.

Major Kata was a trained leader of men. He thus knew it was imperative that he drove his point home before the ball dropped; before they recovered and started spewing forth counter-arguments. The coup issue had to be driven into the collective psyche of those present to give the matter a fighting chance; to give the matter proper consideration. But before he could continue, Nana interjected forcefully.

'What the hell, Major? With all due respect, are you out of your bloody mind? What the hell is this about? Oh, because we probably face death sentences, we should go out there and commit suicide openly? Because from where I stand, a coup and suicide are the bloody same?'

Obo was not far behind in voicing his disagreement. 'But Major Kata, are you saying a coup is our only option? How did we even get to this point? You want us to become international pariahs? Everyone frowns on coups these days! The international community will even impose sanctions! Jesus, but is this really an option? It sounds too far-fetched; much too desperate!'

Nana had not even finished. 'What about the option of sustained civil disobedience? Have we not just proved we can lock down this country and paralyse it with strikes and demonstrations? Is that not a better way? Coups are the absolute last resort.'

Major Kata had his answers ready. 'Gentlemen, let us not be pedantic. Let us think straight. And no, I am not out of my bloody mind, thank you. And yes, we are desperate as well. Your demonstration was successful in large part because of General Yalley sabotaging his own government. But Yalley is about to be a marked man now. He can't repeat that performance. Do you want to risk the hundreds of civilians being mowed down by this maniac of a President this time around? Have you forgotten that you all have death sentences hanging over your heads? You want Saga, Zara and their Orphan youngsters to die after being inhumanly tortured? You all want to die?' he challenged them. Receiving no reply, he continued, 'Coups, like most things, are not black and white. There is something called lesser evil. A lot depends on what you tell the country and people, once you've taken power in a coup, and keeping the promises you make. So what will we do? We will immediately and unilaterally call for a cease-fire to end the bloody war that

354

is senselessly killing our youth. We will completely abolish the National Service decree, which, mind you, is still technically under review. We will lift the ban on political parties and usher in a national democratic dispensation. We'll remove all censorship. We will free all political prisoners. We'll restore freedom of association. We'll immediately declare multi-party democratic elections in nine months. We'll ban and demobilise the Zombie Presidential Guard and BNR. We'll call in Amnesty International to supervise the conditions of those we'll be forced to detain, as well as the thousands we will immediately release. We will immediately re-establish *habeas corpus*, rule of law and due process. Finally, if we are very careful, we may not even have to spill any blood.

'Now, let me ask you all two questions before I stop talking: firstly, are these not the very aims the opposition and true patriots of this country have been fighting for so long? Secondly, how long will it take under the current Regime to achieve all the things I said we will do, such as ushering in democracy? A decade? Two decades? Never? I think "never" is the correct answer here under this Government, which is going nowhere unless we force it out!'

Nana still had fundamental concerns.

'But Major, a *coup d'état* is necessarily a military action, and all we have here are only two soldiers with one retired and the other destined for the gallows. So pray do tell, but who in God's name is going to execute this coup for us? Are we not getting ahead of ourselves with wishful, unrealistic thinking?'

'Mr Nana, please rest assured that I will answer all your questions. But before then, consider this as an opportunity this country has unknowingly been waiting for. We are so uniquely positioned. The President is not as yet looped into Musu's plans, though he will no doubt back it. As such, General Yalley is still in charge of National Security. He still has all his security clearances. He still commands. Everyone in this country still assumes he speaks for the President and that his word is gospel. And Yalley owes this to the nation because, despite his clandestine good deeds, it's not enough atonement for helping to prop up this cancer of a Regime. He must dismantle the evil he helped create and we are here to help achieve this laudable goal. Now, I dare any of you to look into their hearts and tell me I am wrong!'

With that, Major Kata fell silent. He left them to the thoughts that were obviously swirling around in their minds. Tiger spoke for the first time.

'I agree with the Major that we have no other option. He is also right in saying that there is something called the lesser evil. And yes, we are uniquely positioned. Another thing is for certain: even if we initially face the wrath of the international community, we will never face the wrath of the people of this nation, who see Brewman's governance as nothing but a pestilential plague. No one wants to permanently live under the conditions of a raging plague. And the African Union may also back us. One less war on the continent is something they dream of daily. Inviting amnesty and ushering multi-party democratic elections will demonstrate the purity of our intentions. That we are considering this because almost all of us in this room would otherwise face a certain death is neither here nor there. It does not detract from the genuine nature of our intentions. I am a Freemason. To my mind, it is time for us to create order out of chaos. Ultimately, it is my nephew, Saga, and Yalley's daughter, Zara, who have created this opportunity for us. It was their deeds that spurred on Commander Musu to seek our deaths. It is his deeds that consequently spur us on. It is as if this is ordained of God. I have said enough.'

Obo decided it was now his turn to speak. He was now rid of his initial inner turmoil, engendered by the avalanche of stunning information that was literally dumped on him without preamble. He had also come to terms with the fact that though it sounded desperate, a coup may actually be a way forward. He was back to his level-headed self and fully in control of his faculties.

'It is beginning to look like "do or don't", we're damned, so we might as well "do" for the greater good. There are, however, some practical considerations if we decide to proceed. First of all, General Yalley as interim Head of State could generate the impression of a palace coup; a mere rearrangement of the key personnel in charge of the state, a cosmetic change. That is something we will have to immediately diffuse. Also, we will require key civil society organisations in this country to come out immediately to legitimise the new government. I believe that overwhelming support from the students, who are the most determined fighters for democracy in the country, will go a long way in conferring immediate legitimacy. To this end, I believe that a prominent student leader, such as their extremely popular President Kobby, should have a place on the new council, even if it's ex-officio. The Brewman Government also does not have a single woman in any high governmental position, due to the Regime's backwardness. The appearance of women on the new ruling council will demonstrate that we have truly entered a new age. This will also give us the support of the many important female organisations and associations.

'Key members of the opposition, such as my father and uncle, being on the council is a step in the right direction. Also, we all know that the regular professional army is essentially opposed to the ongoing war. This is a huge plus for us. However, the dynamics of turning that concretely into our favour is something I believe General Yalley is best suited to address. And, of course, you can leave the aspect of the critical student support to me. Finally, to my mind, this would be a coup to end all coups. It will be a coup to usher in democracy. Thus, it would be a forcible democratic intervention. We can't call it a revolution. The currency of revolutions has been debased on our continent. Too many so-called military revolutionary types have come along and done just the opposite of revolution and looted, murdered and plundered like everyone else. So let us agree here and now that we ultimately don't call our intervention a coup, but an FDI – a forcible democratic intervention.'

Major Kata had to control himself in order to desist from clapping for Obo. Nana is enormously fortunate with his children. Right here sits a future President of our country. The boy is a natural born leader. FDI? It's simply brilliant, he thought to himself.

'Major Kata, my brother and my son have all scored telling points and made compelling arguments. Obo's FDI is an excellent and original concept. However, all the lofty things we intend to do become possible if and only if it is at all possible to pull this government down through a coup. Civil society organisations can play key roles but that will be in the consolidation and not in the actual execution of the coup, which I say again, is a military matter. As such, before we can go any further, I believe we must hear what General Yalley has to say on the matter. And Major, it is obvious you have thought about this possibility of a coup for a long time and prepared. How else could you deploy 30 trained ex-military types in less than a single hour? I suggest that once we hear from the General, you should also let us know what it is that you have not as yet shared with us,' Nana demanded.

Saga couldn't believe what was happening. He felt like he was watching a movie.

Is this all for real? Am I actually a part of a discussion to overthrow a government that has been in power for so long and is feared by all? Am I actually at the centre of it all? And are Zara and I and the rest of our families going to suffer and die if we don't attempt this coup or Obo's FDI? And will we also suffer and die if this FDI attempt fails?

Saga did not know what to feel or think. At some point, he felt himself starting to shake from pure irrational (or was it rational) fear? But, all said and done, he remained an incurable optimist and he simply trusted the people in the room enormously (apart from General Yalley, whom of course, he simply barely knew). Between his dad, his fearless uncle, his equally fearless brother, together with the inspirational Major Kata, he knew that somehow, there would be a light at the end of this very precarious tunnel they were attempting to traverse.

It was now General Yalley's turn to intervene on the coup issue. They watched him keenly. He was still very much an unknown quantity and still very much part of the Regime. His presence there was a huge risk to all of them. Technically, he could still have them arrested and tried for high treason as well on the unforgivable and dastardly charge of coup plotting. However, Major Kata by including him figured it was worth the risk. He also instinctively knew that the man would go into the depths of hell to save his daughter if necessary. After all, without him, the coup or FDI was a non-starter in the first place.

They all braced themselves to hear from him. Too much depended on him.

General Yalley cleared his throat once and, moving from face to face, looked at everyone in the circle directly in the eye for a few seconds at a time and then began. He sounded almost contrite.

'I am honoured to be amongst you. I am touched that despite my despicable reputation, you have decided to trust me. Major Kata is correct in saying I owe this nation and all its citizens – including your good selves –a great deal. Only God knows how much I have to atone for. And only God knows how much I suffer for my misdeeds as a key protagonist in this oppressive Regime I am very much a part of. I have no doubt that brave, young Saga here can even tell you how much my own beloved daughter hates me. But enough of that. What I will say to start with is that I am completely indebted to those of you here and I will always be loyal to you. I am not a threat to any of you. You can rest assured.'

General Yalley paused. He was becoming visibly emotional, to the amazement of his small audience. They all watched him silently as he struggled to gain countenance. He succeeded after a minute and continued, 'I have thought of myself as many things, but never as a Head of State. It may come as a surprise to you but it never occurred to me to be part of a coup to overthrow President Brewman. But Obo here is right in saying we don't have a choice in the matter. He is also right in saying that we ought to see this as an FDI. Commander Musu will never give up, and the President will, under no circumstances, forgive those who humiliated him so much with the destruction of those vehicles and military equipment. Also, he plans to establish a dynasty with his son in America to rule after him. A coup can succeed. But it can only succeed if we have the cooperation of at least a few of the regular army top brass.

'I will be Head of State if you so wish it, but only in name. Nana and Mr Tiger and their opposition people will have to do the actual ruling of the country for the suggested nine months. Major Kata here can take over the National Security apparatus. I am with Nana in believing that Major Kata probably has all of this worked out in some greater detail and I also want to hear it. I know the Major has already factored in how we are going to get the top army people on our side. Without them, it will be a suicide mission. Let us hear the Major before I give my final version of how this coup or FDI can succeed. Again, I owe you all. Thank you.'

Major Kata again had the floor. 'Yes, I had anticipated that at some point, a coup would be necessary to topple Brewman. It's the only way to be rid of him. And yes, I have prepared. I am the leader of a secret paramilitary group of over 1000 well-trained and very fit older soldiers. Many were officers. Some were senior non-commissioned officers. We have arms and they will obey my commands unto the death. I intend to put them at General Yalley's disposal. They are experienced and loyal. But for purposes of the FDI coup, they will have to be officially deputised and sanctioned.'

Major Kata paused. He was still not used to talking that much. He had to literally force himself. He continued, 'We also have feasible plans to shut down the entire capital city and blockade it within two hours. The main State Broadcasting Corporation will be surrounded and breached for the main takeover announcement. The Presidential Palace will be surrounded and breached if necessary. We can also seal off the two main Zombie barracks for at least 12 hours without reinforcement. We can paralyse the transportation in the city within a couple of hours. Thanks to Saga and his destruction of the Zombie vehicles, their movement and response capabilities will also be severely restricted. We can also take over the State Communications Authority in no time at all. The BRN and all its offices can also be surrounded and placed on lockdown and Musu arrested. The code name to launch this action is Operation Free Zimgania.'

Major Kata paused again. Obo took advantage of this to ask the main question on everybody's mind. 'Major, this is both amazing and, in a sense, troubling indeed. But tell us, how do we get the regular army to back us? How do we co-opt their leaders? From what General Yalley said, that is the most fundamental requirement for a successful FDI in this country.'

Major Kata nodded his head in Obo's direction and continued. 'Like the General here, I am also Sandhurst trained. I went there with a bosom friend of mine. We were inseparable until he died of cancer last year. I saved his life a couple of times on the battlefield. On his deathbed, he made his son swear a solemn oath in my presence that he was never to deny any request from me. The son was to accede to all my demands. The son took this oath in my presence and without fear or coercion. He has known me all his life. He knows I will never ask of him something that is wrong or unholy. The son in question is currently the Chief of Defence Staff of the Zimgania Armed Forces.'

Major Kata paused for effect. He was not given to dramatics, but he also knew that this was the last thing they thought they would hear. Even the General was shocked. Even Saga understood the implications. It meant that potentially, they could have the most senior member of the armed forces on their side. The Chief of Defence Staff was in charge of all the various military services, which comprised of Army, Navy and Air Force. This was indeed an amazing revelation!

Major Kata continued after he noticed that his revelation had sunk in. 'The truth is that I have been meeting with him secretly. He is very much opposed to the war and does not like the President. But he is a professional and may hesitate at the idea of a coup. However, like I said, he swore an oath and is ultimately also a very decent person. I have not explicitly told him about the coup and the support we will need from him. If General Yalley fully comes on board and gives us the green light then I believe I can guarantee the cooperation of the Chief of Defence Staff (CDS) and his senior commanders, who revere him.'

'Gentlemen my position is this: if Major Kata is guaranteeing that he can get the CDS and his service chiefs on our side then I am fully on board. I am your man. However, you must all understand the realities. If we fail, we die. I am still in charge of state security and yes, we may have the support of the regular army but know this: the army is not as well equipped as the Presidential Guard, the Zombies. Furthermore, many of those elite soldiers have received commando training in Israel and have also done the prestigious Rangers Course in America. They are very privileged and some may fight to protect the high status they enjoy. That is what we are up against. What do you think as a military man yourself, Major?'

'You're right. The Zombies are better equipped. But they've also gone a bit soft with all the pampering. They are neither battle tested nor battle hardened. Their main opponents to date have been students with sticks or workers demonstrating and throwing a few stones. I believe we can find a way to neutralise them quite early, once the action begins.'

Nana listened to the exchange between the military men and decided to speak. 'So then, it appears we are all agreed that we are going to topple the Regime with a FDI. I am no soldier, but I believe from now on, everything is strictly on a need-to-know basis. Absolute secrecy and discretion must be observed. Even the opposition groups we lead and the students Kobby and Obo lead cannot be told. Wives, mothers, sisters, family cannot be told. They will all have their roles to play in the immediate aftermath of the coup. We will find a way to prime them to be ready to hit the streets at a drop of a hat, but we will withhold the coup part for now. Saga must, at all times, remain confined to this compound. I am sorry, my boy, but you can't even meet with Zara – I am sure the General will agree. So what next?'

General Yalley got up at this point and started strolling around the large meeting room. The others just stared after him, waiting patiently. He needed space to think. Like Julius Caesar many centuries before, they were about to cross their own peculiar version of the Rubicon, from which there would be no return. It suddenly occurred to him that though a

Freemason himself, he had actually never had the time to visit this particular Temple of Worship in the days Uncle Tiger had made it open to all Masons. He strolled over to the other side of the room to study the iconic Masonic statuary, lined up against the resplendent white walls.

There were two Sphinx statues of wisdom carved in ivory on six-foot pedestals at eye level, two tall 'Working Freemason' statues cast in bronze, and two gold-plated 'Father Time and Weeping Virgin' statues, all placed about six feet apart. This must have cost quite a tidy sum, he told himself, as he walked from statue to statue, admiring the excellent craftsmanship. He wished 'Father Time' could give them more *time* to ponder other options, but that, alas, was just wishful thinking. The die was cast; Major Kata's analysis was virtually flawless. Only a coup could save them, and save their country as well.

He turned and cast his eyes on the opposite wall as he made his way back to his seat. There were pictures, faithful reproductions of other celebrated Masonic symbols, such as the All Seeing Masonic Eye of Providence, the Ark in Solomon's Temple, the Masonic Square and Compasses, to name but a few, all hanging tastefully on the wall. As though seeing these Masonic symbols had suddenly inspired him, General Yalley sat down purposefully and responded to Nana's question with unqualified certainty in his voice.

'Yes, we are all agreed and we have to start planning now. I have two more pieces of information, which I have no doubt Major Kata knows already. The President is secretly out of the country and will be returning exactly in a week on Easter Monday. General Tonton, his Zombie Commanding Officer, is also out of the country representing him at the Regional Security Conference. Mr Tiger here said that our coup action or FDI is ordained of God. I think he may be right, since the circumstances are truly fortuitous. The President must be not made to return. General Tonton must also be not made to return to command the Zombies as well. Without him to command them, they will be disorganised. Gentlemen, Saga, let us begin.'

And with that, the tiny team of four adults and two very young men, one of them still in his teens, began making serious plans for an irreversible change in the destiny and fortunes of their country and of the millions of souls who resided in it. In the process, they were also irretrievably altering the trajectory of their own lives, which could never be the same again.

Saga knew that to some extent, he had to take a bit of a back seat, if not in the planning, then at least in the execution of that which was being planned. Though it would appear on the surface that the day of the Orphan was over, it was not actually the case.

The entire coup initiative was, in the main, primarily a reaction to the investigative findings of Commander Musu into the destruction and demobilisation of the military vehicles at Fort Brewman. And who demobilised those vehicles? It was the Orphans. And was the coup not also being engendered, to some degree, by the overwhelming desire on the part of the chief protagonists to protect the Orphans, who now stood to face extreme retribution for their roles in the Fort Brewman vehicles saga? And with the Government gone, would not the entire population become 'Orphaned' from the dubious and harrowing parentage of Brewman and his party in power, exactly along the same lines proposed by himself Saga, the Chief Orphan, at the start of it all?

The day of the Chief Orphan himself was far from over. With the possible success of the FDI, Chief Orphan Saga surmised that he might now be able, with his beloved Zara, to live some semblance of a normal life in the months and years to come. With the FDI succeeding, then just maybe – even though they were still very young – their love could now at least have a future to grow and to thrive. The day of the Orphan was probably just beginning.

EPILOGUE

On the following Easter Sunday, a Forcible Democratic Intervention was launched at dawn in the Nation State of Zimgania. The chief 'interventionists' had chosen that day, partly for its symbolic significance as the day of Resurrection. They were, after all, aiming to resurrect their failed State. The intervention proved successful and an Interim Democratic Reconciliation Council was formed to govern the country on a provisional basis. The Nation welcomed the Interim Council. In the eyes of the citizenry, a new era of hope was born. And Saga, the Chief Orphan, became hopeful as well.

ABOUT THE AUTHOR

Nat Tanoh comes from Accra, Ghana, and has a rich history of involvement in student and workers movements, which originally emerged from struggles against the institutionalization of military rule in Ghana. During the 1980s, he was editor of a monthly publication for these social movements. Nat Tanoh was educated at the famous Mfantsipim School in Ghana. After graduating from the University of Ghana with an Honours degree, the author undertook post-graduate studies in Development Studies, gaining an MA (Econ) and then a PhD from the University of Manchester, England.

He has since worked as a consultant on Development projects in Ghana and elsewhere in Africa. He also continues to uphold a passion for democratic social development and the fullest realisation of the citizens' dignity, rights and sovereignty. These are lifelong concerns instilled in him from a very early age, growing up as a child in a family living in exile in England, due to his parents' opposition to the installation of a one-party state.

Nat Tanoh is widowed and has a daughter called Natasha.

Find out more at www.drnattanoh.com

ACKNOWLEDGEMENTS

An immense and never-ending thank you to my dearest daughter, Natasha, for being an inexhaustible source of encouragement and inspiration.

Special thanks to my mother, Mrs Alvira Tanoh, and to my dear sibling compatriots – Goosie, Apeaa and Barzini – who have all helped in great measure to make this novel become a reality.

I am sincerely grateful to Mavis Badohu, whose encouragement and goodwill proved tremendously enabling.

Huge thanks to Dr Kakra Condua, Mr Isaac Krampa, Mrs Aden Sapara-Grant, Mr Mochacho Yeboah, Mr Kamson, Ms Mona Taleb, Mr Boom Forson and Commander James Akrong for their contribution in diverse and important ways.

To the doctors and staff of Manvers Ward at St. Mary's Hospital, Paddington, London, and to the doctors and staff of the Renal Outpatients Department, Hammersmith Hospital, London, I say an enormous thank you for your dedication and commitment in recently helping me back to good health at a point when things were proving a touch dicey.

Sincerest apologies to all those who also assisted me in various ways but I'm unable to mention. To you all, I say an immense THANK YOU.

To Leila Dewji, I say a resounding thank you for your commitment, encouragement and above all, for your superlative professionalism. I am of the hope that other budding authors will have the good fortune I have had to work with you.

Printed in Poland
by Amazon Fulfillment
Poland Sp. z o.o., Wrocław